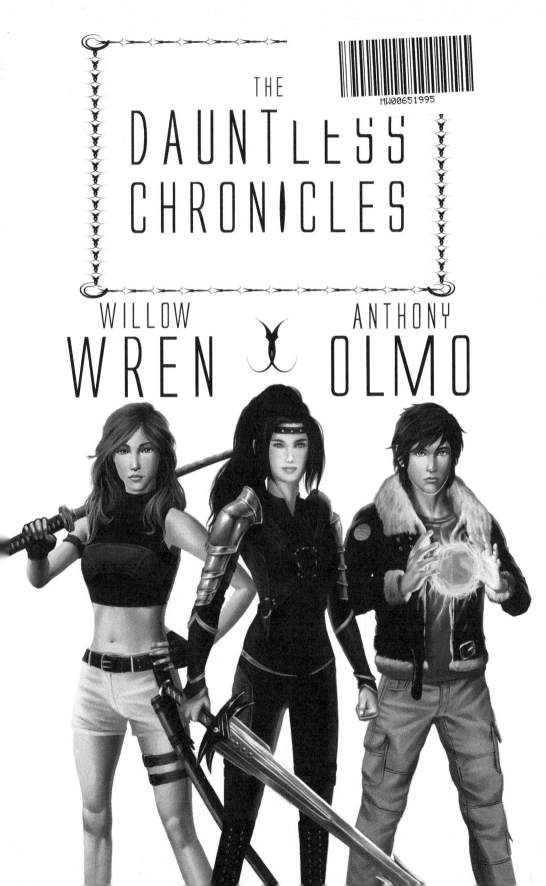

THE
DAUNTLESS
CHRONICLES

W H PUBLISHING, LLC.

REVIEWS & ACCLAIM

Ilene Dillon, MSW, LMFT, LCSW – Radio Host: Emotional Pro, iTunes; Author of Emotions in Motion; Global Lecturer - Australia, China, Europe
Make way, George Lucas, Frank Herbert and J.R.R. Tolkien - Willow Wren and Anthony Olmo have arrived and are *cleverly spinning a space adventure of epic proportions!* It's the story of "teenagers" Destin, Zephyr, and Tessia from Velus, and Andrex from Zaccoth, who are thrust on an interplanetary adventure when Mordrar attacks Velus to make it his. People on these planets are considered adults at age 10. Our authors are not much older, yet here on Earth they've done an amazing job of writing a very engaging story. *What's remarkable about this story is not just the adventure, exploration of superpowers, and depth of character development, but the inclusion of Willow and Anthony's own generation's emphasis on heart, caring and kindness.* This is a first novel, and kept my attention so firmly I read their long adventure in a single sitting. Bring on THE DAUNTLESS CHRONICLES II!

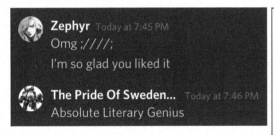

Zephyr Today at 7:45 PM
Omg ;////;
I'm so glad you liked it

The Pride Of Sweden... Today at 7:46 PM
Absolute Literary Genius

Mark MacGregor – Newscast Director, CBS Channel 31, WMBD-TV, Illinois
This heartfelt adventure/science fiction/friendship story told from the eyes of every major character, keeps the action rolling and the imagination fueled. *The intricate detail of both man and machine leap off the page. Just when you wonder how other characters in the scene are feeling, the next chapter jumps right in, continued from a different perspective; the reader feels emotionally attached to, and invested in each character. Wow! I cannot believe two 14-year-olds wrote this!* Such detail and character development. The young authors have set a high standard for their future works. When is the movie coming out!?

Michele Sfakianos, R.N. – Award-winning Author of 11 books including The 4-1-1 Series
What an exciting journey! So much adventure packed into THE DAUNTLESS CHRONICLES. *Saving planets, space travel, ships, and trains – it has it all! A very compelling story full of action, suspense, and riveting plot twists. The brave, young characters* really draw you into the story. *Just when you think things are going their way, new challenges surface.* Don't miss this adventure!

THIS IS SO AWESOME
Danné

REVIEWS & ACCLAIM

Annette Bosley-Boyce, M.A. – Dean, Division of Professional & Graduate Studies, Albertus Magnus College

If you ever wanted to see the cosmos in 2145, then get ready! Wren and Olmo bring you to a future where the infinite power of love, friendship, and kindness reign over the threat of war, fear, and evil. From dragons to ice planets from superpowers to secret escape missions, prepare for a high-tech tale of epic adventure! What are teenagers like from other planets in an entirely different solar system? Wren and Olmo introduce us to Zephyr, Destin, Tessia, Andrex, and Damari—a group of brave and superhuman teens whose silliness, charm, and loyalty will capture your heart in this endearing and heroic story. THE DAUNTLESS CHRONICLES is a must-read for anyone that loves fantasy, science fiction, or a good YA love story.

Anna Meurer – University Student, MIT
THE DAUNTLESS CHRONICLES is a book for the adventurer — *full of action, fantasy, and enchantment. It is a true display of creativity and limitless teenage imagination.*

Sam Rostampour – Cloud Consultant, DevSecOps practices & culture, Toronto, Canada

"Magnificent storytelling by Willow Wren and Antony Olmo drew me inside the heart of the world of gods and goddesses. *The creativity of these two young authors creates an unexpected intimacy between the reader and the characters of this multi-planetary, multicultural universe. Each chapter tells the story from the viewpoint of a different character, creating a 3D hologram of the scenes for the readers.* THE DAUNTLESS CHRONICLES is a fantastic book I highly recommend!

REVIEWS & ACCLAIM

Bryan Post – Founder, The Post Institute;
Top-selling author & coauthor of 13 books
"And so it begins... THE DAUNTLESS CHRONICLES - *what an amazing feat of creativity and brilliant storytelling. This work would make both Joseph Campbell and George Lucas proud."*

Rosa Negrin – Equestrian, Connecticut
An ABSOLUTE page-turner! Wren and Olmo will have you laughing, intrigued, spellbound and completely captivated on their Dauntless journey. *Zephyr, Destin and the amusing Siren will pull you into their gripping world with the neidren's first "puff."*

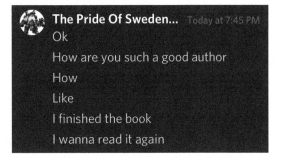

Emilyn Mohebbi – TV Producer, NBC Channel 7, San Diego, California
THE DAUNTLESS CHRONICLES is a compelling and captivating read that makes you feel as if you are in a whole new part of the universe as you dive into the book. The creativity and descriptions throughout this novel paint vivid pictures in your mind, and with those visualizations throughout the book, it feels like you are playing each chapter in your head like scenes from a movie. *One of my favorite aspects of this novel is the way it is formatted. Each chapter is told from the perspective of a different character, which leads to curiosity as you read from various characters' points of view. This unique story will keep you intrigued the entire time -* you won't want to put this book down!

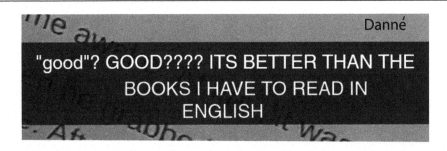

REVIEWS & ACCLAIM

Dr. Jeffrey Bernstein – Top-selling Author of 6 books including Why Can't You Read My Mind?

I'm grateful to have had the honor & pleasure to review THE DAUNTLESS CHRONICLES. Aptly titled, *readers will have almost no time to fasten their seatbelts before being blasted off into gripping tales of out-of-this-world adventure created by two ingenious teen coauthors.* Zephyr and Destin, and other *creatively developed characters, transcend the galaxies as they show indefatigable courage and resourcefulness when facing never ending perilous challenges.*

I heartily recommend this book – *it is so well-written, brilliantly creative, outright amazing and it truly is something "out of this world!"*

Trish Pena – Radiology Tech; Frm. News Anchor & Reporter, WTVW-TV Channel 7 News

Wow! Right from the beginning, Willow and Anthony explained every character with vivid detail. Great storytelling and creativity! I felt like I was right there with the characters. Every detail paints a picture of the exciting moments of the story. *A thrilling journey filled with suspense and heartfelt love for each character. From the moment I opened the book, I enjoyed the adventure. Willow and Anthony make a great team and have done a spectacular job on this saga! I honestly had to remind myself that this book was written by two 14-year-olds.* They are truly talented. Bravo! Can't wait for TDC2.

Nayer Negrin, M.Ed. – Educator, Kayaker, Hiker, Traveler

The fantastical intrigue of THE DAUNTLESS CHRONICLES *had me longing for more with each chapter's cessation. A witty adventure that will capture its readers on the first page.* I couldn't put it down and look forward to reading more from the young authors, Willow Wren and Anthony Olmo.

Alex Danilov – Teen Actor, age 14, New York

THE DAUNTLESS CHRONICLES is a thrilling dystopian novel set in the future. A book with *characters seemingly plucked out of real life, you'll find it hard to put down. New star systems and technologies await, as you take a journey through space* and our own planet. An overall excellent read for all ages!

REVIEWS & ACCLAIM

Holly Sulak Willis, Esq. – Attorney; Frm. Award-winning News Anchor, KVII-TV ABC Channel 7, Texas

Wren and Olmo have done what so many kids and adults dream of doing ... they've written a book! *It is apparent how much they have enjoyed using their imaginations to create a fictional world for all of us to enter, envision, and explore with them.* Those who enjoy science fiction and friendship novels will have a good time exploring the world of The Dauntless Project. There's plenty of rich detail, and the lingo and construction are easy to navigate. Congratulations on this first book to the authors! As a former teacher, this is the passion for creation we always hope to kindle in readers and writers.

Louise Helene – Author, I Saw Your Future and He's Not It

THE DAUNTLESS CHRONICLES is a true page-turner. *These two talented young authors had my attention from the first page. I could not put down this unique, engaging, and exciting tale.* A great read for any young adult, or the young at heart.

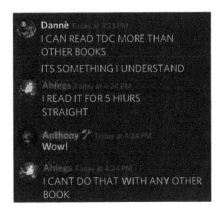

Shelli Dankoff McClellan – OSF Newsroom & Media Relations Supervisor; Frm. News Anchor, WMBD-TV CBS Channel 31 News, Illinois

Engaging, exciting, and intriguing. THE DAUNTLESS CHRONICLES is an enjoyable read. *The action ramps up quickly,* with the chapters written in easy-to-consume bites that kept me turning the pages in anticipation. *The attention to detail is fascinating - everything from the amazing descriptions of the spaceships and Area 51 to the exploration of young love. Perhaps best of all, it didn't end predictably, with a bow neatly wrapped around it. I kept saying to myself 'this was written by two teenagers?!'*

Wow!!! Leia ✦ > Today 09:34

I got to chapter 10 last night I'm totally addicted to it

REVIEWS & ACCLAIM

Logan H. Lindstrom – Avid New England sailor, age 15
THE DAUNTLESS CHRONICLES is an amazing book full of *vivid scenes, nail-biting adventure, and horrifying danger. It is full of cliffhangers and deep characters who are heavily developed throughout the story into complex persons who have strong ties to one another. This book is a masterpiece and one of the best books I have ever read.*

Daniel Martinez – Student, age 14, Connecticut
THE DAUNTLESS CHRONICLES *is a masterpiece of a book with mixed emotions* that makes you want to continue reading. *It captures your attention at every moment. It allows your imagination to grow and lets you create a perfect picture* of what's going on in your mind. *It conjures the absolute description of fighting for what you believe in. There is not one moment where you are not immersed* and want to stop reading. It was awesome.

Frederick Russo – Author, Follow Your Heart
Get ready to meet Destin, Zephyr, Andrex, Tessia, Damari and Siren. THE DAUNTLESS CHRONICLES *is an exciting escapade told by a group of savvy teenagers who will transport your mind and thoughts into a new dimension...and beyond. These friends are supercharged with lots of energy, kindness and compassion.* Be prepared to get engaged in an adventure that is out of *their* world.

Julie Zeff, MSW, CPCC – Author, Vivid Living for Busy Moms: Coach Yourself to an Extraordinary Life
THE DAUNTLESS CHRONICLES was a super fun and engaging read. *Its action-packed, sci-fi focused plot, dotted with twists, turns, romance, and earthly elements, makes this heartwarming and clever story accessible to everyone. The powerful themes of the importance of family, friendship, loyalty, love, and courage flowed* through every page. An enjoyable and creative read for young adults and beyond. I can see it as a major motion picture already!

REVIEWS & ACCLAIM

Harry Bell – Founder & Author, Color a Positive Thought Foundation
I found THE DAUNTLESS CHRONICLES *very entertaining. The coauthors wrote with such detail that this book had me continually guessing what would happen next on this exciting journey* as if I were a character. Wren and Olmo's writing painted a clear picture as I read this book. It was an awesome read!

Vincent Snow Today at 8:15 AM
DESTIN

I still remember your speech earlier, reading chapter 54 and epilogue

and every time I listen to any music that fits the scenario... it actually makes me tear my eyes can't handle the epicness, happiness and happy sadness

Hermine Steinberg – Author, The Co-Walkers: Awakening; Toronto
THE DAUNTLESS CHRONICLES *is an action-packed ride through space written from the unique perspective of 'aliens' who arrive on Earth.* This imaginative and entertaining debut novel written by teen writers Willow Wren and Anthony Olmo will undoubtedly launch their careers in science fiction.

Maddie MacGregor – Percussionist, age 15, Illinois
The daring adventures between Zephyr, Destin, Tessia, Damari, and Andrex were really relatable to me. *Each character reminded me of someone I know.* I got emotional attachments from one character to the next. *The switching between viewpoints kept the book flowing with ease, and caused me to never want to stop reading.* My peers have created a story that's out of this world, literally!

Troy Edge – age 15, United Kingdom
This book is *a stunning read, absolutely brilliant wording and the conveying of the story-line, filled with intense action and compelling subplots, is simply sublime.* Genuinely, a book which could be read over and over again. Absolutely recommended for anyone who enjoys a more action-packed style of writing and totally recommended to anyone! *The second book is already highly anticipated and I simply cannot wait for its release!*

REVIEWS & ACCLAIM

Ron Vincent M. – age 16, Philippines

Filled with sci-fi, action, romance, thrills and so much more. This book takes you onto a whole new level of adventure with aliens, powers, and ships connected with the characters in order to beat a common foe.
THE DAUNTLESS CHRONICLES *gives off an epic vibe* that enlightened my imagination in so many ways. The delineating of the events and the power known as "Mechanical Advantage" makes me want to experience it myself. THE DAUNTLESS CHRONICLES is the perfect book for those readers who seek more uniqueness while keeping an adventurous mood that everyone can enjoy.

Lewie Boyce – age 12

THE DAUNTLESS CHRONICLES *is a masterpiece.* You go on an adventure where you meet these characters that have amazing traits and awesome personalities. *The story progression is the best I have ever read in a book or seen in a movie! I can see this book turning into a television series. This was a story that I will never forget.* I definitely recommend it! :D

Anitta Tilly, M.Div. – Mother of 5

THE DAUNTLESS CHRONICLES by Willow Wren and Anthony Olmo captures the reader's imagination from the first pages of the book. It's as if I was right there in the middle of the story! The writers use ingenious descriptive adjectives, which paint the picture for the reader of an imaginary world with different rules yet deep friendships and close families that fight for each other. *As a parent of 5 children, I find this book refreshing with its values deeply focused on family, friendship, loyalty, and the willingness to give up your life for those you love.*

Zachary B. – Student, age 14

Excitement: *Gallons every chapter.* Steam engines: *Absolutely.* Aliens: *Definitely! Awesomeness: What did you expect? Of course!*

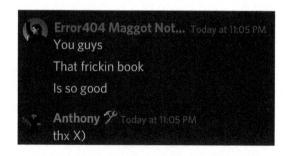

Error404 Maggot Not... Today at 11:05 PM
You guys
That frickin book
Is so good

Anthony Today at 11:05 PM
thx X)

REVIEWS & ACCLAIM

G. Heuer – Artist, World Traveler
There's an art to writing fictional stories - *Wren and Olmo mastered it with their impressive use of an unusual alternating perspective format, exceptional technical descriptions of the spacecraft/ships and locomotive,* wonderfully detailed description of their characters, and articulate use of dialogue. *The characters held their identities throughout the saga, adding to the cohesion of the story and the solidity of the writing.* Wren and Olmo are incredibly talented and creative young people who are very capable storytellers. THE DAUNTLESS CHRONICLES is an *intergalactic journey of adventure and romance* for readers of all ages.

Leia Wilson – age 14, Metro New York
THE DAUNTLESS CHRONICLES is a phenomenal book. *This engrossing story is filled with unique characters, an interesting plotline, and spot-on humor. The well-thought-out world the authors created added realism to the story* and made it very believable. I enjoyed following these characters on their incredible journey. I look forward to reading the next installment of THE DAUNTLESS CHRONICLES!

skywarrior29 Today at 9:47 PM
Zeph, that 54 just gave me ultimate chills
And epilogue was just yes

Willow ✕ Today at 9:47 PM
B))))
I'm glad you loved it

Pat Montgomery – Award-winning Author, Now You Know What I Know; Grandma of 15
Just WOW! The first saga in THE DAUNTLESS CHRONICLES *is magical. I just could not put it down - one of the many twists and surprises kept me engaged* all day and I just finished the book and loved it! *Excellent story with intrigue, action, romance and everything else you need for a great tale. And if you think that you can guess the ending...you would be wrong!* Highly recommend this remarkable book!

The Pride Of Sweden... Today at 7:47 PM
I want it

Zephyr Today at 7:47 PM
Mm book two is soon 😂

The Pride Of Sweden... Today at 7:47 PM
How long is soon reeeeeeeeeee

The Pride Of Sweden... Today at 9:47 PM
I just finished the Dauntless Chronicles
In 3 days btw
That is soo goooooooooooooooood

REVIEWS & ACCLAIM

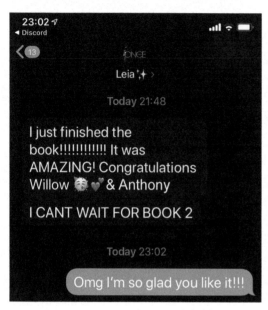

Sara Schaefer – Journalist

Wren and Olmo have created a riveting new world that's rich with detail and imagination, grabbing readers' attention from the opening pages to take them on a magnificent journey through the Cayser solar system and into the lives of its young and brave defenders. Zephyr is a swashbuckling commander with a fearsome command of her sword and Destin is a young warrior determined to protect Zephyr, his family and his planet at all costs. *With its fast-paced plot and teenage characters who exhibit spunk, grace and humor,* THE DAUNTLESS CHRONICLES *is a page-turner that will undoubtedly be a massive hit with this generation of readers!*

Bob Small – Radio Station Manager, WGCH 1490AM

Young authors, Willow Wren and Anthony Olmo present the reader with a *well-crafted, fast-paced adventure with a strong group of main characters that hook you in right away* and keep you interested to the last page and beyond. THE DAUNTLESS CHRONICLES brought me back to my youth, time and again.

I have always enjoyed reading science fiction and I'm pleased to see these young authors keeping this art form desirable and energized!

Zephyr

BumbleBlades, age 15, United Kingdom

Destin & Tessia

BumbleBlades, age 15, United Kingdom

THE DAUNTLESS CHRONICLES

www.TheDauntlessChronicles.com

Copyright

All rights reserved.

Copyright ©2019 by Willow Wren, Copyright ©2019 by Anthony Olmo
Technical Drawings Copyright ©1967 by Hooshang "Jim" Salahshourian
Schematics Design Copyright ©2020 by B. Tyler
Border Design Copyright ©2020 by Phillip GW
Ship Illustrations Copyright ©2020 by Anthony Olmo
Siren Illustration Copyright ©2020 by Willow Wren
Planet Design & Illustrations Copyright ©2020 by Willow Wren & Phillip GW
Compass Rose design Copyright ©2020 by Anthony Olmo
Y ™ Logo Design, Trademark Phillip GW

W H
PUBLISHING, LLC

All rights reserved. Published by WH Publishing, LLC. Writer's INC and associated logos are registered trademarks of WH Publishing, LLC. WH Publishing, LLC., Writer's INC and/or any of its affiliates do not have any control over and do not assume any liability or responsibility for author, co-author or third-party websites or their content.

This book is sold subject to the condition that it shall not, by way of trade or otherwise be lent, resold, hired out or otherwise circulated without the prior written consent of the author(s). No part of this publication may be reproduced, transmitted, decompiled, or stored in or introduced into any information storage and/or retrieval system, or transmitted in any form or by any means in any manner, whether electronic or mechanical, including photographing, scanning, photocopying, recording or otherwise, without written ermission of the publisher. To request permission or for more information, write to WH Publishing, LLC., Attention: Permissions Department, P.O. Box 4323, Greenwich, Connecticut 06831.

This book/ebook/audiobook is a work of fiction. Names, characters, places, incidents and dialogues are products of the co-authors' imaginations or are used fictitiously. Any resemblance to actual persons, living or dead, or events, locales, business establishments or the like is entirely coincidental.

Editor-in-Chief: B. Tyler, Editor@WH-Publishing.com
Worldbuilding & Lore by: Willow Wren & Anthony Olmo
Cover Design: Phillip GW
Cover Image: iStockPhoto - cemagraphics
Character Art: Achnis R.A., Indonesia
Character Art: BumbleBlades, United Kingdom
Character Art: Evelvaii, Indonesia
Character Art: M, Russia
Photographer, Willow's Portrait: Yolanda Perez, New York
Photographer, Anthony's Portrait: B. Tyler
Marketing & Distribution: HGP, New York City
ISBN: 978-1-951943-38-7
Library of Congress Control Number: 2020921244

Printed in the U.S.A.
First Edition published November 2020

Hoggle

wow. you and zeph absolutely hit the nail on the head with that book. It was just incredible, a marvel of literary genius. You both did an absolutely stellar job on it, and I simply can't wait for book 2, so much so I'm gonna read the 1st one again. Well done matey!

DEDICATIONS

*This book is for my wonderful Mom, Dad, and big Brother,
who have been so inspiring and supportive of all my dreams.
With wisdom and grace, they have given me a solid foundation
of industriousness and diligence. I love you so much.*

~Willow

*I dedicate this book to my mother, Caroline, who is behind me
with everything I do, and to The Southport School for their
commitment to their students with learning differences.*

~Anthony

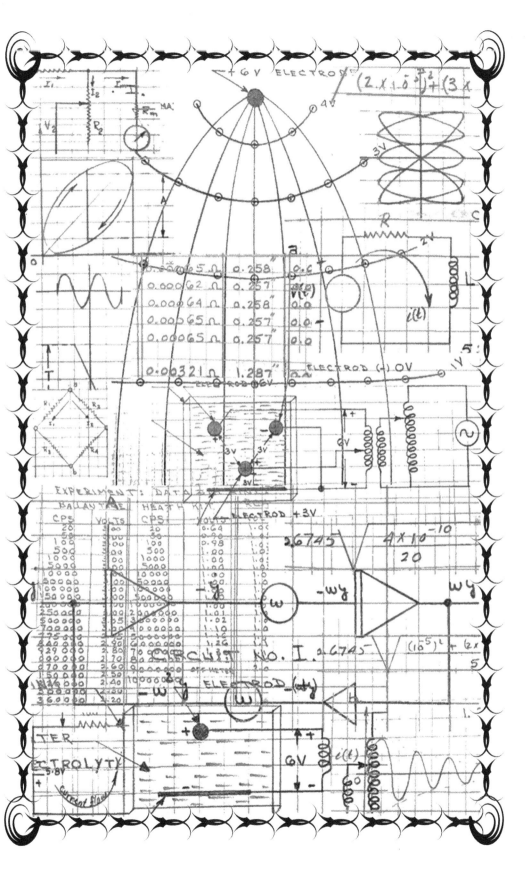

DESTIN, ZEPHYR, TESSIA

BumbleBlades, age 15, United Kingdom

GODS AND GODDESSES

CAYSER GODS/GODDESSES

- **Asrea**, Queen of the Gods & the first being in the universe
- **Xerana**, Goddess of the Sea and Storms
- **Navis**, God of Ships and Travel
- **Idar**, God of Battle
  - Halls of Idar
  - Similar to Valhalla; meant for warriors who died in battle
- **Salutem**, Goddess of Safety and Health
- **Caelum**, God of the Heavens
- **Inferis**, God of Death and the Underworld
- **Eseina**, Goddess of Love
- **Niulla**, Goddess of Honor
- **Shinio**, God of Destiny and Fortune

Asrea was the first godly being created into the universe. She was made from pure matter and gave the universe its stars. She was lonely, so she found a way to create life.

Xerana, Caelum, and Inferis were the first godly children to be born into the universe. Caelum and Inferis worked together to make the planets, and then Xerana used her power of the seas and storms to bring life and fertility to the planets, creating oceans and making plants bloom across the lands.

Caelum and Xerana had two children and named the boy Navis, the God of Ships and Travel, and the girl Niulla, the Goddess of Honor. Navis then married his sister and they had three children: Idar, the God of Battle, Salutem, the Goddess of Safety and Health, and Eseina, the Goddess of Love.

Eseina married Idar, and they had Shinio, God of Destiny and Fortune.

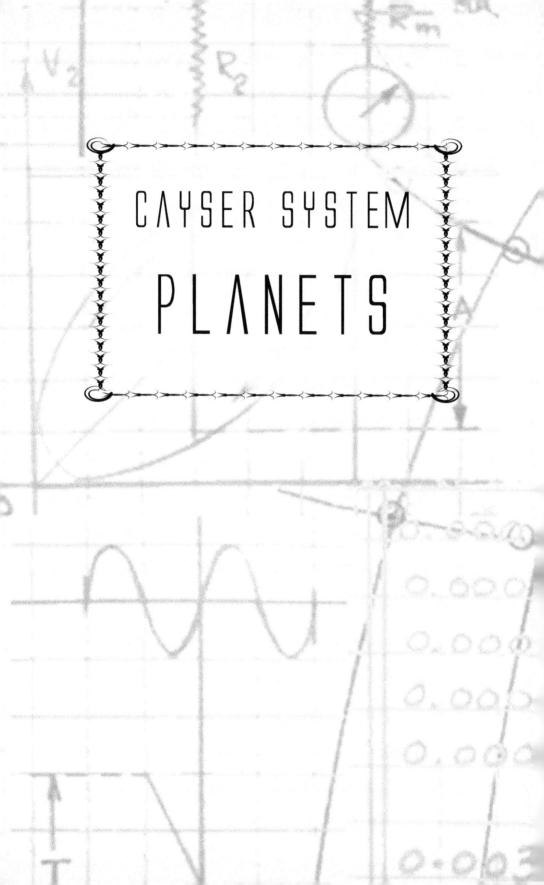

CAYSER SYSTEM

PLANETS

FURTHEST FROM THE SUN: BREI

1. ZACCOTH
2. SAILARA
3. VELUS
4. ORILIA
5. ROCARON
6. OBURNA

LARGEST TO SMALLEST

1. ZACCOTH
2. ROCARON
3. SAILARA
4. VELUS
5. ORILIA
6. OBURNA

ZACCOTH

(Ice Planet)

Zaccothians have very high resistance to cold and can hold their breath for up to an hour if necessary. Their main weapon is a trident made of Zocradian (NOT a metal) and it can freeze or manifest ice at the wielder's will. Fair skin is typical as this planet is furthest from the sun. Hair often is silvery or a light or pastel color. Inhabitants have crystalline markings on their faces that resemble ice. Families tend to have identical or similar markings.   Moon count: 7

(Rock and Mesa Planet)

ROCARON

Physically strong inhabitants, tend to be very independent, and they are exceptional with making jewelry, creating weapons, smithing, crafting, etc. Dark skin with gold markings along their bodies. Men tend to have no hair while women typically have either very dark hair or a hair color that resembles a gemstone.
Moon count: 3

SAILARA

(Ocean Planet)

Sailarans can breathe underwater and excel at swimming. Some even have fins or webbing between their fingers. They can also have the rare trait of bioluminescence and the ability to see in the dark. Hair and skin come in every color, and some inhabitants even have scales. Some deep-water Sailarans' eyes are solid and fully-colored.
Moon count: 13

(Forest/Mountain Planet)

VELUS

Velusans are more military-oriented and tend to be physically stronger than other races in the Cayser System, and their mutations are more powerful. Also home to the Silverclaw Dragons. The inhabitants are the most humanoid of the Cayser races. Hair and skin come in a variety of colors.
Moon count: 2

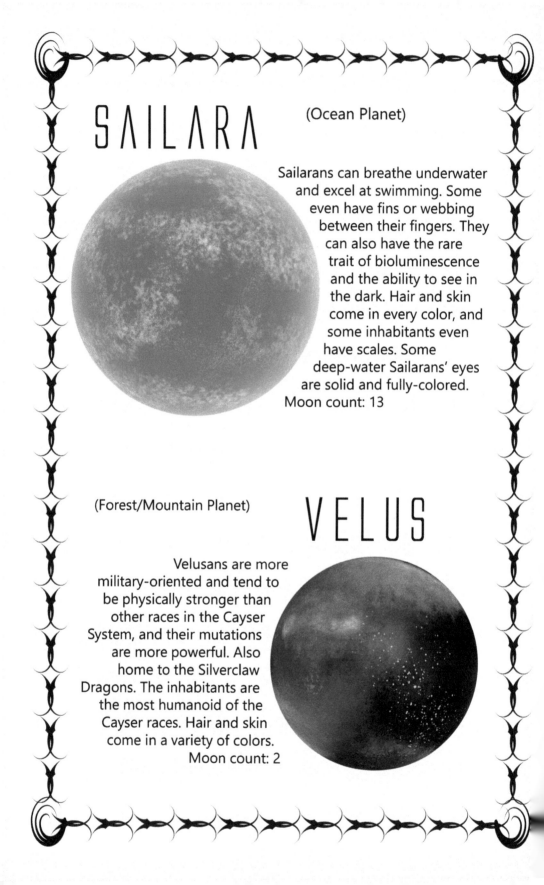

ORILIA

(Tropical Planet)

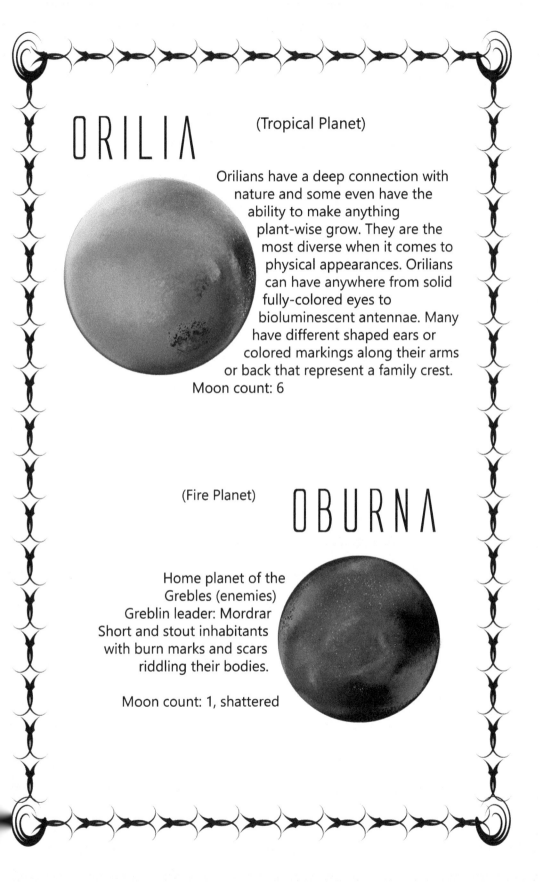

Orilians have a deep connection with nature and some even have the ability to make anything plant-wise grow. They are the most diverse when it comes to physical appearances. Orilians can have anywhere from solid fully-colored eyes to bioluminescent antennae. Many have different shaped ears or colored markings along their arms or back that represent a family crest.

Moon count: 6

(Fire Planet)

OBURNA

Home planet of the Grebles (enemies)
Greblin leader: Mordrar
Short and stout inhabitants with burn marks and scars riddling their bodies.

Moon count: 1, shattered

CAYSER SYSTEM
PENTARCHY

Zaccoth
- Ice planet
- Royal family

Sailara
- Ocean planet
- 95% ocean
- Underwater Empire (emperor and empress)

Velus
- Forest/Mountain planet
- Home to the Silverclaw Dragons
- Ruled in Book 1 by Fleet Admiral Halden (Admiral's rank is as high as royalty or any other rank in the pentarchy High Council)

Orilia
- Tropical paradise planet
- Royal family

Rocaron
- Rock and Mesa planet
- Ruled by the Chieftain and his family (Chieftain's rank is as high as royalty or any other rank in the pentarchy High Council)

TESSIA, DESTIN, ZEPHYR

Evelvaii, age 18, Indonesia

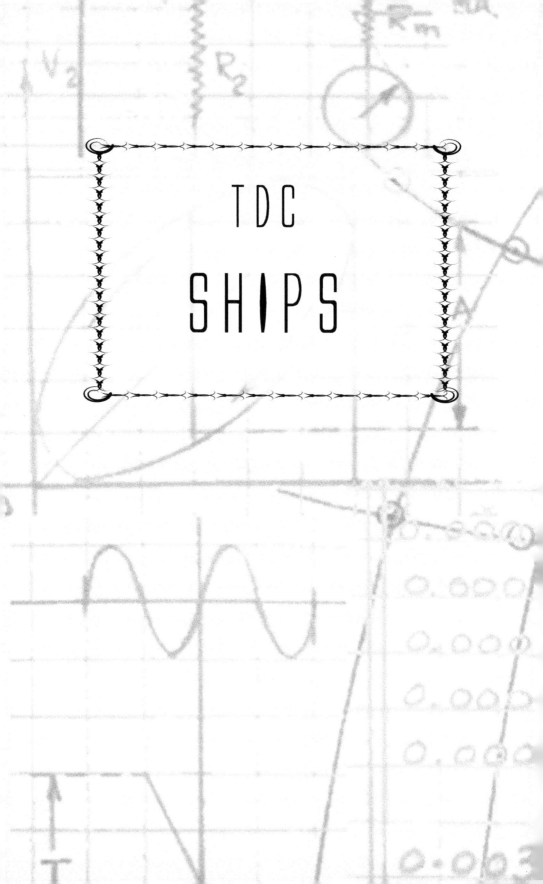

TDC

SHIPS

Caroline

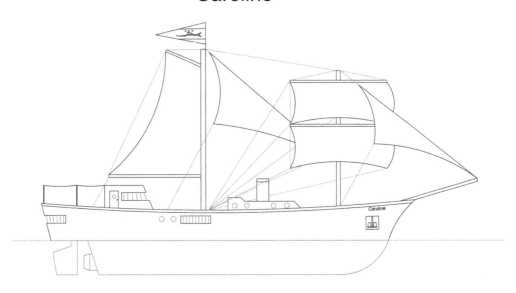

Caroline II

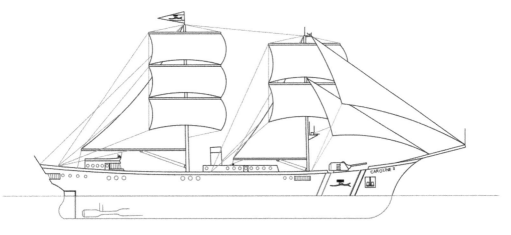

Mennus

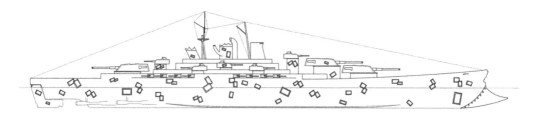

Nautilax

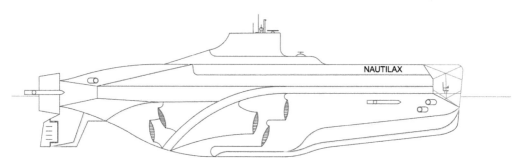

U.D.N.S. Willow (BC 102)

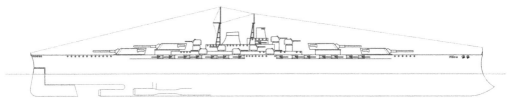

U.D.N.S. Prince of Dragons (SD 05)

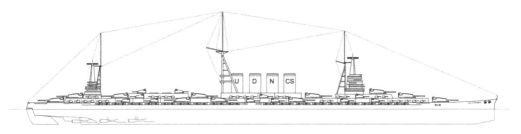

U.D.N.S. Concord (SSL 4)

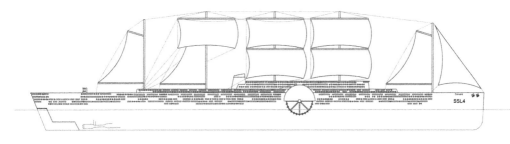

TERMINOLOGY

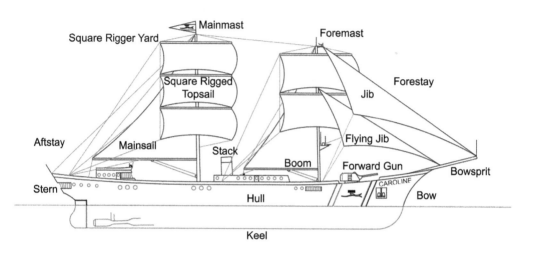

Mainmast

Square Rigger Yard

Foremast

Square Rigged Topsail

Forestay

Jib

Aftstay

Mainsail

Stack

Flying Jib

Boom

Forward Gun

CAROLINE

Bowsprit

Stern

Hull

Bow

Keel

SCALING & TOP VIEW

U.D.N.S. Prince of Dragons (SD 05)

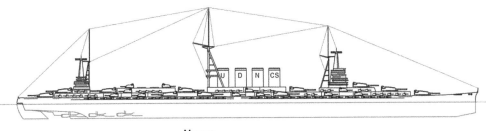

Mennus

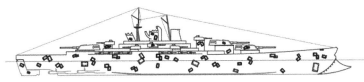

U.D.N.S. Willow (BC 102)

U.D.N.S. Concord (SSL 4)

 Caroline II
Nautilax
Caroline

TOP VIEW

TABLE OF CONTENTS

Prologue

HUMAN YEAR: 2144

A century ago, the wars broke out, and the Cayser System was divided. It was planet against planet, each one only trying to do what was best for its people. The royal family of Orilia, the tropical planet; the chieftain of Rocaron, the rock and mesa planet; Oburna, home of the malicious Grebles; the emperor and empress of Sailara, the ocean planet; the admiral and his family of Velus, the forest planet, home to the Silverclaw dragons; and lastly, the royal family of Zaccoth, the planet of ice and snow. Every leader was pinned against great challenges: finding a way to defeat the Grebles without hurting their people.

The Grebles were parasites; an aggressive race that had fallen from the stars to the formerly uninhabited Oburna, a desolate and deadly wasteland of a planet. Spiteful and power-hungry, they started attacking planets, trying to take over the Cayser System to rule it as their own.

That was when the idea for the Dauntless Project was born: a hyper dreadnought ship the size of a large moon. It would be so powerful that it could decimate an entire planet, along with all of its inhabitants. This ship was meant to stop wars before they even started. The only problem was that no one was strong enough to build such a ship.

Half a century later, the defining Battle of Elofür Bridge on Rocaron pushed the war in favor of the rightful Cayser Council. Shortly afterwards, they won the war, and the Grebles were banished to the fiery planet of Oburna, never to set foot off of it again.

Another thirty years later, a young woman who was strong enough to wield the power of the Dauntless Project made a deal with Admiral Halden, the leader of Velus. Together, with her power and his resources, they started to build the hyper dreadnought, keeping it a secret from the rest of the worlds, knowing that if word spread, another war to subdue the power of Velus could potentially break out.

Halfway through the Dauntless Project, the woman left the planet in search of additional resources, and she never came back. Some said she was dead. Others said that she was captured and that her powers were being abused by those on a greedy planet.

The Dauntless Project was abandoned and forgotten, lost to time. A decade went by, and as the son of the woman grew stronger, so did his power. He liked to call it the Mechanical Advantage. A name for such a power was fitting, and he would train and grow the power on his own, in tribute to his mother. He had the ability to save worlds, but he just didn't know that yet.

Chapter One: Destin

Dealing With Our Fathers

"Hey, Tess! Can you pass me that driver?" I called.

"Yup. Incoming!" Tessia tossed it my way. I caught the tool without looking at it. "Whatcha doin', anyway?"

"Well, if something happens when we're on the *Concord,* you're gonna need a way to defend yourself. And sometimes your katana just won't cut it." I tightened a screw on the grip of the gun and it made a clicking noise. I spun around and handed Tessia the pistol; she studied it.

"This is so cool," she said, taking aim and pretending to fire. Her slim, sunkissed arms extended as she squeezed one of her hazel eyes shut. A strand of hair fell over her shoulder while she swiveled around; it was mid-length and full, dark brown like mine, except her wavy ends were streaked with purple.

"Right?" I smiled, glad that I impressed my big sister. Again.

"HEY DES! TESS! COME OVER HERE! I THINK I BROKE OUR TOASTER!" our Dad yelled at us from across the room.

"What did you do *this time?*" Tess scolded.

I ran over to assess the damage our father had subjected our third toaster to. The thing was still smoking, and I coughed.

"Holy Asrea, Dad! What did you do?!" I exclaimed, referencing the queen of the gods.

"I uh… I thought it would be a good idea to thaw a snack in it since I busted the proen yesterday."

"You did *WHAT*?" I screeched.

Tessia facepalmed, groaning at our father's cooking incompetence. She'd mainly taken over our kitchen after Mom passed away.

Dad's formidable command of the super starliner *Concord* was unmatched, but his cooking or technical skills left much to be desired; he left those to us.

"Fine," I huffed. "I'll start fixing it."

My Dad smiled. "Thanks. I know, I know, I won't do it again." Tall and strong with sandy-brown hair, my father started to walk away toward the direction of the hangars. He was wearing his captain's uniform, the navy jacket unbuttoned. "I need to do some last-minute preparations before we leave."

"Aren't we leaving in four days?" I asked.

"Nope! Tomorrow! Things have been speeding up nicely. The first planet I think we should stop by is Zaccoth."

"The ice planet? You trying to freeze me to death? You know I hate the cold!"

"So you're coming?" Dad's face lit up.

"I guess so. I asked Zephyr to lead one of our escort ships—"

"Wait," Dad cut me off. "Zephyr as in Zephyr Haldensdottir? You mean the admiral's kid? Wow. We haven't seen her in a *long* time."

"I actually saw her a few days ago." I unscrewed the bottom of the toaster. "OH, GOOD GODS, Dad! THIS THING IS *DONE FOR! I swear to the gods themselves*, if you destroy another appliance, I will take the starliner and leave without you."

Before I could say anything else, there was a knock on the door. My Dad turned from the direction of the hangar to answer it. Using retinal scan, he unlocked it and the slab of metal slid open. He blinked at the tall, confident fourteen-year-old girl standing in front of him. On Velus, adulthood starts at age ten.

She had her long, dark brown hair tied up in a high ponytail, her iron pauldrons gleaming in the sun, tall combat boots, and a sword sheathed in a scabbard on her back; there were two belt straps on both legs, each holding a dagger. My friend also had a white rope wrapped around her waist.

"Oh, hey, Zeph!" I called over my shoulder.

"Zephyr?" My Dad sounded more surprised than he should've.

"Good afternoon, Captain Kincaid. It's been a while, hasn't it?" Zephyr smiled, her bright green eyes sparkling. I stood up and walked over to her.

"Nice sword," I said, giving her a high-five.

Born into a military family, Zephyr was training with a sword before she could even walk. Her father, the admiral of the United Dragon Navy, or UDN, and leader of Velus, had shaped her into one of the planet's strongest warriors, even at her young age. She was a born leader and fighter, and adored the idea of traveling to other planets. That was the reason I invited her to join my father's expedition on the *Concord*.

"Thanks," she unsheathed it, giving the blade a swing before putting it back in its case. "It was my mother's first."

Just like everyone else on Velus, I knew that Zephyr's mother, Toriyal, had left the military way of life right before she married. She was still a good fighter, and could be lethal when need be, but nowadays, she mostly enjoyed interior decorating or trying to force Zephyr to wear a dress.

I could see my Dad eyeing the white rope around her waist. Suddenly, a small head with blue eyes poked out from behind Zephyr and gave a small puff from tiny nostrils. Dad jumped.

"When did you get a neidren?" he asked, watching the lithe creature.

"Nearly two years ago." Zephyr unwound the neidren from her hips and placed the scaly noodle on her iron-clad shoulders.

"Hi, Siren!" I said. The neidren puffed at me, and then yawned, revealing no fangs. But it was enough to officially make my Dad decide to leave.

Neidrens were a subspecies of the Silverclaw dragons that inhabited Velus. Adult Silverclaws had large wings, powerful limbs, bodies decorated in spines, and they were about the height of a two-story house. Neidrens were tiny in comparison, measuring more than half the height of an average Velusan adult.

Neidrens had long scaly bodies and no limbs or wings, but their heads were adorned with a small set of icy-blue spines similar to their ancestors. Their tails ended at a whip-thin point, with a fan-like flare coming from either side. The flare had four points on each side, and the colors varied in shades of blue and silver.

Their venom levels were high, and they had retractable fangs; the admiral wanted them removed for the safety of his daughter, however, after Zephyr pulled a few strings, the operation never happened.

"I'm gonna head to the hangar. You two have fun and please… fix the toaster," he waved, leaving the way Zephyr had come.

"The toaster?" Zephyr raised an eyebrow.

I dismissed the subject.

"Just don't ask…" We walked into the living room. "Can I see your sword?"

Faster than I thought possible, Zephyr drew her sword. I stepped back a bit, afraid of being slashed. She held it out to me, and I took its grip in my hand. The leather was soft and strong, and the shimmering icy blue blade looked exceptionally sharp. But for Zephyr, nothing was too sharp. I lifted it and then brought it down quickly, slicing through the air.

"It's really light," I said, swinging it. I nearly hit Zephyr, but she dodged out of the way easily. Siren gave me a look. I didn't even know neidrens could *give* looks.

"Yeah, Diatanium is the best. Light, strong and pretty much unbreakable."

I nodded. "I made the *Caroline* out of Diatanium."

Tess entered the room. I had no idea where she'd been. I didn't even know she'd left.

"Hi, Tessia!" Zephyr waved, her green eyes swirling into purple.

"Hey, Zeph. Hey, Siren. Destin! Put that sword down! Or do I have to remind you what happens when you're with pointy objects," Tessia folded her arms across her chest. I grudgingly handed back Zephyr's sword, and she dropped it into her scabbard.

Siren looked at my sister and puffed, her little black tongue flicking in and out.

"C'mon, Zeph. I wanna show you the magnificent and absolutely glorious *Caroline*."

"Please do," she smiled.

We started walking to the back door of the house, which led to the docks. There were many ships at the docks, but there were also the hangars where my Dad had headed. I knew he didn't like neidrens, which was why he left so abruptly.

While we were walking out of the house, I stopped and turned to Zephyr.

"I have a question for you."

"Fire away."

"What do your eye colors mean? I know they've been shifting for years now, but I've been noticing that they've been more distinct these past few weeks as your emotions change."

"Gray is distressed, blue is neutral, green is happy, purple is excited, and the dark red is when I'm angry."

Note to self, I thought. *Stay away from Zephyr when her eyes are red.*

She's deadly without her weapons. But with them is an entirely different story.

Once we arrived at the *Caroline*, Zephyr gasped.

"Oh, my gods, Des! She's amazing!" The young warrior ran her hand over the strong hull, admiring the handiwork. Our ships were powered by steam and solar sails, and use an Atlas Core to fly. I beamed, happy that she liked it. "How fast can she go?" Zephyr asked.

I patted the Diatanium sides. "Twenty-four knots in the water."

"Nice. Can we take her out for a test run?"

Before I could answer, a strong and commanding voice called, "*Zephyr!*"

My friend's formally violet eyes switched to blue, hints of red at the edges of her iris.

She whirled on the voice that had called her name. It was her twenty-year-old brother, Damari. I've seen the two of them spar multiple times, and even though her brother was older and stronger, she'd bested him way more than he'd like.

As Admiral Halden's second-in-command, Damari Haldenson was broad-shouldered, muscular, and the spitting image of his sister. His dark hair was cut short at the sides, longer on the top. His blue eyes were filled with the same warrior's spark that Zephyr had.

"What, Ari?" Zephyr snapped.

"Where have you been?" he shot back.

"Are you *serious?!* I told Dad I was here to see Destin."

"Not my problem. C'mon, we have dinner with the Orilian Ambassador tonight." Damari grabbed Zephyr's hand and tried to pull her away.

She drew one of her knives and chucked it at her brother. He caught its hilt effortlessly, but then noticed that her eyes were a dangerous red. He dropped her hand immediately.

"Don't give me that," he said, handing the dagger back to his sister. Tessia and I were just watching this like an intense sporting match.

"I'll be there in a few moments." She looked over her brother's shoulder. "Did you *actually* bring like a third of the army to retrieve me?!" She huffed. "FINE. I'm coming, just let me say goodbye."

Damari turned on his heel and left. "Dad's anger is on *your* head, Zeph. Siren, too."

"Don't you drag her into this," Zephyr admonished. She looked at me, her red eyes fading to the same blue as her brother's.

"I know, you have to go. Sheesh, I can't believe the brigade your brother brought to get you. I know you're stubborn, but *really?*"

Zephyr laughed. "Yeah, sometimes. I better go before I'm grounded."

I gave her a quick hug before she sprinted off.

At some distance, I couldn't hear what they were saying, but they were elbowing each other, and then laughing. Zephyr gave Damari a hard punch in the shoulder. He punched back.

They have a strange relationship… I thought. Above me, I heard the boom of a break in the atmosphere, but didn't pay too much attention to it until Tessia tugged on my sleeve.

"Des, look," she said, pointing up at the sky. Battleships accompanied by Destroyers and some Heavy Cruisers had entered the Velusan atmosphere.

I glared at the ships. I hadn't seen those colors before. And they *certainly* weren't the white and gold colors of Orilia.

"Who are they?" I wondered.

Chapter Two: Zephyr

How to Crash a Dinner Party

"Did you have to be *that* obnoxious?" I asked my brother, Damari. We were sitting in the back of one of our Dad's escort vehicles. My brother didn't respond. "Look, I know it's just an act, but you could be a little less of a jerk when we're in public, you know."

The meaner you are to each other, the more the people will assume you could act the same way to them. Life is a contest of power. It's how you assert dominance. My father's words rang in my head.

Damari shrugged and rolled his eyes. "I really don't understand Dad's rule of 'you must be mean to each other in public.' It's so *stupid*."

"I second that," I said, stroking Siren, who was curled up in my lap. "Do we actually have dinner with the Orilian Ambassador tonight?"

"Yup."

"Funnnn. He's just gonna talk about how tropical and wonderful their planet is compared to ours," I muttered.

I thought back to being with Destin and how Damari acted with me. My brother noticed.

"Yes," he said. "It has to be in front of *everyone*."

"But it really doesn't," I responded.

"Well, talk to the admiral about it," Damari said. "Also, change out of your armor. Dad wants you in a dress. So does Mom."

My eyes turned gray. "*What?!*" I exclaimed. "NO. I am *not* wearing a dress, thank you very much." I folded my arms over my chest.

"Well, you can't wear your armor," Damari said, tapping at my shoulder. "Mom already has a dress picked out for you. Be prepared for sparkles."

I moaned. "What are you wearing, Ari?"

He grimaced. "A tux."

I laughed. I had only seen Damari in a tuxedo a couple of times, and it was hilarious how much he didn't like it. Honestly, I was the same way. I would trade sparkly dresses and jewelry for my armor and sword any day.

"At least Siren will be with me…" I said, mostly to the neidren. Siren puffed at me, then slithered up my arm and rested over my shoulders.

"Eeehh…"

"What?"

"Dad said that Siren can't come with you to dinner."

I felt like I got punched in the gut. I have never been anywhere without Siren. Ever since I first got her, we've been inseparable.

There is an injustice in the world and it must be righted, I thought, my eyes flashing between gray and red.

"Siren is coming with me to dinner. I don't care what Dad says." I kissed the top of Siren's head, and she gave me a puff.

An idea sparked in my brain, but I decided not to share it with Damari. He would most definitely laugh.

"You're on your own, then."

I shrugged. "I don't mind that. The only thing I do mind is Siren not being at the dinner with me." I thought about our guests. "Does the ambassador not like neidrens? Is that why Dad doesn't want me to bring Siren?"

"I dunno," Damari said, flatly.

When we arrived at our residence within the Velusan Citadel, Mom rushed out to greet us, black hair flowing behind her. She started telling me that it wasn't good for a young lady to be in armor all the time and that I needed to dress up more often. Then she told Damari that we were late and that he needed to get into his tuxedo *immediately* before the ambassador and his party arrived.

She ushered me into my room and started taking off my armor for me.

"Moooom, I can take off my own armor!" I protested.

"Nonsense. Now, take off all that... black."

"Tactical camouflage," I cut in.

"I'm going to get your dress," Mom finished, ignoring my comment.

I obeyed, grudgingly, taking off my combat boots and the black clothing I wore underneath my pauldrons. In record time, I unbuckled the straps that held my knives, and removed my scabbard from my back with the sword still sheathed.

Mom returned about a minute later, holding an icy blue dress with lace sleeves adorned with pearls. The bottom fanned out, and rhinestones decorated my torso and chest.

I had to be honest with myself. It was a very pretty dress, probably the most beautiful I'd ever seen, and I would wear it if I were forced to, which was exactly what was happening right now.

I put it on and Mom undid my ponytail, letting my long hair fall down to my waist. Then, she took a shimmering hair clip and pulled back any hair that fell into my face. The heels were simple and white, which I was thankful for. When Mom left the room, I took one of my belts and strapped it on underneath my dress with the dagger attached. It was easily hidden by the skirt, and the weight and feel of it against my leg made me feel more secure.

Just in case, I thought.

Then, I took Siren off my dresser and placed her around my neck. My idea from earlier was to dress up Siren as well. I found a box in the back of my closet that was labeled BABY CLOTHES. I found my brother's two-year-old bow tie and tied it around Siren so that the bow was on her underside.

Mom came back, holding a vial of what suspiciously looked like glitter.

NO, I thought. *NOT GLITTER.*

My mother dumped the vial over my head, sending a waterfall of shimmering silver on my hair, Siren, and my shoulders. I batted it away from my eyes, swiping and rubbing at my face. Siren sneezed, sending a cloud of glitter across the room. My neidren looked like a disco light.

"Oh!" Mom breathed. "You look *incredible.*"

"I *feel* suffocated," I said. "Was that really necessary?"

Mom's silvery eyes flashed as she gave me one of her '*you will love it*' Mom-looks. I sighed and stepped out of the room. Mom didn't comment that Siren was on my shoulders, despite the explosive sneeze.

We walked downstairs, into the opulent dining room, and took a seat. The dark wood of the table was the same color as my hair. My head turned to see the smirking ambassador walking in, head held high. He was tall and lean, gliding on spindly legs. The Orilian diplomat had icy blue eyes, bleached hair, and a blinding smile that he flashed at everyone in the room.

You're just as arrogant as when I first met you three years ago, I thought.

"Ah, Admiral Halden. It's good to see you again." The ambassador's voice was smooth and manipulative, and his favorite topic was his own planet and its superiority to the rest of the pentarchy.

I discreetly rolled my eyes in my brother's direction. Damari was sitting to the right of me. He knew just as well as I did that this was going to be a very long and boring dinner.

On my left, the ambassador sat down. I steeled myself, setting my eyes to their neutral blue.

Oh, gods, take me now, I thought. The ambassador reached for my hand and kissed it. It took all my willpower not to jerk it out of his grasp.

"Miss Zephyr," the pretentious ambassador said. "Such a pleasure."

"Please," I responded, trying to look like I was enjoying his company. "The pleasure is all mine."

Siren puffed at the ambassador and his eyes widened. Using this to my advantage, I stroked Siren, telling her what a pretty girl she was.

"You… have a neidren?" One of his eyes twitched. I tried extremely hard to not burst out laughing.

"Yes. She's very good."

"Won't she try to strangle you?" the ambassador questioned, keeping back from Siren.

I shook my head. "Not at all. Would you like to hold her?" I could see that the ambassador was trying to be polite. In an attempt to reassure him, I said, "She won't hurt you. I take her everywhere with me. We're inseparable. She may look intimidating, but Siren is a sweetheart."

The Orilian Ambassador warily held out his hands, and I placed Siren in them. She gave him a puff, then moved around a little bit. The ambassador smiled.

"She really isn't that scary," he said.

"See? She wouldn't hurt a soul."

"You know, the jungles of Orilia have tons of magnificent serpents. Way more than Sailara. All of theirs are probably underwater and you never see them. Orilia is so much better, isn't it. Is that a *bow tie?*" the ambassador asked. I nodded, laughing a bit, trying to ignore his arrogance.

"I thought it would look good on her." I looked over at the head of the table a few seats away from me. My father, Admiral Halden, was looking at me talking to the ambassador. I could see from his expression that he didn't like how I disobeyed him and brought Siren to the dinner party.

I watched as a guard walked over to my father, and whispering something in his ear. My father's eyes widened, and then he excused himself from the table. He was very tall and muscular, with juniper-colored eyes and peppered gray and black hair.

A few moments later, an air raid siren blasted through the house and the city. My neidren slipped from the ambassador's hands to around my neck, hiding her head in my hair. I immediately jumped up, left the table, and ran to my room, unsheathing the dagger along the way.

I stripped off my dress and heels, grabbing my black clothing and buckling on my armor, fastening a belt around my hips. I ripped out the clip in my hair and shook out as much glitter as I could. Tying it into a quick, high ponytail, I then strapped my scabbard to my back, keeping my sword drawn. I unbuckled then rebuckled the belts around my legs that held my knives and laced up my combat boots. Slapping on my gauntlets, I looped Siren around my waist above my belt. She clung on tightly. I grabbed a comm and stuck it on my ear before kicking my bedroom doors open and running into the chaos that had unfolded in the hallways. Everyone dashed to the doors to head for the docks, trying to leave the city.

I tapped my comm. "Ari! What's going on?!"

Static filled my ear for a horrifying moment before I heard my brother's voice. "The Grebles have invaded Velus! Leave… don't wait for… get off Velus… love you, sis…" The comm cut out.

"Ari! Damari Haldenson, answer me! That is an order!" I cried. There was nothing but static. "*Ari!* ARI!"

I tried contacting my Mom. Nothing. I tried my father next.

"Dad! Where are you?!"

"Zephyr! Is that you?" My father's voice filled my ears, and I sighed with relief.

"Yes, Dad! It's me. I'm sorry I disobeyed you–"

"Baby, there's no time for that. Listen to me very carefully. I need you to take your brother and *leave* Velus. The safety of the heirs of Velus comes first. Get on your ship and get out of here!"

I was shocked to hear my father call me that. He hardly ever used endearments. "I don't know where Ari is!" I ran out of the house, seeing bullets and fire raining down from above. Using my sword to deflect the bullets, I ran through the fire, slashing the air wildly.

"Zephyr, head to Orilia. Your brother will meet you there. Just, *please*. Leave Velus."

"Okay, Dad. I love you."

"I love you t–" the comm with my Dad cut out.

"Dad! Dad, please answer! Admiral Halden, answer me!" There was nothing but static. My eyes flashed their dangerous red as I sprinted toward the docks, hoping to at least find Destin and Tessia. I could hear soldiers in the distance, shouting at one another to protect the ambassador and the admiral.

I ran faster and could see the docks just beyond some buildings.

C'mon, Destin. Don't you leave just yet, I thought, racing against the bullets.

I jumped off a wall and hit the dock with a thud. I tucked and rolled, just as my brother taught me to do. I ran to where the *Caroline* was stationed in the waters of Velus, only to see her lifting off into the skies. I heard the roar of her plasma rigid-rotor as Destin throttled up and the ship took off at full speed.

"*UGH!*" I shouted. Siren coiled herself tighter on my waist, and I could sense her fear. "It's okay, girl. We'll get out of here."

I thought back to what my father had said before I lost contact with him. Then, the gear clicked. Of course! My ship, the *Willow!* The one Dad had given to me for my tenth birthday, to mark the beginning of my adulthood on Velus.

I tapped my comm, trying to get Destin, Tessia, or Mr. Kincaid. Finally, on the second attempt, I got through to Destin.

"Des! I'm running to my ship. She's not too far from where the *Caroline* was before you took off because she's right next to the *Concord*. And yes, I watched you lift off."

"Sorry, Zeph. Didn't know you were there. Meet us in orbit. We can land the *Caroline* on the *Willow's* back deck."

"Okay, I'm nearly at the dock. My father told me to head to Orilia with Ari, but I can't find him anywhere."

"We'll see you… OH, GODS–!" Destin screamed while the comm broke up. I watched as the *Caroline* swerved sharply to avoid a missile.

As soon as I got to my ship, I yelled to the lead engineer to start all engines and get us out of here. I looked out of the bridge window to the port side and watched the massive *Concord* move away from the dock and start to lift off.

"What's the holdup?!" I yelled to the engineers.

"I'm sorry, Commander. It takes time for the evaporator cores to steam up. Without enough steam running through the turbines, she won't move!"

"Speed up the process, then!" I snapped. In war, there was no room for politeness, just getting the job done. I turned to the firing office.

"Tell all gun crews to fire at anything Greblin," I ordered.

"Yes, ma'am," the firing officer said in acknowledgment.

Then I turned to the navigator. "Look for an eighty-five-foot brigantine cutter called *Caroline* on the radar!"

"Yes, Commander! What would you like me to do when we find her?"

"Track her! And tell the helmsman to follow her."

Suddenly, out of nowhere, the ship rumbled. I looked out the forward bridge window and saw both of the main guns pointing at a large ship called the *Mennus* off the starboard bow. It was hovering over Velus, spectating the destruction, fires being caused by its flanking ships.

"What is *that*?!" I screamed at the navigator.

"It's the Greblin command ship!" he said.

Gods... help us all.

Chapter Three: Tessia

Escape From Velus

My younger, yet slightly taller brother, Destin, was

at the controls of the *Caroline*, a beautiful ship created by him, named after our deceased mother. His brown eyes narrowed, filled with concentration as he absentmindedly ran a hand through his chin-length hair.

At the moment, we were trying to escape our home planet, Velus, since it was under attack by the Grebles, an enemy tribe of outcasts banished to the fiery planet of Oburna after they lost the Battle of Elofür Bridge half a century ago. My first guess was that they wanted revenge.

"Tessia!" Destin yelled at me. "We need more speed! Get in the A.S.T.S. and set it for race mode!"

"The *what?*" I asked.

"The Automatic Sail Trim System? Didn't I tell you this already?!" Destin shouted.

"Yeah, but you actually expected me to remember all of it?!" I snapped in defense. I looked out the wheelhouse window. There were so many ships. A fleet of small sky whalers caught my eye.

Oh, no, I thought. *Those little things don't stand a chance.*

They were slow, heavy, and unarmed, easy pickings for Greblin plunderers. I silently prayed to Navis, the god of ships and travel, that they would make it out of this mess okay.

"Hey!" Destin said in a stern voice. "We're breaking our atmosphere. You may want to strap yourself in." I nodded and turned, sitting down in the chair next to the desk that controlled the A.S.T.S. computer. At first, it was just a little rattling, but then the ship began to shake violently from the atmospheric resistance. I could hear the four-cylinder single-expansion reciprocating engine struggling to cope with all of the pressure.

"C'mon, Mom. You can do it. Don't give up on me now," I heard Destin say quietly to the ship.

"She'll get us through," I said to my brother with a smile.

As suddenly as it had started, the rumbling stopped, and we were outside of the Velusan atmosphere. Hundreds of Greblin ships were punching through the aerosphere, completely ignoring the *Caroline*. One or two ships fired several times, but they just kept flying past us.

I watched my brother steer the *Caroline* into open space, away from the Grebles.

Suddenly, there was static over the comms, and I could hear Zephyr's voice.

"Where… can't get past the *Mennus*… get away from Velus… go!"

Destin gave me a nervous glance.

"Should we go?" Des asked, and I could hear the obvious worry in his voice.

"Of course not. We'll wait for Zephyr, but we'll get out into the open."

Ahead of us, we could both see the cluster of passenger ships including the *Concord*, which our father was commanding. It was absolutely massive, dwarfing the smaller ships. The cluster was surrounded by protective battleships, cruisers, and destroyers.

"No one's attacking Dad," I joked. Destin didn't laugh. Suddenly, a ship larger than the *Caroline* blasted its horn as it passed us.

My brother whooped and pressed the *Caroline* after her.

"It's the *Willow!*" he exclaimed. "Zeph's okay."

Thank Navis, I thought.

"Look, she's slowing down," I said. There was more static over the comms.

"I thought I told you to go," a stern voice declared. I hardly recognized it as Zephyr. She sounded so strong and commanding, just like her father. She started yelling at the crew and engineers.

"Is the word, 'politeness' in your dictionary?" I asked. Des elbowed me.

I could almost picture Zephyr deadpanning. "There's no room for politeness during war, Tessia. It's us or them, and I *intend it* to be *us.*"

"Okay, okay!" I backed off, rubbing my side, where Des had whacked me with his boney elbow.

My brother landed on the battlecruiser, just aft of the fourth gun battery. A gravity shield was formed around the *Caroline*, and breathable air was filtered and pumped in.

Zephyr appeared from below deck, approaching the *Caroline*.

"We'll keep going, and we shouldn't head to Orilia," Zephyr said.

"What?" I asked. "Why not?"

Zephyr gave me a look that made me wish I hadn't asked.

"Because if the Grebles are attacking Velus, then who's to say they won't attack our neighboring planet and ally as well? Our best bet is to leave the solar system and head to another habitable planet and wait this out. Or until my father goes in guns-blazing and obliterates them all."

"Okay, fair point. Let me radio the *Concord* and let them know the plan," Destin announced.

I watched my brother leave toward the bulkhead that led to the *Willow*'s bridge to contact our father.

I shook my head. "You are your father's daughter," I said. "Maybe even more commanding than he is."

"I doubt that. Also, Siren, please stop suffocating me."

Zephyr unwound the tense little reptile from her waist and placed the dragon subspecies on her armored shoulders.

"Hang on," I said. "You just told her to stop strangling you around the waist. What do you think is going to stop her from strangling you around the *neck?*"

Zephyr laughed. "Because of her love for me, I guess. Otherwise, I would've been dead a year and a half ago when I first got her."

Before I could say anything else, there was screaming and flailing limbs charging out of the *Willow's* superstructure. It was my frenzied brother.

"GUYS! WE NEED TO LEAVE *NOW*. Completely get out of our solar system. Zephyr was right! There are at least half a dozen Greblin destroyers heading toward us."

Zephyr snapped into full military mode and turned to one of the crew members.

"I want the nearest solar system with a habitable planet with resources and oxygen, *immediately*."

"Yes, Commander," the member said quickly, running off to do his assigned task.

"Come on, let's get to the bridge!" Zephyr ordered. We dashed through the vast maze of walkways inside the *Willow's* superstructure, the crew briefly saluting as we darted past. Finally, we entered an elevator that led to the bridge. Zephyr immediately started commanding everyone there. I was fascinated by how easily it came to her, like second nature.

"I want all engines in Overdrive *now*!" she yelled at the helmsman. He acknowledged and responded.

"Yes, ma'am!" The helmsman grabbed both engine telegraphs and slammed them into the flank position.

An alarm blared four times and the bridge's computer declared, "Overdrive requested. Warning: running the ship's engines over maximum capacity could cause substantial damage to the ship's drive train. It is advised that you do not do this for too long."

I could see the *Concord* a few miles off the *Willow's* bow. All of her solar sails were down, and thick white steam was billowing from her single smoke stack.

"Follow that ship!" Zephyr ordered, pointing at the *Concord*. The helmsman spun the wheel hard to the starboard side, chasing after the *Concord*.

"Get next to her so we can board the starliner," I said to Zephyr. She nodded at me and told the helmsman his new directive.

"Acknowledged," he said.

As the *Willow* began to pull up next to the *Concord*, the engines were halted and the ship stopped. "Alright," Destin said. "I guess this is our stop."

"Yup," Zephyr stared out the forward bridge window into the vast expanse that is the universe.

"Hey," Destin walked up next to her. Zephyr had her arms crossed and a stern look on her face.

"Try and loosen up a bit. At least, we're still alive."

Zephyr whirled on Destin, her eyes swirling from gray to red. It was dizzying. "Loosen up? *LOOSEN UP?!* How can I possibly do that?! My Mom might be dead. My brother could be dead. I don't even know if my father made it out of the Citadel! We are at *war* with the Grebles. We have to *leave our own solar system* in order to save our lives! We have absolutely no idea what's going to happen to us! Here, I am in charge of *everyone's* safety, and one *single mistake* could end everything. And you want me to loosen up? I feel *helpless.*"

Zephyr? Helpless? I thought. *Impossible.*

Zephyr pinched the bridge of her nose, looking defeated. My brother and I went on either side of her and put our arms around her. The crew members stood around awkwardly, unsure of what to do.

Suddenly, the helmsman shouted, "INCOMING!"

Explosions rocked the *Willow*, slamming her into the *Concord*. Zephyr stumbled and then regained her balance quickly, her warrior face and authoritative tone back.

"I want every gun trained on our attackers! Defend the *Concord!*" Zephyr shouted. She turned to us. "You guys should probably leave now."

"We'll be on the *Concord* if you need us." Destin and I gave Zephyr a quick hug, then ran off to dock on the *Concord* and join our Dad on the super starliner.

Bombs lit up the expansive, dark sky as we prayed to the gods we'd make it out alive.

T
E
S
S
I
A

Chapter Four: Zephyr

Crash and Burn

"**W**hat is taking so long?!" I shouted at my crew.

"De-activate the gravity shields! Get the Grebles out of the sky! I WANT THOSE SHIPS GONE!"

Everyone was scrambling around, trying to fulfill my demands. Steering the UDN *Willow* away from the *Concord* as far as we dared, I finally got a clear view of our attackers.

The firing officer turned from his desk and said, "Commander! Forward gun batteries A and B are ready to fire!"

"Good," I said. "Let 'em have it!"

I watched out of the main bridge window as the forward two triple turrets armed with deadly twenty-one inch mark seven long guns rotated to the starboard side.

The firing officer shouted, "Gun batteries, Anton and Brono! You have permission to fire!"

A massive flash came from the gun's muzzles followed by a huge boom that rocked the *Willow*. I watched as all six shells sailed straight at a Greblin destroyer, blowing it to smithereens.

"Target destroyed! Reload!" the firing officer directed.

"We have another contact coming off our starboard aft!" The navigator said. "It's the *Mennus!*"

I glared at the Greblin command ship. Mordrar, the leader of the Grebles, had issued the attack on Velus and was most likely on his way to inspect the damage inflicted on Orilia.

The *Mennus* was beaten up and pieced together out of scrap metal. It was beautiful in a horrifying way. I took one look at the firing officer, and he shouted for fire on the *Mennus*.

The Greblin command ship fired at the same time, hitting our shells mid-space. They exploded, causing a blinding light show.

"Commander!" the wireless operator called. "We have a transmission from the *Concord*."

"Answer it," I ordered.

Destin's father's worried face filled the blank space near the window in a massive holographic projection.

"We're going to make a hyperspace jump to the outer rim of our system," Captain Kincaid said. "We're on a course to Zaccoth so we can stock up on food and supplies."

"We'll be right behind you." I seized the wheel, shoving the helmsman out of the way and directing the *Willow* until she was parallel to the *Concord*.

"Ma'am! We have another transmission!"

"Answer."

The Greblin leader, Mordrar, filled the screen. He was short and stout, like the rest of his army, and had burn marks all over his body. His large eyes had no whites, and his pupils were slits. One eye was more pale than the other, signaling the fact that he'd lost his sight in that pupil.

"Is that Zephyr Haldensdottir? My, how you've grown!" His voice was raspy and it sent a shiver down my spine. I held my ground, determined not to show any weakness to this monster.

"What do you want?" I snapped.

Mordrar ignored my curt comment. "Hmm. I'm kind of disappointed it wasn't your father. Then again, he's probably dead!"

My eyes spiraled dark red, and I glared at the grinning Greble. He had teeth knocked out and the rest were rotting.

"We will not be afraid to wipe your race off the face of the universe," I snarled.

"Ooh! You're feisty. Well, let me tell you, dear. Velus belongs to the Grebles now."

Then, all of a sudden, Destin's holographic face appeared right next to the Greblin commander.

"Lemme teach you something about Velusans," Destin began to say. "We do *not* just build ships. We take them apart when they need to be scrapped. And when we do, it is *not* gentle."

"Who on Oburna is this?!" the Greblin leader said to his crew, surprised. The crew was smacking buttons and slamming levers, trying to get Destin off their comm connection.

"Oh, my bad. Allow me to introduce myself. My name is Destin Kincaid, and I possess a superpower I like to call Mechanical Advantage."

For a brief moment, I thought I saw recognition in Mordrar's eyes. The Greblin commander laughed. "You're just a *child*," he sneered.

"One, no, I'm an adult. I passed age ten four years ago. Two, I'm an engineer. Three, looks can be deceiving. And four, *no one* talks to Zephyr Haldensdottir that way!"

I smiled with victorious pride for Destin as there were sounds of metal on metal. I looked out the bridge window to see all three main battery gun turrets being torn off the *Mennus.*

"My ship!" Mordrar screeched. "No matter," he said.

Mordrar shouted at his crew in their own language. Thanks to my mother, I understood multiple Greblin war commands. The one he just issued was for the *Mennus* to ram our ship. Unfortunately, my crew didn't know. The Greblin command ship sped toward us. The helmsman hit the button for the hyperspace jump just as the *Mennus* slammed into us.

"No!" I screamed, but it was too late. We'd been hit. The impact knocked the *Willow* off course, sending us flying into hyperspace. I lost my balance and fell over.

"EVERYONE, HIT THE DECK! Hold on to something!" I yelled. The crew did as they were told. The ship had been knocked to the starboard side, pointing almost at a ninety-degree angle to the *Concord*.

I rushed to my feet and grabbed the wheel, trying to redirect the battlecruiser back to its previous position, but it was too late. The ship was already in the jump, and the auto pilot had locked rudder control.

"Zephyr! Zeph, what's happening?" The connection between the *Concord* was still existent.

"We were rammed!" I yelled. "I can't control her!"

Using all the strength from nearly a decade of military training, I gritted my teeth and yanked the wheel as hard as I could. The hyperspace jump was starting to slow, and I could just make out a blue planet with a ton of land.

That's our best chance of survival, I thought. The *Willow* hit the atmosphere of the planet hard, and heat immediately blasted into the bridge. We were still going too fast.

There was another transmission coming through. I answered it. There was no video. Only audio.

"Please state your name and business or we will shoot you out of the sky," a deep voice proclaimed.

"This is Commander Zephyr Haldensdottir of Velus. I am escaping my home world and my ship is in need of repair. Do I have permission to land?"

"Your name is unknown. You do not have landing clearance. Shoot them down," the expressionless voice asserted.

Out of nowhere, black missiles shot from the land and attempted to hit us. I steered the ship away from them. One grazed the edge and knocked off several gun barrels.

I veered the *Willow* into a nosedive, the atmospheric resistance burning into the hull.

"You're crazy!" One of the crew members yelled at me.

"Nooo, I'm trying to save your life!" I snapped, making a sharp right, aiming for land. From this height, hitting the water would be just as hard as hitting land.

The only difference was that we could sink and drown, or escape the crash and live.

More of the black missiles aimed and missed us as I dodged them, using the nosedive as an advantage to theoretically shrink the *Willow*, making her less of a target. I could see a desert landscape hurtling toward us.

"Brace for impact!" I screamed, pulling the ship up aggressively. The *Willow* hit the sands, spewing clouds of dust everywhere, digging us deeper into the ground, causing a massive crater. Explosions sounded from down below, and the hull creaked and groaned from the impact. "You're welcome," I breathed, finally stepping away from the wheel.

I checked the ship's data computer for oxygen. Once I was sure it was safe and breathable air, I took the elevator down from the bridge to the engine room. The elevator door opened and I saw the three large tubes that the ship's turbines were housed in. It looked like a bomb had gone off. The engine room pipes were broken and bent wires were hanging from the ceiling and dangling from the walls, the frayed ends still sparking. Two out of the three drive shafts leading to the plasma rigid-rotors were broken.

"Commander!" I heard a crew member call. It was the evaporator core room manager, running at me at full sprint. "What happened?!" he asked, out of breath.

"We crashed." I grimaced at the damage. "How are the engines?"

"Core rooms one and two are obliterated. The atlas drive is completely disabled and over half the crew down here was killed on impact."

I winced. *This is worse than I thought.*

"Is the mainland cargo door still operational?" I questioned.

"It depends on how bored into the ground we are," the evaporator core room manager responded.

"Only one way to find out," I said. We walked through several bulkheads before coming to the cargo hold. On the floor of it was the outline of a big door that was used to load supplies when the ship was landed on the ground.

"Are you ready, Commander?" the manager asked.

"Open it."

He pulled on a lever on the wall of the cargo hold and the sound of hydraulic pistons filled the room. The door only opened a few feet because of the ground underneath the ship. I crawled out onto the hot desert sands.

I felt heavy, noticing the difference in this planet's gravity versus Velus's. The blistering heat felt scorching as I dusted myself off. The sun beat down on my head and shoulders, roasting my armor.

Siren, who had remained on my shoulders by wrapping her tail around my arm, lifted her head up and scoped out the desolate lands. She puffed at me.

"I know, girl. Not the best. But, it could be worse. We could be dead."

I put my hands on my hips, squinting in the bright light, seeing nothing but bits of dead brush and powdered rock for miles. A small breeze sent what looked like a ball of weeds tumbling off into the distance.

A chopping noise filled the air. Three pitch black helicopters, heavily armed, were headed my way. Based on the warm welcoming I had received earlier resulting in my crashed ship, I was betting that they were going to be just as friendly.

The sleek machines landed, and I coughed in all the dust that rose from its descent.

Two men in military gear stepped out of the first helicopter. I drew my sword with my right hand, the left one just over one of my knives.

"State your name and business, alien."

"I prefer the term, 'Velusan,'" I responded. "My name is Commander Zephyr Haldensdottir, and I am seeking refuge and medical assistance for my crew."

Siren hissed at the men, her strong body tensing and coiling. I stiffened along with her, unquestioning her instincts. If she didn't trust them, neither did I.

"What is that?!" one of the men shouted, pointing at the thirty thousand-ton battlecruiser that was the *Willow*.

"My ship that you helped destroy," I snapped. The men advanced. "That's far enough." I drew a knife.

"How are *you* a Commander? You're just a teenage girl in a good costume."

I threw my knife, and it hit the first man's bulletproof chest plate. It sank in half way, and their eyes widened, the man crying out in surprise and pain.

"I would advise you not to underestimate me." I went for my second knife.

Another man without the knife in his chest plate grabbed what looked like a primitive comm.

"I need backup!" he shouted. The man with the knife still in his vest hefted his gun, aimed, and fired. I spun my sword, it's Diatanium blade a blur, sparks flying where the bullets hit it.

More men stepped out of the other two choppers and started firing at me. I deflected the bullets, my sword easily taking the powerful beating of the metal rain.

A fourth chopper came toward me, and I could see something dangling from it. I figured that was the least of my worries.

I picked up my second dagger and hurled it at the man who had called for backup. It hit his shoulder hard, and he went down face first into the dust.

I didn't notice that the fourth chopper was directly above me until its cargo dropped.

It looked like a glass box, and the bottom was open. It came down on me, trapping me inside. The sides oozed out some kind of liquid, and as it hit the desert turf, it solidified, creating a strong floor.

I was having *none of this*. I drove my sword against the sides, but it bounced off.

What? I thought. *That's impossible!*

"Siren, waist!" I said, urgently. Immediately obeying, the neidren slid from my shoulders to my waist above my belt and anchored herself there.

Hoping to maybe tip the box over, I threw my shoulder against it. No result. I tried again, kicking at the walls. Not even a scratch. I tried my sword again, slashing and attacking the box to no avail.

The heavily armored men surrounded me.

"How *dare* you," I growled, pounding my fists on the box's wall. They jumped back, startled. "I come here seeking help and refuge, and you *attack* me and trap me in this… this *crate?!*"

"You know where to take her," a man radioed up to the chopper hitched to the cage. The black helicopter lifted off, taking me with it.

No… no this isn't happening. I've got to get out of here. I need to contact the Kincaids and the Concord, I thought.

I looked down at the floor. I scanned the ceiling. There wasn't enough room to jump and bust the bottom open, and even if I did succeed, I'd never survive the fall. Not in this gravity, anyway.

"Maybe we can escape when they let us out," I whispered to Siren. She gave me an affectionate puff and slithered back to my shoulders.

I sat down on the floor, taking in the view of this planet's landscape. There wasn't much to see. The terrain was pretty flat.

After about five minutes that felt like ten hours, I stood up and started pacing, trying to come up with an escape strategy. There wasn't much room to move, and I kinda just wanted to bang my head on the wall, wake up, and hope this was a dream. But it was way too real.

Off in the distance, there was a massive rock formation surrounded by a barrier of trees. The copter flew over the trees and what looked like an electric fence. The top of the miniature mountain opened up, exposing a landing pad. A small hatch door slid to the side to reveal a space small enough for the box below the pad.

The chopper landed, and I was lowered into a brightly lit room. There was nothing in it but the white walls and floor. One wall was a massive mirror. Sword still in hand, I twisted the hilt around, looking for an escape. There was none. The only way out was up, and the hatch was already shut.

"Careful with this one," I heard the pilot say. "She can be a devil."

"Good to know," another voice said.

A door opened, and in came four men and two women wearing goggles and long, white coats with a dozen guards, all as heavily armed and protected as the ones from earlier.

The people in lab coats walked around the box, their eyes wide with amazement. One of them, a female, adjusting her goggles.

"She looks so strong!" the woman said. "This is the second one to come in this month!"

Someone else is here? I thought. *Who*?

"Just *look* at that blade! Fascinating," another remarked.

"She has a snake! And it has eyelids! Oh, this is wonderful," a third exclaimed. The way they said that last line made me sick, but I didn't show it. My eyes were gray turning to red at the words of that third doctor.

"What's a snake?" I cut in.

"That creature around your shoulders. Do you not call it a snake?"

"First of all, she's a *she* and not an *it*. Secondly, her species is called a *neidren*. Not… *snake*."

"Her eyes change color!" a fourth squealed. "Tell me, do they change based on your emotions?"

I nodded apprehensively and backed up, a little overwhelmed. The fifth one, a male, was right behind me, looking at Siren. I spun around, surprised, and struck at him with my sword. He leapt back despite my prison, and all the guards aimed their loaded guns at me.

Siren opened her mouth and hissed, revealing her sharp, retractable fangs that were supposed to have been removed when I first got her. I figured that since she's my partner in battle, she needs a way to defend herself, too. Now, she was clearly agitated. The guards and people in coats left the room. One wall of the box fell open, making me jump.

I left the container, sword raised. I walked around, looking for any way out. The door had completely disappeared, and it looked like a solid wall again. I moved toward the mirror, and put my finger up to the glass, noticing that there was no space between my reflections. Someone was watching me on the other side of the mirror.

I hefted my sword above my head and brought it down on the reflective surface as hard as I could. The glass shattered, sending deadly shards flying in every direction, littering the floor with sharp specks of glittering dust.

The men and women in coats who had observed me earlier had shocked expressions on their faces and started screaming. All but one. A woman with blonde hair tied up in a bun.

"Where am I?" I demanded, holding her at sword and arms length, the Diatanium tip touching her chin.

"Area 51, darling," the woman smiled, but it wasn't cruel. It was nice to see that someone wasn't bent on examining me.

Before I could say anything else, I felt a huge hand on my shoulder. I whipped around, my sword slicing off the end of a gun. A second guard ran to assist, and they tried to grab at me, and when that didn't work, they went after Siren.

Oh, no way in Oburna are they touching her, I thought angrily, my eyes red and flaring.

Three more guards rushed over, trying to pin me down. One grabbed my ponytail and I yelped, surprised. I slashed with my sword, and the guard let go. The White Coats were still screaming and running around like idiots.

Finally, one ended up grabbing my wrists. I tried to twist away, but his grip just tightened. A second snatched my sword and threw it across the room, out of my reach.

"Pin her down!" a third shouted. I freed my left hand and went for one of my daggers, but they were taken away before I could reach them.

A white gurney with iron clamps was wheeled in by a White Coat.

"No!" I shouted, trying to get away from the men. But they didn't let go. They lifted me up and placed me on the table, locking the clamps over my ankles and wrists. Another White Coat brought in a small box with little holes. Siren was taken from me and put inside.

I struggled against the bonds, trying to get out, trying to get to her, but it was useless. The clamps were securely bolted, and I was defenseless.

"*Siren!*" I called after her. Her muscular tail slammed against the walls of the small crate. It didn't crack; it just made a lot of noise.

The White Coats wheeled me into another room with needles and tools for poking and prodding.

They're going to test on me... I thought, my eyes spinning into a dark, agonizing gray. Dread crept in, and I knew I wasn't going to get out any time soon.

A White Coat loomed over me. "Time to see what makes a 'Velusan' tick."

Chapter Five: Damari

Attack on Velus

T hick smoke rose from the city as bombs cascaded
down from Greblin ships. Many were trying to leave Velus
and head to our neighboring planets in the Cayser System,
but the Grebles were practically picking citizens out of the
sky. It made my blood boil, but I couldn't go up there and
help them. I had to stay with my group and protect as many
people as I could here.

I had tied a damp cloth around my nose and mouth to
make sure that I could still breathe. The armory door in the
Citadel had been blocked, and twelve members of the UDN
were trying to bust it down. A massive Diatanium pillar
creaked and groaned, tilting. That gave me an idea.

"Sorres," I said, looking over at my comrade. He was
short and stout, yet fit, with light, coffee brown eyes
complimenting his fair features.

"Haldenson," he acknowledged.

"I need to borrow your rocket launcher," I said. He
passed it over. I looked through the optical sight, aimed, and
fired, right at the base of the pillar. I ordered everyone to

move back against the doors of the armory as the Diatanium crashed to the ground.

"Battering ram!" one of the men shouted. "Good thinking, Haldenson."

"Let's get to work!" I called out. Four men to each side of the pillar, they reared back and rammed it down on the doors several times. On the fifth ram, the heavy doors gave way to the Diatanium. They crashed inwards, smoke pouring in as sand and dust plumed out.

"Why didn't we just use the rocket against the doors?" one of the men said.

I deadpanned. "Hindsight's twenty-twenty. Stock up!" I shouted. The twelve ran into the room. Guns and rifles were being tossed through the air. Rounds were being loaded, the familiar clicking filling the massive room.

A figure came into the doorway, and every man in the room raised their guns, prepared to fire. I held up my hand, palm facing the newcomer. If I closed my hand to a fist, they'd all fire.

"Son," the newcomer said, coughing. I dropped my hand as I recognized my father's voice. Everyone stood down, a little embarrassed that they were just aiming at the admiral, preparing to kill him had I given the order.

"Da– Admiral Halden," I said, remembering my place. I couldn't call my father 'Dad' in front of the UDN while I was on duty.

"Damage report?" he asked, walking over to a rack overflowing with rifles.

"We've moved as many civilians as we could to the Citadel, but the city is in bad shape."

"What about Commander Haldensdottir?"

Even though it had been a year since Zephyr had gained that title, it was still weird hearing it come from my father. To me, she was still my baby sister, despite the fact she's fourteen and considered an adult on Velus.

I shook my head. "No readings or reports. Flight Tower Axon believes she left the system."

He nodded, taking in the information. "Get to Tower A, soldier. You two, accompany him. The rest of you follow me."

"Yes, Admiral," everyone said in perfect unison, saluting him. My father grabbed two swords and a machine gun, along with several knives, before leaving the armory.

Once my father departed with the rest of the group, I was left with Sorres and Dennett. They were my battle companions, and we were to stay together at all times, watching each others' backs. They also happened to be my best friends.

Dennett grabbed a pump-action rifle and rapped his knuckles on it. The hollow sound indicated that it was lacking rounds, so he filled it up. My comrade had dark olive skin, tightly curled inky-black hair, and navy blue eyes that could be mistaken for black. He was around average height and slim build.

"Do you think she left the planet?" Sorres asked me while he was inspecting a knife. Believing it wasn't sharp enough, he reached for a whetstone and started to give an edge to the blade.

I shook my head. "She wouldn't leave unless the admiral told her to."

"She's one heck of a fighter, too. We could use her right about now," Dennett said.

I snorted. "I'd rather have her out of the line of fire, but knowing Zeph, she'd love to be taking down the Grebles."

A bomb detonated next to the armory, rocking the building. More explosions went off. They were trying to bury the armory. Melee weapons fell from the walls.

"TAKE COVER!" Sorres shouted over the noise. The rounds table in the center of the room was our best bet. I motioned for the other two to get under it before going myself. We hugged our knees, drawing in to the center of the table as much as possible. An axe thudded into the worktop, the handle hanging over the edge of the table.

When the deadly waterfall of weapons stopped raining down, we crawled out from under the table.

"We need to get to Tower A," Dennett said, cocking his gun.

I nodded. "Attack to destroy and take no prisoners. Shoot at anything that moves. Specifically, Greblin."

"Yes, Command Sergeant Major Haldeson," Dennett grinned. I punched his bulletproof vest. He hit me back.

"Stick together, work together, fight together," we all said in unison.

I took a deep breath before going to the doors of the armory. I could've mistaken Velus for Oburna; the destruction was immense. I ran out, headed for Tower A, Dennett and Sorres behind me.

"For Velus," I muttered, mostly to myself.

Chapter Six: Tessia

Tracking Zephyr

Destin was on the bow of the *Caroline*, cursing at the comm in his hands. "No luck?" I asked as he came storming into the wheelhouse.

"Nothing! Absolutely *nothing*. It's been three days, Tessia. I don't want to think about the fact that she… she might be…" my brother couldn't even bring himself to say it.

"That Zephyr might be dead," I finished for him. His face was red with anger.

"I *swear* to Asrea, if she's… you know. I'll never forgive myself. I'm the one who asked her to escort the *Concord*. I'm the reason she came. And now she's lost in hyperspace!"

I could see my brother mentally kicking himself, and I knew if he kept this up, it would go downhill from there.

"Des, look at me. She is the daughter of Admiral Halden. If anyone is equipped and prepared to survive out there, it is *Zephyr*. Just because we lost comms with her doesn't mean that she's in the Halls of Idar. Plus, I don't want to think about the rage the admiral will go on if he finds out that Zephyr is… you know," I said.

My brother hurled the comm across the room. It hit the wall of the *Caroline* hard, shattering.

"Relax, Des. We'll see her again," I reassured him. I just didn't know if we'd see her alive, or join her in death.

A message was coming in from the *Concord*. I answered it, and our father's face filled a holoscreen.

"Hey, kiddos. Des, I think I broke–"

"GODS ABOVE, DAD! If you say 'toaster,' I will actually *LOSE MY–*"

"Uhhmm, I was going to say, 'one of the comm networks.' Nothing seems to be working," he interrupted.

I watched as Destin looked over his shoulder at the obliterated comm over by the far wall.

"Heh… I think that was me," he admitted, sheepishly. I burst out laughing.

"Have you had any luck contacting Zephyr?" Dad asked.

Destin shook his head, sorrow filling his facial features. "Three days have passed. I don't want to think about what could've happened."

The *Caroline* and the *Concord* had comm connections throughout Zephyr's jump into hyperspace. We heard the entire thing, including how the planet she asked to land on attempted to shoot down the *Willow*. After Zephyr had shouted the words, 'brace for impact,' we had heard nothing else. The comms had filled with static. I'm pretty sure Destin cried a little.

"Dad, we're going to head into hyperspace and try to find Zephyr. Stay nearby but out of the range of the planet's satellite so they don't detect you," I said.

"Alright. Stay safe, guys. I love you both." The comm between the *Concord* and *Caroline* cut out. I pressed the button for the jump.

Destin set the navigation to find Zephyr's last known location, which was on the planet that tried to take her down, and maybe even succeeded in killing her.

I tried not to think about that as the ship prepared itself to fly at the speed of light.

We were pushed back in our seats as the ship hurtled beyond entire solar systems and through the galaxy.

After a few minutes, we arrived at the planet Zephyr had crashed on. My brother answered a comm coming through. The same voice that had doomed our friend rang through the *Caroline*, and I shivered.

"State your name and business," the voice said.

"This is Destin and Tessia Kincaid of the *Caroline*. We're searching for Commander Zephyr Haldensdottir and–"

My brother was cut off, abruptly. "You do not have permission to land. If you enter our atmosphere, we will shoot you down."

"That's a risk I'm willing to take," Destin said, pushing the ship toward the aerial barrier. The resistance rocked the *Caroline*, and fire engulfed the hull.

"Des! What are you doing? We can't help her if we're dead!" I shouted.

"I have a plan!" he responded. He yanked the wheel to the left as a black missile shot toward the ship.

"*Destin!*" I cried, more urgently this time. "You're going to get us killed!"

"Have you met me?" he shot back. "I'm getting us to the mainland and Zephyr's crash site. We are *finding her*, Tessia."

The *Caroline* sped toward the *Willow*'s distress beacon. Our nav system said her last known location was in a place called the Mojave Desert within a state named Nevada.

More missiles flew toward us. Suddenly, there was a loud booming sound, and Destin cursed. A warning sound echoed throughout the *Caroline* as the lights pulsed red.

"What happened?" I asked.

"The engine room! We've been hit! I won't be able to brake. Prepare yourself, sis. This is gonna be a bumpy landing."

A sandy landscape hurtled toward us. I gripped the armrests on the chair. Destin pulled up hard, trying to cushion our deadly descent. He succeeded in slowing our plummet. We hit the sands, but the *Caroline*'s boilers exploded.

I held up my hand in front of my face to protect myself. Fires raged throughout the bridge. Smoke filled the air, making it almost impossible to see. Shakily, I unbuckled my seatbelt and moved to where Destin was sitting.

I coughed. "C'mon. We need to get out of here." My brother didn't respond. "Destin! Wake up!"

I removed the seatbelt that held my brother in place. He slumped forward, landing in my arms. I slung his arm over my shoulder and made my way to the bridge window. I jumped out, taking my brother with me.

Walking about thirty feet away from the *Caroline* before laying Destin on the desert sands and looking behind me, I put both hands to my mouth, stifling a terrified gasp.

Smoke curled into the blue skies as flames burned through the ship.

I knelt down next to Destin. He coughed and moaned. I breathed a sigh of relief, thankful he was alive.

"We're okay, Destin," I told him, quietly. "Unfortunately, the *Caroline* isn't."

A sound like chopping filled the air. I looked up, seeing three black helicopters heading our way. I still had my sword and gun, and so did Destin. The pistol was sheathed at his hip. I drew my gun and disengaged the safety. With my finger poised over the trigger, I watched as heavily armored men exited the copters and came toward me.

I aimed at the men. They continued their advance. "Stay where you are," I shouted. "Or I will shoot to kill."

The men didn't stop. I fired, hitting one in the chest. It didn't affect him at all.

What?! I thought. *That should've at least wounded him.*

They split up, making a circle around Destin and me. They converged on us. A few took my still-unconscious brother away. I ran to him, but soldiers blocked my way. They grabbed my wrists and pinned me down.

"Destin!" I screamed. I fought against them, but they were too strong. The soldiers ripped my gun and katana away from me. One had a white cloth. He held it over my face. I inhaled a sickly sweet smell, and it made me gag. I tried to get the cloth off my face, but it was no use. I could feel myself beginning to black out. Whatever this substance was, it was powerful.

I mustered all of my might to kick one of my attackers in the kneecap. There was a loud crack, and he cried out and hit the sands. Startling the rest of the group, I used this to my advantage. Twisting out of their grasp, I ripped the cloth away from my face and took in lungfuls of fresh air.

They continued grabbing at me, but I slipped away, running after Destin, who was bound on a gurney and being loaded into a chopper.

Unfortunately, I hadn't gotten that chemical out of my system because the world around me started spinning. I stumbled and tripped, landing on the grainy terrain. On hands and knees, I retched, feeling worse than I'd ever felt in my entire life.

The last thing I saw was the helicopter flying away with my brother before the world went black.

Chapter Seven: Destin

Area 51

I woke up in a strange white room, feeling heavy with the difference of gravity. The walls looked like they were made of padded tiles, and there were multiple cots. I was wearing a white shirt and pants. Tessia was watching me, also wearing white, her just-past-shoulder-length brown hair, messy and tangled. When she saw that I was awake, she wrapped her arms around me and suffocated me in a hug.

"Oh, my gods, I thought I'd lost you…" Tessia cried.

"I'm okay, Tess. Where are we?"

She released me and shook her head. "I don't know. I woke up here, too. Destin… you got knocked out during the crash. The *Caroline* is destroyed."

My head was pounding as her words sank in, but I knew that was most likely the least of my worries, even though my heart ached for my ship. I had put so much into her.

Before I could say anything else, the iron door at the front of the room slid open, and a nearly unconscious girl with dark brown hair that fell down to her waist was dumped into the room by two beefy guards with armor and massive guns. I got out of my cot and walked over to the girl. I rolled her over and gasped.

I knew the girl. She was my best friend, Zephyr Haldensdottir. She was thin, pale, and her half-open gray eyes held none of its warrior's spark. She had bruises up and down both arms, including medical tape and gauze on the kink in her elbow.

When she fully opened her eyes and recognized me, I saw the one thing I'd never thought I'd ever see in Zephyr. Fear. Raw, overwhelming fear.

"Destin… no…" she murmured, quietly, her voice barely more than a whisper. She broke into a coughing fit, and Tess helped me prop her up against my shoulder.

"Zephyr, what happened?"

My friend scowled. "They're *monsters*. They've been using me like an object, experimenting on me, drawing vials and vials of blood. And now they have you…" Her eyes roamed across the room and landed on Tessia.

"Nooooo… Tess, you, too?" I looked over at my sister. Her face was pale at the sight of Zephyr completely drained of her fire and fight.

"I'm sorry, Zeph. But not completely." Tess said. "Now we're together, and we can escape together."

Then, I noticed something. Where was Siren? Zephyr must have noticed my confusion because I could see tears welling up in her bloodshot eyes. I could feel my heart breaking.

"They're testing on her, too. They won't let me see her… it's been days. I don't even know if she's still alive."

Tessia, clearly angered by this, glared at the heavy door, stormed over to it, and pounded on it.

"HEY!" she shouted. One of the guard's faces appeared in the tiny barred window.

"Shut up," he grunted.

"WHERE'S SIREN?" she screamed. The guard looked confused.

"Who?"

"Siren," Tessia demanded. "The neidren? The white noodle-looking creature with the blue eyes? Does that ring a bell? Do you want me to spell it out for you?"

Recognition crossed the guard's face. "Oooh! That space serpent. It looks like a snake, right?"

Zephyr gave him one of her signature death glares. "*Where. Is. My neidren?*" she hissed like Siren, and I could see the gears turning in her head of how to end this man if he misplaced a single scale on her beloved companion.

"Your *pet* is in quarantine. It's being tested for venom levels and sicknesses," the guard answered.

Zephyr was now growling. "She's a SHE!"

My friend seemed so defenseless, laying against my shoulder. It was such a shock to me. I hated seeing her like this. I hated this room. And I *absolutely hated* that Siren was also being tortured.

I had always had feelings for Zephyr because she was always a good person to me. I honestly couldn't imagine a world without her.

She was there for me when my Mom died. She was there when I had first thought about building the *Caroline*. She had always supported me no matter what. She didn't deserve this. I silently vowed to kill everyone in the most painful way possible for what they did to her.

I also held an extreme grudge for the fact that I was defenseless. I couldn't help my sister; I couldn't help my best friend; and, I couldn't help Siren. I couldn't even help myself.

Then there was the thought in the back of my mind that Zephyr wouldn't be in this situation if I hadn't asked her to come. She would be safe with her powerful admiral father and all of his personal guards taking down the Grebles.

"Please," Tess implored. "Can we see her?"

The guard thought about it for a moment. "Yeah, sure. It's just a snake, anyway." He lumbered off, muttering to himself that he despised his job and his roommate or whatever.

I looked down at Zephyr. All of the defiance she had shown the guard was completely gone. Her gray eyes met my brown ones.

"I'm sorry, Zephyr. I'm so, so sorry. You wouldn't be here if I hadn't asked you to come…" I lamented, quietly.

There was a flash of green in her eyes. "It's okay. I needed a break from Velus, but this wasn't exactly what I was thinking of."

My voice cracked. "No, it's my fault. It's *my fault* that you're here. You should be with your father and your guards–"

Zephyr shushed me. "Des, it's really okay. It's not the most ideal situation, but it could've been worse. We could've died. But we're not dead. We're alive and together, and we'll get out of here. Somehow."

She said that last part almost to herself. Tessia walked away from the door and came to my right side, where she put her arm around my shoulders.

"She's right, ya know," Tess said. "We're gonna get out of here, and blow this place to Oburna and back again."

We were quiet after that for a long time. I'm pretty sure I cried a bit.

"Destin…" Zephyr said, softly.

"Yeah?"

"I'm scared."

I thought my heart was going to stop. The words 'I'm scared' should *never* be coming out of Zephyr's mouth. In fact, they shouldn't even be in her *dictionary!*

I inhaled and said, "Don't worry. Somebody's going to be getting a 50 Cal. Multiple times."

She laughed, and for once, I felt not as hopeless as I had when she was first thrown in with us.

"We'll get Siren back, too. You can go full ninja-warrior on anyone you like after that."

Tessia gave me a look. "Nice, bro."

I gave her my evil smirk. "I know, right?"

Now, we were all laughing, despite our desolate situation. Zephyr broke into another coughing fit, and I decided that maybe we should get off the floor and help her get to a cot. I stood up and then pulled Zephyr up after me. She struggled to stand, obvious it pained her. She went limp, becoming dead weight in my grip.

Tessia helped me move her to the third cot in our cell room. As soon as her head hit the pillow, she was out like a light.

I stifled a miniature scream. "Oh, my *gods*, Tessia. I have no idea what to do! We don't even know what planet we're on! And I HIGHLY doubt that Mr. Happy McCheery over there is going to tell us." I jerked my head toward the iron door that held us prisoner here, referencing the guard.

"I have an idea," Tessia said.

"Oh, nooooo, an idea? Tess, I don't have a flamethrower!"

Tessia gave me one of her sisterly looks that wasn't filled with love. "My plan does not involve a *flamethrower*. Plus, that happened when you were FIVE! How do you still remember that?"

I shrugged. "How did you even get your little six-year-old hands on one of those, anyway? It's not like you can walk into the local pyro shop and just say to the store manager, 'Hi! I'm six, and I'd love to launch a flamethrower at my brother!'"

Tess sighed. "Whatever. Here's my idea. You, with your amazing techy powers n' stuff, will find a way to disable the lock in the iron door. Then, you, and already half-dead Zephyr–"

"Whoa, that's a line that you don't cross!" I scolded.

Tess continued. "–will fake being dead, and I can scream my lungs out, 'cause you know I'm really good at that, and the guard will come running. Then after I knock him out–"

I stopped her again. "With what? A *pillow*?"

"Would you stop it?!" she screeched. "Anyway, I was saying that after I knock him out, we could escape–"

"–into the massive prison-test facility that we know nothing about?" I shot. "Face it! There's nothing here to knock out the guards with, and plus, they know this place *way* better than we do! Unless we can get one of those goons to turn on his fellow thugs and help us out, we're trapped here! Zephyr is weak and needs serious medical attention. She'd be dead weight if she's like this while we're escaping, and even if she isn't, we don't have any weapons. Yeah, Zephyr could probably take out half of Velus's army on her own, but not in the condition that she's in, and not against people whom we have no knowledge *whatsoever* on how they fight! We're *doomed*."

Looking a little defeated, Tessia slumped to the floor and hugged her knees to her chest. "You're right…" she said.

Suddenly, something dawned on me, and I moaned in annoyance. "Oh, gods!"

"What?" Tess asked.

"Admiral Halden! He's going to go *ballistic* once he figures out that Zephyr is missing. With any luck, we'll have the entire United Dragon Navy scouring the galaxy for her. And on top of that, he's going to be even more pissed off when he finds out we crashed, burned, and lost a battlecruiser to these cretins!"

"Hopefully, he'll be more relieved than angry once he gets his only daughter back," Tessia said, slightly unhelpfully.

I slid down the wall and sat next to my sister, trying my best to brainstorm escape routes, but it just seemed hopeless.

Just then, I noticed that Zephyr was shivering. Her brow was deeply creased, and I could tell that she was in immense pain.

I stood up and ran over to the iron door and pounded on it, just like my sister had done before. The same guard showed up, and he didn't look happy.

"Please, help her. I know you're all bent on experiments and you should all go to Oburna and die, but *please*. She's in pain. Are you seriously okay with ending her life? She has a family, you know, back on our home planet. Also, her older brother–"

"Okay, okay!" The guard said, cutting me off. "Jeez, you can really make someone feel guilty, can't you?" The beefy man pulled out what looked like a prehistoric comm from one of his many vest pockets and contacted what I was hoping was some help. "Hey, I need a medic in section 78 C, prison cell 13 A. It's the girl that arrived five days ago." He paused. "And, bring the snake-thing as well. These aliens are going insane over it."

"Thank you, but we really prefer the term, 'Velusans,'" I said. The man scoffed and then started to walk away.

"Wait!" I called after him. He stopped.

"What nowwww?" he complained. "I'm not supposed to talk to you! You're gonna make me lose my job, kid!"

I ignored the comment. "Where are we? What planet are we on?"

"You're on Earth. It's basically a giant mudball with too many people and not enough resources, but we're actually pretty cool and manage well enough. Now, if you don't mind, I'm trying to sneak in some sleep before my shift changes!"

Then, out of nowhere, a female medic came speeding down the hallway, holding a box with a white rope in it, and pushing a medical cart. The guard unlocked the door to the cell, and I backed toward Zephyr, standing defensively in front of her.

"Relax… oh, I don't know your name," the medic said, her hair tied up in a blonde bun.

"It's Destin," I responded, quickly.

"Well then, Destin. Relax. I'm not here to hurt your friend." The medic put the box with the white rope down onto the floor, and before I could comprehend what was really inside, Tess dove for it, screaming, "SIREN!"

"Siren!" I exploded, yanking off the lid. I gently lifted the neidren out. "Oh, my gods, we were so worried about you! Are you okay?" I asked. Siren gave a single slow nod. Then, she curved her neck, looking over my shoulder to see Zephyr passed out behind me. She gave several puffs, then slid over my arm, around my neck, and plopped down on Zephyr's torso.

"Um, excuse me, little space snake… Siren, right? I kind of need to get to your owner to help her."

Siren looked at the medic, gave a quick hiss, and indignantly flopped across Zephyr.

"I'll move Siren for you," I said, picking up Siren the way Zephyr had done what now seemed like a millennia ago back on Velus.

I drooped the neidren over my shoulders while Tessia tried to calm her down. Siren wiggled and puffed, clearly unhappy.

The practitioner did a bunch of medic-y things, then took out a syringe filled with a clear liquid. I tensed.

"What is that?"

The woman smiled. "It's a concentrated painkiller. It should get her through the night, at the least."

"Thanks." I watched as Zephyr was injected with the serum, and the difference was almost instant. Her breathing eased, and she relaxed. I let go of the breath I didn't realize I was holding.

Zephyr's eyes fluttered, and slowly, they started to open. They were no longer gray. Her irises were a deep ocean blue. I placed Siren in Zephyr's arms, and her face immediately lit up, her eyes instantly switching to purple.

"Oh, my gods!" she breathed. "Siren! You're okay!" She gave her neidren a gentle hug and then started stroking her scales. She looked at the medic. "It's *you*."

I was confused. Zephyr met this woman before? What happened?

The blonde smiled. "It's me."

"I still don't understand why you didn't run from me like everyone else," Zephyr said.

Now I was even more confused. What went on when she was captured?

"I didn't run because I knew you wouldn't hurt me. You were scared, I understand. The only reason I stay in this place is to help those like you. I try to hamper the experiments as much as I can."

"Thank you," Zephyr's eyes switched back to blue.

"My pleasure. Darling, what is your name?"

"Commander Zephyr Haldensdottir of Velus," she said matter-of-factly.

The medic nodded. "Well, it's good to know that you're alert. I'm going to leave you now and let you get some rest. I'll leave your snake with you as well. There's no reason for you to be separated."

The woman was about to leave when Zephyr called out, "Wait! Can I get your name?"

"Alice," she said, before turning and walking out the iron door that kept us locked in section 78 C, prison cell 13 A.

Chapter Eight: Andrex

Introductions and Awkwardness

Creeping silently through a facility that had trapped me for a month started becoming second nature. This was my fifth escape attempt from Area 51, and I was *so close*. All I had to do was get to my ship, the *Nautilax,* and I'd be home free.

I turned a corner, ducking between doorways and trying to stay out of the view of the security cameras. Men wearing military armor and camo with bullet proof chest plates and helmets walked past me in one of the doorways I was hiding, carrying massive guns.

Suddenly, an alarm went off.

Great Asrea, I thought. They were after me. Again. I sprinted to the confiscated weapons room and yanked on the door handle. It was locked.

"Shoot," I muttered. I didn't want to give away my location. Too late. Guards were running toward me, their booted footsteps echoing throughout the halls.

I darted away from the door, rushing toward the hangar, where they kept all the 'alien' ships. I hated that word. 'Alien.' I prefered 'Zaccothian' in a million different ways.

My home, Zaccoth, was the planet of ice and snow, on the outer regions of the Cayser System. I was studying to be a doctor back on Zaccoth. A remedy I was working on required a plant that only grew here on Earth. But before I even got to a place where the plant was sold or could even find a wild patch of it, I was nabbed by goons in military gear.

They knocked me out and took me by helicopter to this monstrosity of a place. Area 51. For the past month, I'd been subjected to experiments and torture, but about a week ago, they slowed down. Drastically. To me, that could only mean that someone else was here, and they started testing on him, or her, instead.

As I dashed through the hallways, I made a sharp right, and slammed straight into two guards. I fell to the ground, disoriented.

Before I could get up and run away from the men, they grabbed my arms and hauled me to my feet.

"Here he is," the first one said.

"Oh, hey guys! Do you mind? I'm just trying to escape," I said, struggling in their tight grips.

They snickered, dragging me off. We went down a plethora of sterile hallways, taking dozens of turns. I mapped them all out in my head, already planning escape number six.

There was a door ahead of us with a sign next to it that said **Section 78 C**. A guard flashed his ID at a scanner, and it slid open with a hiss.

They dragged me through the long corridor before stopping in front of a cell door labeled **13 A**. The other sentry slid a keycard through the next scanner. There was a click and a green light, then they tossed me through the entrance. I landed on my feet and did a one-eighty to take in my new cell.

Two pairs of wide and confused eyes looked at me. The other girl looked me up and down and then studied my face. I wasn't exactly sure what she was thinking; her expression was incomprehensible. These must've been the newcomers, but by the more beaten up state of the other girl, she must've been the first one to arrive.

"Uh, hey guys," I half-waved at them. "Guess you're my new roommates."

The boy looked about my age. He had dark brown hair that just went past his chin, and he was wearing the same white uniform as me and everyone else in the room.

"Hi," he said, walking over to me. "I'm Destin Kincaid, and this is my sister, Tessia."

The girl who watched me come in joined her brother and smiled at me. "Welcome to Inferis," she said, referencing the god of death and the Underworld. Her hair was tied back in a braid and was slightly lighter than Destin's, but with purple streaks.

I grinned. "I've been here for about a month. Trust me, I know it well. My name is Andrex Nivalis."

The second girl stood up after I said the word 'month.' Her eyes were a deep blue, and they reminded me of home. Her dark brown hair fell around her face and down her back, ending by her hips. She had a white neidren with blue eyes sitting around her shoulders. The creature's black tongue flicked in and out at me.

"So you're the one the White Coats mentioned," she said.

"What did they say?" I asked, intrigued.

"They said that I was the second one to arrive this month. Of course, I didn't 'arrive.' They trapped me and dragged me here." I watched as the girl's eyes switched to a dark red. I was fascinated. I had never seen anything like that before.

"Sorry, I didn't catch your name," I told her.

"Zephyr Haldensdottir," she said. I glanced at her neidren. "That's Siren."

"Where are you from?" Destin asked me.

"Zaccoth. From the Cayser System."

"Nice! We're all from Velus," Tessia walked over to a cot and sat down.

Zephyr was silent, not looking at me. Her eyes swirled into gray as she stroked Siren's scales.

Suddenly, there was a loud banging. Zephyr stood up immediately, her hands in fists, eyes narrowed down on the door.

Eight guards lumbered into the room, two of them for each of us. Two went on either side of us and grabbed our arms. One reached for the neidren around Zephyr's shoulders before grabbing her. Zephyr leapt at the guard, her heel connecting with his jaw. There was a cracking sound, and the guard doubled over in pain.

"Siren stays with *me*," she snapped, her red eyes filled with hatred.

Note to self. Stay away from Zephyr when her eyes are red. Also, never get on her bad side, I thought.

Siren slithered down from Zephyr's shoulders and twined herself around Zephyr's waist. She was almost invisible; white scales on a white shirt.

"Move," one of the guards shoved me.

"Okay! Jeez, someone didn't get their beauty sleep," I muttered. The guard scowled.

We were all dragged out of the cell corridor and into a massive room. It was at least fifty feet tall. At one wall, behind glass were White Coats, as Zephyr called them, holding clipboards and pencils.

There were four doors on the wall ahead of us. We were each sent through one of them. Inside the room, I saw my clothing, my whalebone bow, and my quindent. All of my arrows were accounted for.

"Awesome!" I breathed, quickly changing into my blue and black long-sleeved wetsuit, and slinging the quiver over my shoulder. Since I lived on Zaccoth, there was a lot of swimming. I had a belt with several Bowie knives attached.

I walked out of the room. Destin and Tessia were still in their rooms, and Zephyr was standing outside her door already.

She had gleaming silver pauldrons that went over her shoulders and down to her elbows, straps over her chest and back in an X to hold it in place. Her long hair was tied up in a high ponytail, and she had on a leather headband with studs. A belt with a blue gem rested on her hips, Siren right above it. She had two straps on both legs. They were holding one dagger each. Her gauntlets were black with blue trim, and she had tall black combat boots that went up to her knees. They were laced, gold studs holding the strings in place.

I had to be honest with myself. It was attractive in a scary but beautiful way. I couldn't stop staring.

I didn't hear Destin walk out of his room until he was right behind me.

"Whatcha lookin' at?" Destin asked, smirking.

I whipped around, startled, my bow with a loaded arrow directly in his face. He backed up, surprised.

"Hey! It's just me!" I looked Destin up and down. He was wearing beige work pants with a bajillion pockets. His dark brown work boots matched the color of his hair. So did his aviator jacket. He had a large pistol holstered at his left hip.

Tessia walked out last. She was in shorts with boots like her brother's. She had a black and gray mecha crop top, and her hair was now out of its braid and held up in a bun that sat on top of her head. Her sword, which looked like a katana, was at her right hip, and she also had a pistol. It was on her left hip, and it was smaller than Destin's.

A loud voice boomed throughout the room.

"This is another experiment for your combat skills. Begin!"

Ugh, I thought. *I've already done this. They're gonna send in these fat little targets and–*

My train of thought was abruptly cut off as one of the walls slid open. At least a hundred robots with swords and guns rolled out.

"What?!" Destin yelled.

Zephyr's eyes switched to red as she ran headfirst into the brigade of robots.

I turned to Destin. "Is she always this brave?" I asked.

"Dude, you should've watched her command her ship. She's a freaking *powerhouse*." Destin drew his pistol, and it extended into an auto-rifle. He pulled on the gun's slide, cocking it and firing on the bots.

Okay then… I thought. I grabbed three arrows from my quiver and loaded them onto the bow. I fired, nailing my oncoming attackers.

Tessia grabbed her katana, and it made a satisfying *shhhhink* as it flew out of its sheath.

I decided not to waste my arrows. I grabbed my quindent and as soon as it was in my hands, it started to glow a bright blue. Using its length to my advantage, I slashed through the robots easily.

I looked over at Zephyr. She was tearing through these robots like they were made of thin air. I had no doubt that she could take them all on her own. She grabbed one of her knives and threw it with the force of the gods themselves, yelling her war cry.

It sailed straight through two of the oncoming bots, disabling them both.

A bot came up behind her. Like a sixth sense, she whipped around, her sword slicing the head clean off. I watched her fight; if something came up from behind her, her back would tense, and then she would turn around and attack. I realized that Siren must give a slight squeeze to help Zephyr during battle. The two of them made an impeccable team.

I remembered her telling me that her last name was Haldensdottir. I recognized her father's name, and seeing her in action made me realize how much training she must've gone through.

Destin blasted any bot that came his way, his auto-rifle in full assault mode. We continued fighting until all of the bots were obliterated. Zephyr retrieved the knife she had used during the battle.

"Good. Now, you get to face each other," the White Coat that had spoken before said.

A
N
D
R
E
X

Oh, you've got to be kidding me, I thought.

"Can I just ask something?" Destin shouted. "Why are you all so crazy?"

"Excuse me?" the White Coat demanded.

"You're all incredibly stupid! You're experimenting on living, breathing beings that have families and lives. Take my good friend, Commander Zephyr Haldensdottir, for example. She asked for medical help for her crew and what do you do? You put her in a *box* and fly her to this dump!"

The White Coat looked taken back. He struggled to say his next words. "You can sit out this round." He then turned to his co-workers, but forgot to turn off the mic. "Is he right?" the White Coat said.

"Um, HELLO?! You left your comm on!" Tessia yelled.

I turned away from the glass, laughing. The White Coat straightened himself out and said, "Andrex Nivalis and Commander Zephyr Haldensdottir, you're up first."

I watched as Tessia and Destin were dragged to one side of the arena and were placed in what looked like a glass box. Tessia slashed at it with her sword, but the strong material didn't even scratch. She started shouting, but I couldn't hear her through the soundproof box.

I turned back to Zephyr. She unbuckled her scabbard from her back and tossed it to one side of the room. I realized that her sword was in it. She held up her hands open-palmed, her soldier's stance strong and intimidating.

"Don't you go easy on me," she said, her eyes blue and incomprehensible. She smiled, but it was like a victory smile. Like she'd already won. It kind of unnerved me.

"You sure you want to do this?" I asked her. "It doesn't seem like a fair fight."

"Keep your quindent," Zephyr said, nodding at the long weapon.

Out of my peripherals, I could see Destin throwing his head back in laughter. That just made me feel even more confident. Oh, joy.

"*Begin!*" the White Coat shouted.

We started to circle each other, our footsteps silent. I watched as Zephyr's eyes swirled. It was dizzying to watch, but the number one rule in fighting is to never take your eyes off your opponent.

I sheathed my quindent and replaced it with my bow, nocking an arrow in it. I fired, and Zephyr leaned to the side, dodging it easily. I shot another arrow. She ducked, and the feathered bullet sailed over her head and bounced off the wall behind her.

"Why did you drop your sword?" I asked, trying to find a way to distract her.

She shrugged. "You can't always rely on your weapons in battle. Sometimes you need to fight without them."

"You're a good fighter," I said.

"Thanks. You're not so bad yourself."

"You took down those robots like they were nothing."

"They were just small obstacles," she replied.

I launched another arrow. She spun out of the way. I realized that she still had her daggers, but she didn't use them.

I removed my quiver and dropped my bow, taking my shimmering quindent as my choice weapon instead. We both advanced on each other, the attack circle closing. At the same time, we lunged at one another. Zephyr unsheathed two of her daggers faster than I thought possible and blocked my quindent.

She knows she can't touch the quindent, I thought. *She knows the cold temperature will burn her.*

I was surprised to see how *strong* she was, despite the fact that she had just been put under the same experiments I was subjected to. She was incredible.

Zephyr pushed back my quindent with her daggers and then slashed at me. I dodged, then struck, trying to force her back. She moved backwards from me, all the way to the other end of the room. Then she resheathed her knives and ran at me, full sprint. At the last second, she put herself into a slide, going straight between my legs.

"Whoa, what?!" I shouted. I suddenly felt pain shooting up through my right leg as Zephyr landed a hard snap kick to the back of my knee.

Then she grabbed my quindent and pulled it over my head. Twirling it like a baton, she struck me in the back and I hit the floor hard. I heard the clattering of the quindent as it landed on the floor. She took the risk of burning her hands holding it, but she knew how long it took before she had to drop it.

What the— What just happened? I thought, dazed. I could feel something cold and thin against the back of my neck. I knew immediately that it was one of Zephyr's knives.

"Have you had enough?" she asked.

"Uhhh, yeah. Is surrendering an option?" I felt Zephyr lift her dagger from my skin. She offered her hand and pulled me up.

I seriously thought I was going to go flying. Her grip was solid Diatanium. She still held her knife in her right hand. Zephyr backed up, and poised it to throw.

Oh, gods, I thought. *This is the end of me.*

Instead, she hurtled the small blade at the White Coats at the top of the arena. The dagger flew straight through the glass, shattering it. It hit one of the White Coats in the shoulder, and absolute chaos reigned.

"ARE YOU HAPPY NOW?!" she screamed, her formally blue irises a dark and deadly red.

Even without fighting, she was still incredibly intimidating, her commanding military voice soaring across the arena.

"Um, yes. We have our results," one of the scientists said, shakily.

Zephyr was enraged. "How *DARE* you make us fight! Just because you are the hierarchy of this nation doesn't mean you have the right to be conducting torture! We asked for *help* and you responded with *experiments*. We asked for *landing clearance* and you responded by *shooting us out of the sky*."

"Guards!" the scientists screamed. "Guards!"

Three men ran in and surrounded Zephyr. She tried to fight them off, but they were relentless. Grabbing her arms, they pinned her against the wall.

For some reason, this made my blood boil. I nocked an arrow and let it fly. It hit a guard in the arm. He let go of Zephyr, and she twisted out of the other one's grasp. She ran to her sword and removed it from the scabbard.

"Thanks," she huffed. Her gray eyes had a mixed color I hadn't seen before. Gold. Flecks danced in her irises like tiny stars.

More guards entered the room. We stood back-to-back and started taking them down.

"Guess we're a team now," I said to her.

"Yeah. I guess we are."

Chapter Nine: Tessia

Siblings who Actually Have a Bond

"**O**h-ho-ho, maaaan!" Destin shouted. "Andrex just got *totally smoked* by Zeph!"

"I know! Now look at them. Fighting back-to-back," I said. "I so ship!"

"I know, right? But did you *see that?* SHE DIDN'T EVEN USE WEAPONS EIGHTY PERCENT OF THE TIME!" my brother raved.

Grinning, I turned to my little brother. "I'm aware, Des. Remember, I'm trapped in this box with you."

"This should be viral," he said.

We continued to watch as Zephyr and Andrex were taking down guards left and right. More entered the room. One grabbed Andrex and Zephyr snap-kicked him in the groin. The man doubled over in pain and let go of Andrex.

"Holy Eseina," I said, referencing the goddess of love. "This is so cute it hurts."

"Like, actually though! I just wanna scream, 'DATE!' at them, but I'm pretty sure Zephyr would kick me in the shins."

I laughed quietly, knowing that statement would be entirely true if it ever did happen. It didn't matter that he was taller than the three of us and downright handsome with his tousled blonde hair and gray-green eyes. A pale blue, crystalline marking resembling ice formed two lines that curved down from his right temple along his upper cheekbone; his family's mark of Zaccoth ended in sharp points about two inches from his nose.

Guards converged on Zephyr and Andrex, and two gurneys were rolled through the doors. Zephyr noticed, her eyes widening. She shouted.

All amusement from before was replaced with horror as we watched our friends being strapped down. Zephyr wasn't having any of it. She fought like a cornered dragon, her knives flying. They grabbed her and forced her onto the rolling table. The clamps locked around her ankles and wrists, and Siren was removed from her waist, where she'd been the entire time.

Andrex, Destin, and I watched as Zephyr tried everything to get back to Siren. They were both taken out of the room, and Andrex was pulled out next. Everything went silent.

"Gods…" Destin said, quietly, his eyes wide. The door to the arena slid shut.

I realized that Zephyr was going to get herself into a lot of trouble in Area 51. She was probably the most dangerous one here, but it was her upbringing. Her mindset. She was a soldier, and a really good one at that. She was fighting to protect those she loved, and didn't care about what happened to herself, as long as the rest of us were alive and okay.

Destin knew this, too. I could see it written all over his face. We were all concerned about her, but even if she took a bullet during an escape attempt or while fighting, she'd probably ask us to leave her so we could get away.

The door to the box slid open, and my brother and I both stepped out. The arena had been cleared of the wounded guards, and there was blood on the floor. I shivered, unnerved.

"Siblings Destin and Tessia Kincaid! You will face each other! *Begin!*" the White Coat shouted. He really didn't need the microphone anymore. We could hear him perfectly fine since Zephyr destroyed the window.

Destin huffed. "You guys *actually* expect us to fight each other? Wow. You're really more stupid than I thought."

The White Coat's face turned red. "Begin. Fighting. *Now.*"

"You can't make us," I challenged.

I watched as Destin pulled out his pistol and dropped it on the ground. He kicked it away from him.

"I forfeit."

"You *what?!*" the White Coat raged.

"Me, too," I affirmed, kicking away my sword and gun.

Then again, we could've just shot the White Coats through the broken window and be done with the experiments, but that would probably just cause more problems for us.

"You're siblings! Don't you *want* to kill each other?"

Destin gave the scientist a look. "You see, we're siblings that actually *care* about each other. Is that in your dictionary? The word 'care?' You know, it might be good for you to do that every now and then."

TESSIA

The scientist scoffed before yelling at guards to come get us. The men hesitated, hoping we weren't going to put up as much of a fight like Andrex and Zephyr did. When they saw that we were compliant, they took us by the arms and led us somewhere to change back into our white prison uniforms. Then they dragged us back to our wonderful cell.

"Well," I said, once we were behind bars again. "That was eventful."

I noticed that Andrex was the only other person in the room with us. Zephyr wasn't back yet. That scared me.

Andrex was sitting on the edge of a cot, his head in his hands. He looked up at us. He was back in his white clothing, same as us. "Hey, guys."

"Where's Zeph?" Destin dared ask. I could hear the worry in his voice.

Andrex sighed. "I don't know. The tables were split up into different hallways."

"Zeph's a soldier. A warrior. Even though she hardly knows you, I can already tell she cares. That battle back there was to protect *you*. And Siren," Destin said.

Siren… I thought about the little neidren. *Is she okay?*

We were all silent. Destin and I moved about the cell and eventually flopped on our cots, contemplating life.

"We need a plan," Andrex said, after a while. "An escape plan. You know, I was put here because that alarm was me. It was my fifth escape attempt."

"Your *fifth?*" I shrilled.

Andrex nodded. "I was so close," he said. "I tried to get to my bow and quindent, but I got caught. I've practically memorized this place."

Destin and I exchanged glances. This was good news. If Andrex knew his way around Area 51, then that completely boosted our chances of getting out of here.

I stood up and started pacing, trying to think of a way out of here. So far, I had nothing.

Every head in the room turned as the door opened and Zephyr was thrown in. She was unconscious. Her hair was down and messy. Andrex looked at all of the bruises on her arms and the gauze from the blood draws.

"She's digging herself into a hole," Destin said. "Put down the shovel, Zeph," he whispered to her. "Stop fighting for once."

Andrex walked over and lifted her up. He had a pained expression on his face mixed with something else. I knew what it was, but I didn't say anything.

He brought her over to a cot and placed her down. Her breathing was shallow, but at least she was still alive.

I shifted my gaze to Destin. He had a dark look in his eyes, and I knew he was blaming himself again for Zephyr being with us.

I put a hand on his shoulder. "It's *not* your fault," I told him. "She's actually alive because of you."

Destin snorted. "Oh, really? How's that?"

"She would've stayed on Velus to fight with her father and brother if you never asked her to come. The Grebles could've killed her. She also defended Dad and the *Concord*. They're also safe because of her."

I watched as my brother took in this information. "True."

"So…" Andrex said, not turning away from Zephyr. "Any thoughts?"

I felt like I was hit by the *Caroline*. The idea was so crazy, but so brilliant, it just might work. "Destin reveals his powers to Area 51."

"I *what now?*" my brother exclaimed. "Tess! Are you *trying* to get me killed? You could've done that in the arena, ya know."

I gave him a look. "Just think about it! When the White Coats are about to experiment on you, you take their tools and make something out of it! When they figure out you can build with your mind, they'll use it to their advantage, but unbeknownst to them, you're going to actually build our *escape* vehicle."

A smile grew on my brother's face. "That just might work!"

"Whoa, hold up. You have powers?" Andrex looked shocked. "You can build stuff with your mind?"

"Uh, yeah. Guess I forgot to mention that," Destin shrugged.

I continued. "With Andrex's knowledge of the layout of Area 51 and you 'working' for the White Coats, we might just get home!"

Destin was jumping up and down now. "Tess! You're brilliant! We're gonna go home!" My brother suffocated me in a hug.

"I know I am," I said, flipping my braid over one shoulder. The boys laughed.

"Hopefully, my sixth attempt, and your first, will get us outta here. Man, I really miss the snow," Andrex admitted.

"Just give me my sword and daggers and I can clear a path," Zephyr's weary voice came from the other end of the room.

"Zeph! You're okay," Destin exhaled a sigh of relief.

"Zephyr, you're in absolutely *no shape whatsoever* to fight," I said.

I watched as Zephyr sat up slowly. She winced and put her hands up to her head.

"No," she said. "No, no, I'm fine. I'm perfectly fine."

"Would you stop that?!" Destin shouted. Everyone froze and looked at him, our eyes wide, including Zephyr. Her irises flashed gray.

"Stop what?" she asked, hesitantly.

"Stop *killing yourself*, Zephyr! You are putting yourself through too much! Area 51 will experiment on you until you die! When I first got here, you were barely conscious! And you're just speeding up the process of dying. You fight to protect us, but what about yourself? You need to stop thinking about us for once and start caring about your own well being!"

Silence. No one knew what to say. Zephyr exhaled.

"You're right," she said.

"And another– Wait, what?" Destin was now the shocked one. So was I. We didn't expect her to agree so easily.

"I said... SIREN!" she suddenly yelled, startling all of us. "Where's Siren?"

Zephyr swung her legs over the side of the cot and stood up, faltering a bit. She took one step and fell to the floor.

Andrex ran over. "You okay?"

She gave him a look. "What do you think? Oh, I swear to the gods. I'm going to take the entire UDN and demolish this place."

"I'll be right behind you," Destin said. "I want this place gone just as much as you do."

Zephyr's gray eyes spun into a light green. I saw her glance at Andrex for a brief moment. During that half second, I noticed a color I had never seen before. Gold. There were only a few flecks of it though. As soon as she looked away, they disappeared.

Interesting... I thought. Maybe it was a side effect of the experiments, but something in my gut told me it definitely wasn't.

Our warrior of a friend stood up slowly and sat back down on the cot.

"How are we gonna get Destin to the lab? It's not like some guard is gonna suddenly walk in and grab him for experiments," Andrex stated.

The cell door then opened, and a guard walked in. He grabbed Destin and dragged him out of the room.

"Well, that just happened," Zephyr said. We all flinched as the door slammed shut.

A split second later, it opened again, and another guard walked in. "You, too." He wrapped his beefy hands around Andrex's arm and hauled him off.

"Check ya later," Andrex said, saluting and winking as he left the room, escorted by the guard. I could've sworn that both gestures were aimed at Zephyr.

It was just me with Zephyr now. "You *like* him," I said.

"Who, Andrex? Yeah, he's nice. I mean, there's no reason why I wouldn't like him. Of course, I like him, but not like that. You know. Why wouldn't I like him? That's ridiculous!" Zephyr scoffed.

I blinked. *Was she babbling? Since when does Zeph babble?*

More sentries came to take us away. Zephyr stiffened, and it looked like she was about to fight the man, but an expression I couldn't quite recognize crossed her face, and she held out her wrist instead.

I was just as shocked as the guards. She didn't even try to get away. As we were moved out of the cell, I turned to Zephyr.

"What was that?" I whispered.

"Destin was right. I would only get in more trouble with these people. I won't fight them anymore."

"Wow, Zeph. That's... unexpected."

"Yeah, I'm saving my strength for when I *really* get to nail these bastards."

"Aaaannd there it is," I sighed. We both laughed.

Off in the distance, there was a scream.

"That sounds like–" Zephyr started.

"*Destin!*" I cut her off, breaking away from our escorts, and running down the hallway.

The guards chased after me. Zephyr didn't; I knew she was too weak, but there was no way she'd admit that.

I followed the sound of the yelling and busted through a doorway. I stood in a massive hangar filled with at least four ships, wandering White Coats, and guards at every corner.

The first thing I saw was the wrecked *Caroline*. The second thing I noticed was my brother crying.

Oh, no... I thought. *Oh, my gods, no.*

I rushed over to my brother and put my arms around him. He turned away from the ship and faced me. His eyes were bloodshot and his face was wet.

"I'm so, so sorry, Destin. I know how much you love her. I know," I said, embracing him. He buried his face into my shoulder.

"She's gone, Tess," he sniffed. "S-she's gone…"

My heart ached for my little brother. I wanted to take him far away from this place on the fully intact *Caroline*. But that wasn't going to happen.

"Good lord," my escort said when he finally entered the hangar. "I've never seen someone so upset about losing some hunk of metal."

I eyed him over my shoulder, glaring daggers of cold fury. Just from my facial expression, he knew he messed up. Big time.

"Well, if you spent half a year building her and then named her after your mother who died, then just *maybe* you would understand," I snapped.

I saw Zephyr enter the room behind the guard and watched her eyes land on Destin, who was still crying. Her eyes blazed red, which mirrored exactly how I felt. I made a quick prayer to the gods that she wouldn't attack the guard. Mainly because I wanted to.

"What did you do?" she hissed. The guard looked back and forth from the two of us and knew he wasn't going to be getting out of this situation any time soon.

"I don't understand why someone would be so upset about a machine. You can't be *that* attached to a ship," he said

"You *idiot.* Do you have *ANY* idea what you've done?! You have officially succeeded in getting the award for the *biggest moron* to ever exist in the universe." Zephyr advanced on the guard, poking a finger into his bulletproofed chest.

You go, girl, I thought.

"The amount o*f work* and *effort* and *time* that Destin has put into this *'machine'* is incomparable to whatever your pathetic human species can accomplish. Then there's the emotional factor. He named this after his *dead mother.* I just want you to take a moment and appreciate the fact that I don't have my sword right now."

I let go of Destin and helped Zephyr corner the guard. Using a move that would immediately admit me into the UDN, I kicked the man in the knee, then elbowed him right below his chestplate where the diaphragm was, then struck him across the face with the back of my hand.

"Now you listen to me," I raged. "If you *ever* say or do anything like that again, I will not hesitate to *end your life.*"

"Oh, don't worry, Tessia. He won't be."

I whipped around. My brother's eyes were glowing a bright electric blue. I had only seen them glow like this a few times.

There was a screeching noise of metal being torn. I watched as a small and sharp chunk of the *Caroline*'s hull ripped off. The shard flew toward the guard.

"Tessia, watch out!" Zephyr jumped across the space between us and knocked me to the floor, shielding me with her body. A split second later, the piece of burnt metal nailed the guard in the chest. He was dead before he hit the ground.

I didn't realize I was shaking. *That could've been me.*

My gaze shifted back to my brother. His eyes had returned to their normal brown. They went wide as he saw the dead man, Zephyr and me laying on the floor, and every

White Coats' head facing him. He then clutched his stomach and fell to his knees.

"What happened?" he rasped.

"You don't remember?" I asked, getting up and making my way over to him.

"It's blurry… but you were fighting him," he pointed at the body, "and then there was yelling and a metallic sound. That's pretty much it. Gods, I feel nauseous."

Zephyr came over. "Oh, yeah. Thanks for saving my life, Zeph," I said.

"No problem. It's in my job description."

"MY SUB!" Everyone jumped. Andrex broke away from a couple of guards and bolted through the hangar.

Three ships away from us was what looked like a subship. It would've been beautiful if it hadn't been so stripped for parts.

Zephyr left me with Destin and went to help Andrex. Or to slap him back to his senses.

He was flailing his arms and exaggerating whatever he was saying. Zephyr grabbed his shoulders to calm him down. For the first time, I noticed that he was taller than her. When Andrex was sane again, they hugged.

"Those two seem to be getting along *swimmingly*," Destin grinned, referencing Andrex's Zaccothian heritage.

I sucked in air through my teeth. "Yikes. That was…"

"Yeah, I know. I feel kinda *gill*-ty now."

"You're too *finny*," I cracked up.

"Oof. You may wanna work on your puns."

"Well, if you have any better ones, let *minnow*." We both laughed for a good, solid minute. When we were silent again, Destin's face went stern.

"Tess, something happened to me when I went all crazy," he admitted. "I heard Mom. I *swear* to the gods I heard Mom. She was telling me to harm that guard... to protect her memory."

I was speechless. "Des, Mom's been dead for seven years. That's impossible."

"I know what I heard, Tessia. It was her. It had to be *her*."

"Okay then. But I don't understand why Mom would ask you to hurt someone, even if it's to protect her memory."

Destin shook his head and squinted, like he was trying to think clearly.

"You need rest, Des. I still don't know what that electric blue eye-thing means, but I don't think it's good," I said. My brother ignored me. "Des! Did you hear me? C'mon, let's go." Still, he wouldn't move. He was lost in thought. He held up his hand to me. "Don't you silence me!"

Destin looked up at me with a serious expression. What came next I wanted to believe, but it just seemed impossible.

"Tess... I think Mom's alive."

Chapter Ten: Zephyr

A Subship

Andrex wasn't happy. His ship, the *Nautilax*, was a family heirloom, passed down for four generations. It was called a subship. It could travel underwater like a submarine and travel through space as well.

The subship was stripped of its outside material and most likely whatever Andrex kept inside it as well. The Diatanium hull was removed of its lights. At least the windows were intact.

The *Nautilax* had six large intakes; three on either side of the ship.

"What are those for?" I asked.

"The *Nautilax* runs on saltwater. Living on Zaccoth, we got a lot of it. It uses the intakes to draw in water and uses zinc and graphite to create a salt water reaction, which produces an electric charge to power massive Uranium ion batteries which supply power to a giant Rotorax ten-thousand horsepower electric motor which then turns the plasma rigid-rotor."

"Wow. You know, Destin's the tech guy. He
practically supervised the creation of my… my ship. Oh, my
gods. Where's my ship?" I started looking around the hangar.

"Didn't you crash it?"

I exhaled. "Yeah. Didn't help that a Greblin ship
rammed me right before the hyperspace jump."

"True, but the bonus is that I met you," Andrex
smiled. I returned the smile, unsure how to answer that. I
could feel my face start to turn red, so I turned my back and
faced the subship instead.

"What were you doing here on Earth anyway? Is
Zaccoth under attack, too?"

"No, Zaccoth is fine. I'm a doctor. An ingredient for a
medication I was working on only grew here. Before I could
even get to it, I was snatched and brought to this
godsforsaken place." Andrex grimaced.

I put a hand on his shoulder. "I know. Me, too. I can't
wait to get out of here."

"What happened back on Velus?"

"My father had a dinner with the Orilian Ambassador
and the Grebles attacked our planet. It was *ridiculous*. My
Mom forced me to wear this blue gown with like a bajillion
sparkles. It was really pretty, but I'd rather wear my armor.
In the middle of the dinner, an alarm told us to evacuate the
city. I escaped with Siren since she was with me, but I have
no idea if my brother or parents are alive."

"I'm sorry, Zeph. We'll all get home. As soon as
Destin completes a way outta here, we'll be home free."

"I'm glad you're positive about it. Uh, and sorry
about your knee in the arena," I smiled.

"Eh, I'll live. Besides, I've been through much worse. You put up a good fight without your sword."

"Thanks. We make a pretty good team when we're not against each other," I admitted, remembering how we fought off the guards in the arena.

"We do. Actually–" Andrex was cut off by Destin, who had walked over. I cursed myself for not realizing that he was there; that meant I let my guard down.

"Hey guys," Destin said, his eyebrows going up and down. "Whatcha talking about?"

"The *Nautilax*," I pointed at the ship. Destin took one look at her and his eyes widened.

"OH. MY. GODS. She's *magnificent!*" he shouted. "Where did you get her?"

"Family heirloom. She belonged to my–"

"How fast can she go? What's her main source of power? *DOES SHE HAVE TORPEDOS?*"

"Yeah. Six tubes. Four forward, two aft," Andrex managed to get a sentence in.

"What's the operational range? How many passengers can she hold? WHAT DOES THE BRIDGE LOOK LIKE?!"

"Slow down, Des!" Tessia said, coming over. "Give Andy some time to answer."

"*Andy?*" Andrex grumbled, clearly not amused.

"Yeah."

"Please never call me that again."

Tessia nodded in response. A White Coat ran over to us holding a clipboard.

"How did you do that?" she asked Destin, pushing her heavy glasses up her nose.

"Do what?"

"You tore metal off that ship without even *touching it*. It was amazing!"

I watched as Tessia and Destin exchanged looks. It was almost like they had a telepathic connection.

"I can create and control any machine with my mind," Destin replied.

"Fascinating," the White Coat said, eyes wide, scribbling on her clipboard. "How long have you been able to do that?"

"All my life," Destin responded.

"Oh, this is wonderful! Do you know what we could accomplish with your power? The things we could build!"

The White Coat ran off to spread the word around Area 51. Little did they know they'd fallen straight for our trap; the plan for our escape was in motion.

"That was too easy," I said when we were back in our homey little cell.

"I know, right?" Tessia agreed. "Gods, humans are *stupid*."

"If we told those scientists that dragons existed, they'd probably be on a ship to Velus right now to study them," Destin scoffed.

"What do you even plan on building?" Andrex asked.

"I'm going to make a new ship strong enough to bust out of here and carry us to the ocean," Destin said.

I could almost see the gears turning in his head. I honestly didn't care what the ship looked like. I just wanted it to be operational, and, of course, the obvious: able to get us out of here. *Fast*.

"But how do you just start building a ship that normally takes months of planning and–" Andrex was cut off.

"Have you met me?" Destin laughed. "I have shipwright heritage in my blood. My…" his voice trailed off.

"You okay?" I noticed Destin's eyes flash the dangerous electric blue.

"Des?" Tessia asked, worry clearly evident in her voice. Her brother just stood there staring at the wall. Then all of a sudden, he collapsed to the floor. *"Destin!"* Tessia screamed.

We all ran over to him. His eyes were open, glowing that electric blue. It was extremely creepy.

"D-Destin…?" I looked him up and down, trying to figure out what happened. Slowly, he blinked. His eyes shifted back to their normal brown. I exhaled, relieved.

"What was that!?" Tessia screeched.

"She's alive…?" Destin breathed, almost to himself. He got up slowly and started pacing around the room.

"Who is?" Andrex asked, confused.

"No, that's not possible…. it can't be…" Destin whispered to himself.

"What is?" I said, trying to get a straight answer.

"My Mom!" he yelled. All of us moved back a little, surprised by Destin's outburst. Cautiously, I walked over to him and put my hand on his shoulder.

"Des, you need to calm down. Your Mom's been–"

He slapped my hand away; my eyes went wide. "NO!" he screamed.

Instinctively, I moved my stinging hand to my chest, protecting it, shielding it with my other arm. I moved away from Destin, confused by his sudden rage. Andrex moved in front of me as a motion of defense.

Destin shook his head and squeezed his eyes shut, like he was trying to clear his mind. When he opened his eyes again, he noticed all of us trying to stay out of his way. His eyes landed on my hand, which was fine now, and he looked at me.

"Sorry, Zephyr," he said. His tone was sad and genuine. "What... what happened?"

"Gods, it's getting worse," Tessia murmured. Andrex and I whipped our heads to the right and stared at her.

"You *knew about this?!*" Andrex blurted. Tess nodded.

"It's happened a few times in the past several years. Just the glowing eyes, but... he's never spaced out like this."

"Um, hello? You guys are talking as if I'm not here. I'm right in front of you!" Destin frowned.

"Well, Glowy McBlueEyes, guess we know what to expect the next time you go into possessed-mode," Andrex said.

We all cracked up. "I'll forever call you that," I said.

"...Really?" Destin's facial expression was unamused. That just made us laugh even more.

Destin deadpanned. "Thanks, guys..."

"Ahhhh, we needed that," Tessia sighed. "Do you have any plans for the *Caroline II?*"

"Hey, that's not a bad idea! I'll remake the *Caroline*, but bigger, better, and stronger than before! And this time, I'll make sure she has guns." Destin's eyes lit up, but in an inspired way.

"Let's bust outta here!" Tessia grinned.

Chapter Eleven: Damari

The Wrong Conversation

My father, Admiral Halden, slammed his fists down on the desk of his office and swiped off all of the papers. I was standing next to a bookshelf with Captain Kincaid beside me. It had been almost a week since the Grebles attacked, and there was still no sign of my sister or the Kincaid siblings. My father and the United Dragon Navy had driven the Grebles out of Velus, but they were also on Orilia and Zaccoth. Attacks and missiles were fired on us each day, but the Citadel held, and the UDN never wavered.

"WHERE IS SHE?!" he shouted, his commanding military voice booming through the office. He walked over to the weapon's wall and drew two swords. He drove them into the desk, completely impaling it. I flinched as he took an axe and hurled it toward the bookshelf. It landed about a foot away from my head.

I loved my father, but to be quite honest, sometimes I was afraid of him. Even though I was his son, he treated me like a soldier. To the rest of the UDN, I was just another man who was willing to sacrifice his life for his planet.

Captain Kincaid leaned into my ear, whispering, "Is your father okay?"

I gave the captain a look. "Define 'okay.'" Captain Kincaid's eyes widened a little bit. "Just give him a minute."

My father took down every close-range weapon from the wall and either hit another wall, the desk, or shattered the window. That was our seventh window.

Once he was out of sharp, pointy objects, including pens – he threw those, too – the admiral took a deep breath, and turned to us.

"Where is she?" he repeated, but quietly this time. "Where is my daughter?" He tapped his index finger on the desk, thinking. "I bet that bastard, Mordrar, has her." He slammed his hand down. "Soldier, open the comms. Get me the Greblin leader!"

"Yes, Admiral," I said.

On the inside, my heart ached for my sister; I had absolutely no idea where she was, and I missed her. For all I knew, she was dead. On the outside, however, I was stone-faced and head-strong, knowing the risk of casualties in battle.

I walked over to the side of the desk and pressed a button. An AI voice asked who I wished to call. I typed in the name of the Greblin leader. After a few rings, Mordrar answered. His ugly face filled a holoscreen.

"H-How does this work?" he muttered. "How do I know if it's on?"

"Uh, sir?" a Greblin soldier said. "You're visible."

"Oh. *Oh.*" Mordrar cleared his throat. "Admiral Halden. I would say it's good to see you, but I'd be lying."

My father hissed. "Where is my daughter?"

"Mmmmm... who?"

"ANSWER ME, MORDRAR!" the Admiral roared.

Oh, he's in for it now, I thought.

"I don't have your brat, Halden."

I tensed, wishing I could kill Mordrar through the holoscreen.

"I swear to the gods. If you so much as *touch*–"

Mordrar cut him off. "I said I don't have her. But gods, you two are so related."

"So you have seen her?" my father pressed. "Where is she? How do I know that you're not lying?"

"Because I rammed her ship myself, Halden," Mordrar snapped.

My father's wide eyes were angry, and one of them twitched. "End this conversation," he ordered through gritted teeth.

"Your kid is dead, Halden! You're never gonna find her!"

"There is the Dauntless Project," Captain Kincaid voiced. We both turned to the captain, who had been silent this whole time.

"Kincaid, you're promoted," my father declared.

I smothered a laugh.

"I what?" the captain looked confused.

Mordrar blinked. "Well, that was unexpected."

My father growled at the Greble. "Mark my words, Mordrar. You will not win this war."

The Greble snorted. "You'll never–"

I shut the comm down, cutting Mordrar off. My father sighed. "That brought us nowhere."

"Actually, Halden," Captain Kincaid said. "I just got a ping from a crew member on the *Concord*. They discovered that her last-known location is a planet called *Earth*. All they know is that her battlecruiser was rammed by a Greblin ship before jumping into hyperspace and that her distress beacon went off after she crashed."

"I want to know if she's alive," my father snapped.

Cautiously, the captain moved toward the admiral and put a hand on his shoulder. "I know, Halden. I know. Destin and Tessia followed her. I don't know if they're alive either. All I want right now is for them to be with me, but the gods haven't made it so." He paused, a sad look on his face. "They're all I have left of Caroline."

I could feel tears pricking the back of my eyes, but I quickly blinked them away. Soldiers *never* cried. Hearts of steel were forged under the power of my father to make sure we had what it took to get the job done.

I cleared my throat. "Dad? Why don't we take the UDN to Earth and find Zeph, Destin, and Tessia? Or at least a search party. I am well aware of the Greblin threat facing Velus and Orilia."

My father thought it over. "Good idea, Damari. You will lead the search party at dawn and head for Earth. Take the *Prince of Dragons*. The rest of the UDN will stay behind to defend the Cayser System. Especially *Orilia*." He spat out the planet's name. I knew his distaste for the Orilian Ambassador; I felt the same way. So did most of the Cayser System.

To *everyone's* surprise, the ambassador had made it out of the battle alive and unscathed. I kind of wanted to end the Cayser System's suffering and just finish the Grebles' job for them when it came to the ambassador, but I knew I couldn't.

My father dismissed me to gather soldiers for the search party. I gave him a slight bow of my head with my hands behind my back and exited the room.

I started determining party size and debating what supplies to bring. I'd select four top soldiers to command the ships.

I figured we would have twenty soldiers to each of the five ships, including medics, and crew members. We would also need food, medical supplies, weapons, ammo, and battle armor. We had no clue what Earth would throw at us, and I needed to be prepared to lead men and women into battle if that's what it took to get my sister back.

I realized I forgot to tell my father about a message I had received earlier from Sailara about a weapons shipment. I hustled back through the halls and stopped in front of my father's office. I raised my hand to knock, but stopped. It sounded like Captain Kincaid and the admiral were deep in conversation.

Pressing my ear against the thick door, I heard a very old but familiar name; Dauntless. I heard my father's voice.

"I want to restart the Dauntless Project."

"*What?!*" the captain hissed. "Are you crazy?! Halden, with all due respect, I strongly advise against that."

"You're the one who mentioned it!" my father's voice hissed back.

"I wasn't *serious!*"

"Destin has Caroline's gift. It should be harnessed and he should be trained so he can get better. Your son possesses the Mechanical Advantage! We could get the project going again! Do you have any idea what that would mean for us? For the Grebles?"

"Do *you* have any idea what that could do to Destin? He's a *kid!*"

"He's past age ten, am I wrong?"

"No, but–"

"Then he is no longer a child. You know the rules just as well as I do. When a child of the Cayser System passes age ten, they receive their pennant as a way of welcoming them into adulthood. He is an adult. A very capable adult."

I'd heard about the mention of Destin's ingenuity when it came to building ships and machines, but I never considered calling it a power. To me, it sounded like my father wanted to use Destin against the Grebles and end the new war. I was all for ending the war and getting my sister back, but at what expense? I learned very quickly at a young age that a soldier must be willing to do whatever it takes.

"Look, Halden," the captain said. "You may be the admiral, but that means nothing for the Dauntless Project. I have a say in what happens to *my* son, and reopening the project is too *dangerous*. It *killed my wife*, for gods' sake!"

I stepped away from the door, the gears in my head spinning. From what I just heard, Admiral Halden wanted to restart the project that got Destin's mother killed. More importantly, he wanted Destin to complete the project *for* him.

I knocked on the door, slightly shaken by my father's words and how he wanted to restart such a deadly project. The conversation immediately ceased. My father's voice filled the silence.

"Come in, soldier."

Chapter Twelve: Destin

The *Caroline II*

Everything was unfolding in front of my eyes. I could see schematics, blueprints, ideas for a new ship that would be strong enough to handle the travel back to Velus after busting down the walls of Area 51.

The *Caroline II* was going to be better than her sister, and she was going to blow this place to Oburna and back. She would have the hull design of a Brigantine and the rigging of a Schooner, which would give her a top speed of forty-six knots. She'd be powered by two prototype engines. The T.E.S.T. engine, designed by my mother, but as far as I knew they were never built. And the *Caroline II* would be armed with two eighty-eight millimeter guns put in a set of two on a single forward turret.

The only downside about my ability was that I couldn't write down or draw my ideas out. Everytime I tried, I would get splitting headaches that would knock me out. So, everything was stored in my brain. Those around me couldn't see the numbers and translucent gears that would appear before my eyes guiding me through the construction, but all that mattered was that I knew they were there – and that I could complete what my mind had set out to accomplish.

"Destin? Hello? Don't you space out on us again," Andrex's voice cut off my train of thought.

"Sorry," I said. "I'm just excited! We have absolutely *no idea* what the humans and this Earth are capable of–"

"Aside from primitive tech," Tessia interrupted.

"*Capable of*," I repeated. "They probably don't even know the full extent and potential of their resources! I dunno, maybe they actually have something useful that we don't."

Zephyr scoffed. "That's highly unlikely. Have you *seen their comms?*"

"Yes, but that doesn't mean anything about their resources! Maybe they just don't know how to make proper comms," I said.

Andrex looked at me in shock and laughed. "Are you actually *defending* these guys?!"

"No, but–"

"They're our captors! I would have my stupid Earth plant by now and be back on Zaccoth if it weren't for them!"

"Remember," I said. "You're talking to a master engineer."

"Glowy McBlueEyes is right," Zephyr flashed me a teasing grin. "Even though they're our captors and an utterly useless race, there's probably more they could do with what they have on this mudball than they realize."

"You're never gonna stop calling me that, are you?"

Zephyr laughed. "Of course not!"

I facepalmed. *Thanks, Andrex*, I thought.

"OH, MY GODS!" Tessia exploded. We all jumped, startled. "Des, you know how you can't write anything down *physically* when you have ideas that involve your abilities?"

"Yeah. So? You want me to write them down *mentally*?" I was totally confused.

"Exactly! Use your mind to control the pen like you would a machine! Have your brain write down your ideas *for you!*" Tessia was practically bouncing off the walls.

"Tess, that's brilliant! Great Navis, that would've made my life so much easier!"

"Well, it's not too late to start," Zephyr said. "Anything worth sharing during that brainstorm you had a few minutes ago?"

I gave Zephyr my evil engineer smirk, showing that I might have something that'll save us all.

"Alright. Someone get me a pen and paper. Let's do this!"

Zephyr walked over to the door. "Um, excuse me, Mr. Guard? Can we have three pens and fifty pieces of paper, please?"

The guard scowled. "For what?!"

"We're bored," Andrex said, matter-of-factly.

Zephyr turned away from the door to hide her smile. Andrex had a pretty good bored face.

"Fine. I'll get you your fifty pens and three pieces of paper," the guard muttered.

Zephyr was unamused. "Fifty *sheets of PAPYRUS* and three *INK STICKS*," she said. "Ya know. *Pens?*"

The guard grabbed his comm and said, "Uh, our inmates need 'fifty sheets of pancakes and three pens.'"

"PAPER, YOU MORON!" we all shrieked in unison.

"Fine."

"*Thank you*," Tessia breathed. "About time."

"That took long enough…" I said. Moments later, paper and pens slid through the little slot in the door.

"Well, that was unexpectedly fast," Andrex stated.

I nodded, laying out three pieces of paper in front of me. I put the pens to the right of the paper. "Alright. Let's see what my Mechanical Advantage has come up with!"

"Go for it," Zephyr said enthusiastically.

We all sat down cross-legged around the paper. I closed my eyes and focused on the pens in front of me, imagining what I wanted them to do. I saw the *Caroline II* in every detail from the tip of the bow sprint to the end of the transom, from the top of the highest mast to the bottom of the keel. It was unfolding so perfectly. I could imagine the huge T.E.S.T. engines that would help propel the ship to forty-six knots: its theoretical top speed.

"It's working, Des!" Tessia exclaimed. "Keep going!"

My brain was working like a computer. There were thousands of numbers and statistics swirling through my mind, almost as if they were writing themselves down. Technically, they were. I could see the bow and the stern so clearly in my mind, as if I could reach out and touch them. There were the masts and booms rising up on the deck, the square riggers coming to life on the page before me.

When I opened my eyes, everyone was staring at the sheet of paper. In front of me was a full-blown drawing of the *Caroline II*, a beast of a ship that would take us through the stars and back home where we belonged.

"She's beautiful," Zephyr breathed, admiring the ship.

"She's gonna get us home," I said, satisfied with my work.

Andrex stood up and walked over to the door. "Excuse me, but we need to see the White Coats. We have something that would interest them greatly."

I was taken away from the others to the hangar by two guards. My breath hitched in my chest when I saw the wreckage of the *Caroline* again, but she was going to be a big help when it came to the construction of her sister, the *Caroline II*.

After the White Coats had seen my drawing, they immediately rushed me to the hangar where they wanted me to commence the construction as soon as possible. Using some of the salvagable parts from the *Caroline*, I pictured creating the new ship. Then, a stroke of reality hit me, and it made me want to kill every White Coat and guard. Or cry. I couldn't tell. The *Caroline* was only a few months old, and they had *destroyed* her. Completely demolished her. I tried to connect with my ship, but there was no response. All it did was make me more angry. My eyes burned with tears.

I shouted at the White Coats. "MAY THE GODS CURSE YOUR SOULS AND SENTENCE YOU TO LIFE WITH INFERIS!"

I held my hands out in the formation of claws at my ship. "You. Will. Be. REBORN!" I screamed. As if I were tearing something apart, I separated my hands in a yanking motion.

The *Caroline* parted, metal screeching and sparks flying. Blue electricity crackled in my eyes as I turned to the White Coats.

"Let me make something *very* clear to you. When you hurt *anyone* I love, you take a look at what I did to this ship, and then you take a look at yourself and thank the gods or whatever deity you worship that you're still in one piece," I seethed.

The White Coats nodded, eyes wide with shock and fear. I turned back around to face what was left of the *Caroline*.

"Now leave me alone to work in peace! And get Zephyr, Tessia, and Andrex in here!" No one moved. "ARE YOU *DEAF?!* Bring them to me!"

The White Coats scrambled around, issuing orders to the guards. A few minutes later, my friends arrived in the hangar, looking confused.

"Destin!" Zephyr shouted, running toward me. Her gray eyes darted around the hangar, looking at all of the destruction. "Wha… what… did you do this?"

"Are you okay?" Tessia cried, running up after Zephyr.

"Oh, yeah, I'm just *fantastic*. Absolutely, one hundred percent *A-OKAY*."

"Duuuuuude," Andrex said, quietly, surveying all the damage that used to be the *Caroline*. My eyes were still glowing their dangerous neon blue, electricity sparking.

"Destin? Hello?" Zephyr waved her hand in front of my face. "Are you in possessed-mode or are you here? Like, 'here-here?'"

"Yeah. Yeah, yeah, I'm here," I shook my head, trying to clear and organize my thoughts. Behind my friend were White Coats whispering to each other, and by the looks on their faces, I didn't like whatever they were talking about.

One of them signaled in my direction for two guards dressed entirely in black to take something away in my general direction. When they came and grabbed me, I wasn't too surprised. After all, my reaction to seeing the *Caroline* again wasn't exactly pretty.

"Hands off!" I snapped.

"Your presence is requested," one of the guards said. His voice was deep.

"Request? No one ever *requests* here."

"You're coming with us," the other guard demanded. I glanced at my friends; their facial expressions showed concern.

Tessia gave me a knowing look, as if to tell me I'll be okay. Somehow, I doubted that.

Chapter Thirteen: Destin

Call me Braindead

"**W**here are you taking me?" I asked the guards.

They didn't respond. They weren't wearing their normal Area 51 government-issued military garb. Instead, they were all in black, masks completely covering their faces; all except for their eyes. It was pretty disturbing, to be quite honest.

"To an experiment," one finally said. I tensed in their grips.

"What."

"You heard me."

"Can I just not?" I tried twisting away from them.

I was led down endless hallways, constant corridors of white streaking past me, the bright lights glaring and overwhelming.

Once several minutes passed, they brought me – sorry, *threw me* – into a dark room. I hit the floor on my knees. Getting up swiftly, I ran to the door, but they slammed it shut. I hit my fist against the surface. Nothing.

"Hey!" I shouted. "What gives?"

I looked around me; blinked a few times, too. My eyes wouldn't adjust. The room was so dark, I couldn't tell if my eyes were open or closed. I couldn't see my own hand in front of my face.

Reaching out with my arms, I felt around the space, trying to look for some kind of object, or at least a wall.

Just then, blinding light filled the room, making it completely white.

"*GODS!*" I screamed, covering my eyes and head with my arms. The pain behind my eyes was immense.

"Destin Kincaid," an eerie voice said. I only assumed it belonged to a White Coat.

"What do you want?" I snapped, rubbing my face, trying to get used to the lighting. The room was so white, I couldn't even tell where the walls were, or where the ceiling started.

"This is a more extreme version of a basic psychology test we perform on humans," the voice continued. I heard a buzzing noise behind me and I whirled around.

Tessia stood before me, perfectly still, eyes staring ahead. She was in her normal clothing; the kind she would wear back home. Jacket, mecha crop-top, denim shorts, sandals, and a low-hanging ponytail.

I waved my hand in her face. Not so much as a flinch.

"Tess…? What did you do to her?"

No response.

"HELLO?!"

Silence.

I walked in circles around my sister, trying to figure out why she wasn't moving. I reached out my hand. It rested on her shoulder, like she was actually in front of me. Her head turned in my direction before she disintegrated. I grasped at her, trying to make her stay.

"TESSIA!" I was horrified. What was this for an experiment? Why would they do this to their own race? Not to mention how strange this supposed test was. What did they expect from me?

"GIVE ME MY SISTER BACK!"

Humans are monsters, I thought. I figured that they wanted to test my mental range, thinking it would be different than the others since I had my Mechanical Advantage power. There was another buzzing sound. I turned my head to see Zephyr. She was in her full battle gear, UDN-issued, teeth gritted, eyes red, hair in a tight battle-bun, sword raised for a finishing blow. She had one foot off the ground, almost in a running position. The thing that really bothered me was the fact that Siren wasn't with her.

I stepped in front of Zephyr. She looked so *real*. And so angry.

"You're not Zephyr," I said, quietly. "You're not real."

The frozen Zephyr suddenly moved. I dodged out of the way of her sword, just narrowly missing its blade. It came down hard on the ground, a few sparks flying.

Zephyr blinked and looked around. "What's going on?" she asked.

Don't fall for it. This isn't real. None of this is real, I thought, trying to tell myself that this wasn't actually Zephyr, no matter how much it looked and sounded like her.

"What are you?" I asked.

Fake Zephyr gave me a confused look. "I'm Zephyr. You know, your best friend? Did you hit your head while working again?"

This was too much. "No, no you're *not* Zephyr. The real Zephyr is in the hangar. With Tessia and Andrex." I shook my head. "GET OUT!"

Just then, the room went dark like it was when I first got there. I heard a gunshot, the sound of a sword falling to the ground, and a thud. When the lights flicked back on, Zephyr was on her knees, clutching her stomach, blood staining her hand and darkening her shirt.

Even though my brain told me it wasn't real, my heart told me otherwise. It hurt the way I thought it could never hurt again; it was like losing someone as important as my Mom.

I ran over to her and knelt by her side. She looked up at me, breathing heavily, her gray eyes filled with so much pain. It broke my heart. It broke my heart into a million pieces.

"No," I cried. "No, no, no! Not you." My voice cracked. "Not… not you."

"I'm not afraid to die, Destin," she said, softly. I could hear her trying to hide the strain in her voice.

"But I'm afraid of losing you."

She leaned her head against my shoulder, and I pulled her to me, a lump rising in my throat as I fought back tears. Finally, I just couldn't help it anymore. I cried. Right there. Holding Zephyr, dying in my arms. There were a long few seconds before she stopped breathing.

"Z-Zephyr? Zephyr, please say something." I looked at her, expecting her ocean blue eyes to open and meet my brown ones. But they didn't. I buried my face in her neck, sobbing, grieving for my best friend. "ZEPHYR, WAKE UP! Please… please *wake up*…"

The lights flicked off again. When they came back on, Zephyr was gone. There was no blood on my clothes. I swiped at my face, trying to clear my mind. Ahead of me stood Tessia, Andrex, and Zephyr. There was a small table between them and me. On the table was a single knife.

"Choose one," the White Coat said.

I jumped, forgetting he was there.

"Choose one what?" I sniffed, angrily. "I swear to the gods, if you even *touch* her–"

"Pick up the knife," the voice cut me off. "And choose someone." Realization hit me like a punch to the gut. I didn't know how much more I could take.

"I'm not going to take one of their lives," I said, standing up. I picked up the knife.

Maybe I can use this to defend myself, I thought.

"Wouldn't Andrex Nivalis be the obvious choice?" the voice prompted.

"Excuse me? How could I take the life of someone who could *save* lives? Unlike *you*," I snapped.

The White Coat ignored the comment. "But isn't he your competition?"

"For…?" I waved my hands dramatically in the air, trying to keep him talking. I knew the answer to the question, but in a way, I didn't really want to believe it.

"Zephyr Haldensdottir's heart."

Hearing the words out loud hurt, but I knew that Andrex was better than me in more ways than one. And Zephyr was my best friend. She probably thought of me like a brother.

I shook my head. "I won't."

"Then wouldn't Zephyr Haldensdottir be your next choice?" the voice said. "She's not your blood. She could–"

"No," I stated, firmly, my voice echoing through the room. I *really* wanted to strangle whomever was on the other side of the wall.

"Tessia Kincaid may be your sister, but–"

"Great Navis, you're crazy!" I shouted. "I'm not gonna hurt any one of them, because I know they'd do the same for me. I'm not gonna hurt Tessia; she's my *sister*. I'm not gonna hurt Zephyr; she's my best friend. And I'm not gonna hurt Andrex, because I believe he can make Zephyr happy."

"Choose one," the voice urged.

"You want me to pick? Fine. I choose myself."

Chapter Fourteen: Tessia

The Big White Bugs Need to be Squashed

"**C**an you not?" I snapped at the White Coat

behind me. He had some kind of measuring tool and was trying to get the length of my back.

Andrex, Zephyr, and I were just sitting around in the hangar doing absolutely nothing. The White Coats were trying to measure all three of us, but whenever they got close, we just batted them away. They were like really annoying bugs with their big glasses.

"When's Des coming back?" Zephyr asked. She was lying on her back on the hangar floor, playing with Siren, who had been given back to her.

Andrex shrugged. "Only the gods know."

"I'M. SO. *BORED*," I announced, rolling on the floor next to Zephyr. Siren didn't even turn her head to look at me.

"We all are," Zeph said, sitting up. "Gods, I just wanna go hooooome."

"Ditto," Andrex mumbled.

On the opposite side of the hangar, one of the many doors opened, and in came Destin escorted by two guards. We all sat up and faced him, but he didn't look at us. His head was down; hair hanging in his face.

"Des?" My sixth sense told me that whatever the White Coats did to him was affecting him greatly.

Destin walked past us and slowly lifted his head, as if in a trance, and started to work on salvaging the *Caroline*.

"Dude, you okay?" Andrex stood up.

Destin didn't respond.

Zephyr and I exchanged concerned looks. She passed Siren off to me before walking over to my brother's side.

"Destin?" she asked, softly. He turned to her at last, and I could see his eyes were red from what looked like crying. Zephyr put a hand on his shoulder, and he stopped his work.

"Y-You're not real," he said, shakily.

Andrex and I advanced, keeping our distance. We could all clearly see that he had experienced trauma.

"I'm real," Zephyr urged. "I'm right in front of you."

"You died, Zephyr. You died in my arms." Destin closed his fists, knuckles white. A single tear fell down his cheek.

"No. No, I'm right here. I'm alive."

My brother's voice broke. "You were killed. By *them*. They shot you."

Zephyr shook her head. "Whatever they did to you, that wasn't real. But I am. And I'm alive." She put her arms around him. "You're okay." He leaned his head against her shoulder, crying.

I went over to the other side of Destin and did the same. "She's right. Whatever you saw isn't gonna happen. It was... a simulation or something like that."

Destin was shaking. "Don't you ever leave me, Zephyr. Please, don't ever."

She chuckled, trying to make the situation lighter. "I don't plan on it." Destin kept sobbing. "Hey," Zephyr said. "Look at me." Destin swallowed back some tears and looked up at her. "I'm not going anywhere. Not for a *long* time. I *promise*."

"I know. But... what if you–"

"Shhh. No. A million times no. Whatever you saw was fake."

"*But it looked so real.*"

"That doesn't matter, Des. What matters is that I'm here with you now, and that I won't ever leave you." Destin nodded slowly, swiping at his face.

"Dude, these guys are just absolute bastards," Andrex piped in. I realized it must be a little awkward for him to just stand there while I was hugging Destin while Zephyr was trying to support him.

Destin laughed inwardly. "Ya don't say."

"We'll blow this place to Oburna and back," I declared. "Wipe it off the face of the universe."

Zephyr stood up. "C'mon, Andrex. Let's give them a minute."

They walked away from the both of us, talking quietly. Destin's gaze followed Zephyr as she made her way across the hangar with Andrex.

"What happened back there?" I asked him, quietly.

"They wanted to see what it would take to break me," he responded. He turned to the *Caroline* and started to work, his hands moving like they had a mind of their own.

"And?"

"They succeeded," he muttered, angrily breaking off a piece of something burnt from the side of the hull. "They tried to make me kill one of you. I-I couldn't do it."

A million thoughts of the White Coats injuring Destin after he refused to do their experiment rushed into my mind. He must've noticed the change in my facial expression.

"That doesn't mean I didn't 'kill' anyone," he said.

"Huh?"

"I took my life instead. I could never do that to you guys. I care way too much. And I know that's going to bite me in my future; it already has."

I bit my lower lip, trying to think of some way to comfort my brother, but as long as we were in this place, there was no complete promise of fully reassuring anyone.

After a long minute, I finally said, "Here, how about this: you stop worrying about whatever happened in there and we get to building our way out of here."

"Yeah, let's do that!" Andrex called from the other side of the hangar.

"Let's build ourselves a *Caroline II!*" Zephyr agreed.

"Haven't you two ever heard of something called a *private conversation?*" I shouted back at them. I failed to hide my amusement, and I could have sworn I saw a small smile on Destin's face. I turned to the White Coats. "You want this ship built right? Well, we're gonna need a few items from you. First things first, our stuff. Especially his tools," I pointed at Destin.

"Yeah, my tool belt has pretty much… everything I need. And it probably includes some tools that you guys on Earth don't have…"

The White Coats' eyes were wide with wonder.

I nodded. "Yeah, that. Second, this place is gonna need a crane."

"What?!" a White Coat shouted.

"Hey, just because I have a Mechanical Advantage doesn't mean I can lift *everything,*" Destin said, flatly. The White Coat sighed.

"Okay then."

Zephyr walked up behind the White Coat. "Also, do you happen to have any Diatanium…?"

"Huh? What's… Diatanium?"

Zeph deadpanned. "An extremely strong metal alloy compound made up of diamonds and titanium. Duh."

"And you would need this why…?"

She shrugged. "It's only needed to build the entire ship's exterior and frame."

The White Coat blanched. "I-I'm sorry to tell you, but we don't have Diatanium on Earth."

"Useless *and* primitive tech? How have you people stayed alive for so long?" I needled.

"Relax, guys. I'll just have to make some," Destin said, dismissively. "You wouldn't happen to have a forge and rock crusher, would you?"

I thought the White Coat was going to pass out. "Uhh, we can get that for you, too," he squeaked.

"Good."

Several hours later, the government officials of whatever nation on Earth this was ordered an operational crane, forge, and rock crusher, and had it moved into the hangar. Andrex stared in amazement at the massive machines, marveling at their size.

"Have you never seen one before?" I queried.

He shook his head. "We don't use machinery for construction. We build everything out of ice, on land and underwater. Quindents can take water and shape it, freezing the water into structures like buildings."

"Whoa," I said. "That's really '*cool*.'" Andrex deadpanned. "I'm sorry," I laughed. "I had to."

There was a loud bang off to my right, and a burning smell filled my nostrils. I spun around to see a coughing Destin with a smoking device.

"Bro! What the actual–"

"Chill, Tess. I'm just experimenting with this… eePhone. Or however you pronounce it," he muttered, examining the thin, small device.

"It looks like a polished rectangle," Zephyr uttered, flatly.

"Yeah. It looks like a holoscreen with a metal backing, a glass front, and… ooh! Is that a Logic Board?" Destin waved at another White Coat. "Hey, can I have another eeFune? I think I broke this one."

The White Coat's face was impassive. "It's *iPhone*. And, no, those are expensive."

Destin snorted. "I could build one ten times better in thirty seconds."

"I'll be right back," the White Coat sauntered off, huffing.

"Uhhhh, what's a phone?" Zephyr asked. Another White Coat grabbed a clipboard and a pencil and dashed over to us.

"You don't know what a phone is?" the new White Coat's eyes were wide with excitement.

"Well, I wouldn't ask if I knew, now would I?" Zephyr snapped. "We don't have… eeFunes."

"iPhones," the scientist corrected.

"Yeah, that. We don't have iPhones. We have comms, holoscreens, holoshots, transmitter subspheres… what are you doing?" Zephyr scrutinized the White Coat, who was furiously scribbling down everything she said.

"Please, continue," he said without answering her question. "Oh, and what is a transmitter subsphere?"

"It's what the Cayser leaders from our system use to communicate over for critically important conference calls."

"And what is this… Cayser System?"

"HAH!" Des called from the other side of the hangar. "WOULDN'T YOU LIKE TO KNOW."

"Yes, I would. That's why I'm asking."

No one answered the White Coat. I had to turn away to hide my laughter, although I think it was quite evident.

"Hahahaha, no," Destin said. Andrex snorted, laughing. A few moments later, five guards wheeled in a bunch of spare parts for machinery. Destin's eyes lit up, and he smirked.

"This is gonna be fun!"

Chapter Fifteen: Zephyr

The Matchmaker

"So, uhh… Des?" I asked, a little nervous. Destin

was very good with his Mechanical Advantage, but
sometimes he could be a little reckless.

"Mmm?" he said, a little absentmindedly, focusing on
fitting all the spare parts into the right place to create the
T.E.S.T. engine, or the triplex expansion steam turbine
engine.

"You know what you're doing, right?" Destin gave
me a look from the top of the huge T.E.S.T. engine he was
standing on - one of the gigantic brass piston cases that
housed one of five pistons on the massive engine, which was
at least two stories tall. We were lucky the hangar was
considerably taller.

"Right!" he cried, enthusiastically. "We are ready to
fire this bad boy up!"

I deadpanned. "I love how you just *ignored my
question.*"

"Wait. You're gonna start it?!" Tessia called. She was
at least ten feet away from me, working on the forge, getting

it ready to begin processing the Diatanium. Destin gave me his 'evil engineer smirk.'

"Did you forget who you are talking to?"

"Uh... no," Tessia said, without looking at him. "You're my nutty brother with an obsession with machines and you just so happen to be able to control them with your mind. Huh. Why would I be worried at all?"

Andrex and I exchanged a look before bursting out laughing. The relationship that the two Kincaid siblings had was sweet, ridiculous, and funny.

Destin walked over to the edge of the engine and slid down a ladder that was leaning up against it. He walked over and stood next to me, hands on hips, looking at the side of the huge engine. White Coats started to gather around us, their huge eyes taking in every detail; writing down everything they could on their stupid little clipboards.

"Whaddaya think?" Destin called over his shoulder to the others. Siren, who was on my shoulders, lifted her head, blinking the sleep out of her eyes. She looked at the two-story engine, yawned, and flopped back down again, unamused. I scratched her small head with one finger absentmindedly, studying the engine's structure.

"It looks good," I told him. "But... if you start it up... won't we all go deaf?"

The White Coats surrounding us started to slowly back away from the engine in an attempt to keep their hearing.

"WHAT," Andrex shouted from the other side of the engine.

"Yeah, I'd like to be able to hear my brother's annoying voice every now and then," Tessia added.

Destin scowled. "Thanks, sis."

"Anytime," she responded, waving a dismissive hand our way without looking at us. Siren undulated off my shoulders and down my arm, poking her head up into the air like a scope. She puffed at the massive engine, scanning it with her stormy blue eyes. Her small black tongue flicked in and out, catching the strong metallic scent of the engine and the burning coals in the forge.

"Earth isn't *too* different from Velus, is it, girl?" I cooed, softly. She puffed at me, looking a little sad. I knew what she was thinking. "I know, me, too, girl. I miss home just as much as you do."

She eyed me skeptically, like yeah, you're having a *little* fun here manipulating these humans.

"Okay, yeah," I laughed. "It's certainly been... an experience. I guess the best part so far was the arena."

The arena... I thought, remembering my fight with Andrex. *Andrex...* I reflected on our battle. He was one of the strongest guys my age I've ever fought. Granted, I was the youngest of the group, but he was the closest. Tessia was the oldest at fifteen, and then Destin, Andrex, and me at age fourteen. Apparently on Earth, they have shorter years, so Tessia would actually be around seventeen and the rest of us would be sixteen.

I looked around the massive hangar, my eyes landing on Tessia and Destin. I've known them for as long as I remember; we've always been together. Then I shifted my gaze to Andrex. I certainly hadn't known him for that long, but I had this weird feeling in my gut that I couldn't shake.

Siren smirked at me, and I playfully blew on her snout. She shook her head before wiggling to my right shoulder and settling in the crook of my neck. She moved her head around a bit, bumping my chin with her forehead and flicking her tail on my other shoulder.

"What do you know that I don't, darling?" Siren gave me her renowned deadpan stare before pointing her tail toward Andrex and then Destin.

"Siren! What–" I started. She cut me off with a sharp hiss, pressing her tail against my neck, as if urging me forward. "What is it, girl?" Her only response was applying more pressure. I complied, walking to the left, since that was where she wanted me to go. Throwing caution to the wind, I put faith in my battle-buddy's intentions.

Her pressure led me to the side of the massive engine, where Andrex happened to be. He had one hand on the engine, his neck craned, looking up at its height. Siren pressed me closer.

"Hey," Andrex said, looking at me. Siren nodded at him, and he smiled. "I feel like she's up to something."

"Hyeah, tell me about it," I said, laughing. "She practically *pushed* me over here."

With that line, she pushed against my neck for the fifth time, urging me closer to him.

"*Seriously?*" I hissed at her. She just continued her hard-press, puffing at me, as if to say, "yes."

"Sorry?" Andrex asked, confused.

"Hmm? Oh, I didn't say anything." I smiled, and moved so that I was leaning against the massive engine's piping. I felt Siren moving off my shoulders and onto the engine.

What are you up to? I thought. To be honest, I wanted to see where this was going, but something in my gut told me I should be wary.

Andrex took a step closer to me, and I could feel my heart beating faster. I sensed Siren's lithe body moving over my waist as she returned from the engine. She laced herself around my hips as well, but for some reason, I couldn't feel her on my back. It was just cold metal.

Metal? I thought with a start. Carefully, I attempted to take a step forward. Siren tensed, her powerful muscles contracting. *She tied me against the engine!* Again, I tried to pull away, but I didn't want to hurt Siren. She clung on like a vice, trapping me.

"I-I'm stuck," I muttered. "Andrex... I'm *stuck*."

"Here, let me," he moved closer, taking hold of Siren's tail. After a moment, he furrowed his brow and looked like he was trying to get his hand off of something. "Uhm, Zeph?" Andrex said. "Siren's grabbing my wrist..."

Just then, Andrex was pulled forward by her tail. We were just inches apart, my face burning. I hated myself for blushing, and I didn't know what to say or do, for I had never been in a situation like this before. Honestly, I don't think anyone has. It was just me with Andrex... and Siren. Staring into each other's awestruck eyes. He had beautiful eyes. Wait, what was I thinking? I'm a soldier, not some head-over-heels princess! But I couldn't lie to myself. It was nice. Really nice... just enjoying each other's company. It was a warm and comforting feeling I hadn't known before. I didn't know what to call it.

Siren just kept pulling him closer to me, until our noses were almost touching. My heart pounded, and it seemed like I couldn't breathe, but in a good way.

Almost automatically, I put one hand on Andrex's chest, feeling his heartbeat. It thundered like mine; powerful and unrelenting. It was terrifying but thrilling, all at once.

"GUYS!" Destin shouted. I inhaled sharply, startled by the outburst. My eye contact with Andrex broke. "We're gonna move the engine outside. Sound good?"

That one moment was all I needed to break out of the trance. "Siren, let go," I ordered. She gave me a gentle squeeze, refusing my demand. "Siren! Let *go*."

With an almost sigh-like motion, she released both Andrex and me. He laughed a little.

"Guess we better get ready to go deaf, right?" he said.

"Sorry," I muttered.

"For what?"

"For...*that*," I said, pointing at Siren. She didn't look happy, and her tail was lashing back and forth. She whacked my bicep.

"Oh, please. She was just pulling a prank. She's a very smart neidren, you know," Andrex winked at me before walking off.

I slid down the engine's side, head in my hands, elbows resting on my knees. Siren gave me a puff. "What just happened?" I asked, mostly to myself. Siren opened her mouth and yawned. "This is your fault, Si," I scolded. She closed her eyes and wiggled around on my shoulders a bit, like a shrugging motion.

"Zephyr?" Tessia's head popped around the side. "Hey, you okay?"

"Uh huh," I said, not looking at her.

She frowned, but said nothing else. "C'mon. Last thing we want is you going deaf. Ya know, you being a soldier and all, you kinda need your hearing."

I nodded and stood up slowly, still trying to contemplate Siren's actions. *Oh, Siren,* I thought. *What do you know that I don't?*

Chapter Sixteen: Andrex

Test the T.E.S.T.

W hat just happened? What in the worlds just

happened? I took in several deep breaths, trying to collect my nerves. I knew that Siren was a smart neidren. Was she trying to act like a matchmaker or something?

We were so *close* to one another. We could feel each other's heartbeat. And her *eyes*. They were blue at first, but once Siren grabbed me, they were like ice. I figured out a while ago that blue was her neutral eye color, but there were these golden spark-like colors that seemed new. I'd seen them in the arena, and now here, and it was driving me crazy trying to figure out what it meant.

"Dude, you good?" Destin asked, cutting off my train of thought. "You look a little… distracted."

"Huh? Oh, no, pfft, I'm fine," I said, flippantly.

"Where's Zeph?"

I looked over my shoulder, but I couldn't see her anywhere. Confused, I advanced toward the side of the engine, wondering if she were still there.

I felt a tap on my shoulder, and I whirled around. Zephyr was standing behind me, and once again, I noticed her blue eyes blooming with gold. It fascinated me.

"Andrex, are you coming?" she prompted. "We don't want you getting squashed by the... whatever the machine that moves the T.E.S.T. is called."

"IT'S CALLED A S.P.M.T.! A Self-Propelled Modular Trailer!" Destin corrected.

"Yeah, that," she returned. Before anything else could happen, I grabbed her hand and pulled her off to the side. "Hey, what gives?"

"Are we... just gonna act like nothing happened?" I asked, quietly. For a moment, I thought the golden sparks in her eyes got a little bigger.

"I mean... well..." Zephyr kept talking, trying to think of something to say. For some reason, I couldn't focus on her words. Instead, my mind was pinpointed on what felt like a rope making its way around my waist.

Siren was moving across my arms now, like she was trying to pin them to my body. Unconcerned, I turned my attention back to Zephyr. She was still babbling.

"Okay, stop," I said, cutting her off. "Certainly, it was strange, but–" Suddenly, Siren tensed, wrapping herself tighter around me. The only thing I hadn't noticed before was that she had done the same with Zephyr, too.

We were pulled together, our faces about an inch or so apart. Our eyebrows went up as we practically relived what happened a few minutes earlier. Zephyr blinked. I didn't. We were both surprised, and blushing.

"Siren!" she scolded. "Cut it out!"

The neidren raised her head to look at the both of us, a satisfied expression on her small white face. I deadpanned in her direction. Instead of releasing us, Siren just made herself tighter, pressing us against each other.

"Andrex! Zephyr! Are you guys coming? Where did you guys g–" Tessia came around the side of the T.E.S.T. engine, and her jaw dropped.

"We could use a little help," I said. Tessia had the same gooey expression on her face that Siren did. What was going on with everybody?

"Yeah, I'll help you. But first, Destin needs to see this."

"NO, HE DOESN'T," we protested at the same time.

"What do I not need to see?" Destin called from the other side of the T.E.S.T. He poked his head around the engine, took one look at us, and burst out laughing. We both deadpanned.

"GET US OUT!" we shouted.

Destin, in silence, walked over to us with a smug look on his face and gave Siren's tail a high-five. I felt like I was missing out on a *much* bigger picture.

Cautiously, Destin and Tessia unwound Siren from around us. Her small black tongue flicked in and out in frustration. In a way, it looked like the Kincaid siblings shared the same feelings with Siren. I exchanged a look with Zephyr; she looked awkward.

Without warning, Siren slipped off of us easily and entwined herself around Destin's arm, raising her head and glaring at Zephyr. She stared right back, the Battle of the Unblinking commencing.

Siren opened her jaws, revealing her fangs, and hissed. Zephyr moved her head back a little bit, one eyebrow raised, clearly judging her neidren. Firmly, she pointed her index finger at the little creature.

"You and I are going to have a serious discussion about this later, *missy*," she snapped. In response, Siren hissed at her before burying her face in Destin's tousled dark hair.

"Right, then…" Destin shifted the conversation. "Now, can we stop getting distracted and actually move this thing outside so I can start it?!"

It took a while to actually move the massive engine outside. The Area 51 guards had driven the S.P.M.T. into a large courtyard. It must have been late in the afternoon because the sky was blooming with hundreds of different shades of pastel purples and golds. Only the brightest stars speckled the sky.

The guards positioned the gargantuan engine into the center of the courtyard. Destin looked it over one more time, making sure that everything was there and that all of the moving parts were well oiled. The White Coats then hooked up what seemed to be some kind of monitoring station. Destin eyed them carefully making sure they didn't do anything to screw over this test.

A White Coat walked up to Destin. "How are you going to control it? You have no way to."

Destin laughed. "You kidding me? I was born with a way to control it!" The scientist raised an eyebrow. Destin's irises suddenly flashed the dangerous electric blue and the White Coat backed away slowly.

Destin turned to the engine and then to us. "We may want to move back," he called. We walked to one of the courtyard walls, then, Destin turned to the engine. It was now completely lit up with spotlights. "Okay," Destin sighed. "Let's do this."

"Don't hurt yourself," Zephyr said.

"Yeah, please don't. You're kinda our ticket out of here," Tessia said, jocosely. Destin didn't respond, and I noticed the way he and Zephyr shared a look. It was hard to explain, but it was there.

Destin then closed his eyes and raised his right arm at the engine, his hand in a claw formation. "Ignition!" he shouted.

There was the sudden sound of what I assumed to be the electric starter motor. The engine's pistons moved into a starting configuration, followed by a heavy *chug*, then another and another after that. There was also what sounded like a consistent whining noise, which I guessed was the turbine. Both noises were getting louder and faster with every second.

The ground was vibrating; I could feel it in my chest and in my bones. It was a powerful and terrifying feeling all at once.

"This isn't even maximum output!?" Tessia cried, glancing at the gauges on the White Coats' monitoring station.

"I know what he's doing!" Zephyr shouted. "Destin is going to push the engine as far as it will go!"

A pang of concern surged. "Well, how far can it go?!" I asked.

"I think that's what he's trying to find out!" Tessia responded. It had already been several minutes and the engine continued increasing in speed, thick white steam billowing out of the temporary exhaust. I looked at Destin. His hand was still out, palm parallel to the wall of the engine.

Then, as if he were turning a dial, he twisted his wrist. A sudden bang came from the machine.

"What was that?!" I shouted.

"He just locked the steam valves in the fully open position!" Tessia shuddered. "He's running the engine in *overdrive!*"

Zephyr's eyes flew wide, and I saw her mouth the words, *'great Idar, no.'* "HE'S GONNA GET HIMSELF KILLED!" she screamed. "DESTIN! DESTIN, STOP IT!"

Destin didn't show any form of acknowledgment. "DESTIN!" Tessia cried. "STOP! THAT'S ENOUGH! YOU GOT THE DATA YOU NEED; TURN IT OFF!"

I walked up to him and shook him by the shoulder. Still no response.

"DESTIN! COME BACK FROM WHATEVER WORLD YOU'RE IN!" Zephyr screamed again. I swear I saw Destin mouth the words *almost there.* He kept twisting his hand. Sparks of blue lightning crackled around his hands and head.

"GOT IT!" Destin cried.

His eyes flew open and he thrust his hand toward the ground. An arc of light blue electricity spewed from his palm, stretching high into the air before coming down on the enormous engine. It gradually got quieter, the chugging of the pistons and thrum of power slowing down with every passing breath. Destin grinned. "See? I knew it would…"

His eyes rolled into the back of his head as he staggered and fell. Since I was the closest, I caught his arms before he hit the ground.

Everyone in the courtyard shared a terrified glance, our ears still ringing. The White Coats were the first ones to break out of the trance. They gathered around me, still holding the unconscious Destin, and started sharing theories. One of them held a small silver cylinder that looked like some form of injector and moved to place it somewhere near Destin.

Tessia stormed over and slapped it out of the White Coat's hand. "And what do you think you're doing with that? To *my* brother?" she demanded.

"Touch him," Zephyr snarled at the scientists as her eyes flashed dangerously. "I dare you."

They all backed away slowly, leaving us to the guards instead. Two men took Destin away from me, and I could tell both Zephyr and Tessia wanted to go after him, but they also knew they couldn't.

We were all forced back to the cell, analyzing what had just happened. We all knew how to get out of here. We just needed to make sure we didn't kill ourselves in the process.

Chapter Seventeen: Damari

Mission: Earth

Preparations for the Velusan command ship, the

Prince of Dragons, were finally complete. I was finally leaving my home planet to search for my sister and her friends. Sorres and Dennett were behind me, fooling around with some of the equipment from a firearm package. Thank the gods, I put on the safety.

I cleared my throat, and they stopped immediately. "Take this seriously, guys," I cautioned. "We're about to leave our solar system to head to a completely unknown planet."

Sorres put a hand on my shoulder. "It's gonna be okay, Haldenson. You know how crazy your sister can be. And when she's with the Kincaid siblings, it's even worse. She can fend for herself."

I snorted. "That's what I'm worried about. She can be a bit too reckless and courageous for her own good. Ever since… well, you know, she practically dedicated herself to protecting everyone else."

Dennett tilted his head, giving me a look I couldn't quite identify. "That was six years ago, Haldenson. She knows when to break."

"Does she?" I asked. "She still blames herself." I opened my mouth to keep talking, but my father walked into the hangar. Every soldier in the vicinity stood at attention, eyes straight ahead. Sorres, Dennett, and I snapped to, hands behind our backs, feet slightly apart, heads held high, faces completely void of emotion other than the smoldering warrior's spark in our eyes.

"At ease, soldiers," my father's voice commanded, echoing throughout the hangar. He strode over to the *Prince of Dragons'* mainland cargo door. Sorres and Dennett stayed in place, as if frozen in Diatanium, mimicking my stance. "At ease, soldiers," he repeated.

My battle buddies relaxed, but didn't leave. The admiral just gave them a curt nod, letting them know that they were dismissed. Together, they picked up the firearm package and carried it onto the *Prince of Dragons*.

"Admiral," I started. My father cut me off, his voice deep and quiet.

"Damari, my son, just come home safe with your sister and the Kincaid siblings. I can't lose another child. You are both my legacy; everything I have worked to create on Velus. I love both you and your sister very much."

I stood frozen, unsure of what to say; it was very rare that he would show such affection like this, especially during on-duty hours.

"I'll come home safe, Dad. With Zephyr and the Kincaids."

My father pulled me into a hug. "May the gods bless your travels," he said, pressing a small metallic object into my hand. I closed my fist around it.

We broke away and I nodded at him reassuringly before turning to the mainland cargo door and running up the ramp, looking over my shoulder at my father before the hatch clicked shut. I opened my palm and glanced down at what my father had given me.

I recognized the object immediately. It was Zephyr's favorite pendant, one she had gotten on her eighth birthday. Of course, she never wore it because of her intense training, but also because it reminded her of what she had lost so long ago. It was half of a whole, the twin with the other owner.

The carving of a Silverclaw dragon holding Adahemite, a blue, star-like gemstone found only on one of Sailara's moons, matched an identical Silverclaw that could connect by a thin string of white magnets on their backs. I held one half of the pendant - this dragon with his gem, and the other owner had its match.

I didn't notice Dennett coming down the hallway until he was right in front of me. "You good, Haldenson? We're about to take off, and the Captain is wondering where you are."

My head snapped up and I cleared my throat, tucking the pendant in the buttoned pocket above my heart. *You're coming home. Whatever it takes.*

"I'm good," I said. "Let's head to the bridge."

"Race ya," Dennett challenged, a glint in his eye. I caught him off guard by shoving him against the wall before sprinting ahead of him down the corridor and up the stairs. "NOT FAIR, HALDENSON!" he called after me, following my footsteps.

I reached the closed door to the bridge first, laughing as Dennett came next. He punched my arm and I hit him back.

"You owe me," I said, smirking. Before Dennett could respond, I turned to the door and straightened my uniform. Then, I placed my hand on a scanner, and the door panel slid open with a soft hiss. Everyone in the bridge stopped talking and stood up.

"They're all yours," Dennett whispered, clapping me on the back before walking off to his station and standing at attention.

"Everyone to your posts!" I shouted. "Start all engines! And load all guns! We have a planet to search and stars to cross!"

The bridge was instantly filled with commotion as soldiers moved to their posts. Out the forward bridge window, I watched the massive doors to the hangar open. The ship lifted off and began to move into the skies. Several tug ships hooked up gravity cables to help the massive *Prince of Dragons* maneuver out of the hangar.

The ship had just left the planet's atmosphere when a transmission from the newly promoted General Kincaid came in. "I'm following suit with the *Concord*. Meet you in two klicks," he stated.

"Noted," I said, pressing a button on the panel in front of me, moving the comm to broadcast. I turned to Sorres. "Set radar to Earth."

"Yes, Haldenson," he nodded.

"Braxton, head down to the East Wing and make sure all star charts are set to MAP. Rondier, you're in charge of weaponry and attack calls. Seeing anything remotely Greblin is an automatic call to arms," I ordered. The two men saluted and left the bridge swiftly. I turned to a female soldier this time. "Merai, what is the first system we are crossing to?"

She shoved a strand of her auburn hair behind her ear as she bent over the panel. Her amber eyes scanned the radar. "Looks like the first system after Zaccoth is the Euthenia Nebula."

"How long until we arrive within borders?"

"A few days tops without hyperspace," Merai said, turning away from the panel to look at me.

I bit my cheek, realizing that it was likely going to take a week or so to get to planet Earth. Since it wasn't on any of the UDN's star charts, that rendered us unable to hyper jump to its location. We could've used the distress beacon as a navigator, but it fizzled out just moments after it went up.

To me, that meant nothing. I was getting my sister back. No uncharted star system was going to stand in my way. *Whatever it takes,* I thought.

A small smile cracked across my lips, for I felt confident that the mission would be successful, and that I would get Zephyr back home safe and alive.

"General Kincaid, we will cross-board in two klicks, just out of Orilia's atmosphere," I affirmed.

"That's a copy, Command Sergeant Major Haldenson." Consider us your unarmed escort," the new general ribbed.

I chuckled before clearing my throat. I nodded in Dennett's direction.

"All engines, full ahead!" he ordered. The *Prince of Dragons* pushed forward, gathering speed with each passing breath.

In a commanding voice worthy of my father's praise, I gave the rallying announcement to kick-start our journey.

"Alright, strap in lads. We've got the Kincaid siblings and a commander to save. Let's bring them home!"

Chapter Eighteen: Tessia
Another Close Call

Unpainted yet still stunning, the *Caroline II* was almost complete. Everyone had been working as a team for almost two weeks straight, both day and night to continue building the ship. I had overheard several days ago that there was to be a race to test out my brother's creation; an annual competition called the Great Atlantic Run. Unbeknownst to them, it was also a wonderful opportunity for *us* to test the *Caroline II*, so we knew exactly what she was capable of to get us off planet Earth.

Zephyr had climbed, ladderless, to the top of the forward mast to fasten the headstay there. Andrex had carefully walked to the end of the bowsprit, tying it to a large eye on the end, making sure it was taut. The last thing we wanted was the mast falling over during the race.

Destin was standing like a statue, eyes open and blank. I knew that expression by heart. It was his Mechanical Advantage at work, showing him which parts belonged where. He then blinked and moved forward, knowing exactly what to do.

I was working on fastening the wheel to the pedestal; Area 51 officials had supplied us with a dark wooden wheel, already fitted with the spokes and handles.

A White Coat approached Destin. "How much–?"

"Sh-sh-sh," he said without looking at the man, holding one hand in front of his face to silence him. "I'm *thinking*."

"Uh… okay…" the White Coat complied, taking a step away from the *Caroline II*.

Still ignoring the scientist, Destin looked around the deck. Zephyr and Andrex had finished fastening the headstay, and I was almost done with the wheel. Trying not to be too obvious, I poked my head around the side of the wheel to see what was going on between my brother and the White Coat.

Out of the corner of my eye, I could see Zephyr climbing further up the mast. She pulled herself up and sat on the small surface at the top of the spar, legs swinging. Elbows on knees, fingers laced, she glared at the White Coat.

Andrex walked over to me. "Is she safe up there?" he asked quietly, pointing to Zephyr sitting on top of the mast at least four stories above us.

"Yeah, she's fine. She can catch herself."

Before Andrex could respond, another one of those S.P.M.T.s, as Destin had called them, rolled into the hangar. On it was a long metal pole, and I knew exactly what it was. The aft mast for the *Caroline II* had just arrived. Destin eagerly slid down the ladder that was leaning against the *Caroline II's* hull and went to inspect the new component.

"It's perfect." My brother ran his hand over the smooth pillar. He moved back from it and folded his arms over his chest, studying the aft mast. "Alright, let's put 'er up!"

"C'mon down, Zephyr!" Andrex called.

"Be right there!" she shouted back. Swinging her legs around the side of the mast, she used her momentum to flip around on her stomach and slide down the mast.

"You're crazy," I said as she approached me.

"Maybe I am," she smirked. "So how are you going to get this one up?"

"Yeah, this one is definitely bigger than the first one." Andrex proclaimed.

"We use the crane!" Destin pointed at the large machine.

The last time we used it was to put the engines in the *Caroline II*, and that *went well*.

Destin hooked up the crane's four cables to the top of the aft mast. He then gave the signal to have it lifted toward the *Caroline II* so it could be placed on her deck. His expression went blank as he made his way onto the *Caroline II*, following the new mast as it was being lifted up.

Zephyr bumped into my arm, but I didn't really notice it until she did it again.

"What?"

"That's not supposed to look like that, right?" She pointed up at the cables that were holding up the aft mast. There was a slight screeching sound, and the cords looked strained. One of them snapped.

"Oh, no," I glanced down at my brother, who was standing below the mast on the deck. A second cable snapped, and yet no one seemed to notice.

What happened next seemed to be in slow motion. Zephyr screamed out my brother's name, and started to move toward him.

Andrex, understanding what she was doing, lunged out and wrapped his arms around her waist, pinning her against him. She struggled, but he refused to let go.

Destin moved backwards to look up at the falling mast. That was what saved him. The aft mast of the *Caroline II* came crashing down toward him. Destin cried out as the spreader ripped into his arm, the rest of the mast holding his body down on the deck.

Wide-eyed, I jumped off of the stairs and ran to his side, leaping over the mast in order to get to him. There was blood all over the aft mast and deck. I put my hands under the spar and pushed against it, trying to get it off my brother. Zephyr rushed over to help me. Together, we shoved the aft mast off of Destin.

I knelt down next to him, one hand over my mouth. It felt like someone had punched me in the gut. My chest tightened, and it felt like I couldn't breathe.

Guards, medics, and White Coats swarmed the *Caroline II* and boarded her. They brought up a gurney and surgical supplies, but decided to bandage his arm before lifting him up.

Shaking, I sat on my knees, still in shock about what had just happened. Zephyr put her arms around me, but there was no way I could be comforted.

"Zeph, I–" Andrex started. I jumped, not noticing he had come up behind us.

Zephyr let me go, stood up, and whirled on Andrex, her red eyes flashing dangerously. "How *could* you?!" she snapped. "How could you stop me from saving him?!"

Andrex frowned, clearly upset. "Excuse me? You would've been crushed!"

"Honestly, I would rather be crushed and Destin would be fine than being in the situation we are in right now." She spun on her heel and stormed off the *Caroline II*, following Destin.

Andrex helped me up. "You did the right thing," I said. "Even if she hates you, she's still alive, and so is Destin."

He shook his head and chuckled. "She had absolutely no regard for her own safety…"

I let out a breath of laughter. "That's Zephyr for you. She never puts herself first."

"At least you got Destin's attention in time. I'm sure he'll be okay," he put an arm over my shoulders in an attempt to reassure me.

"Thanks," I looked down at the blood that covered my hands. "I hope so, too."

TESSIA

Chapter Nineteen: Destin

The Soul Harness

Chaos reigned all around me, but I couldn't

comprehend any of it. White Coats were screeching, guards were shouting orders, and I thought I could hear Zephyr snapping at everybody, but she sounded so far away.

I had never been in so much excruciating pain. My entire arm burned; it felt like someone had poured molten lava into the wound, making it blaze.

Above me, the fluorescent lights embedded in the flawless ceiling flashed as I was wheeled past. It hurt my eyes to keep looking at them, but for some reason I didn't want to close my lids. It was almost a distraction from my throbbing arm.

"Do you think he'll be okay for the race?" a White Coat asked.

"Are you serious?!" I could hear Zephyr's angry voice, but I couldn't see her. I didn't need to look at her to know her eyes were dark red and she was smoldering. "Is that *all* you care about? He could've been killed!"

"Stop being so dramatic," a guard huffed.

"Stop being such an insensitive blockhead," she snapped back. I snorted, catching some of the White Coats off guard.

"At least he's conscious," the White Coat that had spoken before said, pushing his glasses up his nose.

"Yeah," I strained. "But I might not be for much longer."

I felt someone grab the hand on my non-mauled arm and squeeze it. Knowing it was Zephyr, because if it were a White Coat that would be downright weird, I squeezed back, trying to find any distraction from the agony of the gash.

"In here," a female voice directed. The gurney took a sharp turn to the right and I was brought into a room decked out with surgical supplies.

"Ma'am, we're gonna have to ask you to leave the room," a White Coat said, politely.

"Don't you *ma'am* me," Zephyr snarled. "I'm not leaving this box until I know he's safe.

There was a sound of the pocket door sliding open and slamming aggressively into its slot. "There you are!" Tessia exclaimed. "Thank the gods."

She ran over to my side and pushed my bangs out of my eyes. "Hey, Tess," I said. "Stop mothering me."

She laughed. "I can 'mother' you all I want. Especially after what just happened."

A White Coat shoved a piece of plastic tubing under my nose and flipped a switch. Tessia tore it away from my face and threw it back at the man.

"What was that for?!" he yelled.

"You're not putting that anywhere near my brother," she hissed.

"It's an anesthetic! It's supposed to make sure he's not in pain while we fix his arm!"

"Well then, why didn't you say that in the first place!" Tessia huffed.

The White Coat carefully put the thin tube back under my nose. A cool jet of air pushed its way into my nasal cavity. It had no scent, but I started to feel drowsy, and I could feel my consciousness slipping away. Zephyr said something to me, but I couldn't comprehend it. I opened my mouth to respond, but the room spun, and black engulfed my vision as the world disappeared.

"You can't do this to Destin! He is way too young!"

"I don't care, Fynn. Have you seen what's happening to him?! He has the power!"

My ear was pressed up against the door to my Mom's office. These arguments were becoming more frequent between my Mom and Dad. I still didn't understand what they were talking about, but my name was always being mentioned. And this thing called the 'Dauntless' or the 'Dauntless Project.'

"Fynn, please listen to me. He has the power of Mechanical Advantage, and I know you have seen the Dauntless. Now, think about what will happen if I finish the Dauntless Project! We can both control her! Velus will have the most powerful military in the Cayser System! Gods, maybe even the galaxy! People won't have to die anymore to the Grebles! Fynn. We can finally *end the war."*

"Yes, Caroline, I know. But he's only seven! And I've seen your power surges. Some of them have almost killed you! I don't want to have that happen to Destin."

"Okay, yes, but I designed a machine to prevent that." There was the sound of crinkling paper as my Mom pulled something out of one of her many drawing holders. *"It's called a Soul Harness. This will allow Destin and me to transmit power to one another, and with it, the harness should prevent deadly power surges."*

"How do you know that?" Dad sounded annoyed but concerned simultaneously. I pressed my ear harder against the door, trying to make out every bit of their conversation.

"You see, that's the thing. It should *prevent surges, but I don't know for sure..."*

"That's reassuring..." Dad mumbled. I could hear his boots clicking against the floor as he paced. I couldn't hear them saying anything else, so I took in a deep breath and knocked on the door to the office.

"Mommy? Can I come in?" I asked.

"Yes, sweetie, come in." I opened the door slowly and peaked my head in.

My Mom was wearing a white T-shirt and black shorts. There was a pen tucked behind her ear and she was standing behind a huge drawing table. Blueprints and papers covered the wide space.

Behind her, hanging on the wall, was a gigantic drawing of a ship. There was a gold plaque over it that read: The Dauntless. On the far wall, there were little tubes where Mom kept all of her drawings.

Standing in front of my Mom's desk was my father. He was wearing his black captain's uniform, and I knew from eavesdropping on another conversation that he was supposed to be leaving for a trade and passenger route to Rocaron on the Concord in a few hours.

Dad approached me and lifted me up from under my arms before sitting me on his hip. I laughed, unaware of Mom's tight smile and the tired lines under Dad's eyes.

He took his Captain's hat from the table and placed it on my head. It fell down my face, catching on the bridge of my nose.

"Are you gonna try and stow away on the Concord?" Dad teased.

I laughed. "Noooo. I'm gonna stay with Mommy and help her win the next race!"

"Ah," Mom said. "Looks like we've got a future racer on our hands, don't we, Fynn?" She walked around the table and stood next to my Dad, ruffling my hair.

Before Mom could say anything more, there was a knock on the front door of our house.

"MOMMY," my sister screeched. "THERE'S SOME GUY AT THE DOOR AND HE LOOKS REALLY OFFICIAL."

My Dad burst out laughing as he followed my Mom out of the office, through the hallway, and down the staircase. Tessia was flopped over the back of the couch, not bothering to sit up in our presence. She just lifted one hand and pointed at the door.

"Thank you, Tess," Mom said with a smile. She unlocked the front door and let the panel slide open.

My sister was right. The guy did *look really official. But I didn't think much of it. I glanced over at my Mom, and I could see recognition cross her face. She knew the man at the door.*

The officer standing before us was young and clearly in the UDN, his military uniform and badges showed he was of high status.

"Mrs. Kincaid. Admiral Halden is requesting your presence immediately," the young man announced. "It has to do with... the project."

"I'll be right there," Mom said.

"The project?" Tessia bounced up from the couch. "That sounds fun."

Mom laughed. "In a way, I guess it is. I'll see you guys later, alright?"

She came over to us to kiss both Dad and me, and then walked over to Tess to kiss her on the head.

"Come home soon, okay?" Dad said.

"I'll be back before you know it. I promise."

My family watched as Mom grabbed her jacket and left the house. Little did we know that would be the last time we'd ever lay eyes on her again.

Chapter Twenty: Andrex

She is Reborn

Kicking myself mentally, I felt terrible for holding

Zephyr back when she tried to save Destin from almost being killed by the aft mast. Even though I knew I did the right thing, it still hurt for her to be mad at me. Why did I care so much about how she felt?

Off to my right, Zephyr was muttering something under her breath, probably a death threat, while the Area 51 guards shoved us toward the hangar. She still refused to look at me, and every time I tried to apologize, she would walk away.

The person-sized door to the hangar slid open and the very first thing that my eyes landed on was the fully-painted and stained *Caroline II*. She was an absolutely beautiful ship, and I could completely see why Destin was so attached to her, aside from the fact that she was named after his deceased mother.

"WHAT DID YOU DO TO MY SHIP?!" Destin shrieked from behind me. I jumped three feet out of my skin, completely taken off guard by the explosion.

Destin shoved his way past me and ran over to the *Caroline II.* Tessia slid down the ladder of the ship and walked over to her brother. "Whaddaya think?" she asked, grinning.

He ran only one hand over the hull, his eyes wide. "She's... oh, my gods... did you do this?"

Tessia smiled. "With a little help," she nodded toward Zephyr. Of course. That's where they'd been going for the past few nights.

Even though I was suspicious of the guards taking them for hours and they wouldn't return until I woke up, I never asked, fearing I'd get elbowed in the face by Zephyr.

Not even glancing at me, she walked over to Destin and put an arm around his shoulders. "She's ready for the ocean *and* space."

Destin's face broke out into a massive grin. "OH, MY GODS, YES!" He practically tackled his sister in a hug. Well, as best as he could since the other arm was in a sling.

I approached, moving closer to Tessia and Destin. As much as I wanted to make amends with Zephyr, I knew she hated me. So I decided it was best to avoid her until she calmed down a bit.

Placing his good hand on the hull, Destin closed his eyes and said nothing. The entire hangar went silent, as if everyone knew what was about to happen. I could've sworn I saw a spark coming from his palm.

A humming sound filled the air as electric-blue circuit markings flooded over every inch of his skin, covering his face, arms, neck, and hands.

"Wake up, Mom," he whispered. Electricity shot from both hands and the *Caroline II's* engine fired up, making the entire hangar vibrate and resonate with the powerful sound.

I could hear the soft scraping of pens on paper as the White Coats scribbled their notes on everything they could. Slowly, the markings faded, and Destin turned back to us, grinning.

"She lives!" he announced, beaming. He practically bounded over to the White Coats. He almost reminded me of a younger child. "WHEN CAN I TAKE HER OUT FOR A TEST RUN?"

The scientists, not used to seeing one of their... *test subjects* so elated, were completely confused, and they took a wary step backwards.

Since the White Coats weren't responding in comprehensible sentences, Destin returned back to his ship. He just stared at it as if it were something he had lost long ago, but it had just been found. He put his hand on the hull again and whispered to the ship, "You rest now. It will be your time soon enough..."

The engines seemed to rev in agreement, and then there was a small pop as they slowed and powered down.

"Alright, back to your cell," one of the White Coats directed.

Destin grumbled. "Why can't I stay with her?" he complained, clearly annoyed.

The White Coat that had ordered us to be taken back smiled, wickedly. "Because we have another test planned."

A
N
D
R
E
X

Chapter Twenty-One: Zephyr
Black Light? Glow Red

Furious and slightly confused, I paced around the

cell, trying to think about everything that had just happened. There was the episode with Siren and Andrex, and then Destin passed out. After that, Destin almost gets killed by the aft mast and Andrex stops me from saving him.

"I need to hit something," I growled, still walking up and down the length of the cell. Siren's tail flicked around my shoulder, irritated.

"Zephyr…" Destin groaned. He had been subjected to bedrest by order of the White Coats.

"Yes?" I said, not stopping my stride.

"Would you *please* stop pacing!"

I ceased my traipsing back and forth, and slammed my back against the wall before sliding down it. Briefly, I shot a glance toward Destin. He looked fine now. His arm was all stitched up and he was sprayed with this strange substance that had healed his flesh almost instantly. It was miraculous, but it was also Area 51. He was practically as good as new, and while he was healing and resting, Area 51 personnel had taken his blueprints - those were the technical drawings and sketches the pen automatically wrote from his thoughts as he finished completing the *Caroline II*.

Andrex walked over and sat down beside me. I didn't look at him.

"Hey. C'mon, just listen to me, at least," Andrex said. I positioned myself to prepare to stand up. He grabbed my hand. "Why are you being so stubborn about this? We're all we have in this place."

I shot him one of my death glares and he let go. "You stopped me from saving Destin. Of course, I'd—"

"You would've been crushed by the mast," he said, cutting me off. "By me grabbing you, you're both alive and safe."

"Barely," I muttered.

"Look at me, Zephyr. I don't want to lose someone in this place, alright? We need to watch each other's backs and keep one another safe, okay? That includes you, Commander."

I bit my bottom lip. "Why are you making it so hard to be mad at you right now?" I complained.

Andrex grinned. "Is it because I'm so charming?"

I scoffed and swatted his shoulder. "Yeah. *Charming*."

There was a slam on our cell door that made all of us jump. Destin winced as a guard lumbered in. "All of you, get up. Now."

The guards were still walking us down the long hallway to whatever experiment they were going to put us through next. Moving my head slightly to the right, I stole a look at Destin, who was nervously wringing his hands, his eyes wide with what looked like fear.

"You know," I said. "Earlier, I was debating whether to call the guard an Orilian or an insensitive blockhead. But then I realized they were the same."

Destin chuckled, but he still looked troubled. "Hey," I whispered. "Are you okay?" He nodded slowly, but I know when he's upset. I've known him all my life; I could tell when even the smallest thing bothered him.

Then, he leaned over to me and said very quietly, "this is the same hallway they took me down for the test where they… t-they…"

It was obvious that it pained him to finish the sentence, so I let him trail off. *What did they put him through to make him act this way?* I thought, my concern for everyone in our group growing. *What are they going to put us through now?*

Behind me, I could hear Andrex and Tessia talking in hushed tones, the other guard's heavy bootsteps muddying up their words so I couldn't make out their conversation.

Finally, we came to a large white panel lined in gray on the left wall. To my right, I could feel Destin tensing, nervous energy radiating from him like gamma. The panel slid open, revealing nothing but white beyond it. A sharp intake of breath from Destin told me that this was most definitely where he had been taken before.

"Move," the guard ordered, hitting Andrex's back with the butt of his rifle.

"Gods," Andrex groused, rubbing his spine. "So testy."

Warily, I stepped into the room, my eyes trying to take in every detail; the problem was that the only detail was

ZEPHYR

blinding light. I couldn't see anything beyond the mass of bright nothingness. I felt Siren tensing around my waist, clearly sensing danger. I turned around, but all I saw was Andrex and Tessia. It was like the door had disappeared.

"What even is this?" Tessia asked, taking several steps forward. Suddenly, the lights went out, and we were submerged into suffocating darkness.

"Zephyr?" Destin called out. "Zephyr, where are you?"

Remembering that he was on my left, I blindly reached out and grabbed his hand. "I'm right here, Des." He was so tense, I thought that even the slightest squeeze would break his fingers. He was trembling, and his breathing was getting faster.

"Destin?"

"No… I want to leave. No, Zephyr, *you* need to leave. Get out of this room," he said, shakily.

I frowned, even though it was quite evident that no one would see it. Just then, as quickly as the lights had turned off, they came back on, and we all shielded our eyes, trying to protect them.

"GODS!" Andrex shouted, taking a step back. When my eyes finally adjusted and I could see without squinting, I noticed that there was a table a few feet in front of us. On it were all of our weapons. My sword, Destin's auto-rifle, Tessia's katana and pistol, and Andrex's bow and quindent. I moved toward the table, forgetting that I was still gripping Destin's hand. He pulled back on my arm, surprising me.

"Don't," he warned. "They're not real."

"What are you talking about?" Andrex picked up his quindent and spun it around. "Feels pretty real to me."

Destin shook his head. "That's how they trick you. That's how…"

"They broke you," Tessia finished for him, unafraid to say those three blunt words. Even I winced at them.

"It'll be okay, Des," I said, picking up my sword and examining its blade. Siren touched her nose against the flat edge of the Diatanium before pulling away and giving her head a quick shake. "What do you think, girl?"

Siren looked up at me and gave a short nod, believing that the blade was real.

"This will not be a test of fighting," a female voice said. We all jumped, forgetting that the White Coats could just listen in on us whenever they felt like it.

Destin came up beside me and took hold of his pistol. He pulled back on the slide, a small bullet casing ejecting itself from the gun. It clattered to the floor, a significant and physical sign that the gun was loaded. With a hiss, the pistol extended into its assault auto-rifle form. "*What do you want now?!*" Destin thundered.

"This is a test of black light," the female White Coat replied.

Tessia frowned. "So, which is it? Are you putting us in darkness or keeping us in the light?" Andrex laughed.

"Neither," the female White Coat responded, flatly. There was a clicking sound as the lights dimmed, the blackness engulfing us. I could hear a hiss from afar, but didn't pay too much attention to it.

"*Zephyr!*" Destin shouted. A moment later, I felt an arm around my torso, and I was thrust to the ground, my sword knocked out of my hands. The blade, clattering to the ground, echoed in the darkness. Someone had their arms around me protectively, shielding me with their body. I didn't fight it. A feeling in my gut told me that the person was Destin. I noticed he was shaking.

"You guys okay?" Andrex's voice sounded from the darkness.

"Uh, huh," I said, sitting up. Slowly, the pitch blackness around us gradually shifted to a dark purple. Siren started glowing, a silvery blue outlining each individual scale, making her look like something out of a dream.

I could make out the outline of Destin kneeling next to me. He fired a single shot into the indigo lights of the room. A bright blue bullet streaked across the room, sparks flying as it hit the opposite wall.

"Whoa," Tessia breathed, pulling the slide on her own pistol and taking a shot. Instead of the electric blue of Destin's, her's was glowing bright white.

"Um, guys?" Andrex asked. "Is this supposed to happen?"

We all turned toward the sound of Andrex's voice. We could see the outline of his body. The only difference was now he was glowing, and it was getting stronger and brighter. Brilliant green markings of lines and circles covered his face, hands, and arms, looking like a circuit board. It was clear the markings were all over his body, since we could see that he was glowing green beneath his clothing.

"Hey! It's happening to me, too!" Tessia exclaimed. The same type of lines and circles covered her body, except this time, they were a vibrant indigo with lines of white streaking through, like a comet passing in the night sky. Her katana also started to radiate the same coloration; her pistol, too. Same with Andrex's quindent and bow.

I looked down at myself and noticed that the markings were all over my body as well, except they were a vivid red. *All of these colors belong to our pennants*, I thought, realizing that it must have some connection to our illumination. Out of the corner of my eye, I saw the same electric blue light of Destin's bullet as well as neon orange, coming from my friend's body. We all looked like rainbow circuit boards.

"Wow," I exhaled. The markings were beautiful in a mysterious kind of way.

"Guys," Tessia said.

"Who knew these were on us?" Andrex marveled.

"I got to admit, it's pretty cool," Destin muttered, rubbing at his arm. The scar that went down the entire length of his arm was a thin glowing line.

"GUYS," Tessia shouted. "Do you hear that?"

"Hear what?" Andrex asked.

"Wait… what is that?" Destin wondered. "There's a hissing sound…"

"Gas," I realized, as it finally clicked. Everyone turned to me. "They're gassing us. Cover your faces!"

It was too late. The damage had been done. The world swirled as one-by-one, all of my friends dropped to the ground, unconscious.

Chapter Twenty-Two: Destin

On Freedom's Doorstep

Bright sunlight filtered through the window in a

cabin on the *Caroline II*. My head pounded, and I sensed something was different, like the *Caroline II* wasn't on dry land. I sat up on the bed and looked out the cabin window. I almost couldn't believe my eyes. The ship was in the *water*. Vast blue ocean stretched out before me as far as the eye could see. For a moment, I thought I was on Sailara, but then everything came back to me. Area 51, the testing, the fighting, building the *Caroline II*, and the death of the guard I killed. I remembered the dark room and the gassing, my mind reliving my injury with the mast.

I jumped out of the bed and looked around the cabin, absentmindedly flexing my arm. It felt completely fine, like it hadn't been mutilated by the aft mast.

My gun was in its holster on my tool belt, which was on the desk next to the bed. Somehow, I was in new clothing similar to the ones I was wearing when I first arrived on Earth. Hanging on a chair next to the desk was my dark brown aviator jacket.

Quickly, I put them on, opened the cabin's thin mahogany door, and poked my head out into the long hallway that ran the full length of the ship. I heard chatter coming from the galley and mess hall at the back of the ship. I pushed open the door and closed it behind me. Briskly, I walked past the other cabins before coming to the very stern of my ship, where the mess and galley was.

What I saw before me made my blood boil. Andrex, Tessia, and Zephyr were all sitting at the table looking at papers, but that wasn't what bothered me. What did, however, was the fact that there were three unwelcome guests. White Coats. I stopped and drew my pistol.

"What are they doing on *my* ship?" I snapped, pointing my gun at the White Coats. The former din of conversation stopped and everyone looked up from the papers on the table.

"Ah," a male White Coat said. "You're awake. *Finally.*"

I gritted my teeth. "*Get. Off. My ship!*"

"Des," Zephyr said, standing up. "Just sit and listen." She gestured to the one empty chair at the table. I was shocked. It was a very un-Zephyry thing for her to say. The fact that the White Coats were on the ship and not tied up or knocked out surprised me even more.

I walked over to the table and dropped my large pistol on it. It landed with a heavy thud as I sat down. Tessia was next to me. A hand rested on my back, and I realized it belonged to my sister. She leaned over to me and whispered something in my ear.

"I know you're gonna hate this, but please listen. We may be able to use this situation in our favor." I nodded in acknowledgement and looked out of the big picture window to my right that presented the view out of the back of the ship. I noticed that we were in a port and there were other ships and boats docked around us. Turning my head to the White Coat that had spoken to me earlier, I shot him a death glare that would make Zephyr proud. He needed to know that he was not welcome on my ship, nor would he ever be.

"Before we start this conversation, I have some questions. Where are we, what's happening, and *why are you on my ship?*"

"Well, this is a test," the White Coat began. "Not only is it an evaluation for you all, it's a trial for–"

I slammed my hand on the table, cutting him off. "Holy Navis! You guys just don't know when to quit, do you?" I shouted. "WOULD YOU JUST STOP WITH THE GODSFORSAKEN TESTS AND LET US GO HOME? We just want to *go home*."

The White Coats said nothing, their eyes wide with disbelief. "Destin," Andrex said, his voice filled with warning.

"At this point, you are just torturing us. You launch my ship without my permission, drag us to this port, and now you're acting like my ship is yours!" I felt everyone staring at me. "Ya know what? To Oburna with this!" I continued. "I'm starting this ship and leaving this planet, and you three idiots are going to get out of here before I keelhaul you!"

I picked up my gun, left the table and walked out the way I came in. "Destin!" Tessia called after me.

"If you need me, I'll be in the engine room!" I called back. Fuming, I walked down the hallway until I came to the door that led into that room. I slid the door open. This area was much different than the rest of the ship. In front of me, there was a catwalk that spanned a huge gap. Under me were the two huge T.E.S.T. engines. I could see the tops of the huge brass piston casings for the massive machines.

I climbed down a ladder onto the engine room floor. Then, I walked over to the triplex expansion engines. They alone were about two stories tall, while the turbine casing tubes were about as tall as me.

My eyes drifted over the casing tubes, examining them. Shifting my gaze over to the four gear boxes and drive shafts, I started to first check the oil inside of the gear boxes. Especially the ones that connected the triplex expansion engines to the turbines, since they were under the most stress. Once I confirmed that they were fit for running, I moved to the turbines. I opened a hatch on the side of the casings and stuck my head inside. There, I unclipped a flashlight from my tool belt and let the beam of light shine inside the turbine blades, making sure none of them were cracked or warped.

Finishing up with both turbines, I moved to the triplex expansion part of the engine. I had purposely saved it for last, because that was the most complex section of the machine. I was so focused on my work I didn't hear Zephyr come in.

"Hey," she said. I jumped, startled, hitting my head on a piston connector rod and dropping my wrench.

"Gah…" I rubbed my head and then turned to my friend. She was cringing.

"Sorry," she grimaced. "You okay?"

I cleared my throat. "What do you think?"

She was wearing a red tank top, a black belt with one knife stuffed in a leather sheath, and black pants, her tall combat boots coming up to right below the knee. Her dark hair was tied up in its usual ponytail. I noticed that she wasn't wearing any of her armor, even though there were White Coats on board; it was nice seeing her look more like a civilian than a soldier.

Siren was draped over her shoulders, her coils of white scales glinting in the light. I picked up my wrench and continued my work.

"Look, I really hate this, too. Do you have any idea how badly I just want to throw them overboard? But," she sighed, "you should listen to what they have to say."

"What do you mean?" I asked, climbing onto a valve stem rod to tighten up a bolt.

"I happen to know you love sailing, right? And I also know you love racing."

I stopped working. "They want me to race for them," I scoffed. I already knew that they wanted me to, but I didn't fully consider it until now. I was racing for *myself*.

Although, Zephyr was right. I loved racing sailboats. I had been a sailor all my life. My Mom was the one who got me into it. She had a huge two hundred and fifty-foot four-masted racing schooner called *Destiny*. Apparently, I was named after her. She had won the annual Velusan Regatta six times in a row. That's how my family met Zephyr's. It was during the awards ceremony.

"They want to test the ship," Zephyr shrugged. "But so do we." I shuddered at the word *test*. I officially hated that word with a burning passion. I chucked my wrench across the room. It bounced off a valve stem rod on the other engine across the room.

"WHY?!" I shouted. "I am sick and tired of this! It's just test after test after test!"

The only person that was allowed to test my machines was me and me alone, especially after what happened to the original *Caroline*. I didn't want any White Coats within a hundred mile proximity of my *Caroline II*.

"I wish Tessia killed me in the arena!" I screamed.

Siren shot me a glare. Zephyr's eyes flared red before switching to gray. "Don't say that!"

I felt tears welling up in my eyes. "I just want to go home…" I mumbled, practically crying. I sat down next to the huge engine and buried my face in my hands. The scent of grease and oil filled my nostrils, and it reminded me of home. Zephyr sat down and put her arms around me. We were silent for a few minutes.

She pulled away and looked at me, her eyes as blue as the ocean outside. "Des, I know this is hard, but if we do this we can discover the limits of the *Caroline II* and finally escape this wretched place." I lifted my head slightly.

"That's true. I mean, do we even have to do the race at all? We could just take the *Caroline II* all the way back to Velus! We could go straight home."

Then there was the sound of footsteps. The three White Coats were standing over me, clipboards and pencils in hand. I got up and drew my pistol at the one who spoke to me earlier.

"Alright," I began. "I'll do your stupid little test and I'll listen to what you have to say, but after that, I don't want to see you on my ship ever again!"

The White Coat smiled a wicked grin at me. "We'll see," he derided. I cocked my gun.

"Oh, yes. We will see…"

Siren hissed at the White Coats as we walked out of the engine room and back to the galley where Andrex and Tessia were still waiting. Tessia was now standing, looking out of the big picture window. Andrex was still studying the papers that were on the table.

"So," I started. All eyes turned to me. "Let's see what this race has to offer."

DESTIN

Chapter Twenty-Three: Zephyr

The Great Atlantic Run

I was always able to tell when Destin was up to

something, and right now, I could tell there were big plans
for the *Caroline II.*

I could almost see his brain working, the gears inside
his head churning with an idea for the escape plan. The only
obstacle: our getaway plan might need to involve three White
Coats that we would need to eliminate later. I, personally,
would prefer to just leave them behind and be done with it.

Andrex stood up from his place at the table and
walked over to me.

"What can you not do?" he asked. "Seriously, tell me.
I wanna know."

I gave him a confused look. "What?"

"You got Destin to emerge from his... state. I don't
really think that's the right word for it. You can also fight
insanely well, you're smart, you're a freaking navy
commander, you–"

"Okay, okay! I'm not good at *everything*. Just what I
was trained to do."

Andrex stumbled back in mock shock. "What? Is this possible?"

I gave him a light punch on the shoulder. "I have flaws, ya know."

"Please," he said. "Enlighten me."

"Well, look at me. *Really* look at me. What do you see?"

Andrex looked me up and down, his eyes finally landing on my face. "I see a ninja-warrior military commander who can take down an army all on her own."

"That's not–"

"But I also see that you lock yourself away from the world, because you're afraid if you open up, you can be hurt."

Rendered speechless, my gut and my heart told me he was right, but my brain refused to believe it. Sure, I wasn't the definition of an open book, but I wasn't closed off either. Right?

Something behind Andrex caught my eye. Tessia was holding her hands up in the shape of a heart. I made sure she knew I was looking at her before I let my eyes flash red briefly, letting her know I was unamused. She moved herself closer to the window before walking behind me and tugging on my ponytail.

"Hey!" I said. Siren, still around my shoulders, gave her a puff.

"Oh, loosen up, would ya? Stress is not good for you," Tessia removed the tie that held my hair in place. I started to turn my head to protest, but she just pushed it back. Andrex was obviously trying not to laugh.

"What are you doing?" I asked.

Tessia took the strands of hair that fell in front of my ears and tied them behind my head, making a half-crown braid, tying it with a spare hairband from her wrist, while letting the rest of my hair hang down. Then she braided the small ponytail, tying it with a spare band from her wrist. She stepped away to admire her work, nodding in approval.

"There," she said. "Much better."

I deadpanned. "That was completely unnecessary."

"Oh, thanks, Tessia!" she mimicked. "This looks great, Tessia. I should let you do my hair more–"

I pressed a finger to her lips. "Don't push it."

Destin came over. His gaze snapped over to my new, and apparently, improved hair. "Nice work, Tess."

"Thank you! At least *someone* appreciates my skill."

Destin scoffed. "Yeah, I appreciate it when you use it on someone other than *me*."

I burst out laughing, and so did Andrex. Destin waited until we'd settled down before saying that he was going to do the race. The White Coats looked happy about it.

"You see, we will be traveling with you," a White Coat said.

"WHAT," Destin's eyes flared.

"Well, we can't let you escape, now can we?" The White Coat snapped his fingers, and two guards came through the door. They went on either side of Tessia and restrained her.

"Excuse me! Hands *off*," Tessia scowled.

"We will be taking one of your own and placing ourselves on board to make sure you don't do anything *rash*." The White Coat looked at me as he said those words. I looked at Destin. His face was red and his nostrils flared. His hand was over his gun in its holster. My shoulders tensed and my fists curled. Siren slid down from my shoulders to my waist, sensing a potential fight.

"Your call, Des," I said. There was a moment of silence while he exchanged glances with his sister.

"Stand down, Zeph. It's not worth it." Then, all of a sudden, a rumble came from deep within the ship. The guards dragged Tessia out as the ship's autonomous voice said, "Starting engines." Destin turned around and walked up a set of stairs to the wheelhouse. Andrex and I followed him, the White Coats right at our heels. I leaned into Andrex's ear.

"I *really* wanna take them out," I whispered, unwinding Siren from my waist and placing her on my shoulders again.

"Me, too. At least you have one of your daggers. Still can't believe they gave it back to you."

I smiled. "I told those gullible White Coats that my knife was significant to the functioning of the *Caroline II*."

Andrex flashed me a grin. "Well, aren't you a clever one."

We followed Destin up the stairs and into the wheelhouse, then he opened the door on the side and walked out onto the main deck. "Right," he said. "Andrex, do you know how to undock a ship?"

Andrex laughed. "Of course! I have a subship, remember?"

"Good, you can start undoing the dock lines. I'll be on the bridge," Destin pointed at the top of the wheelhouse.

"Aye, Captain," Andrex said, saluting Destin. Destin smiled.

"Please," he said. "Call me Captain Des." We all laughed. Then, Destin turned around and walked back to the wheelhouse, climbing a ladder which led to the ship's bridge.

The *Caroline II* had two helms. One inside the wheelhouse for flight, and an open bridge on top of it for sailing on a planet. Destin headed to the open bridge; I followed him up. Siren gave me a curious puff.

Destin ran his right hand over the large mahogany wheel and placed the left one on the engine throttles. He looked out over the deck.

"Right!" his voice boomed. "I don't care who you are, but when you're on *my* ship and when *I'm* at the helm, you answer to *me* and only me. Also, you don't just sit around as rail meat on my ship! You do something useful! That means you, too, White Coats. I don't care if you don't know how to sail. I don't care if you don't know how to use a winch. I don't care if you don't know how to operate a steam engine, just do something productive. But don't even *think* about sabotage because everything that happens on this ship, I can feel!"

This was a side of Destin I hadn't seen in a long time. It was the captain's side of him. Nothing like the shy boy I knew half a decade ago. I realized that he would be a good commander in the UDN.

Andrex looked up from a cleat on the starboard side. "All dock lines released, *Captain Des!*" he affirmed. Destin smiled as he spun the wheel to port side and grabbed the engine throttles.

He pushed them forward a little, and was a clunk as the engines went into 'ahead slow.' There was the steady chugging of the triplex expansion engines, and the slight whine of the turbines. I looked out ahead of me, vast blue waves sparkling in the sun. White steam billowed from the single exhaust funnel in between the *Caroline II's* two masts, a sign that the engines were running well.

Destin's eyes flitted around the ship, checking to make sure that everything was working properly.

"You there!" Destin pointed at the one White Coat who had ordered Tessia to be taken away. "Where is our heading?" The White Coat gave Destin a confused look. He rolled his eyes. "*Where are we going?*" he asked again.

The White Coat opened his mouth as if to say 'oh.' I had to turn away to hide my snicker. The man pointed just past a low stone wall in the water. A short distance from the end of the wall was what looked like the outside of a huge circular arena.

"That's the starting point," the scientist said. I noticed a hole in the wall big enough for ships to sail through. I turned to Destin. He looked at me, and then looked forward again.

"Let's get this over with," he grumbled, just loud enough for me to hear.

He grabbed the engine throttles and pushed them further forward. The chugging of the engines got louder; so did the whine of the turbines. We passed the wall and the waves got bigger. They were beginning to rock the ship. White caps dotted the ocean. Destin turned the wheel to maneuver the ship through the opening. As we sailed closer to the arena, I started to hear two male voices that sounded like announcers. I noticed Andrex sitting on top of the forward gun turret. He looked back at me on the bridge. We exchanged worried glances as we sailed through the opening.

One of the announcers yelled out, "And there she is, folks! The *Caroline II!*" The place was absolutely *massive*.

I watched Destin's eyes widen as he looked around the huge arena. There were thousands of Earth's civilians watching us. He leaned over to whisper something in my ear.

"I have a feeling this is more than a race," he forewarned. I noticed that there weren't many other sailing ships, and it looked like they were fueled by pure engine power.

"Let's talk about the *Caroline II,* shall we?" Announcer One said.

"Yes, let's," Announcer Two began. "She is a custom-built brigantine cutter–"

"She's a brigantine *schooner.* Not a *cutter,* a *schooner*," Destin cringed, interrupting the announcer.

I watched as he grabbed the throttles and pulled them back. The ship began to slow down.

"She was apparently built by a sixteen-year-old named Destin Kincaid from the planet Velus," the announcer continued. "And get this, everyone… she is powered by steam!"

"I'm *fourteen* in Velusan years," Des mumbled, rolling his eyes.

"Yeah, it's crazy! She will apparently get up to forty-six knots on engine power alone! Plus, she also has something called *solar sails.* It's just like an ordinary sail, but with solar cells embedded in the fabric. Not only do these sails provide power like a normal sail, they also charge a battery which powers an electric overdrive! Don't underestimate her speed!"

The announcers were giddy to the point where I just wanted to smack the grins off their faces. Andrex and I exchanged a look, and I knew he was thinking the same thing.

I looked out across the water, and noticed three other ships. The one closest to us was a huge, funky-looking silver ship without a mast or sails. It didn't even look like it had an exhaust for a steam engine, what Destin assumed it was powered by. I could see a male around the same age as my brother, Damari, but with tan skin, sandy blonde hair, and green eyes, waving to us. Unsure of how to react, I just kinda looked at him. He had a strong build, and was wearing a leather jacket with jeans and some kind of shoe I hadn't seen before. I believe the White Coats called them *sneakers*.

"Hey there," the stranger called, flashing a grin.

"Hi," I responded, nonchalantly. Siren gave the unknown man an indignant puff, clearly disliking him. I trusted her instincts. After all, she was my partner in battle.

"So you're from another planet? What's that like?" he asked.

I shrugged. "It's better than here. Not as much gravity. We definitely have better technology than you when it comes to comms, travel, and weaponry, but the only downside is that we don't have jets."

"What about fairies? Elves? Dragons? Mermaids?" The man rattled off several names I didn't recognize. The only one I did know was 'dragons.'

"We have Silverclaw dragons. They're on the Velusan flag."

"DO YOU RIDE THEM?"

I was offended. "Excuse me? We don't *ride* the dragons. We *respect* them. Just the thought of putting them under reins and saddle is purely *savage*."

"Oh," the stranger said. He nodded in Destin's direction. "Is he your brother?"

Destin wasn't paying attention to this conversation, and I was glad. He needed to focus on getting the *Caroline II* ready to race. And win.

I shook my head. "No."

"Your boyfriend?"

"Wha– no. He is not my boyfriend," I responded, irritated by the question.

"Are you single?" the man asked, smirking.

"Why don't you mind your own business," I snapped. I was starting to see why Siren didn't like him. He was nosy and annoying, just like the White Coats. I let my eyes flash red.

The man held up his hands in mock surrender. "Just trying to make conversation with the competition," he said. His grin was overconfident.

You're cocky, I thought. *Egotistical. Well, that shall be your downfall.*

"What's your name?"

"Commander Zephyr Haldensdottir," I said, formally.

He scoffed. "*You?* A Commander? You're probably only several years younger than me!"

I spread my arms. "If you want, I'll spar with you."

"Sure. Right after I demolish you in the race," he winked. Siren tensed and opened her mouth to hiss. Her reaction mirrored exactly how I felt. The mystery man eyed Siren, warily.

"What's your name?" I asked.

"Aiden Wright," he grinned, boldly. "But you can call me Breaker. Everyone does. It's my racing nickname. You know, since my family's won this race *thirty-six* times in a row. We are undefeated."

Something to the left of the man caught my eye. It looked like a girl with braided brown and purple hair being escorted by two guards onto the ship. My jaw dropped. It was *Tessia*.

"Yes, yes, I know. Quite amazing," Breaker continued, oblivious of Tessia.

"What? Oh, no, I'm not amazed at your 'feats' of racing. You're gonna get crushed by Destin. But what's *Tessia* doing on *your ship?*"

Destin heard that, and his head swiveled toward Breaker's ship. "WHAT?!" he exploded. He turned to a White Coat, grabbing a fistful of his collar. "Why is my sister on that ship?!"

"She wanted to watch the race," the White Coat squeaked.

Breaker turned to walk over to Tessia. I studied his arrogant stride and haughty stance. I watched him talk to Tessia as she glared back at him, clearly, unamused.

"What is that for a ship?!" Destin said, pointing at Breaker's craft.

"Ah, you like it? It's my *motor yacht*. This baby has won this race with my family *thirty-six times in a row*," Breaker smirked, presenting his ship.

"What's her power plant?" Destin asked.

"Four Cummins Diesel engines that each put out twenty-five hundred horsepower," Breaker announced, proudly.

Destin snorted. "HAH! You ain't got nothing on me."

Breaker gave Destin a befuddled look. "Your ship is powered by *steam!*" Breaker screeched.

Now, I know you never *ever* mock something Destin has built. I looked at him, studying his facial expression. He was *not* happy.

"One hundred and fifty-five thousand horsepower on each engine at maximum output *not* including the electric overdrive…" Destin stated, flatly.

Breaker said nothing. There was nothing *to* be said. Tessia just burst out laughing.

"Dude, you are gonna *looooose*," she taunted. Breaker composed himself.

"Oh, we'll see about that. After all, you can't bluff in racing." His confident smirk was back.

It was my turn to laugh. "He's not bluffing. *You'll* see."

I realized that the only sounds I could hear were the waves and the engines on the ships. Everyone had ceased their own conversations to listen in on ours. The announcers were also eating this up, their eyes wild with excitement. When they realized that the banter had ended, they told everyone to prepare for the start of the Great Atlantic Run. It would be a standing start, meaning that all ships had to straighten up on a line to begin. Destin maneuvered the *Caroline II* to our position on the starting line.

"Setting sails!" Destin yelled as he pressed a button on the control panel to the left of the wheel.

Then all of the sails on the *Caroline II* began to unfurl. The huge square riggers on the forward and aft masts dropped down, and the Bermuda-cut sails rolled out of their masts onto the booms.

"*Caroline II,* set A.S.T.S. to race mode!" Destin announced.

"Setting Automatic Sail Trim System to race mode," the ship's automated voice responded. The ship began to heel heavily to the starboard side as all the sails adjusted to catch the most wind.

Even though I've known that Destin had his Mechanical Advantage his entire life, I still found it mindblowing how he could piece together a ship in a week that would take someone else about two years to create.

A deafening foghorn sounded and the ships set off, gathering speed as we moved away from the port. Suddenly, I saw Breaker's ship start to come toward us. I noticed his heading compared to ours. Both ships were on a solid collision course!

"Des...?" I inquired, nervously.

"Yeah, Zeph?" he replied, still looking forward.

"That doesn't look right," I said, pointing at Breaker's ship. Destin turned his head to look at it.

"Yeah. That *doesn't* look right!" Suddenly, there was the sound of a horn. Destin shouted, "I'M UNDER SAIL! I HAVE RIGHT OF WAY!"

I saw Breaker flash an evil grin from his bridge. "He's not altering course, is he?" Destin voiced aloud. Without warning, his ship made a sharp turn toward us.

"Destin!" I yelled. His eyes widened.

"WHAT THE– BRACE FOR EMERGENCY TACK!" Destin spun the wheel frantically to the starboard side. There was the sound of metallic clicking of the winches adjusting as the sails flipped to the other side of the ship.

"ARE YOU TRYING TO KILL US!?" I shouted at Breaker in his bridge as our ships passed within mere inches. Destin grabbed a comm hanging on the wheel post and flipped up a switch so his voice could be heard on broadcast outside of the *Caroline II*.

"PROTEST, PROTEST, PROTEST!" Destin shouted. "VESSEL *ELLERON* HAS CUTOFF VESSEL *CAROLINE II* UNDER SAIL!"

Then a quiet male voice on the other end said, "Protest acknowledged. Protested vessel will be penalized accordingly."

Andrex walked over to Destin, who was at the wheel. Destin didn't look at Andrex; he mapped a path ahead of him that would ensure our victory just to wipe the smirk off Breaker's face. We'd already gotten him penalized, a glorious bonus.

"Why don't you use your Mechanical Advantage to screw with Breaker's ship?" Andrex whispered, making sure the White Coats didn't hear him.

Destin's eyes glinted mischievously as he accepted Andrex's idea. "Zeph," he said. "Take the wheel."

I gave a slight bow of my head before taking hold of the mahogany wheel. Destin stepped away and closed his eyes, connecting with Breaker's ship. From my periphery, I could see the ship lurching, going fast and then slowly, repeatedly.

"Not too much!" I warned. "Tessia is still on that ship."

Then, Destin quietly said, "Boom." A second later, an engine blew up, smoke rising from the ship. I stifled a laugh.

"Dude!" Andrex clapped Destin on the back. "That's awesome."

Destin grinned. "All in a day's work."

I noticed how there were no other ships in front of us or next to us. The *Caroline II* was powering ahead, easily overtaking any competitors. The White Coats were fascinated; madly scribbling on their clipboards.

"*Caroline II*, ahead thirty-four knots," Destin announced. The ship sped up a bit, the waves slapping against the hull. The wash of it was coming on board, soaking the forward deck in saltwater.

Siren looked out at the endless sea. She gave me a small puff before resting her head on one of the coils she had made on my shoulder. I heard the crackling of static before Tessia's urgent voice filled the bridge.

"Des? Zeph? Andrex? Do you copy?" Tessia called.

"Loud and clear," Destin answered.

"Oh, thank the gods. Aiden is an absolute *nightmare*."

"Yeah, I can tell!" Destin said. "He clearly doesn't know the rules of right of way!"

"No, Destin. That's not the worst part. He's... *hitting on me.*"

"WHAT?!" Destin exploded. "He's doing *what?!*"

"This just got personal," Andrex said, quietly.

"Oh, you bet it just did," Destin fumed. I could almost feel Siren smiling at the fact that Breaker was going to get crushed by Destin.

Chapter Twenty-Four: Damari

A Little Reckless

"**H**aldenson!" Sorres shouted. "There's a distress beacon on our sonar. It's almost identical to the one the commander has, but it's the wrong planet."

I walked briskly over to my comrade's station, glaring at the sonar. He was right; the beacon was excruciatingly close. I frowned, contemplating whether or not to investigate the signal.

"Your call, Haldenson," Sorres murmured. That only made my frown crease deeper down my face. Everyone on the bridge of the *Prince of Dragons* was silent, awaiting my command.

I straightened myself and turned to everyone in sight, pushing a button to my left to activate the comms.

"We'll head down to this planet to check out the beacon. If it is legitimate and it is the commander, then that's good news for us. If it is anything else, we get out of there immediately. Understood?"

"Yes, Captain," the crew and soldiers said in unison.

"That's a copy, Haldenson," General Kincaid said.

The *Prince of Dragons* dove down to the planet within the vicinity of the distress call. Out of the bridge window, I could see that this planet did not possess much life. It had red sands and high mountains, dead shrubbery poking out of the ground in random places. There was a crashed ship burned beyond recognition, half buried in the rust-colored sand. It was the same size as her battlecruiser, but no one could tell if it was the one that belonged to my sister.

Maybe this was a mistake, I thought. Still, if this were my sister, I had to know. Several soldiers followed me out of the bridge to the main cargo landing door. It slowly went down, hot air blasting into the Velusan command ship.

I cocked my gun and walked down the ramp warily, my eyes taking in everything as fast as I could. My ears picked up a faint buzzing in the air, but no matter where I looked, I could see no source.

Stopping at the bottom of the ramp, I held up my hand. Those behind me froze.

"What is it?" Dennett asked.

A chill rocketed up my spine, making me shiver, despite the heat. "I can't help but feel like we're being watched."

"There's no life here as far as the eye can see," Merai said. "I think we're okay."

Dennett huffed. "Famous last words," he said, shaking his head. Merai shot him a brief glare before following me to the crashed vessel.

We had almost approached it when the buzzing noise started to get louder. "Something's wrong," I said. "Something is very, *very* wrong."

"Is that sound getting louder?" Sorres asked.

"It is," Merai cautioned. "Everyone, on high alert!"

Behind me, Dennett shrieked. I whirled around to see the source of his fear, only to feel my stomach rise into my throat. At least a hundred bandits had surrounded us without our knowing. Their red and black headscarves had blended into the desolate planet's landscape perfectly. Roughly, fifty of them were riding massive insects, their copper heads glinting in the light. The buzzing sound was coming from their translucent wings rubbing together. Two huge black pincers adorned each claw, and a third served as a beak for the creatures. Their light brown bodies hummed in the heat, only adding to the noise of their wings. Piercing blue eyes narrowed in on us. The bandit on the biggest bug raised a crossbow and fired a warning shot into the air.

"It's an ambush," I tried to keep my voice steady. "This crash never happened." Everyone cocked their guns, pulling on the slide. I tapped the comm in my ear, radioing the *Prince of Dragons* and the *Concord*. "Attention all crew and soldiers. We have been ambushed. Requesting backup immediately."

"Haldenson, we need to get you back to the *Prince of Dragons*," Dennett urged. "You run while we cover you."

I blinked. "Are you crazy? I'm not leaving you guys to deal with these monsters!"

"Dennett's right," Merai pressed. "You have to live. For Velus."

"No, no, I'm not leaving you," I insisted. "I made a promise the day we were bonded. I fight to the death beside you."

Sorres smiled. "We love you, too, man. But we're not all getting out of this one alive."

"Oh, yes, we are." I hit the comm again. "All units, engage and *destroy* these bandits. We're obviously not getting off this planet without a fight. Rondier, you have permission to fire."

The primary armament turrets on the *Prince of Dragons* turned toward the bandits. With a huge bang, one of the massive 110-inch guns went off, killing at least fifteen of the enemies and their mounts. The leader screamed, ordering those alive to fire with intent to kill.

"Sorres, Dennett, Merai, GO!" I shouted. Everyone ran toward the *Prince of Dragons'* ramp. I followed last, making sure everyone got into the command ship.

More arrows kept coming, and there was more buzzing as the copper bugs leapt into the air. Some of the riders left their mounts so they could ram the *Prince of Dragons.* More Velusans continued to show up at the cargo door frame, shooting the monsters from the sky.

The beasts got under the ramp and hit it with their heads, launching Dennett and Sorres into the ship. I drove my sword through the floor, holding on to the hilt and keeping myself steady. Merai wasn't so lucky. She lost her balance and stumbled toward the side of the ramp. An arrow flew past me and hit her shoulder. She cried out before tumbling off the side.

"MERAI!" I shouted. "I'm going after her!"

"HALDENSON, NO!" Sorres called. He reached out to grab me and drag me back inside. Too late. Evading his reach, I drew my sword and jumped off the inclined plane, hitting the sands and rolling to ease my fall. Merai was on her back, struggling for air. The arrow was lodged in her shoulder, and there was splattered blood on the sands beneath her from a fresh gash on her cheek, clearly caused by the rock beside her face.

Another arrow shot toward us, but I slashed it out of the air with my sword, cutting the thin missile in half. The bug that had knocked into the ramp screamed before lunging, its massive black pincers snapping at me. I feigned left before dashing right, bringing my sword up to chop off the claw. It dodged and swiped at me, cutting my forehead. The monster reared and struck again, but I was faster. Gritting my teeth, I dove under the beast and drove my sword into its gut. It screeched and twisted, but couldn't get away. I turned my sword and wrenched it down the creature's abdomen. It snapped at me, but couldn't reach.

With one final rotation of my blade, the massive being shuddered and went limp. I pulled out my sword and rolled out sideways before it could crush me; wiping the blade clean on the sand, I dropped it back into my scabbard.

"Haldenson," Merai gasped. "What are you doing?"

"Saving your life." I stood up quickly and ran over to her side, snapping off the arrow shaft, leaving the head in her shoulder to make sure it didn't bleed further. Offering my hand, she grasped it and I helped her stand, slinging one of her arms over the back of my neck.

"Stop, Haldenson. You–"

"Less talking, more moving," I said, cutting her off, not wanting to be shot by bandits. "Shut the doors!" I shouted up to the crew.

"But–" a crewmember started.

"*I SAID, SHUT THE DOORS!*"

Dennett and Sorres slid down the ramp as we approached it. There was a hiss and a click, and then it started to move up slowly. By the time we reached it, it was about seven feet off the ground.

"You're crazy!" Dennett snapped.

"I don't care; you can yell at me later. Take Merai!" I directed.

"No, you go first," Merai protested. Regardless, I lifted her up.

"Not a chance," I said. Dennett and Sorres took each of her hands in theirs and pulled her up.

It was now my turn, but the ramp was so high, I couldn't reach it. "JUMP!" Sorres shouted.

Idar, help me, I thought as I jumped as high as I could, this planet's stronger gravity threatening to tug me back down to the sands, leaving me at the mercy of the bug riders.

My comrades grabbed my wrists and arms, pulling me up and out of the way of the soaring arrows. I could feel the shots bouncing off my armor as they hauled both Merai and me back inside the *Prince of Dragons* just as the door slammed shut. There was a loud thud on the hull as the copper brutes slammed into the exterior of the command ship, trying to break in.

All four of us lay on the floor, breathing heavily. Despite that near-death experience, I was grinning. Everyone had gotten out alive and without many injuries. I put a hand to my ear and tapped the comm.

"I need medics to take Merai to the medical bay immediately," I ordered. "We need an arrow head pulled out of her shoulder."

"We don't get paid enough for this…" Sorres muttered.

A few moments later, two medics came down the corridor and transported Merai to the bay to treat her wounds. I watched her leave, content with the fact that she was still alive. The cut in my forehead was finally starting to ache now that the adrenaline rush had subsided.

Dennett whirled on me. "You are *insane*," he fumed. "Do you have any idea what you could've done?! You're next in line for Velus, man! You're not allowed to die!"

I shot him a glare. "And what would you want me to do in a situation like that? Just let *her* die?! Or worse, become a slave to those… those bug riders? No soldier left behind. You know I would've done the same for either of you or anyone else on this ship."

"I know," Sorres sighed. "You have a good heart. Just wait for backup next time, okay?"

I nodded and gave a mock-salute to my friend. "Yessir," I said, grinning.

We had left the strange planet and system a while ago, and I hadn't seen Merai come out of the medical bay. My forehead gash had been cleaned and stitched, leaving me with just a dull throb. I thought it would be best to check on Merai, or at least with the medics.

Was she more seriously injured than I thought? I wondered, ergo deciding to check on her. If it were necessary, I would take her from active-duty and place her on the *Concord*.

I walked down the corridor and took a left in the east wing of the *Prince of Dragons*. Fiddling around with the button above my heart, I opened the pouch and took out Zephyr's dragon pendant absentmindedly, just rubbing the creature's engraved scales with my thumb.

Then, I took another right, and crashed straight into Merai. She winced, putting a hand to her shoulder.

"Watch it, y–! Haldenson? I'm sorry, I didn't realize it was you." She looked down, her face turning a little red.

I smiled. "Don't worry about it. How's your shoulder?"

Merai's gaze suddenly turned cold as she lifted her head to look at me, her amber eyes staring straight into my blue ones.

"You were a fool to come after me," she said.

I was confounded, and a little angry. "Excuse me?" I snapped. "I saved your life!"

She shifted her weight as I gritted my teeth in frustration. What did she expect me to do at a time like that? Just leave her? "*You* endangered your life at the expense of mine! What would become of Velus if you were killed?" Her gaze softened, and she almost looked sad. "For all we know… you're Velus's only living heir."

That really hit me. We both knew she was right; so did everyone on the *Concord* and *Prince of Dragons*.

"Don't say that," I said, harshly, glancing away. "She's alive. She *has* to be."

Merai raised her good arm and put her hand on my shoulder, smiling. "We'll find her." I noticed how she didn't add the words, '*dead or alive.*' Still, what she said before nagged at me.

We were quiet for a few moments, but once we realized we were out of conversation, Merai took that as a cue to leave. She gave me another smile before walking past me and down the hall. She was about to turn the corner when I called out to her.

"Anisa, wait!"

Merai tensed and froze mid-walk, and for a moment I almost regretted using her first name. I thought she was going to walk away, but instead, she turned to face me, one eyebrow raised. "Yes, Haldenson?"

"If it meant saving your life, I wouldn't hesitate to do it all again."

Her eyes widened as she blushed before looking down and smiling. "Thank you," she said, quietly. "I never got the chance to tell you that."

"You're welcome," I said. Merai nodded and moved past me, bumping into the hand that held the dragon. Since I was holding it loosely, it tumbled from my grip and clattered to the hallway floor.

Merai stooped to pick it up, her amber eyes examining the dragon clutching the blue Adahemite between its gleaming talons. It was clear she recognized it.

"Half of a whole…" she muttered. "Who owns the other starstone?"

I looked down at the pendant as she handed it back to me and said nothing, guilt and sadness washing over me as I felt my heart break.

"Wait a minute," Merai said, realizing the truth. "The other pendant… it's… it's in the soil of Velus, isn't it? Because it belongs… to *her*."

Chapter Twenty-Five: Andrex

The Storms Brew

Vast blue ocean stretched out before my eyes as far as I could see. Glinting and sparkling in the golden sunlight of Earth, the white caps swished against the hull of the *Caroline II*, making her rock in the deep waters ever so slightly.

Behind me, I heard a very long and exasperated sigh escape Destin. Ever since Tessia had been transferred to Breaker's motor yacht, Destin had been in… a mood. He had tried everything in his power to get her back, but the White Coats refused, even his threats.

There was also the faint sound of chatting between Destin and his sister over a comm that she'd taken from Breaker, and I could tell by Destin's annoyed tone that Breaker was probably hitting on Tessia again, and not the way that would make her feel flattered.

I breathed in the clean, salty air; the chilled winds and the sound of rushing water reminded me of home. Zaccoth, the Cayser System's farthest planet from our sun, was a stunning world of ice and snow. To me, it seemed like a very sleek design of blues and whites, and the darkness of our oceans and seas. I had grown up playing under those waters with my little brother and his friends. I couldn't really say that I missed them, though. In some strange way, it was nice being so far away, like it was a world only I knew about, despite the fact that I had met Destin, Tessia, and Zephyr.

"Hey," Zephyr's voice said behind me. Startled, I jumped.

"Must you be so silent?" I said, putting a hand to my chest as if that would calm my surprised heart.

"Sorry." She came up next to me and crossed her forearms on top of the railing on the *Caroline II*. Out of the corner of my vision, I eyed Siren, warily. She was sleeping around Zephyr's shoulders, but after what happened a few days ago, I wasn't too sure.

I exhaled, running a hand through my hair.

"What are you thinking about?" Zephyr asked, not turning her head to look at me. I noticed she had taken out the braid Tessia had put in earlier and had changed the style back to her normal high ponytail. Her dark hair whipped in the winds.

"I'm… thinking about home."

Zephyr nodded. "Zaccoth." She paused. "Do you miss your family?"

I scoffed. "Can't fully say that I do. It's nice being away for once, even if it means being trapped in Area 51."

She tilted her head in my direction, her oceanic eyes studying my face. She turned around, resting her elbows on the top rung, her upper back leaning against the railing. "Are you an only child?" she asked.

I shook my head. "A younger brother. But he's… *a character*, to say the least."

Zephyr smiled. "Does this *character* have a name?"

"Aspen," I said.

"Aspen," she repeated. "That's a nice name."

I grumbled. "Yeah, more like Ass-Pain." I paused for a moment before continuing a new train of thought. "You know, it's strange. I know all about your family because you're the daughter of Admiral Halden. But you know nothing about mine."

"That's true."

"I know of your older brother, Damari. He's a CSM, right?"

Zephyr briefly nodded. "Command Sergeant Major."

"And I think… correct me if I'm wrong here, but I think that there is a–"

Zephyr cut me off with a cold gaze, her blue eyes sparking with hints of dark gray. "You're wrong," she said, sharply.

I was taken aback by the sudden change in tone. "Sorry," I replied. "I didn't mean to offend."

Zephyr looked up at me, her eyes returning from their stormy stage. She then frowned, looking past me. "What is it?" I asked. I turned around and saw the source of her concern.

Thick black clouds were off in the horizon, at least five miles away. I could hear the faint sounds of the clouds clashing, creating rumbling thunder.

Together, we climbed up the ladder that led to the bridge. Destin and the White Coats, surprised by our sudden arrival, jumped out of their skins.

"What is it? What happened?" Tessia's voice said from the comm in her brother's hand.

"Well," Destin exhaled. "Andrex and Zeph just scared the life out of me. What's up, guys?"

"There's a storm at least four nautical miles out," Zephyr said, pointing out of the bridge window.

Destin swore under his breath. "That's great," he muttered, sarcastically. "*Caroline II*, furl all sails and start engines!"

"Request acknowledged," the *Caroline II's* voice system responded.

There was the rumble of the engines as the *Caroline II* started up, no longer using her sails to move forwards. The white canvases rolled themselves up to be tucked under the yard, a horizontal pole which crosses the mast where sails are set.

"I SEE THERE IS A STORM BREWING!" Breaker's obnoxious voice screeched from the other side of the comm. Destin cringed and scowled.

"WOULD YOU SHUT YOUR FACE?!" Tessia shot back. "I'm gonna go help Breaker not sink his ship. Not to help him; to make sure I'm still alive when we do cross the finish line."

I laughed. "Have fun, Tess."

"*Kill me*," she muttered, and then turned off the comm.

"Right," Destin said, clapping his hands together. "Here is the storm procedure: depending on how bad it is, or unless you have a death wish, do *not* run around on the deck! And I need someone in the engine room in case everything backfires and the emergency fail safe dies on us. FYI, those engines are going to be under 'extreme load,' so it's gonna be hot down there."

None of the White Coats said or did anything. There were a few silent moments before Zephyr raised her hand. "I know enough about the engines to fill that job."

Destin bit his lower lip, clearly wishing one of the White Coats had volunteered instead. After a long second, he sighed. "Okay, Zeph. Please be careful," he advised. "One wrong step and those engines will chew you up."

"Oh. *Lovely*," she retorted, sarcastically as she climbed down the ladder that led to the bridge.

I moved to follow. "I'm going with her."

Destin put his hand on my shoulder and stopped me. "She can handle herself. Right now, I need you to handle the deck work. Sorry to say this, but you really have the best chance of survival if you get tossed overboard."

"What are we doing then?" one of the three White Coats asked. Destin whirled on them.

"You're gonna shut up, sit tight, and stay the heck out of my way. Got it?" The scientists nodded. "Andrex, I'm gonna need you out there. Be very, *very* careful."

I grinned at him. "I'm practically a fish! I'll be fine, don't worry."

Destin shook his head. "Famous last words, my friend."

Deadpanning, I said thanks before leaving the bridge the same way Zephyr had. The thick black clouds had gotten much closer, and I could see the dense wall of rain underneath it.

Oh, great. This is gonna be fun, I thought. I walked over to the aft mast and gripped it, the rough waves slapping against the hull and rocking the ship more than I'd like. The first few droplets of rain made their way toward the *Caroline II*. I put a hand over my eyes to shield them from the bright sun, looking as far into the storm as possible.

The waves were getting higher with every passing current, and thunder cracked above us as the clouds clashed.

Judging by the ominous gray waves and dark skies, I knew for certain that this wasn't going to be pretty. I silently made a prayer to Navis, the god of ships and sailing, and Xerana, the goddess of the sea and storms, that we would all make it out of this storm in one piece.

Chapter Twenty-Six: Tessia

Hit or Miss, I Really Hope He'll Miss

"Up ahead!" Breaker's obnoxious voice shrilled,

shattering my nerves. "I see there is a storm brewing!"

"Would you shut your face?!" I snapped, angry that I had to be stuck with this moron. He flashed a grin at me.

"Stop talking to the competition. It's not like they're gonna win, you know."

I smirked. "Is that why you're in second place?"

Breaker turned bright red and glanced away from me, trying to hide his bruised ego. As long as he was hitting on *me*, I would be hitting his pride.

I turned back to the earthen comm I held between my hands. "I'm gonna go help Breaker not sink his ship. Not to help him; to make sure I'm still alive when we do cross the finish line."

On the *Caroline II*, Andrex laughed. "Have fun, Tess."

"*Kill me*," I muttered before switching off the comm and slamming it down on a table in the bridge.

"You just couldn't resist talking to me, could you?" Breaker said as his green eyes flashed with egocentric energy.

Deadpanning, I said, "No, I just don't want to die in this storm."

Breaker's overconfident smile never wavered. "But you're already in heaven, Tessa."

"It's *Tessia*," I snapped, suppressing my urge to retch. When Breaker wasn't talking about himself, he was hitting on me. When he wasn't hitting on me, he'd continue to brag about his wins. I didn't know which bothered me more.

"Alright, Breaker. We're gonna be sailing into the storm in about a half an hour and we have no idea what it's gonna be like. I know back home our storms at sea are always much worse than they look," I said, walking over to the bridge window.

"North Atlantic storms can be pretty nasty," he said. "Luckily, you're with the best racer and sailor this world has ever known."

"Wow. And for a moment there, I thought you were going to act like a normal human," I muttered, even though I had no idea what a "normal human" was like. Since arrival, I'd been surrounded by experiment-driven White Coats, angry Area 51 guards, and now this crack-pot. Not to mention the two insanely giddy announcers at the beginning of the race.

"Whatever do you mean?" he asked, the grin still plastered on his face. I was getting sick of looking at it.

Ignoring him, I questioned, "What's at the end of this race, anyway? Where are we going?"

"Belfast, Ireland," he said. "Once the winner crosses the finish line fifteen yards from shore, the ship docks in the harbor and the awards are handed out. Later that night, there's a huge ceremony and dance party to formally address the winners."

Huh, I thought. *I guess you can act normally.*

Ahead, droplets of rain from the closest edges of the storm made their way over to the bridge, sprinkling across the window. With the storm almost on top of her, I could just make out the *Caroline II* through the haze. She had just entered the downpour, and even though we were hundreds of feet away, I could see that Destin must have started the engines because there was a tower of steam billowing from her single exhaust funnel, huge waves tossing the brigantine schooner around. I sent a quick prayer to the gods that they would be okay.

Walking over to the wheel, I shoved Breaker aside.

"Hey, what are you doing?!" he shouted.

"Showing you how a Velusan handles a storm, you pathetic excuse of a human."

Utterly shocked by my blunt statement, Breaker took a step back and let me take the wheel. He looked like he wanted to take control of his ship again, or at least say something, but I shot him down with an icy glare.

"Tessia, this is an *Atlantic* storm. They are normally worse than they look. Do not underestimate it," Breaker said, giving up regaining control and walking over to the bridge window instead.

If this storm is anything like the disaster on the Day of Xerana, then we are in huge trouble, I thought, trying not to let any distress show.

"Why don't we play a little ice-breaker?" he said. "Get to know each other a little better?"

I scoffed. "Why?"

"Well, we're gonna be stuck with each other for a while. Might as well make the most of it," Breaker said, winking.

Wrinkling my nose, I stared him down, but once I realized that I wasn't getting out of this, I sighed as loudly as I could, making sure my annoyance showed. "FINE. What's this 'ice-breaker?'"

"I ask you a question, and you answer it, and then you ask me a question. It could be anything at all."

Resting my elbows on the wheel and placing my face in my hands, I shrugged. "Go for it."

"How long are your years? Are they also three hundred and sixty-five days?"

I almost slipped off of the wheel. "Three hundred and sixty-five?! That's so short! How do you get anything done?"

Breaker raised an eyebrow. "So…?"

"Our year has five hundred and eighty-two days. We have eighteen months in a year. Even our days are longer than yours."

"EIGHTEEN?!" Breaker screeched. "We only have twelve. So how old would that make you on Earth?"

"Nuh-uh. My turn," I said. "You already asked your question."

Breaker pouted, folding his arms over his chest. "Fine."

It took me a moment before I realized what I really wanted to know about this planet. "What's your favorite thing about Earth?"

"Humanity," he said, after a long moment. I suppressed my disgust, and let him continue. "The way that when someone is in their darkest hour, masses of humans can come together. And when that happens, anything can be solved. Just one big unanimous decision that doesn't have to be said aloud, yet action is taken."

I blinked, completely in shock. "Wow. Really?"

He nodded. "Our race has managed to survive for millennia somehow. Now, my turn. How old would you be here versus your planet?"

I rolled my eyes. "Seventeen here, fifteen there. Happy?"

He grinned his obnoxious winning smile. "Ve–"

An enormous and powerful lone wave slammed into the hull of the ship. The motor yacht rocked, knocking Breaker off balance. I gripped the wheel and spun it, managing to stay on my feet and keep control of the ship.

"That was a rough wave?" I said, my voice much pitchier than I would've liked.

Breaker nodded and gritted his teeth. "This is gonna be a fun storm…"

TESSIA

Chapter Twenty-Seven: Destin

Tossing and Turning

The *Caroline II* powered over another swell,

pounding into the angry and foaming waves below. "BRACE!" I yelled to Andrex.

He immediately grabbed the handle of the forward gun turret as the bow came crashing down, completely submerging. It rattled the rigging so much I thought the bowsprit was going to snap off. What also didn't help was that everything the *Caroline II* felt, I felt, too - another strike of the churning waters forced me to double over, clutching my stomach in pain.

The White Coats looked greener than Orilia's flora. To be honest, it was quite hilarious, and I would laugh if I had the strength. My arm was starting to burn where the mast had ripped into me; I needed to make sure I didn't reopen the wound.

Coughing salty seawater from my mouth, I looked up only to see the *Caroline II* falling over another wave. There was a moment of weightlessness before the bottom of the ship collided against the seething ocean.

Andrex swept dark red seaweed from his hair. It landed on a White Coat's neck, and he screeched. "Oh, quit complaining!" Andrex said. He looked over at me and frowned. "Are you getting seasick?"

I laughed painfully. "Since I was born on a boat, I don't get seasick. This… this is just sheer agony. I take every beating the *Caroline II* does. I just…" With another slap of thick-foamed waves against the hull, I realized something that *did* make me seasick. "ZEPHYR!"

"Is she still in the engine room?!" Andrex shouted over the roar of the swells.

"Is she still *alive?!*" asked one of the White Coats. I shot him a glare, knowing they weren't asking that question because they cared about her.

"Thank you for volunteering," I said. The scientist frowned, clearly confused. "Congrats, you get to go down into the beating heart of this ship."

"Wha… why?!" he protested.

"BECAUSE YOU'RE *EXPENDABLE*," I snapped, staring him down until he stumbled off, not wanting to get in my way. As soon as he left, I felt a surge of power rush through my veins as my vision tinted bright blue. Zephyr must've hit something in the engine room.

"NO, DESTIN! YOU'LL ELECTROCUTE ALL OF US!" Andrex screamed. I opened my mouth to respond, but the *Caroline II* was tossed into the air before slamming down into the sea.

Flashes of blinding pain erupted behind my eyes, and a splitting headache emerged from the base of my neck, rendering me almost unconscious.

"Navis... what did I do to you?" I rasped, gripping the wheel until my knuckles were white and aching.

"That's it. You're not driving anymore," Andrex said, moving me out of the way. He yanked the wheel aggressively to starboard, avoiding another massive torrent. I collapsed to the ground, wanting to get up and help, but I just couldn't move.

"Andrex... the sails..." I muttered.

"They're secure, don't even worry about it," he said, eyes ahead on the storm.

Clumsily, I stood up, leaning heavily against the dashboard. I lifted my head, looking at nothing but pouring rain so thick, you couldn't see six yards out. What looked like a miniature tsunami reared up, threatening to drag the *Caroline II* down to the sea floor.

Andrex and I exchanged terrified glances before the wave slammed into us, completely enveloping the *Caroline II*.

Chapter Twenty-Eight: Zephyr
The Heart of the *Caroline II*

Down in the engine room, it was boiling and loud

since the two engines were under extreme load. I'd almost been burned twice, and whatever was happening above deck with the raging waters was most certainly not helping. Unfortunately, Siren was freaking out from the ocean and engine, so she started to tense around my waist, unintentionally strangling me. I grabbed a pipe to prevent myself from slamming into the wall.

"Siren," I said, exhaling. "Please... I..." she immediately slackened her grip, but still remained tense and nerve-wracked while I tried to keep my balance. This storm was most certainly a hundred times worse than we'd formerly anticipated.

My elbow slammed into something and a surge of power erupted in the engine room. I gritted my teeth, a strange numb sensation shooting through my arm. *Great Asrea*, I thought. *I hope whatever I just hit doesn't hurt Destin.*

Off to my left, I could barely make out some shouting over the roar of the engines. A bundle of white clothes and flailing arms came screaming down the hallway, bursting through the door to the engine room and barreling into me. Completely taken off guard, I lost my grip on the pipe and crashed to the floor with the blathering moron on top.

"Get off me!" I snapped, pinned beneath the White Coat's body. I shoved him away and rolled in the opposite direction.

"WE'RE ALL GONNA DIE!" the White Coat wailed. I tugged on my ponytail to tighten it before rising to my feet and brushing myself off, not bothering to help up one of my captors.

"Stop being such an Orilian. This storm is absolutely *nothing* compared to the one Sailara got on the last Day of Xerana," I said, nonchalantly. The man just blinked at me in utter confusion, still sitting on the ground. "Why are you even down here? You could've killed us both! You heard what Destin said. Or are you deaf as well as dumb? This engine can chew you up and spit you out like you're *nothing*." I gestured toward the massive T.E.S.T. engine, its monstrous pistons pumping dangerously under the extreme load.

The White Coat didn't get up. "I'm just here to make sure you're still alive."

I deadpanned. "Because you care? That's rich."

I grabbed his collar and dragged him through the engine room and into the hallway, sliding the door shut behind me. The silence of the passage compared to the roar of the engines was deafening.

"It's… it's awful up there," the White Coat trembled. "I don't think we're gonna survive this s–"

I clamped a hand over his mouth. "Do you want to jinx our odds and have the gods curse our souls? I, for one, would rather die in battle and in honor so that I may one day join my ancestors in the Halls of Idar."

"Like Valhalla?" he asked, jerking his head away from my hand so that he could speak.

"Is Valhalla a place where warriors go when they fall?" The White Coat nodded. "Then, yes. It's like Valhalla. Gods, you humans have the most *unusual names*. Although I will admit that this place has a nice ring to it."

The *Caroline II* was thrown by another swell, and the scientist flew forward. I side-stepped him so that he would crash into the wall instead of my face this time. Siren wiggled around my waist, tense and nervous. She hissed, and I could feel her powerful, lithe body contracting as she stiffened herself.

"Me, too, girl. We've gotta get to the bridge." I ran down the hallway, not waiting for the White Coat to pick himself up.

The ship rocked again, hurling me against the wall. I gritted my teeth as I let my left shoulder take the brunt of it, ensuring Siren remained unharmed. "What is going on up there?" I wondered aloud, continuing my way through the passage.

I reached for the dagger I had tricked the White Coats into letting me have and began to pull it out, planning to impale the wall in order to steady myself. As soon as the knife was halfway out of its sheath, I shoved it back in, remembering that everything the *Caroline II* felt, Destin felt, too.

ZEPHYR

"Gods," I muttered before falling into the far right wall.

"WAIT FOR MEEEE!" the White Coat howled, afraid to be left on his own, even though it would probably be safer for him. Then again, I didn't want him messing around near the engines.

I walked back, clamped my hand around his wrist, and hauled him with me, trying to stay balanced in the swaying ship.

Somehow, we managed to get to the bridge, mostly unscathed. As I spat saltwater out of my mouth and swept my soaked hair from my eyes, the first thing I noticed was Destin on the ground and Andrex steering the *Caroline II*.

"What is going on here?!" I shouted over the thunder of the waves and the cracks of lightning that illuminated the sky. I gripped the wheel so Andrex could take a break.

He hesitated before letting go. "We can't go on like this for much longer. Half of these waves have nearly sunk us," he said, kneeling next to Destin.

Crazy Mechanical Advantage, I perceived, knowing that Destin wasn't as strong as the *Caroline II*, yet he felt every wave that bashed us around and he was still conscious.

"What if we *lifted off?*" I asked, trying to make sure the White Coats didn't pick up on the *Caroline II*'s ability to fly. "We could go above the storm and get a break—"

"No," Destin strained. "That would be… cheating."

"YOU WANT TO RISK OUR LIVES OVER THE FACT THAT WE *COULD* BE DISQUALIFIED?!" I snapped.

One of the White Coats grabbed my shoulder. I shrugged him off, too busy eyeing the storm while yelling at Destin.

"Well, when you put it like that…" Destin said.

"I agree!" Andrex stood up, using the wall as support.

Siren tensed as the White Coat seized my arm this time, shaking it. I turned to him. "What is it?"

"I think the storm is clearing over there!"

I squinted, trying to look past the white caps and slanted downpour. He was right. The storm was starting to clear, but not soon enough. It seemed the closer we got to the edge, the higher the swells got, trying to keep us trapped in the squall. Trying to drown us.

"Everyone, brace! I'm putting her in overdrive," I ordered, spinning the wheel to soften our battering against another surge of saltwater. "We're almost there…"

Chapter Twenty-Nine: Andrex

Too Far From the Finish Line

Just out of reach, the edge of the Atlantic rainstorm seemed far away. The waves were getting larger and more aggressive, like they wanted to keep tossing us between their watery fingers forever.

Zephyr activated the overdrive for the *Caroline II*, trying to get us out of the monstrous weather as soon as possible. I could just make out the roar of the *Caroline II*'s engines over the angry seas. It was like an unspoken battle, yet it was so evident that it was there.

A massive gush of water flooded the *Caroline II*, dousing all of us. It was getting more and more difficult to hold on to anything since we were all slick with salty seawater.

"C'mon, *Caroline II*. Just a little further…" Zephyr coaxed, yanking the wheel hard to port, making our collision with another wave less harrowing.

The other two White Coats on board had hardly said anything. They were just holding on for dear life. Everyone was completely soaked, and the gale-force winds and heavy rains felt like they were trying to assist the ocean in pushing us under.

From behind us, a massive wave lifted the ship, hurling us in the direction we were heading, tripling our time. We burst from the edge of the storm and Zephyr veered left, moving us away from the swell. We all collapsed to the deck, laughing with relief.

"Oh, my gods. Let's never do that again," I said, thankful we were finally out of danger. Everyone muttered in agreement.

"I'm… gonna go nap. And if you need me, you don't need me. I'm *napping*," Destin mumbled, standing up slowly. "Talk to the ship."

"Ah," Zephyr said, unwinding Siren from around her waist. "Don't worry, *sir*. We shall make sure you are not disturbed."

"Good…" he said, leaning heavily against the wall as he left the room.

I glanced over at the White Coats. All three looked completely nauseous. One of them left the bridge to retch over the side of the *Caroline II*.

"I can't believe we survived that," I said, sitting up. Zephyr looked at me.

"I know… Gods, I can't wait until we're done." She turned to the two other scientists still in the bridge. "How much longer until we get to the finish line?"

"Hhhhh… we probably have another five days…" The White Coat said, still a little shaken. I rolled my eyes.

If only I could actually drown… I thought. We'd almost died in a single storm. What would the next five days bring?

I stole a look in Zephyr's direction. Based on her scowl, I knew she was thinking the same thing. Siren's tail whacked her arm, and she deadpanned.

"I need to hit something," she muttered. I spread my arms in invitation. She gave me one look and shook her head. "Not you. Preferably one of them," waving her hand at one of the White Coats. Luckily for them, they were too busy being seasick to notice.

Turning to one of the men and tapping him on the shoulder, I asked where the finish line even was. He said it was in the harbor of a place called Belfast.

Well, I hope we're fast *enough to get there before the Caroline II sinks*, I thought, frustrated. It would've been so much quicker to just use her flight system, but that would be "cheating." Frankly, I was more concerned with keeping everyone safe.

Chapter Thirty: Damari

Ghosts From the Past

The engine room in the *Prince of Dragons* was absolutely massive. It was a fascinating place to me. Every pipe and piston was impressive. On the catwalk that overlooked the PoD's four massive main drive turbines where I stood, their defining whine perfectly reflected the power and might of this command ship.

I remembered back to the conversation I had with Destin and his mother, Caroline, about the construction of this ship so many years ago. Destin knew everything about the PoD since he was his mother's apprentice. It was rumored that he had actually had the idea for the ship to be fitted with the hundred and ten-inch Mark III Carronade guns; the PoD's primary armament.

I started to think back to the time I first met Destin. He was a shy kid and didn't say much, but he knew his stuff. He learned everything technical from his mother.

"So I've heard of your new project, Lead Engineer! You sure the task isn't too much?" I asked, in a half-joking manner.

Caroline Kincaid gave me a serious look. "Not at all. It's just another battleship. Nothing too special about her."

I nodded. "Not even her size?"

She laughed. "It's not like I haven't built anything bigger." I nodded again, remembering the Dauntless Project.

We were at an awards ceremony, and Mrs. Kincaid had just won the annual Velusan Regatta for the fifth time. My father, mother, and little sisters, Zephyr and Evya, were all aboard a two hundred and five-foot racing schooner called the Destiny. Alongside us were Mrs. Caroline Kincaid, Captain Fynn Kincaid, Destin and Tessia. The admiral was congratulating Mrs. Kincaid while the kids ran around the deck.

Zephyr tackled her twin, Evya, and they crashed into Tessia. The girls all started laughing as Tessia attempted to untangle them.

"Hey!" Evya complained. "No fair!"

Zephyr just laughed and rolled out from the pile, helping up the other girls. I looked over to my left and saw Destin leaning against one of the masts. He was so shy, and his body language suggested how uncomfortable he was with all the people on board the Destiny.

I watched as Zephyr walked over to him and started up a conversation. At first he shied away from her, but the longer she stood there, the more he warmed up to her.

"Damari!" my mother shouted. I jumped out of my trance, turning back to my parents and the Kincaids.

"Yes?" I responded.

Captain Kincaid cleared his throat. *"We were thinking of making the project more… open."*

I frowned. "What do you mean?"

My father lowered his voice to make sure the kids on deck didn't hear. I was only twelve at this point, and I wasn't exactly sure what information he was about to entrust me with.

"We add more ships to the project. Make it equal for every planet this time. Think of it as… a deterrent," the admiral said.

My eyes widened. "War preventions?"

Mrs. Kincaid nodded. "Think of the possibilities. The Grebles would no longer be a threat. Entire star systems would have no reason or chance to go against us."

"It's the perfect weapon," I muttered.

"They are the perfect weapons," Mom corrected, putting emphasis on "they."

As the adults kept talking, I started to tune them out, listening in on the kids instead. Destin had opened up a little and was talking with Zephyr. Tessia had started braiding Evya's hair; they were at a distance so each could have their conversations separately.

Destin was telling the story of how he was born on Sailara, the ocean planet, instead of Velus. He was named after the ship he was born on, hence, the similarities between their names.

I shifted closer to the four so I could watch over them. Tessia had finished braiding and they'd walked toward Zephyr and Destin. The twins started elbowing each other until Evya pushed Zephyr just a little too hard and began a grappling match.

Evya was slightly larger than Zephyr, but they were both matched in strength due to the year's worth of UDN training they'd received since their fifth birthday. I smiled, amused, wanting to see how the fight played out, but I also wanted to make sure that my sisters didn't hurt themselves.

I made my way down from the bridge and onto the deck, pulling the two apart. Tessia wrapped her arms around Zephyr's waist to drag her away while Destin did the same to Evya.

I gave my best powerful older-brother look at the two of them. "Guys, this is a celebration. Not a battle. You can hammer it out in the arena tomorrow, okay?"

They both nodded to appease me, but I could see the quick, competitive glares they flashed at each other. The Kincaid siblings released them. Destin left, heading up to the bridge silently, unbeknownst to the adults that he was approaching them and their classified conversation.

He made his way over to the wheel. I chuckled a little, seeing that he was only about half the size of it. Zephyr followed him up, and even though I couldn't understand what they were saying from this distance, it was clear he was teaching her how to sail.

The adults had stopped talking, noticing that the two of them were now at the wheel. I followed my sister's path, making my way up to the bridge along with the other two.

"Mommy?" Destin asked. "What were you talking about?"

I could see Mrs. Kincaid freeze as she tried to think of a quick excuse to cover up the project.

"We were talking about the PoD," my mom fibbed, using the acronym for the new Velusan command ship rather than saying her full name.

Evya piped up. "The Prince of Dragons?" She folded her hands into a finger-gun. Zephyr mimicked the position and the two of them went back-to-back, pretending to shoot at the bridge's controls.

Tessia joined in, shouting a command that meant enemies were in sight. My dad laughed at the three of them.

I opened my mouth to speak, but heard someone call my name and I turned around, seeing no one.

"Damari?" the voice said again. I recognized it immediately as I snapped out of reminiscence and turned around.

Merai was moving down the PoD's catwalk, approaching me. She raised an eyebrow. "I've been calling your name for the past minute."

I laughed. "Sorry. I guess I was… never mind."

She tilted her head, an unspoken question about the end of my statement written all over her face. I didn't have the guts to complete it. Despite the joy of that memory, it also still hurt me, knowing how much both the Kincaids and I had lost.

Merai moved beside me, looking out at the engine room. "Which one?"

"Huh?"

"Who were you thinking about?" she said, rephrasing the question this time.

I scoffed, quietly. "Both of them…"

She put a hand on my shoulder. "The commander is alive. If anyone is equipped and prepared to survive out there, it's her."

"What makes you so sure?" I asked, doubtful.

"Well," she said, grinning slightly. "She has the most powerful Mechanical Advantage individual in the Cayser System with her and she's a wicked fighter, so…"

It was my turn to smile. I looked at her, seeing the scratch on her cheek from the fight with the bugs. Her amber eyes sparkled in the light of the engine room. I opened my mouth to speak, but suddenly, a full-ship comm rang out.

"CSM Haldenson, you are needed in the bridge immediately," the announcement said.

Merai exchanged a worried glance with me, knowing they wouldn't have done full-ship unless it was urgent. Without saying a word, we both took off at full sprint down the catwalk, heading for the bridge of the *Prince of Dragons*. My mind raced as my heart pounded, wondering what news I'd hear next.

Chapter Thirty-One: Destin

When Ships Do Handbrake Turns

Years of sailing at the helm of any ship I was allowed
on had prepared me for so much more than I could've hoped
for, especially for the long days we spent here out at sea.
Even though that storm took a huge chunk of energy out of
me while giving the *Caroline II* a good beating, I was still
standing. The deep blue waves that smacked against the hull
started shifting to a stormy gray that reminded me of
Zephyr's eyes when she was shot in that simulated
experiment.

I shook the thought away, looking up at the clouds
instead. They were lighter than the sea, but they didn't
exactly make me feel better.

I sighed, missing the sunny skies of Velus. Closing
my eyes and listening to the waves lapping softly against the
Caroline II, I thought I would absolutely burst when I heard a
White Coat say that he saw land.

Above me, Zephyr was sitting on one of the
spreaders. She confirmed that our destination, and the finish
line, was ahead of us. Then she stood up and turned around;

even though she didn't say anything, I recognized that facial expression. Pure annoyance and distaste.

She slid down the mast and ran up to the bridge while Andrex was out by the bow, shouting at the White Coats in general.

Zephyr tugged on her hair briefly to tighten the ponytail before exhaling. "It's Breaker," she said. "He's catching up."

I thought my brain was going to explode. "He WHAT?!"

She just shrugged. "His ship was meant for calmer seas, and now that we're out of the storm, he's closing in on us. Fast."

Scowling, I opened up a full-ship comm and held the device to my lips. "Andrex, I need you to open the sails! White Coats, stop being useless and do whatever Andrex tells you."

I cut the comm line and turned to Zephyr. "I'm gonna do something stupid and crazy, but I don't want you to stop me."

She deadpanned. "Well, if you say something like that, you know I'm going to try to stop you."

Laughing, I shook my head. "Not this time. This one is gonna work. And," I said, grinning. "It's going to make us win the race. Just a liiiiiiiittle something my mom invented."

"So… a Crazy Kincaid?" she said, laughing. I nodded, my evil engineer smirk widening across my face.

This is going to be GREAT, I thought, already using my Mechanical Advantage to search through the power of the *Caroline II*, plotting my movements. This had to be *perfect*.

One wrong move and it would mean the obliteration of the Belfast Harbor.

The *Caroline II* was approaching the harbor, fast. I waited until the entrance was at a forty-five degree angle to the *Caroline II's* bow.

"Destin?" Zephyr asked. "What are we waiting for…?"

Ignoring her question, I quietly said to myself, "Hold… hold… hold…"

"Des?" she said again, more urgent this time. I narrowed my eyes on the port, and then when the harbor entrance was at the correct angle, I shouted.

"BRAKE!" I spun the wheel hard to the port side, all the way until the clunk of the max turn angle. I grabbed the port engine throttle and slammed it into reverse, activating the *Caroline II's* differential thrust. "DROP PORT ANCHOR!" I yelled to Andrex.

"Wha–" he began.

"DO IT!" I snapped, cutting him off.

He grabbed the lever and yanked, dropping the anchor. The clattering of the massive chain thundered from the *Caroline II'*s side and sank to the ocean floor. There was a brief moment until the heavy metal anchor landed and caught the sandy seabed.

We could all hear the groan of the ship's hull as the bow of the *Caroline II* dipped toward the sea and the stern of the ship began to swing out to starboard. It was almost like the *Caroline II* was doing a handbrake turn. The engines and the ship's hull strained to cope with the stress of those maneuvers.

"WATCH OUT! CRAZY IVAN!" I heard Breaker yell from his ship. I didn't notice until now how *close* he had gotten to us.

I waited until bowsprit was pointed directly at the harbor entrance. "CUT THAT ANCHOR CHAIN!!" I ordered Andrex.

"WHAT?!" he screamed back.

I deadpanned. "JUST LET THE LINE DROP!"

"GOT IT!"

Andrex just let the chain run to its end, the metal links completely falling overboard into the depths of the stormy gray seas. I then grabbed both engine throttles and slammed them into 'ahead flank.'

"DROP THE SAILS! ACTIVATE ELECTRIC OVERDRIVE!"

The A.S.T.S. immediately went to work, setting all the sails for speed. The white canvas solar sails started glowing a coppery gold, collecting the power of the sun. With the electric overdrive activated, the engines roared louder than they ever had before. It was the sound of the *Caroline II* being pushed to her limits.

C'mon, girl. You've got this... I thought to the ship.

The ship responded with her engines revving higher as thick white steam billowed from her exhaust. It was as if she were saying, *"YOU CALL THIS A CHALLENGE!?"*

The *Caroline II* accelerated faster than any human ship ever had. I looked at the ship's pitometer. It was going faster than her originally planned forty-six knot top speed. I stood there in shock. My ship was commanding herself! Setting her own limits! I felt like a proud parent.

She pulled into the Belfast Harbor, sending out a large wave that exploded against the docks, spraying everyone and everything within range.

Without me pressing any buttons her horn sounded as if to say, *"I win! This is what happens when you mess with me!"*

Out of the corner of my eye, I could see Zephyr staring at me. Her breathing was fast, like she was scared but relieved all at once. I burst out laughing, walking over to my best friend and giving her a hug.

She hugged me back, Siren hissing in my ear from her shoulders as if scolding me for that insanity I just pulled.

"We did it, Zeph!" I exclaimed. She laughed and tightened her grip, exhaling.

"And now," Andrex said from the bridge doorway. "We get to go home."

Zephyr released me and ran over to hug him as well. Outside on the deck, the White Coats were celebrating that their god had spared their pathetic lives. Off to the starboard side, Breaker's motor yacht came in. He stormed off of his ship and onto the soaked docks, absolutely furious that he lost the race.

Behind him, Tessia walked off of the ship and onto the *Caroline II*. The three of us ran down to greet her, hugging and laughing, but suddenly Breaker bellowed.

All noise in the harbor stopped as he screamed at the top of his lungs.

Chapter Thirty-Two: Tessia

Ships Have Feelings, Too

"**N**o! They cheated!" Breaker roared. "They should be disqualified! They're not even *human!*"

"Does that matter?" Andrex asked. "I mean, to me, you look like an Orilian."

Off to my side, Zephyr choked and Destin burst out laughing, leaning on the wheel. It shifted and rotated, and my brother hit the deck face-first, too busy cackling to care.

"Isn't that a place in Canada?" Breaker said, looking confused. Zephyr laughed even more.

"What's a Canada?" Destin said, still lying on the deck.

Breaker deadpanned. "It's a country, but that's not important. THEY CHEATED! They used unregulated tech!"

Destin snorted, standing up to brush himself off. "What are you talking about? First of all, you're the one who cut me off under sail, which is a big fat nautical no-no, last I checked. Second of all, if the tech we're using is unregulated, that's not technically cheating."

Breaker's face turned bright red as he stormed onto the deck of the *Caroline II*.

"HEY! What do you think you're doing?!" Destin shouted, his hand on his pistol in its holster. "GET OFF MY SHIP."

"Oh, yeah?" Breaker challenged. "And who's gonna make me!"

Destin grabbed his pistol, and in a quick draw, removed the suppressor and fired a shot into the air. A deafening boom and echo followed, cutting off the din of chatter on the docks. Everyone turned their attention to my brother and his foreign weapon. He then lowered it so it was level with Breaker's chest.

"Please don't make me," Destin said. "As much as I hate you, I don't want to kill you."

In unison, Zephyr and I said, "I'll do it." If Breaker's eyebrows rose any higher, they'd meet his hairline.

Zephyr sighed and advanced, stretching her arms. "You ready for that sparring match, Wright?" she asked, nonchalantly.

"W-Wait, you were serious about that?" Breaker stuttered.

"You weren't?" she said. "Does your ego bruise that easily?"

Breaker scoffed. "Well, who am I to fight a girl?" I laughed under my breath, knowing that Breaker was going to seriously regret underestimating Zephyr's fighting skills that had been primed and perfected since the Velusan age of five. I also knew his pride and oversized ego was wounded after he lost the race, and he didn't want to lose the sparring match either.

I switched my gaze over to the left of me on the deck of the *Caroline II.* Zephyr's eyes flashed a brief red before changing to the neutral ocean blue. She rolled her neck, stretching the other arm as well.

"You're not fighting a girl," she said, cracking her knuckles, face as impassive as stone. "You're fighting a soldier."

Andrex started laughing. "Dude, I feel badly for you." Breaker moved his arms behind his back, lacing his fingers together, stretching his biceps.

I strode over to Zephyr. "Kick his butt for me, will ya?"

Zephyr grinned. "It would be my pleasure." She unbuckled the belt around her hip that held her knife and placed both on the deck. Giving her hair a quick tug to make sure the ponytail was tight, she advanced almost at the same time Breaker did.

I studied his stance. He was clearly a trained fighter, but compared to Zephyr, it wouldn't be anywhere near enough. The two of them circled, Zephyr's steps clear and precise. Her eyes were calculating and cold, completely void of any emotion, except for the small sparks of red that signaled her distaste toward Breaker. He feigned a step forward, trying to make Zephyr strike first. She didn't. One of her fists twitched slightly, and she stared lasers into his eyes before flitting her gaze around his body.

She's looking for exposure. Somewhere she can hit. But what is she waiting for? I thought. *Take him out already!*

Just then, Breaker lunged, his moves quick and decisive, but not enough. Zephyr leaned back, easily dodging the blow. She turned to him head-on, face calm and steady.

He, on the other hand, was wasting his breath trying to make a show out of the fight.

Breaker attempted to land a punch, grinning the whole time, trying to go for Zephyr's gut or shoulder, but she blocked him easily, catching his fists and whacking his forearm with hers. Something shiny in Breaker's boot glinted in the sunlight, something that obviously shouldn't be there. The curved lines and flashy silver edges made it clear it was a knife.

I glanced back at Zephyr. She almost looked bored. She glanced around at the crowd, blocking him without looking, knowing his every move. Then, she shoved Breaker back, clearing at least ten feet of space between them.

"Alright," she snapped. "Show's over. No more play time. You wanted a match, I will give you a match."

Zephyr and Breaker went for each other at once this time. Zephyr let her body go loose as she dropped low, easily missing a blow to the head. She crouched and sprung forward between Breaker's legs, rising up before he could turn around. Then she kicked him in the side, his hip cracking as her heel forcefully collided with it. He grunted and spun around, catching Zephyr's shoulder and forcing her to the ground. As her upper back hit the deck, she threw her legs out and locked them around his torso, twisting her body so that he would come crashing to the floor next to her.

It turned into a grappling match. Without hesitation, Zephyr jumped Breaker and pinned him down, one boot on his forearm. He lifted his face and twisted, but her fist struck his nasal bone and his head flew back, smacking against the deck. Blood seeped from Breaker's nose. He gritted his teeth and jammed his elbow into her calf, knocking her leg off balance just long enough for him to shove her off. He moved to pin her to the deck, but she was prepared. Using both feet like a spring board, she launched him backward, away from her body.

Rolling to the side, she put both hands behind her, elbows bent, back hand-springing upward, using the force of the jump to move herself into a standing position. The two rushed each other, blocking punches and kicks. Zephyr caught him in the chest with her knee, and he put a hand to his sternum just as she chopped her hand upward on his throat. He started gasping for air. One of his hands dropped down to his boot.

The knife! I remembered. How could I tell Zephyr without distracting her?

Breaker's right leg was bent. Zephyr used the bent leg as a booster, pushing herself up and over Breaker's back, using her momentum to flip him over her body without hurting herself. They both landed on the deck. Breaker finally showed his knife, thrusting the blade toward Zephyr's head. Recognizing it's metallic flash in the sun, she brought her arm upward in another chopping motion, catching Breaker's wrist. He cried out and dropped the blade, only to catch the hilt in the opposite hand and slash again, missing her neck by just inches.

Now Zephyr was angry, her eyes dark red and smoldering. Off to my right, I could hear a clicking sound, and I knew what was coming. The winch to the boom on the aft mast was turning; the clicking was the sound of it locking in place. I looked up to the boom over my head and noticed that the sail was partially unfurled and catching wind. I knew that all Destin had to do was press the tack button on the control panel to let it fly. I shared a grin with my little brother, knowing the fate Breaker was going to meet.

Andrex and everyone else watched the sparring match with wide eyes, cheering whenever Zephyr would dodge a blow. The White Coats were recording the fight and scribbling furiously on papers, fascinated.

Breaker caught Zephyr in the shoulder with his elbow, knocking her off balance. He brought down the knife, slashing her left bicep. She hissed and spun, bringing her leg up high to kick him in the jaw. His head snapped to the side and he stumbled.

"BREAKER! MY SHIP HAS SOMETHING TO SAY TO YOU!"

Rubbing his chin and swiping at the blood on his lip, Breaker scowled at Destin. "Ships don't talk, alien."

Destin's eyes cracked with blue sparks. "Oh, this one does. HEY, ZEPHYR! *DECK!*"

Zephyr dropped to the ground as the winch released, the clicking sound clear over the silent crowd. The boom vang swung out, catching Breaker in the head, knocking him over the port-side railing of the ship. There was a satisfactory splash as he tumbled into the water, the spray sprinkling my face.

Zephyr was on one knee, a hand pressed over her bleeding arm to stanch the flow. "You took away all of my fun," she grinned. "Wow, Earth's gravity is heavy…"

Destin smiled. "That cheating bastard had it coming. And anyway, I have final say on *my* ship. Now, let's get you patched up. I don't want your blood on my freshly-stained deck."

Zephyr laughed. "Okay, *Captain Des*. As you say." Several White Coats approached her and started chattering excitedly. One of them, a blonde with glasses and hair tied in a bun, grabbed Zephyr's good arm and led her away to a medical tent off of the *Caroline II*.

Andrex leaned over the railing where Breaker had tumbled into the sea. "Uh, shouldn't someone get him out?"

Destin sighed. "AhhhhHHHHHH, *FINE*."

Andrex hopped the railing and dove over the side of the ship, his jump neat and almost splashless in the churning waters.

"Andrex!" I shouted, rushing over to the railing. "Destin, I didn't think he was going to *jump!*" Destin's eyes were wide with shock, too. I grabbed a spare rope from the deck and ran back, scanning the water, looking for any sign of life. Some White Coats were screeching behind me, but I just tuned them out.

About fifteen feet from the *Caroline II*, a hand rose out of the water, and Andrex's head followed. "I got him!" he shouted.

Exhaling with relief, I threw the rope to him, and with my brother's help, hauled both Andrex and unconscious, but alive, Breaker onto the deck. "You're *crazy!*" I chastised. Andrex just shrugged.

"I wasn't going to let him die. And plus, I've missed swimming." He beamed, shaking the water out of his messy blonde hair. I held up my hands in front of my face to prevent getting wet. Destin and I laughed.

"Dude, you are so lucky Zephyr didn't witness that. She would be shouting at you for it," my brother said.

Andrex smiled. "I save lives. She... well, you saw just now."

"She saves lives, too, but not in a medical kind of way," I said, chuckling. Below us, Breaker coughed and sputtered, salty seawater coming up from his lungs. He opened his eyes slowly, took one look at me, and grinned.

"Hello, gorgeous," he said. He scowled at Andrex and Destin. "Alien losers," he muttered. "You're ALL LOSERS. You should just hang yourselves and leave Earth in peace."

Andrex deadpanned, asking himself why he saved Breaker; Destin glared daggers, claiming to shoot Breaker, and I bent down on one knee and punched him in the face. The back of his head hit the deck and he went out cold.

"If I wanted to do myself in, I would climb your ego and then jump to your IQ," I said, solidly, my voice steady and even. Standing up, I stretched and cracked my knuckles. "Gods, that felt good."

Andrex and Destin laughed. "Ah, that's my sister!" Destin clapped me on the back. He put his arm around me, smiling at the harbor.

"We did it," he said. "Now, let's go home."

Chapter Thirty-Three: Zephyr

Seamless

Medics herded me into a tent off the docks and sat me on a table to get a look at my arm. I was still angry Breaker had caught me off guard long enough to disrupt my balance and cut me.

My bicep stung, the blood refusing to stay within the confinement of my palm, trickling through my fingers even though it was pressed firmly against the wound. I looked up as a woman with a blonde bun told everyone to leave the tent. It was the same woman who hadn't been afraid when I threatened her on my first day at Area 51. She had saved my life the day Destin and Tessia arrived.

"Alice," I said, coldly. "Where have you been?"

She smiled at me while opening the drawer to collect some white cloth. "They deployed me across the world to another facility in Austria."

Another facility? I thought, my mind racing. *Are there more like us? Trapped? Being experimented on?*

The sweet scientist seemed to read my mind. "No, no. It's only dedicated to lab results. But that's besides the point. I'm here now, and I'm going to help you."

"Thanks..." I muttered. When she approached, I took my hand off my arm. Fresh, unrestricted blood pulsed from the slash mark. The woman frowned before pressing the white cloth on the wound.

She grabbed a small metallic bottle, a clear bottle, and some bandages. "I'm going to clean it first. It might sting a bit."

She opened the clear bottle and poured some of the liquid on another white cloth before dabbing it on the lesion. Alice was right. It *did* sting. A lot. "Why did you make the other White Coats leave?" I asked, quickly, trying to distract myself.

"Well, they would want this opportunity to draw your blood. I didn't think you would've wanted that," Alice replied.

"What about you?"

She laughed. "Remember what I said to you what seemed like forever ago, commander? I try to help those like you. That's why I'm going to get you out of Area 51. I also assume you have a plan."

I blinked. "How did you...?"

"Oh, come on, sweetie. I wasn't born last week. You revealed Destin Kincaid's power to us, *knowing* they would experiment on him. Now, either you suddenly hate your best friend, or you have a plan."

I let out a breath of laughter. Alice was smart, I'd give her that. "Yeah. We had him propose to build something for

Area 51, but instead, it would be our escape," I said. About to open my mouth to continue, I clenched my jaw instead.

Why am I telling her this? She's still a White Coat! I thought, scolding myself. Maybe I'd lost more blood than I'd thought.

Alice finished cleaning the cut, next raising the metal can. She pushed a tiny button on the top; a clear film shot from a small funnel on the can, covering the wound.

Before my very eyes, I watched as my skin melded back together, the only evidence of the former injury a thin scar. "How did you do that?" I marveled, staring at the can.

She shook it. "We're Area 51. We've got a lot of new battlefield technology to help wounded soldiers."

"That's actually… pretty smart," I admitted. I then remembered Destin's accident with the aft mast, and how his arm had healed so quickly.

She smiled, wrapping the bandage around my arm. "Your skin will still be unstable for a little while during the healing of your inner tissue. Keep this on until you have to change for the awards ceremony."

I stood up, thanked her, and walked out of the tent, slightly shocked at how much I revealed, and how much she *knew*, but what surprised me most was her supposed willingness to help us. This human wasn't like all the others. She had a good heart… and I was hoping that my heavy trust in her would outweigh my judgement of the White Coat population in Area 51.

Gods, Zephyr, I thought. *You'd better be right about this…*

Chapter Thirty-Four: Destin
The Grand Awkward Ceremony

After we had won the race against Aiden, and Zephyr had obliterated him in the sparring match, there was an awards ceremony that apparently came with a *dance*. The one thing I do not do whatsoever. Unfortunately for us, the White Coats had measured and fitted us for *tuxedos and dresses* at some point… probably when they were experimenting on us and we were laden with a ton of anesthetics.

Although I continued to protest, I was shoved into a changing room and locked in until I put on the tux, complete with a bow tie. To be honest, it was a nice fit, but I already missed my work clothes.

Two guards escorted me, grudgingly, to a sleek, black vehicle with four wheels. It was longer than any of this kind of transport I'd ever seen. I remember the White Coats had called it a limo.

I took a seat. Andrex was on the other side, eating one of the assorted candies offered in the vehicle.

"Hi," he said. He was also in a tux with a bow tie.

"What are you doing?"

He swallowed. "Eating."

"Uh, that could be poisoned!"

Andrex waved a dismissive hand at me. "Eh. I tried all of them. They're safe."

I gave him a look as if to say, 'what the heck.' "Dude," I said. "You're nuts." Andrex just gave me a thumbs up.

The limo door opened again and in came Zephyr. She was wearing a crimson dress that came down to her knees. It didn't have straps on the shoulders so that it showed the clavicle, but instead wrapped around the tops of her arms. The entire outer layer of the dress was a floral pattern in lace; the same color as the rest of the outfit. She was wearing sparkling silver wedges. I had to be honest with myself... it was really attractive.

"Hey, guys," she said, sitting down. Siren was wrapped around her neck and chest like a scaly necklace. Her facial expression was a little guilty, like she had hurt someone she cared about.

"Wow," Andrex and I said at the same time.

"You look... great." My engineer eyes took in every detail of the dress. Zephyr's normally pin-straight hair was wavy. She looked really pretty.

Even in the dim lighting of the limo and the setting sun outside the blackened windows, I could tell Zephyr was blushing, her former expression melting away. I decided not to question it.

"Thanks." She unwound Siren from her neck and placed her on her lap instead.

Tessia entered last. She wore a white dress about mid-thigh length that showed off her figure. The top of the dress wrapped around her neck and had an open back that stopped about two-thirds of the way down her spine. She had the same shoes Zephyr did, except they were white and not silver. I hated to admit it, but the White Coats were *really* good at picking out dresses.

"Tess," I said. "You look fantastic."

My sister gave me a friendly punch on the shoulder and smiled. "Thanks. You don't look so bad yourself."

The limo started moving. It felt nothing like the steam-powered land cruisers we had on Velus. I didn't hear the chugging of a steam engine, but instead, a steady buzzing noise of what sounded like a very quiet engine.To understand what it was, I closed my eyes and quickly connected to the vehicle. It was also powered by a liquid fuel, but it wasn't water. I was being powered by a chemical that was made up of oil and a new highly-combustible liquid. Octane.

After about fifteen minutes, we arrived at a club on the coast of Belfast, Ireland. On one of the dry land docks rested the *Caroline II* in all of her winning glory. Within the club were bright flashing lights that changed color every other second. Loud music carried all the way to the limo.

"I guess this is our stop," Andrex said, popping one last chocolate in his mouth before opening the door to let us all out. Zephyr's eyes flashed purple. She was excited about this, but I had no idea why.

"C'mon!" Zephyr grabbed Andrex's hand while Tessia took mine. The girls ran inside the building, pulling us with them. Once we got inside, cheers immediately overpowered the music. It surprised me; these other humans were reacting so well to us, considering we had been greeted on this planet with guns pointed at our heads.

Lights sparkled all around the walls and ceiling. White tables with enormous floral arrangements dotted the massive room.

"Whoa," Tessia breathed. "Maybe Earth isn't so bad after all."

"I know. Only Area 51 is terrible," I added. The girls let go of our hands and ran onto the dance floor, laughing.

"That's the happiest I've ever seen them," Andrex said, watching them dance and spin each other around.

I nodded, staring at the strobes flashing and the disco ball sparkling. Humans continued their dancing while Andrex headed toward the buffet. I decided to head outside to the dry dock to admire my masterpiece.

Small golden lights decorated the hull, masts, booms, and square riggers. It bothered me that the humans had decorated my ship without my consent, but that didn't distract me from the fact she had won the race. I patted her hull, a slight metallic sound echoing from the contact. She was absolutely magnificent, a thousand times better than her sister, the original *Caroline*. She was a beast out on the waves, telling others what for. She was built to race.

I always believed that you should respect a ship or any kind of machine as if it were a living, breathing being. Because in a way, all of those components within make them almost like a metal creature. If you treat them with respect, they will help you. I knew the main reason we crushed the *Elleron* in the race was because Aiden had mocked the fact that the *Caroline II* was powered by steam.

I heard the door to the club open and close, the music growing louder and then softer as the sound carried itself farther outside. There was the soft clicking of heels on the pavement behind me, but I wasn't concerned.

"Des," a voice said. "You're missing out on the party."

I looked up at the *Caroline II* instead of turning around. I knew it was Zephyr behind me. "I'm missing nothing. I'm happy right here. With her."

Zephyr moved next to me and stared at the ship. Without turning her head, she looked at me from the corner of her eye, studying my facial expression. "You love her, don't you?"

I laughed, putting my hand on her hull and feeling her power coursing through my veins. "Of course, I do. With all my heart."

Zephyr smiled. "Don't forget about Tess."

"I have to love her anyway; she's my sister."

We were quiet for a few moments, just watching the *Caroline II* and feeling the cool night breeze, the waves crashing below us. It was almost like we were back home.

"Why don't you come inside and dance?" Zephyr offered.

I snorted. "No way. I don't dance."

Zephyr raised an eyebrow. "Everybody dances."

"Well, this particular Velusan right here doesn't." I pointed at myself.

"I'll teach you to dance."

"No, no, no, no, no. I don't dance. No. Just *no*," I protested.

"C'mon! Let's at least have a little fun while we're on this planet. We're finally out of Area 51! Living and being alive are two completely different things," she said, smiling.

"Are they, though?" I complained. Zephyr gave me a pleading look.

"Pleeeeease? For me?"

"Errrr… ahhhh…mmmm… FINE. Just let me say goodbye first."

She nodded and took a few steps back. I pressed my forehead to the hull, the cold metal stinging my skin. *We'll get you home. You'll fly free*, I thought to the ship.

Yes. The ship responded. *I will get* you *home safely. The White Coats are no match for my power.*

I smiled. *I know. You're amazing, Caroline II. I love you.*

I'll see you in the stars.

I took a deep breath and turned around. "Okay. Let's go… dance."

"Yay!" Zephyr grabbed my hand and pulled me back inside the club. I could see Andrex and Tessia talking at one of the tables. Of course, Andrex had a full platter of food in front of him. Siren was curled around my sister's shoulders, her little face looking proud.

"Do we *have* to?" I whined.

"Oh, don't be a baby. It's fun!" Zephyr led me onto the dance floor.

"I thought you prefer to fight," I told her. "You know, since you're in the military."

"Yeah, but I'm also the admiral's daughter. Therefore, I was required to learn how to dance. And I actually enjoy it. You will, too."

She brought me to the middle of the floor. I looked over my shoulder. Andrex and Tessia had stopped talking and were watching us. I couldn't read Andrex's expression, but Tessia had a huge grin on her face.

Oh, gods, I thought.

Zephyr took my right hand and put it on her waist. Her right hand took mine and held it up; her left hand rested on my shoulder.

"This feels weird." Zephyr ignored my comment.

"This was the first dance I was taught when I was seven," she stated.

Zephyr started directing me with different steps, telling me which way to move. At first, it was just walking in a box shape. It wasn't too bad. I spun her around once, but instead of putting her hand back on my shoulder, she took my hand and we opened arms before coming back together again. Following her lead, she quietly told me to separate from her. We joined forearms, walking in a circle before switching to the other side. I had to admit, I was enjoying this. I even caught myself smiling.

"See? I told you you'd have fun!" Zephyr laughed. Her eyes were a bright and vibrant purple, a color I'd nearly forgotten she had. It was when she was excited, and ever since we got here, desolation and despair had been the main mood.

"Yeah, okay. I'm having fun!" I spun her around, remembering the steps, repeating the motions again and again.

When the song ended, I realized that every pair of eyes in the room was watching us. The dance floor had almost been cleared, and we were in the center of a massive circle of humans. Zephyr grabbed my hand and took a bow. I bowed, too, awkwardly. It completely blew my mind how comfortable she was in a setting with *so many people*. Then

DESTIN

again, being the admiral's daughter put her in a lot of social settings where she had to actually talk and engage, since she was a member of the admiral's family. Large crowds were not my forte. I've always tried to avoid them to the best of my abilities.

"Okay, that was pretty fun," I said. She smiled.

"Right?" Zephyr hugged me. I felt a rush of happiness that I've missed for a very, very long time.

"Remind me to go to *every* dance party thing you have at your place!" I said. Zephyr burst out laughing.

Andrex and Tessia walked over.

"Wow, Des. I didn't know you could dance," Tessia smirked.

"Uh, yeah. Neither did I."

"Everyone loved the performance," Andrex affirmed. He then took Zephyr's hands and whirled her around so her side was against him, arms crossed around her torso. He dipped her and said, "May I have this dance?"

Zephyr giggled. Wait. *Giggled?* ExCUSE me? Zephyr Haldensdottir most certainly does not *giggle*. Come to think of it, this might be the first time.

Her purple eyes lit up with little golden sparks as she replied, "You may." I almost wanted to say something, but the music started up again and everyone resumed partying, filling up the strobe-lit dance floor. Tessia took my hand and dragged me back to the claimed table. I took a seat while Siren slithered off of the trophy and gave me a friendly puff, curling around my hand and arm.

"Hey, Siren," I stroked her small head with my index finger. It was good to see that even a neidren was impressed with me.

"You like her," Tessia said.

I was completely taken off guard. "What?"

"Oh, come on. I'm your sister. I notice these kinds of things. You. Like. Zephyr."

I turned away from Tessia. "I have no idea what you're talking about."

Even Siren gave me a look, as if to say, "Seriously? I noticed, too."

"Really? You, too?"

Tessia smirked. "It's kind of obvious."

Realizing I wasn't going to win this, I sighed. "Ahh, okay, fine. I do. I like Zeph. Are you happy now?"

"Yes."

"Good. I just–"

"Why don't you come and dance with me? I haven't seen you smile in a long time. It was good to see you so happy." Tessia stood up.

"Sure. Let's go dance."

Chapter Thirty-Five: Andrex

Rewards and Returns

Just as the music got quiet and the dance lights turned off, I spun Zephyr around, dipping her in the almost pitch-black room. Gradually, the lights came back on, but they weren't the strobes of the dance floor. A pale glow lit up the room dimly, just enough light so that our eyes wouldn't be hurt.

I bowed to Zephyr and took her hand in mine, kissing it while grinning. She laughed, giving me a curtsy of her own. I watched as her purple eyes bloomed with specks of gold. Before I could ask about it, I saw from the corner of my eye the Kincaid siblings approaching us.

Tessia linked arms with Zephyr and the two of them ran ahead of us, laughing and talking. I couldn't make out anything they were saying over the din of conversation and music playing in the background.

Destin and I walked over to the buffet and started filling up four plates with food. We chose an assortment of meats, fruits, and other strange human food they were offering at the ceremony and returned to the table. I placed one plate in front of Zephyr and sat to her right; Tessia was on her left. Destin placed his sister's plate in front of her and sat on her left.

"Thanks!" they both chimed. Siren slithered across the table to Zephyr's place and stuck her nose in front of one of the thick meat slices. Her small black tongue flicked in and out, like a little taste test.

Zephyr picked up the knife from the table and spun the blade between her fingers rapidly before bringing it down and cutting off a piece for Siren to eat. Behind me, I heard the clatter of something hitting the floor, and I turned to see one of the human waiters staring at Zephyr with wide eyes.

Destin also took notice of this and started choking from laughter on his drink; something called Coca-Cola.

Zephyr blinked in uncertainty. "W-What?" she asked. "What did I do?"

Tessia put a hand on her shoulder, also cracking up. "Oh, you're just being yourself. Never change, got it?"

She nodded, still confused as to why humans were staring at her. Her eyes swirled crimson as she flashed them all her famous death glare to get them to back off; they did straightaway. When she turned back to us, her irises were blue once more.

We continued eating and talking, and after we finished our meals, we decided to remain seated for a bit. Siren slithered up to Zephyr's shoulders and curled around her neck, closing her icy blue eyes and letting out a little puff of air.

Suddenly, the room went pitch black. Everyone went silent as the music stopped and the soft strobes shut down. I heard Zephyr grab the knife and stand up, preparing for any source of danger.

"Ladies and gentlemen," a voice boomed from the DJ booth. "We present the winners of the Great Atlantic Run. Captain Destin Kincaid, Doctor Andrex Nivalis, and Commander Zephyr Haldensdottir!"

Personally, I was a little annoyed that Tessia's name wasn't said, but I knew that since she was on Aiden's ship, which got second place, she wouldn't be mentioned for first. There was more clapping and cheering from everyone in the room.

Zephyr put the knife down slowly as a spotlight lit up our table in the dark club. Destin and I stood up on either side of her. The voice said to send a member of our table up to the stage to claim the trophy. Destin pushed his chair out a little more and made his way over to the three humans holding models of the *Caroline II* in gold, the *Elleron* in silver, and the ship that came in third place was cast in bronze.

The human holding the *Caroline II's* trophy handed it to Destin on a dark wooden platform. There was a little plaque on the wood that said: *The Caroline II Takes 1st Place: Great Atlantic Run - Year 2144*.

"Smile for the cameras!" another human said, holding up some strange contraption that resembled our holoshots.

Destin turned around, looking a little uncomfortable in the spotlight, but held up his trophy and smiled regardless, and even though he was nervous, he was practically radiating with joy for winning the race and beating Aiden.

The "camera" flashed, capturing Destin's image. The announcer spoke once more, saying that it was time to leave the club and head outside to view the winning ship. I watched as Destin's smile dimmed.

"Hold up," he said. "You're doing what now?"

Everyone in the club stood up and started making their way to the doors, excited to see the *Caroline II* and her interior.

Zephyr, Tessia, and I walked over to him. He was close to fuming. His voice lowered dangerously as he turned to look at Zephyr through narrowed eyes.

"Make sure they don't get to the bridge. If they see the flight controls, it's all over," he growled. Zephyr's eyes flashed between blue and red as she gave a curt nod. Siren's head rose from her coils and she hissed as Zephyr spun on her heel and strode after the humans. We were all very close behind.

They're probably gonna want to see the engine room. If they go in there, that could also mean that they'll see the Atlas Core. If they see the Atlas Core... I thought, trailing off.

"Oh, no," I muttered. Destin raised his eyebrows at me. Tessia's eyes widened as she realized what I was thinking of.

"The Core, Des! What about the Atlas Core?"

Destin's face morphed from shock to fury. "If the White Coats see what makes the *Caroline II* fly, we are done for."

We all started walking a little faster, shoving our way through the mass of humans in order to get to the ship. Zephyr got there first and stood in front of the *Caroline II* with her legs and arms spread defensively. Her eyes narrowed in on the crowd as Siren's head rose. Everyone stopped advancing toward the *Caroline II*, afraid of Zephyr and what she could do to them. Honestly, that was the smartest move. We shoved our way through the throng and took our places beside her.

"No one goes onto my ship," Destin snarled, glaring at the White Coats along the edges of the crowd. "I will not have it be *trampled* by destructive humans."

Out of the corner of my eye, I saw a White Coat turn his head to another before nodding at the guards. I switched my gaze to the Area 51 guards in their pitch-black uniforms standing in the shadows beyond the bow of the *Caroline II*. The blue LEDs all along the side of their rifles lit up as they pulled on the slides, advancing on us. Zephyr spun around and growled at them, pulling one of her daggers out from underneath her skirt. I stared at her. How did she hide it so well?

Shaking my head to clear my thoughts, I took up a fighting position at her side, watching from my peripherals as she spun the hilt so the blade's tip pointed at the ground.

"Stay back," she hissed. The guards didn't heed her warning, continuing their advance. Off to my right, one of the humans yelped, and I whipped my head around to see even more guards coming up behind us.

"EVERYBODY, GET DOWN!" Zephyr shouted. Without a moment's hesitation, the humans hit the docks as Zephyr turned at blinding speed and struck down the nearest guard, plunging the dagger into his exposed shoulder. The guard screamed and pulled the trigger, bullets exploding from the muzzle.

There were more cries from the humans as they covered their heads in an attempt to protect themselves. Zephyr opened her palm and thrust her hand into the guard's face, catching the bottom of his chin and exposing his windpipe. With her other hand, she brought the broad side of her dagger's hilt down hard on his throat. He dropped his gun and clutched his neck, falling to his knees trying to breathe.

She spun on the next guard, rearing up before letting her leg fly out in a spin-kick. Her heel connected with the rifle, knocking it from the man's grasp.

Figuring she could handle herself, I turned around to fight the guards I originally saw, ducking down beneath their gunfire before springing forward to tackle one. Behind me, I could hear Tessia cursing at one of the Area 51 sentinels as she broke away from his grip and snap-kicked him in the kneecap.

Then, there was a massive boom from the *Caroline II* as Destin fired the forward gun turret. Shocked, I craned my neck to look up at the smoking 88mm barrel above us. He just fired a blank shot.

I turned my head even more to see Destin's formerly brown eyes glowing blue and crackling with electricity as his Mechanical Advantage took over and fueled him. He was very clearly furious.

"Now," he said, quietly. "Get away from my ship before I fire a *live* shot."

There was silence, no one wanting to get in Destin's way, then one bold White Coat shouted an unknown command at two guards. Without a moment to spare, three guards converged on Zephyr and disarmed her, pulling her wrists away so that she couldn't fight back. The third guard holding her dripping dagger pressed the razor-sharp point against her back.

Destin, Tessia, and I shot death glares at the White Coats and guards. The scientist that had issued the order approached Destin and lowered his voice as he spoke into his ear.

"You are property of Area 51. You belong to *us*."

"Oh, yeah?" Destin snarled in reply. "And who's gonna enforce that?"

The man grinned and took a step back. "Come with us without any more strife and we won't have to take the commander to one of our... *dissection labs*."

Tessia ran over to her brother's side and put her hands on his chest and shoulder to prevent him from doing anything stupid. I approached as well, standing defensively next to them. The White Coat straightened up and snapped his fingers.

"Sedate them. Now."

More guards appeared and wrapped their large hands around us before pressing syringes against our necks and injecting an anesthetic. I struggled in their grips, but it was too late. I looked up at the star-lit sky, wondering if I'd ever see it again. A flash of blinding white light streaked past the atmosphere, lighting up all of the Belfast Harbor.

The last thing I heard before blacking out was a female voice coming from Destin's mouth.

"You have no idea what I am capable of... consider that a warning shot."

Chapter Thirty-Six: Tessia
The Alternate Motive

Ever since the incident in Belfast, my little brother had been consumed in his own moody world while his eyes flashed between their Mechanical Advantage, or MA, electric blue and his normal genetic brown. He was angry and every time someone tried to talk to him, he'd stare them down or just walk away.

During this time, Andrex was trying to get past my brother's Diatanium wall while Zephyr pulled me aside. She had the same facial expression as when we were being escorted to the GAR Awards Ceremony. Guilt.

"What's wrong?" I whispered.

"It's… one of the White Coats…" she muttered, her gray eyes not meeting mine. My heart rate sped up, wondering what could've possibly happened.

Zephyr… I thought. *What did you do?*

"She… she's onto our plan. I… I don't know why b-but I just let everything come out and–"

I pulled Zephyr into a hug, trying to calm her down. She stood there in a moment of shock before wrapping her arms around me and shaking.

"It's okay," I said, quietly. "Everything–"

"No," she said, tearfully, cutting me off. "It's not okay. I've betrayed you… all of you. All because I opened my mouth to a White Coat who wears the most convincing smile in the universe…"

Unsure of what else to say, I just kept hugging her, trying to calm her down. I'm sure the last thing she wanted was to tell the boys that she'd exposed us to a White Coat of all humans.

There was a quiet beep before the cell door slid open. Zephyr pulled away from me and turned away from the door to hide her face. Siren bopped her tiny nose against her cheek as a form of comfort, and Zephyr bent her head toward the neidren.

Instead of the expected Area 51 guards, a female White Coat with blonde hair tied tight in a bun walked into the room. The cell door slid shut behind her.

"I froze the camera and microphone, but it won't be long before the system recognizes that and shuts it down," she said, her voice hushed.

Zephyr stiffened and turned around. "Alice?"

"I'm here to get you out."

Destin squinted at Alice from his dark corner, his glowing eyes the only really defined feature. "Why?" he growled.

"Because I hate everything about Area 51 and how they're treating you. You deserve to be free."

"Well, you do treat us like creatures here," Andrex said.

She nodded sadly. "And I apologize for that. But there's something you need to see. The only way out of Area 51 is by rail. If you try to fly away on your ship, our camouflaged missiles will shoot you down. They just salvaged an old Russian locomotive around two hundred years old from the mid-1950s. It's powered by steam."

Destin completely perked up and emerged from his shadowy corner of the cell, his eyes back to brown and practically glittering from excitement.

"SHOW ME!" he exploded, bouncing up and down.

I chuckled. "Someone's happy." I walked over to him and elbowed him in the side. "You're gonna help us escape?" I asked, looking at her suspiciously through slit lids.

The White Coat nodded. "We must hurry. I can get a keycard to you later, but you need to construct your escape first. Come with me."

Alice left the cell and beckoned for us to follow her. Zephyr walked out first, her eyes darting around the hallway. She turned back around and shrugged, signaling that she saw nothing and that it was as "safe" as Area 51 could be.

We followed Alice. She led us down a long hallway into a room we had never seen before. There were large wooden boxes stacked to the ceiling. She continued walking, leading us behind one of the large stacks.

There was the locomotive, massive and timeworn.

"Whoa…" Destin said, running over to it. He rested his hands on the dark metal exterior, eyes wide with excitement and fascination.

"Yes, she's quite beautiful, isn't she?" Alice remarked. "I don't know where they found it or how it got here, but it's pretty impressive… and I think it will make a pretty good base for what you're going to do with it. I just don't have any information on this old iron horse. Maybe–"

Just then, Destin turned to the locomotive and his eyes flashed Mechanical Advantage blue, or MA blue, cutting off Alice's train of speech.

"She's a Russian P38 Class, type D2′ h4, one of 4 locos built by Kolomna Locomotive works in 1954."

We all stared at him.

After a long moment, I said, "'Cause we totally know what that means."

"Hold on, you got that all from looking at it?" Alice questioned, astonished.

"Well… no. I asked her," Destin said.

"Wait, wait, wait. You *asked* the locomotive?!" Alice stared in confusion.

Destin shrugged. "Part of my MA is that I'm able to 'talk' to machines."

Alice nodded slowly, backing up toward us so Destin could do his thing.

"What do you need us to do?" Andrex asked.

My brother turned his head over his shoulder and smirked at us before clapping his hands and rubbing them together.

"First things first," Destin said, holding out his hand to the locomotive, a bright flash as his eyes lit up.

There was the sound of screeching metal as the locomotive tore itself apart from the inside-out. The entire train completely collapsed, every bolt, screw, and individual piece of metal falling to the ground. We all flinched backwards, not wanting to be hit by a stray piece of shrapnel.

"Well, then," Zephyr said, looking at what used to be the Russian P38 Class locomotive.

Destin turned around and grinned at us. "Let's get to work!"

Chapter Thirty-Seven: Damari

Flipping Tables and Losing Sanity

Merai and I sprinted to the bridge of the PoD. I was faster and raced ahead, practically crashing into the walls if I had to take a sharp turn. I shouted at the PoD's AI to open the door. It hissed and slid to the side as I ran through, Merai hot on my heels. All the soldiers in the bridge turned and gave a brief salute.

"Haldenson," Sorres said. "We've located Earth. We're only a day away."

Whether I was breathing heavily from relief or from sprinting through the command ship, I didn't care. I was one day away from discovering if my sister was alive or not. I was only one day away from bringing her home.

A beeping sound rang out before General Kincaid's voice came over the comms and echoed throughout the PoD's bridge.

"One day?" he said. "Then what are we waiting for? Let's head into hyperspace and get there already!"

I took a deep breath, straightening myself out and brushing off my uniform. "Yeah, why don't we?"

Dennett pressed down on the comm button and leaned over the mic. "No can do, General. The PoD is much faster than the *Concord* by a longshot. If we went into a jump, the starliner would have to push her engines to the limit to keep up. You'd snap her drive shafts in half and essentially destroy the ship."

There was silence in both bridges for a long moment before the general finally spoke up again, clearing his throat. "So what, we just travel the day?! That's one more day that the commander and my children are endangered. That's one more day we could have them back with us and safe from whatever could happen to them on Earth."

Again, no one said anything. There wasn't much *to* say. After some time, I cleared my throat as I looked out of the bridge's window.

"It's the only way. We have to take the day's journey and pray to the gods that nothing will endanger the commander and the Kincaid siblings," I declared, my eyes narrowed, scanning the stars.

Sorres approached me, speaking up. "Haldenson. What if we went ahead of the *Concord?* We could be in and out no problem. Grab the commander and the Kincaids. Then leave."

There was a slamming sound from the *Concord's* end of the comm. Some of my men flinched as I remained stone-faced, understanding the general's rage. I seriously wanted to flip a table or throw my sword into the wall, but was I going to? Gods, no.

"You need the *Concord*. You are not going to a planet we know absolutely nothing about without us. You saw what happened with those... those BUGS!" the general shouted.

"We are coming with you whether you like it or not. We have to take the day."

Internally, I agreed with Sorres. Sending the PoD or a scout ship out before the *Concord* was the best thing to do, but since the general was my superior, I couldn't exactly just say no to him.

Glaring out at the void of the galaxy, I exhaled. "Yes, General. As… you… wish."

Merai came up behind me and I shook my head slightly, trying to clear my thoughts. Her presence at that moment acted as a comfort for me even as my fingers twitched discreetly, my muscles itching to attack something. Anything.

She subtly bumped her hand against mine as a motion of reassurance. Out of the corner of my eye, I saw her raise herself up slightly.

"We can spar later," she whispered. I looked down toward her, raising an eyebrow. She smiled at me, nodding. I hid a scoff behind the mask all soldiers learn to wear. It was like Merai could read my mind. For some reason, I was completely okay with that.

"Alright. We will continue to travel for the day and reserve our fuel. Like the general said, we have no idea what we are going to be up against."

I looked out at the stars once more. The general said something into the comms again but I ignored it as he continued to shout at his crew. I understood his pain and I could fully relate to how badly he wanted his children back. I knew I couldn't bear to lose my sister. Especially not after what happened six years ago.

Absentmindedly, I put a hand against the pocket over my chest that contained Zephyr's pendant. I knew everyone in the bridge was staring at me, but I didn't care. They all knew what happened. The entire Cayser System knew.

Without bothering to excuse myself, I turned on my heel and walked out of the bridge, removing the pendant from my pocket as I did so. No one followed me.

As soon as I got to the lift that would bring me to my room, I couldn't take it anymore. One tear started the waterfall.

I pressed my forehead against the cold steel wall and gritted my teeth, letting out a sob, squeezing the pendant in my fist. The spines of the dragon dug into my palm, but I didn't care. I punched the wall out of frustration, ignoring the blooming pain in my knuckles. The lift's door opened and I wiped my eyes, storming out and returning to my room, breathing heavily.

"Whatever it takes."

Chapter Thirty-Eight: Destin
The Silver Dragon

Being inside of the new Silver Dragon's boilers was like crawling in a huge metal tunnel. I was there to finish laying the heat rods. Once working, they would glow red-hot to boil the water to create pressurized steam to flow to the piston boxes and running gear. I crawled all the way to the back end of the boiler and started wiring up the cabling inside the tight space to power the heat rods. Suddenly, I heard Zephyr's voice coming through the smokebox door.

"Is everything okay in there?" she called.

"Yep! Almost… almost… done!" I beamed, proud of my work. The work that was finally going to set us free.

I shuffled back from the boiler and slid out, dusting myself off.

"What are you here for?" I wiped my hands on my pants.

"The new tender just arrived," she responded.

My face lit up. "Oh, perfect!"

I climbed down the front of the huge locomotive. By now, it was far beyond recognition from its former state. It looked nothing like the old P38 Class locomotive. I had reworked almost everything except for the frame. Its old black steel streamlining had been replaced with shiny Diatanium plates, which shined and reflected the light in the hangar brilliantly.

"Alright. Then let's hook up this tender."

Together, we walked toward where the tender was being unpackaged by Area 51 guards who thought we were working on the train for the facility's benefit. It was absolutely huge. It was taken from an old 4-6-6-4 Challenger Class, apparently some sort of American locomotive from a few centuries ago. Personally, I was surprised this planet even had technology two centuries ago.

However, the tender looked good. It had a 6-14 wheel arrangement, and was the perfect size for the new locomotive. It would have more than enough room to hold all the fuel for the new Silver Dragon. It was the same shiny Diatanium as the *Caroline II*'s hull.

I walked over to the huge tender. It was about the same height as the locomotive, but only half the length. This was normal for a locomotive tender, seeing as it didn't need to have all the important running gears on it. The tender would be positioned on the rails behind the locomotive. Once in place, I'd have to hook up the water infeed pipe and a few of the electrical connections, and boom. The tender would be filled with water to fuel the locomotive. It was a perfect system. And that perfect system was going to get us home.

"Guys, help me move this to the back of the Dragon," I said, going behind the tender.

"Wouldn't it be easier to back up the locomotive?" Andrex asked, coming up beside me.

"Nope. I couldn't even start this thing without fuel. Plus, the axle boxes are so well balanced that you could just easily push it," I responded.

"Then let's give this a go," Tessia said.

We began to push the tender until we heard the clunk of the locomotive's coupler, signifying that they were now locked together. I walked around it and crawled into the gap between the locomotive and tender, connecting the air hoses for the air brakes, the main water intake pipe, and the many electrical wires.

"Right! That's the loco done!" I announced. "Now, we need the *Caroline II* and the *Nautilax*. We're putting them on flatcars. And we need a passenger car. For, y'know, *passengers.*"

Alice approached us, smiling. "Lucky for you, they brought both of those in, too."

My face lit up. "Perfect! Where are they?!"

"They followed your design when they remodeled the flatcar and passenger car. They're just waiting to be hooked up to the couplers."

Out of the corner of my eye, I could see Tessia practically deflating with relief. I felt the same way, and I'm sure the others did, too.

Five Area 51 guards came up behind Alice and surrounded us, telling us to move back to our cell. As I passed Alice, I locked eyes with her, nodding inconspicuously. The look in her gaze was more than clear.

She was going to get the Silver Dragon connected and ready for travel. Before the guards could take us away, she came right up to us. She lowered her voice as we all leaned in.

"Once you slip out, take a left and keep going twenty paces. When you reach the fork in the hallway, take a sharp right. Find the heavy iron door. Slip the keycard into the lock and get your gear," she muttered, hastily.

Before we could respond, the guards shoved us off, throwing us back in our cell and locking the heavy door.

Now all we had to do was wait.

Chapter Thirty-Nine: Tessia
Who Knew Keycards Brought Pain

We were all restless within our cell, completely antsy waiting on Alice to slip the keycard under the door. I was tapping my foot against the floor, Zephyr was anxiously playing with Siren's whipping tail, Destin was wringing his shirt in his hands, and Andrex was pacing back and forth.

"I think I'm about to explode," Andrex grumbled. "I can't take this."

I looked over at him, deadpanning. "Dude. None of us can. This is like the definition of torture!"

Zephyr exhaled and hung her head as Siren rose up to bump her tiny nose against her forehead. She snatched her pillow and threw it at Destin out of boredom. He smacked it out of the way, flashing a glare at her.

Exhaling with frustration, my narrowed eyes flicked back and forth between the two of them. "Will you two knock it off? This is just the anticipation getting to you g–"

A small rectangular object slid underneath the cell's door. All of us stared at the thin white object, trapped in a brief moment of shock. Almost simultaneously, we snapped out of it, all hastily making our way over to that slim piece of whatever it was made out of. That thing was our way out, and we finally had it.

I bent down to pick up the card, staring at it like it contained the power of the gods. This small object was the key to our freedom… and I was holding it between two fingers.

Zephyr's face broke out into a smile as Siren wound herself around her waist, giving us all a small puff of air before resting her sleek head on her coils.

"Let's get out of this pit," Zephyr whispered, plucking the keycard from my hand and slotting it into the hidden lock Alice had been so gracious to show us.

I held my breath, expecting the door to remain shut, but it slid open soundlessly. Around me, I could hear everyone exhaling; even Siren.

Zephyr took a step out into the hallway before waving at us that it was all clear. We stepped out, grinning with happiness over the thought of freedom.

"Remember," Andrex whispered. "This is a stealth mission. We get our supplies, and then we book it. Got it?"

We all nodded and started running down the hallway. I could almost hear Alice's voice in my head as she gave us the directions.

Left… keep going twenty paces… sharp right… my mind went over. *Find the heavy iron door. Slip the keycard into the lock and get your gear.*

We had all memorized the instructions, telling ourselves over and over what the correct path was. As the sharp right came, we skidded to a stop to turn and dash down the corridor. Ahead of us was the heavy iron door. Just like Alice had said.

Keycard in hand, Zephyr took it and slipped it through the lock. The door hissed as the hydraulic pistons released and the air-tight seal cracked. It moved back slightly, clicking before it slid to the side into a slot, revealing a room full of weapons. Standing near a table in the middle was a woman with blonde hair in a tight bun. She turned around and smiled at us.

"Alice," Andrex whispered, catching his breath.

"Good," she said. "You're here."

To everyone's amazement, Zephyr walked straight up to the good White Coat and gave her a hug. Alice stood there for a moment in shock, her action reflecting all of our expressions, before she returned the gesture.

Zephyr pulled away, looking Alice dead in the eye. I hadn't noticed until now that they were just about the same height.

"Thank you," Zephyr said. "For everything you have done for us. I was right to trust you."

Alice smiled warmly at her. "I'm not done quite yet, Commander. I have stocked the locomotive with enough food and medical supplies to get you to the ocean. There are also mattresses, blankets, and pillows, including other equipment should Destin need it."

I stared, awestruck. "How did you manage to pull that off alone?" I asked.

"I wasn't alone. There are very few of my co-workers who share my view on this entire facility and what it stands for. We are happy to help you get home."

Turning my attention away from the conversation, I looked at the weapons in the room, and saw all of ours.

Zephyr's sword and armor, my brother's jacket and auto-rifle, my katana and pistol, and Andrex's bow, quiver, and quindent. It was all here.

On the table that Alice and Zephyr were standing next to was all of our clothing. The others appeared to have noticed as well. Andrex started to take off his shirt.

"Whoa, whoa, whoa! Hold it!" I said, putting my hands out in front of me. He gave me a confused look.

"What?" he defended. "Last I checked, there aren't any changing rooms in here. If you wanna get out with all of our supplies, just turn around and deal with it."

Rendered speechless, I grudgingly pivoted on my heel and left the boys to change, taking off my own Area 51 prison uniform and putting on the clothes I had arrived in.

Zephyr changed as well, sliding into her gauntlets and strapping on her pauldrons. She beamed as she finished tying up her hair, and I could practically feel the power radiating from her. Her eyes swirled into purple, which, I'm sure, reflected how we all felt. Excited. Hyper psyched to get out of Area 51 and finally return home. I could still hardly believe this was happening. It seemed so surreal.

Zephyr turned to us. "Now, remember. This is a stealth opera–"

From the corridor, there was the bang of a rifle as a bullet whizzed past my ear, almost nicking it. Everyone froze except for Alice, who hastily pulled a set of cuffs out from her jacket.

"Quick," she whispered. "I thought of the alternatives. One of my coworkers could've leaked the plans. Just chain me to the table and promise me you will get out of here."

Without a second thought, Zephyr sheathed her sword on her back and whipped around, shoving Alice to the ground for show and locking her wrists around the table leg. Luckily for us, the table happened to be bolted to the floor.

"I can't thank you enough," Zephyr said in hushed tones. She drew her sword once more and moved to the doorway. She exhaled, Siren hissing and tensing around her waist.

"What now?" Destin queried, looking out at the group of guards starting to clog the hallway.

The young warrior turned around, her eyes pulsing between purple and red.

"Now, we do this the hard way."

T
E
S
S
I
A

Chapter Forty: Zephyr
Liberatory Shots

It was absolutely *amazing* being back in my own armor again. The feel of my cold iron pauldrons through my shirt, the worn-down leather grip of my glorious Diatanium sword, and the comfort of my gauntlets against my wrists made me feel more powerful than I had in weeks.

The chill of my knives against my legs was invigorating as I finished tightening the straps that held them in place. My headband was finally back where it belonged, holding back my hair so I could stare my enemy directly in the eye. Siren was wrapped around my waist above my belt, holding on tightly, knowing there was danger ahead. The comforting smell of my black leather combat boots brought me right back to being in the arena with my brother, he and I sparring with fierce enthusiasm.

My eyes spiraled into their deadly dark red. Without a moment's hesitation, I dashed into the hallway of my prison, Tessia, Destin, and Andrex right behind me, holding their weapons that were confiscated when they were taken to this gods-awful place. Guards fired at us, their bullets ricocheting throughout the hallways. Spinning my sword wildly, I powered through the fire, deflecting a few stray bullets toward the gunmen. They hit home, knocking down three of them.

"Hey, *princess!* Hasn't anyone ever told you that you never bring a knife to a gunfight?" one of the guards shouted, looking at my daggers.

"First of all," I seethed, throwing one of my knives straight toward him, "I am *not* a princess. I'm your *worst nightmare.*" I continued to deflect bullets while my taunter took a hit and dropped dead. "Second, you guys have terrible aim."

I saw Destin out of the corner of my eye, his pistol clicking as its ends expanded, reverberating as his gun transformed into an auto-rifle. Full-assault mode. He was taking out our enemies left and right, causing some of the attackers to back off, rethinking their moves.

But two guards cornered him. "Where do you think you're going?" one of them asked.

Destin gave Tessia a look, and she threw him her gun. His auto-rifle quickly transformed back into a pistol. "That way," he said, crossing both arms, confusing the guards. Fingers on the triggers, he pressed. With loud bangs, his advancers hit the floor. He tossed the gun back to his sister. She caught it with one hand, shoving it back in its holster.

Tessia looked like a flurry of rage with her sword flying. She threw it, impaling one man's bullet-proof vest. "Didn't anyone ever tell you not to bring a *gun* to a *sword fight?*" Tessia yelled, redrawing her pistol and firing like the amazingly protective sister she was. I realized that her later action contradicted her words, but it didn't matter right now.

She and Destin were fighting back-to-back like a sibling powerhouse.

Andrex had his quindent strapped across his back, his whalebone bow the choice weapon at the moment. He was reloading and shooting faster than I ever thought possible. As soon as he was out of arrows, he drew his quindent, and it glowed blue in his hands. Twirling it like a powerful beacon of death, he struck down everyone in his path, icing a few guards to the wall or floor as he passed.

Sparks of gold danced in my eyes through the red. Realizing I was engaging in a major warrior's no-no, I stopped myself from being distracted by Andrex and focused on my own side-mission: getting everyone out safely, even if it meant the cost of my own life.

I grabbed my second dagger, throwing it with the force of a missile, my aim more powerful and incomparable to any adversary. Their technology was primitive compared to Velus's, so I was pretty sure their aim was just as bad. Luckily for us, it was.

"We've got one shot to get out of here!" Destin shouted over the deafening thunder of gunfire.

"Let's make it count!" Andrex called back, his quindent rapidly reducing the number of his attackers.

I was dodging bullets, flying through the storm of fire that faced me. I ran directly up to one of the gunmen. He didn't even see me. He was too busy trying to nail Destin. Once he noticed me, it was too late.

I thrust my left hand as an open-palm straight into his chin, snapping his head backward before sending him to whatever afterlife the humans worshipped.

"Tessia, on your left!" I called. She moved as my third dagger whizzed past her. It landed in the man charging up to her, and he hit the floor face-first.

Siren tightened around my waist. I whirled just in time, spinning my sword to block the rain of bullets directed at me.

"How do we kill them?!" a man shouted. "They're gonna tear us to pieces! Or *she* will!" He pointed his gun directly at me as I sprinted toward him.

Someone was trying to radio for backup, but Andrex whacked the communication device out of the fighter's hand with the butt of his quindent. It went flying through the air and landed at the end of the hallway where we first started the escape. It was supposed to be stealthy, but fifty gunmen in your face doesn't exactly say, '*You're getting out of here without a fight.*'

Suddenly, Destin yelled, "EVERYBODY, STOP!"

To my surprise, everyone did. Guns stopped firing. Andrex paused for a moment before punching his attacker. He went out cold, but nobody really noticed.

Destin was red in the face, and I immediately saw the reason for his distress. One of the sentinels of Area 51 closed his fist around Tessia's neck.

Instantly, Andrex had his quindent poised to throw at the man. Destin had his auto-rifle loaded. The hand that held my sword tensed while my left one was inching toward my final dagger.

Even if it means I get killed, I can't allow Tessia to die, I thought.

I had to act fast; her face was turning blue. I prayed to Idar, the god of battle, to bless my aim. I dropped my sword to create a distraction. The man let down his guard for only a second, but that was all I needed. I threw my dagger to my opposite hand before hurling it with the force of the gods themselves. It hit my intended mark, and the man dropped to the ground. Tessia, released from his death grip, fell to the floor gasping for air. Destin ran to her. We all exhaled in relief as I stomped on my blade, catching the hilt as the sword flicked back up.

Our victory was too early. A single shot was fired, and I felt a blinding pain as a bullet hit my back just inches below my left lung, barely missing Siren. Any higher, and she would've been dead. Any higher than that, and I'd be dead.

"Zephyr! *NO!*" Destin screamed, his eyes meeting mine for a brief moment. In them, I saw pure terror. I remembered what Destin had told me back in the hangar what seemed like so long ago: *"You died, Zephyr. You died in my arms."* Destin closed his fists, knuckles white. A single tear fell down his cheek.

No, I thought. *I'm not going to die. I made a promise to him, and I'll make sure I see it through.*

A burning sensation filled my entire body and I put my hand out to the wall to steady myself, but the wall wasn't there. My sword slipped from my grasp and clattered to the floor as my muscles refused to support me. I stumbled and fell to the floor. Someone caught me before I hit the ground. I tried to get away from the person who had me, thinking it was a guard, but their grip was strong.

No… no, I'm not going back. I'm so close, I thought. Eventually, I relaxed, the pain overwhelming all of my senses.

"Zephyr! Zephyr Haldensdottir, stay with us!" I couldn't tell who was talking to me. Every noise in the room was muddled together. Then more quietly, I heard, "*Stay with me*."

Fire opened up again, and I could hear Destin.

"You wouldn't listen to me, would you? Now let me show you what happens when you mess with an engineer that has a home-built gun that fires fifteen hundred rounds a minute." I heard a click, and his gun's automated voice saying, '*Overdrive activated.*'

"We need to… get to the Silver… Dragon," Tessia coughed. I could hear her gun pumping out bullets, and I knew she was back to fighting.

It seemed like an eternity before the noise died down. I could just barely make out the words Destin was saying. It felt like hundreds of blisters were searing my skin around the gunshot wound.

"Is she… is she alive?" he asked. Someone pressed their ear to my chest and two fingers on my neck.

"Just," Andrex said. "C'mon. We need to leave before more thugs show up."

Somebody lifted me up. My entire body felt like it burned with the heat of a thousand suns. I could feel hot blood flowing against my skin from where the bullet struck me. I was bleeding out.

"No…" I forced myself to speak. "L-Leave me here. I'll only s-slow you down."

"Not a *chance*, Zeph. When we made our plan to escape, it included *all* of us," Destin said.

"C'mon! There's our ticket outta here." Tessia pointed at the Silver Dragon. The magnificent sleek train designed and built by Destin loomed ahead of us. Behind the locomotive was a passenger car, and behind that were two low-loader flatcars. Covered by tarps were the *Caroline II* and *Nautilax*. Alice really had done everything to help us.

Everyone boarded as the grounds lit up. Bullets were bouncing off the Dragon's tough exterior. More government goons had appeared, and they were trying everything in their power to keep us at Area 51.

"Andrex! Take Zephyr a car down. The supplies should be in the passenger car," Destin said.

"Right," Andrex acknowledged.

Once we got to the car, Andrex placed me down on the floor and started searching for supplies. His right sleeve was soaked red from carrying me. My vision was fuzzy, and I knew I was losing blood quickly. I struggled to stay conscious.

"What's Zaccoth like?" I asked, my voice quiet. Andrex looked at me.

"It's amazing," he told me. "Ice towers so tall they look like they can touch the skies. Stars so brilliant they reflect off the snow during the night. Incredible snow deserts for miles. Animals the size of a hill covered in thick fur from head to hooves."

"You miss it," I said, trying to hide the strain in my voice.

"I do," he responded, grabbing a white box with a large red cross.

Andrex knelt down, rolling me onto my side to examine the wound. He inhaled through his teeth, the universal sign for, '*That doesn't look good.*'

He put me flat on my back again and ran a hand over my torso, searching for something.

"Gods above…" he breathed.

"What?" I murmured, concerned. I heard him whisper a quick prayer to Salutem, the goddess of safety and health. That just made my worry grow.

"There's no exit wound. I'm going to need to perform surgery to get the bullet out before it gets infected."

"What's my… other option?"

"You die."

Chapter Forty-One: Destin

My Mechanical Advantage

My stress levels were maxed out after just

witnessing my worst nightmare become a reality. I thought everything would be okay. I really thought that we would get out unscathed. The simulation shattered my heart, but actually living it was a million times worse.

I stumbled into the locomotive cab with Tessia hot on my heels.

"K-KEY!" I shouted to her.

"Wha–"

"THE KEY! I NEED THE KEY!" I demanded, cutting her off.

"OH!" She tossed me the key to start the Silver Dragon, but my hands were shaking so badly I missed the catch. The key clattered to the floor and fell through a vent. I cursed, furious and rattled.

"DESTIN!" Tessia grabbed me by the shoulders and shook me. "COME ON, DESTIN! PULL YOURSELF TOGETHER! Forget the key! Unless you can magic it up here, you gotta start her the hard way."

I nodded and dove for a panel under the locomotive's monitoring station, and using brute force from my adrenaline and Mechanical Advantage, I tore the Diatanium plate clean off its screws. I stuck my head in and grabbed the ignition cables, tearing them off the starter cylinder. Using my teeth, I ripped the insulation off the wires and jammed them together, sparks flying from the wires as fifteen thousand volts of electricity passed through them. It burned both of my hands and my hair stood on end. I completely ignored the pain, letting my MA take over.

"START!" I yelled to the locomotive. "Tessia, open the steam valves!" My sister turned to the front of the cab and grabbed two valve controls and opened them. "COME ON! LIVE!"

The locomotive thundered to life. I stood up and ran to the train's main controls and slammed the Johnson Bar all the way forward. I grabbed the throttle, and because of stress, I accidently shoved it completely open, releasing *all* of the locomotive's eighty thousand horsepower. The massive pistons began to pump back and forth with the might to move a mountain. The huge drive wheels on the train spun for a brief second, shooting sparks out of the bottom of the Silver Dragon. A split second later, they found traction and grabbed the steel rails as the train began to move.

I could still hear bullets attacking the outside of my beautiful mechanical child.

None o' that, I thought. I heard the heavy chug of the piston boxes and the roar of the compressors. Then there was the sound of metal on metal as the massive drive wheels on the locomotive ground against the rails. Below it, sparks flew from the huge wheels as the train began to pick up speed. I noticed the enormous door leading away from Area 51 to the outside world was closed.

My eyes glowed MA blue.

"That's not gonna stop me." I pulled on a cable hanging from the ceiling. The sound of the Silver Dragon's horn ripped through the room.

The train burst through the giant metal doors of the hangar, sparks flew, fires raged, and we were all home free. I couldn't be prouder.

Suddenly, I heard someone scream, "Send in the 'copters!"

I ignored the gunmen as more orders were shouted over the pandemonium.

I will push everything *to the limit… and beyond… for Zephyr,* I thought.

I turned on the huge headlights of the Silver Dragon, closing my eyes and holding on tightly to the Johnson Bar.

Feeling the vibrations of the machine, I imagined myself inside the wiring of the train's computer. Through my mind's eye, I could see myself swimming in the gigantic tanks that supplied water to the evaporator cores to make steam. I could see the running gear on the side of the locomotive as I felt myself becoming one with my machine. It was a good feeling. A feeling that I've missed.

Then, I told the locomotive, *give me everything you've got!* I felt the train speed up even faster. Almost as if the locomotive were responding to me, it seemed to say, *"Will do!"*

Suddenly, Andrex came dashing into the room.

"You good?" I raised an eyebrow.

"Do we have any fever medication or something?" he asked. "I can't read Human."

"Errrr," I wavered. "I'm not sure, why?"

"It's for some form of pain relief. She *did* take a bullet."

"Oh, no... is it bad?" I knew Zephyr was tough, but when someone tells me that she needs a pain killer, it must be really bad.

I started to feel guilty again. *This is my fault, this is all my fault, my best friend is going to die because of my actions*, I said to myself over and over again.

"Hey," Andrex consoled. "Don't worry. Zephyr's one of the toughest girls I've ever met. She'll live," he put his hand on my shoulder. It felt as if he read my mind.

"How can you be sure?" I asked.

He laughed a little. "Dude, I'm a doctor. Trust me, I know."

I nodded and turned back to the Silver Dragon's controls. I tried not to think about it too much, deciding to focus on the constant chugging noise of the Silver Dragon's running gear instead. I concentrated on it so much that I didn't even notice Andrex left the cab. I stuck my head out the window and stared at the vast expanse of the Nevada Desert. I looked forward to see the front of the locomotive, its massive headlights cutting through the darkness. I watched my pennant flapping around on its pole at the front of the train. Looking back, I saw the passenger car trailing behind the locomotive, and the low-loader flatcars that carried the *Caroline II* and *Nautilax*.

We will get you both to the ocean. I promise, I thought.

It felt good to have the wind running through my hair again. Being in control of a machine was my most favorite feeling in the universe. I moved away from the open window and looked at the speedometer. It read two hundred and five MPH. I smiled, then looked at the water gauge and my grin was replaced with great worry. Running the train over its maximum capacity had caused us to burn through almost all of our fuel; only thirty-five percent remained. That got me thinking about what kind of toll this might have taken on the running gear. I grabbed the Johnson Bar and pulled it back gently. Then I seized the brake and tugged.

Tessia walked in. "We have the thread and we found tweezers. Somehow. Now all we need is a needle, a scalpel, and sedatives, but we might need to sub the scalpel with a dagger, knife, or even a sword," she said. "Then again, we don't exactly have any knives with us since Zeph lost hers in battle… wait, why are we slowing down?"

"It's the fuel. We're running out. Quickly," I said.

"Yikes." Tessia looked at the gauge. Andrex came running in again and dropped Siren around my shoulders. I only noticed now that his arm was covered in blood, but it was obvious it wasn't his.

"O-Oh, hey, Siren! I'll watch her while you help Zeph," I told him.

"THANKS," Andrex blurted. "She won't leave Zephyr alone– Wait. What is that?" Andrex bent down and found a broken piece of thin, sharp metal. With all the commotion, I had completely missed it.

"Perfect," the young doctor said. "I think we'll be okay. Tess, I'm gonna need your sword."

"That's fine," my sister replied. Then they both left to attend to Zephyr. I kept pulling on the cord, hearing the hissing of the air brakes and the squeal of the brake shoes on the giant metal wheels. I opened the right cab door and waited for the train to come to a complete stop before I jumped down onto the desert sands. It was creepy seeing nothing but blackness around me. The only light was the dim glow shining through the windows from the headlights of the train.

I unclipped a flashlight from my tool belt and turned it on to examine the undercarriage suspension and running gear. There was the constant hissing of the steam deflectors venting excess steam pressure. Inspecting the running gear closely to make sure there were no faults in the driving rods, I stuck my fingers in the joints to confirm there was grease so a fire wouldn't start. Making my way to the back of the train, I checked that the *Caroline II* and *Nautilax* were properly strapped down on the low-loader flatcars. The inspection continued with the trucks and axle boxes. The axle boxes needed more grease on both cars; they weren't designed to run at a constant two hundred and five MPH.

I went to the Silver Dragon's water tender and opened a little hatch door on the undercarriage. Searching for a rag and a grease gun, I made my way back to the flatcars. Attaching the end of the grease gun to a little node on the top of the axle box, I inserted a stick of grease in the gun and began to pump the handle back and forth. Siren was startled by the sound of it. Her little head popped up.

"It's okay, girl," I soothed. "It's just one of Uncle Destin's tools." The neidren looked at me, then the grease gun, then me again. She tucked her little head away in her coils as I continued my work on all twenty-four axle boxes. By the time I was done, the moon had shifted a decent amount.

I put my tools away and was about to climb back aboard when I noticed something odd - on the right middle set of the running gear where the main rod meets the eccentric crank, the main pin was gone.

You can NOT be serious, I thought. *That's the one spare part I don't have.*

The main pin attached the eccentric crank and rod, which was linked to the gear connecting rod which moved the valve stem back and forth in the piston box, which also controlled the train's direction of movement. Without the main pin connecting everything, the train couldn't move. We were stuck in the middle of a desert with Area 51 guards hunting us down. I cursed at the top of my lungs. Tessia must have heard me because she poked her head out the door.

"What just happened?" she asked.

"This set of running gear is missing its main pin." I growled. She jumped down, knelt beside me, and looked at the poppet valve gear.

"Oh, yeah," she said. "That's a problem. Can you fix it?"

I laughed. "Can I fix it? Yeah! Just not here because I don't have a spare." My sister had a worried look on her face. "I'm going to have to improvise or else disable this set of running gear," I explained.

"Is that possible?" she asked.

"Yeah. It's a switch in the cab. I have to turn off running gear set two. And besides, we would save water running on only the forward set. The problem is that the eccentric crank and rod can fall off, even though there is no power being applied to the wheel set."

"Well, how do we fix that?" Tessia's eyes roamed over the desolate landscape.

"We take off the eccentric crank and rod," I said.

"Or…?" Tessia began. "We make a new main pin!"

"But I need material!" I shouted. "There's *nothing* here, Tess! We're in the middle of godsforsaken nowhere!"

"Can't you use a different spare part and modify it to work here?"

I thought for a minute. "That could be possible…" I said. "I need to see what I have." I got up and walked over to the ladder to climb into the cab of the Silver Dragon.

Through a door at the back of the cab, I walked via the compressor room into the water tender and finally to the passenger car, moving all the way to the back of it to my little workshop. On one side were shelves and bins fully loaded with spare parts. On the other side were tools and machines. I rummaged through the bins, but found nothing.

"Terrific. Just *perfect!*" I slammed the door to my workshop. For once, I felt like I had failed at my own super power. I grabbed a red rag hanging on the wall of my workshop and wiped my hands.

What would Zephyr say? I thought. She'd probably tell me that I can fix it easily using… something to improvise. But what?

Outside of the window, I saw beams of light penetrating the darkness. Black choppers shone searchlights down from the night sky.

They were coming for us.

Chapter Forty-Two: Andrex

The Passenger Car

Zephyr had rolled over and was laying on her stomach now, unconscious. Her face was pale, and her breathing wasn't as steady as it was before. The bullet had taken an obvious and fast toll on her health. I had to get it out of her body before it caused any further damage.

Carefully, I removed Zephyr's belt, armor, and shirt so I could get to the gunshot wound. She was just in the bindings around her chest now. I took a deep breath and with Tessia's sword, cut an X shape across the entry wound. The powerful muscles in Zephyr's back contracted as she exhaled. She didn't make any sound, though.

How are you so brave? I thought. From what she'd told me of the training her father had put her through, she must've had to endure a lot of pain and defeats to get to where she is now.

Using the tweezers Tessia had found tucked away in the medical kit, I moved the sharp metal pincers ever so carefully under her skin, searching for the bullet. The tweezers finally clicked against something solid.

Maneuvering the tiny tongs around the lead, I squeezed the object, pulling it out quickly. Fresh blood spurted from the wound.

Zephyr's breathing became more shallow and rapid. Threading the needle, I worked faster, noticing she was starting to wake up. I stitched the wound on her lower back and sealed it, tying the string before cutting it off. After, I reached into the medical kit and grabbed a roll of bandages, swiftly wrapping them around her waist to keep the wound from leaking.

I relaxed at last, knowing that Zephyr would live. I hadn't noticed that her eyes had opened.

She tried to move, using her arms to push herself up, but she only fell back down again, wincing.

"Hey, Zephyr. Just relax, okay? You'll be fine. The bullet is out," I said in my most calming voice.

She rasped. "Great Asrea. This is probably the worst pain I've ever been in since–" She cut herself off, her eyes a dark gray.

It felt wrong to ask, so I didn't. "I bet. The stitches should hold you steady until we can get you some proper medical help at a hospital where they have all the right tools."

She grimaced at the word 'hospital,' but nodded, her face flushed. "Thank you," she breathed. "Thank you for saving my life."

"Well, I certainly wasn't going to let you die." We were quiet for a while before I stood up. "You should rest now."

"Okay," she conceded. I could tell that she wanted to add something more, but it looked like it was hard to say.

I opened the door to the car. Just as I was about to leave, she called out.

"Wait. Can… can you stay with me? At least until I fall asleep?" Zephyr asked. I smiled at her.

"Of course," I said. It felt like the world could hear my heartbeat. I couldn't tell if it was from adrenaline or something else.

Zephyr nodded, then rested her head on the floor. Now that surgery was completed, I pulled one of the mattresses Alice had stored for us and carefully helped Zephyr get onto it. Her eyelids fluttered.

I laid down next to Zephyr and put my arms behind my head. She shifted slightly from her stomach onto her side to lean her head on my chest, and I put my left arm around her, careful to avoid her bandages.

While my hand was resting on her upper back, I touched something raised in a jagged formation. It felt like a scar. Curious, I followed its line diagonally across her back. I hadn't fully realized that it was there before, since I was so focused on saving her life.

"May I ask what happened?" I lifted my head and saw three deep, rigid scars that stretched over her shoulder blades and spine.

I felt her nod against my chest. "You know how Velus is known for its dragons?" she asked.

"Yeah, I guessed that's why Destin called the train the Silver Dragon."

"I, uh…" Zephyr trailed off. It felt wrong to press her, so I stayed silent. After a long while, she spoke again.

"I used to have a twin. I was eight a-and mad at something or someone. I'd stalked off to find somewhere to be alone. I didn't realize how far I'd gone into the forest until

I was lost, and didn't know that my sister had followed me. I had been told to never go near the forests during the dragons' mating season. If a female sensed a presence other than her own flesh and blood, she would attack to kill."

I could tell that this memory was painful for Zephyr to relive and tell. I almost knew where this was going, but I said nothing.

"Apparently, I had gotten too close to a nest, and a mother dragon came out from behind the trees," Zephyr continued. "My sister jumped out and tried to save me, but I stepped between her and the mother, getting these scars. She trapped both of us under her claws. She tried to suffocate me, and broke three of my ribs. She would have succeeded in killing me if my father hadn't followed us into the forest. He didn't kill the dragon, even though he could have. She was just trying to protect her young from danger, like he was. My Dad fought her off and brought me back to the Citadel. But… my sister was… she didn't… I-I couldn't save her."

I was speechless and heartbroken. Very few people have faced angry dragons, let alone mothers, and lived. Zephyr was only eight when that happened. And to lose a sibling…

"That's awful," I said at last. Zephyr pressed her head against me, and I felt her start to shake a bit. At first, I thought she was cold from the surgery, until I felt something wet on my shirt. She was crying. That was when it finally clicked. She protected others to the fullest extent because she blames herself for the death of her sister.

"I wanna go home," she said, her voice barely even a whisper. I squeezed her shoulder gently.

"We'll get you home." I wished that I could add the words 'I promise' to the end of that sentence, but I couldn't. As long as we were on Earth and the Grebles were conquering planets, we weren't safe, and any promises were empty.

Zephyr shifted her head so she could look at me. Her stormy eyes sparkled with golden flecks. I couldn't believe how stunningly breathtaking they were, and how beautiful I thought Zephyr was, even in her emotional, wounded state.

"What does the gold mean?" I asked, changing the subject. She frowned, confused. "Your eyes. They're gold."

"Oh. I don't know. I've never had that color before," she admitted. She moved her head back down to its former place and curled up.

When I was certain she was asleep, I whispered to her, "You're safe with me."

Zephyr's breathing was steady, and her face was no longer creased with pain. From the story she told me, I was sure her pain then was way worse than it is now.

Destin walked in to check on Zephyr, and saw me with my arm around her, her head on my chest.

"Uhhmm… am I interrupting something?" he asked.

I cleared my throat. "No, no, not at all."

He raised his eyebrow. "If you say so. How is she?"

"Better," I said. "The bullet is out. It's gonna ache for a while, but she'll be fine."

Siren's head lifted from Destin's shoulder. I watched Destin's eyes move to my hand on her shoulder and then to the three scars. Destin's eyes widened at the sight of them.

"Good gods… I'd almost forgotten about that," he said. I remembered that Destin and Zephyr had been friends for years, and that he knew her loss and pain. Seeing that the mood in the car was a little depressing, I decided to ask Destin the question that had been bothering me for ages.

"What does the gold mean?" I asked. "In her eyes."

Destin laughed.

"Dude! You seriously haven't noticed? Zephyr's eyes only change to that color when she's around *you!*"

Realization dawned on me as I grasped the meaning of Destin's words.

"She is in love with you!"

I felt my face burn. "Wh… what?"

Destin and Siren both deadpanned. "It is *so* obvious. You guys are honestly so adorable it hurts. I saw the looks you gave her in Area 51."

"*You saw those?*" I blurted.

"Dude, I'm an engineer. I'm probably one of the most observant people in the universe!" Destin laughed.

"Right."

"Man, I kinda wish I had a holoshot. I sooo need a photo of this."

I gave him a look. "No, you don't."

Tessia walked in. "Ohhh, am I interrupting something?"

"That's what I said!" Destin exclaimed.

"Where's Zephyr's shirt?" she asked.

"I had to remove it to get to the bullet!" I whispered very loudly, so I didn't wake her. "It was either remove it or rip it. And I'm pretty sure she'd prefer the first option."

Tess held her hands up in a heart. "I totally ship."

"Wow. Now I *know* we're related. I said the same thing! Just, different phrasing." Destin was grinning.

Siren puffed.

"You had doubts?" Tessia asked. Destin shrugged. She then bent down and picked up her katana. It still had blood on it. "I'm gonna go clean this off." She left the car.

I realized that Destin had stopped the train, and I asked why.

"HAH! Can you believe this? THE TRAIN BROKE DOWN. Witless humans… I suspect sabotage!"

I jerked my head at Zephyr, who was still out like a light. "Quiet!"

"Sorry. But the thing is, I don't have the spare part to fix it. We're stuck here in the middle of the desert with nutjob scientists hunting us down and we have minimal food. Also, there's the fact that Zephyr just had freaking *surgery* and is probably very weak, although she'll never admit to that."

"Well, aren't you just a positive little ray of Brei," I said, referencing the Cayser star. Destin narrowed his eyes at me.

"We're also stranded on a different planet with NO CLUE where home is!" he screeched, softly.

"Look, Des. If anyone can get the Silver Dragon up and running again, it's you. I'm a doctor, Zephyr's a soldier, and Tess is an artist; she's also probably your best option for an engineering assistant. If you need me to freeze anything in place, that's doable. But we've got lives at stake. If you're looking for more of a pep talk, head to your sister. I'm just telling you what is and isn't. I believe in you and your skills. You can fix this train."

"Thanks," he smiled. "That means a lot."

"Of course."

Destin hesitated before speaking again. "Hey! I think I know what to use to fix the train, but you might not like it."

I raised an eyebrow, prompting him to keep talking.

"Can I have your bow, shave it down and use it as a main pin?"

"Can you *what?*" I exclaimed. I inhaled, grudgingly, and said, "Yeah, sure. Do what you need to do to get us home."

Destin ran off excitedly to butcher my whalebone bow. I felt Zephyr's hand curl up into a fist, and I glanced down. It seemed like it was trying to close around something. My first thought was her sword. She goes nowhere without it. My second thought was Siren, who was still with Destin.

Zephyr inhaled sharply as her eyes flew open. Her hand went to where her scabbard would be, but there was nothing. Her eyes widened as she noticed her bandages. I took her shoulders and turned her to face me.

"Hey! Hey, hey, Zephyr. Relax." I felt her tense shoulders slacken as she remembered what had happened. The power grab on her planet, the crash, the testing, the race, the fighting, the bullet, and the Silver Dragon.

"Why have we stopped?" Her eyes were alert. They were an icy blue with golden flecks as they flitted around the passenger car. The color reminded me of the sun reflecting off the snow.

This was the soldier's side of her, checking for every exit, looking around at the supplies to see what could be used as a weapon.

"The train broke down."

"You're kidding!"

"I really wish I were."

Zephyr rolled to the edge of the mattress and stood up slowly.

"My sword... where's my sword?" Zephyr was searching the car. "Siren! Is she okay?"

I jumped up after her. "Siren is fine. She's with Destin. Tessia picked up your sword when you dropped it back at Area 51."

Zephyr's eyes were unfocused. She was thinking. "We need to get to the ocean. How much time until Destin can f-fix..." she stumbled and I caught her.

"You don't need to worry about Destin. He knows what he's doing. What you *do* need to do is think about yourself for once. Sit down and rest! I just pulled a bullet out of you."

"I hate this..." she muttered.

"I know, but you need rest. Doctor's orders," I told her.

She laughed a little, and her eyes swirled to green, the gold lights still dancing. "You know I don't take orders, right?"

It was my turn to laugh. I sat her down on the mattress again. "I know, but you need to. Can you do that for me, please?"

She nodded.

"Okay, good. I'll be right back. I'm gonna go check on Destin's progress on the train."

I left the room, hoping Zephyr would follow directions and stay put. On my planet, there was a name for the type of girl that Zephyr was. An Avalanche. Unpredictable and unstoppable.

Destin's words still rang in my head. *"She's in love with you!"*

I jumped out of the train. Destin didn't notice me. Instead, he was cursing and smacking his wrench on the driving rods of the Silver Dragon.

"Des! How are the preparations?"

"Lousy and slow," he grumbled, not looking at me.

"Delightful," I said. "Zephyr's awake. Thought you should know."

"That's great! How is she?"

"Disoriented and weak."

"Oh."

"I thought I'd bring Siren to her since she's somewhat coherent."

"Nice. I'll come with you. I need a break from this hunk of glorious metal."

We climbed back up onto the train and entered the passenger car. Zephyr was standing up, leaning against the wall, her bare and scarred back to us.

"What did I *just* tell you?" I scolded. "You're supposed to be sitting and *resting*."

She turned to us. Her face lit up when she saw Siren. Destin handed her over and the little neidren curled around Zephyr's shoulders and arms, puffing happily.

"I know what you said, Andrex," she responded, stroking Siren. "But I also told you I don't take orders from anyone. I hate doing nothing. It makes me feel fidgety."

"Dude, you actually thought that you could get the Queen of Stubbornness to listen to you?" Destin coughed.

"...Yes."

"You look a lot better," Destin said to Zephyr.

"I feel like I was hit by the Silver Dragon," she confessed.

Zephyr turned her back to us again, and Destin frowned at her scars, but didn't say anything.

"Zephyr, you really shouldn't be standing up." I walked over to her. She tensed when I took her arm. "It's for your own good."

I glanced at Destin for backup. He was just grinning. Instead of helping me convince Zephyr to help herself, he just slipped out of the car.

Thanks... I thought. Zephyr's dark blue eyes locked onto my gray-green ones.

"I hate this planet," she said.

"I know. Me, too." She leaned into me and I put my arms around her. She pressed her head against my shoulder and shivered.

"We all do," Destin said.

I jumped. "Where did you go?" I snapped.

"Eh. I thought you guys could use a moment." His grin never disappeared. Zephyr raised an eyebrow. Destin backed out of the car again.

"Sorry," she murmured. "Sometimes Des can be a little... well, you know."

I smiled. "Yeah, I do know. We shared a cell."

I coaxed her back onto the mattress. Once we sat down, I took a deep breath and said, "Destin told me what the gold means."

She looked at me with her eyes, but didn't turn her head. "What did he tell you?"

"Do you love me?"

Zephyr's cheeks turned red. She looked away, her expression sad. "Andrex, I can't have attachments like this. I could never ask you to take that risk."

"You didn't have to ask."

ANDREX

"Andrex..." her eyes didn't meet mine. The gold had completely enveloped her irises. They looked like miniature suns. I took her face in my hands.

"I choose to take the risk," I told her.

In that quiet moment, as if in slow motion, our faces moved closer until our noses touched. Slowly, our lips met. We fell into a kiss, and the entire world melted away behind us. There was no war. No wounds. No pain. No crazy government officials chasing us down. It was just Zephyr, me, and the dimly lit room of the Silver Dragon's passenger car.

I wrapped my arms around her upper back and pulled her closer. Her hands slipped over my shoulders. Our bodies pressed together. It was like there was no one else in the universe but us.

Zephyr's grip tightened. Her hands moved to my hair, tangling her fingers in the short locks. I felt like I couldn't breathe, but in a good way.

We broke away after an eternity, smiling.

"You're beautiful," I whispered. She blushed as a strand of hair fell into her face. I brushed it away, tucking it behind her ear. We kissed again, but more passionately this time.

Zephyr's hand moved down my back over my shirt. My arms pulled her to me, and we were lost in an entirely other world. When we stopped to breathe, we put our foreheads together, eyes closed, just enjoying each other's company.

She shifted and rested her head against my shoulder as my arms enveloped her body, cradling her against my chest. Exhausted, she relaxed and sighed, exhaling softly.

She didn't draw in another breath. It took me a second too long to notice.

"Zephyr?" I said, stunned. She didn't respond.

I shook her shoulder gently. There was no reaction. "ZEPHYR! ZEPHYR, WAKE UP!"

Chapter Forty-Three: Damari

A Soldier to Cry On

Reeling and pacing around my room wasn't exactly helping me, but doing nothing made me want to scream. Glancing over to my left, I saw the tablets I'd swiped off the desk. Luckily, none of them broke. I knew my Dad would go ballistic, knowing he's damaged a lot of technology himself. Especially before that 'conference' he had with Mordrar.

There was a knock at my door. I stopped pacing and turned to it. My hands twitched again, still aching to hit something else to release the repressed frustration stored deep within.

I decided not to answer the door, not wanting to talk to anybody. Resuming my pace, I kept trying to clear my head, although that seemed impossible. My thoughts were consumed with finding my sister and making sure she was safe. Other outcomes started pushing their way into my mind. Darker realities. I just wanted to risk all and disobey Captain Kincaid; take a battlecruiser or anything else at this point and just race to Earth. Yet the soldier in me was compelled to obey.

The knock sounded again.

"Haldenson?"

It was Merai.

Exhaling heavily, I went over and pressed my hand against a panel next to the door. It scanned my palm and flashed once before the door slid open. Merai stood in front of me, her expression weighted with clear concern.

"Hey," I said, my voice emotionless and dry.

Merai sighed. "I'm so sorry… the captain made the wrong call," she said. "We should've taken the PoD ahead."

Anger filled my features as I slammed my palm into the door frame. I ignored the pain and pressed my forehead against my hand, gritting my teeth.

"I swear to the gods… if we get to that planet and I find my sister dead knowing she'd be alive had we left now–" I choked on my words, using every ounce of emotional strength to hold back tears.

Merai stayed silent.

"…I'll kill him… I don't care if that's treason, I–" I exhaled angrily. "I can't lose her, too, Merai. I am helpless and powerless here… I can't–" I cut myself off again, squeezing my eyes shut and letting out a sob.

Part of me hated myself for crying in front of another soldier when I was supposed to be the strong one. I was their leader. But another part told me it was okay. I was allowed to be upset and angry. I was allowed to cry.

Finally, I couldn't take it anymore and just let all the emotion I had been bottling up flow out of me. I slid to my knees with my forehead pressed to the wall, and I cried. Right in front of Merai.

Still silent, Merai knelt down beside me and wrapped her arms around me, pulling me into a hug. I didn't try to fight her off, even though that one little rule in the very back of my mind screamed *"No signs of affection on duty."*

"Damari, it's okay… we're going to find her. She's stronger than you give her credit for," she said.

I let out a half-laugh, half-sob. "She's my baby sister. I can be as protective as I want."

Merai put her hand over mine and squeezed it gently. "Just breathe," she said, quietly. "Just breathe…"

I pulled away from the hug and swiped at my face. Merai just smiled at me. It was a warm smile that lit up her amber eyes and almost seemed to brighten the room around us. She squeezed my hand again, giving me a reassuring nod. I suddenly felt a bit better, and I believed her. We were going to find Zephyr, and she was going to be alive and safe.

After a long moment, I finally spoke. "You're right. But don't you dare try to stop me from killing the captain after all of this is over."

Now it was her turn to laugh. Her positive attitude was contagious, and I could feel a small smile starting to form on my face as well.

"Alright, Haldenson. Deal. I'll bring the snacks and let the whole crew know."

Over to my right, I could hear some murmuring before Sorres and Dennett came around the corner.

"Yo, Haldenson, we–" Dennett started. Sorres whacked him in the gut, shutting him up. Dennett doubled over. "Dude, what the–"

Dennett saw me kneeling on the floor in my doorway in front of Merai. He grinned as Sorres smirked.

"Awwww, you guys are adorable," Sorres said. Merai's face bloomed into an embarrassed blush as she averted her eyes down and away from them. She muttered something under her breath about killing them later in the PoD's arena.

I rolled backward and grabbed two tablets from the floor, throwing one of them at my friends. Sorres caught it, laughing.

"Glad to see you're doing better," he said.

"Oh, get out of here before I keelhaul you both," I said, chuckling as well. Dennett held up his hands. Heart-shaped.

"You two are looking a little re– UFF!" Dennett yelped as I threw the next tablet at him and hit him square in the stomach.

Sorres cracked up, Dennett whacking him over the head. Merai started laughing as well, although it was clear she was trying very hard not to.

"Now gettout!" I shouted, laughing. "Or I will throw you from the PoD's top deck when we land on Earth."

Sorres, still cackling, shoved Dennett back down the corridor from which they came. Merai and I both exhaled and then looked at each other, laughing. Her face was still red.

She cleared her throat. "Well… that was…"

"Interesting?" I finished for her. "I mean, with those two idiots, you get used to it. I'm sorry about that, though."

Merai smiled. "I-It's fine. I don't really mind it." She stopped, staying quiet and averting her gaze away from mine. It was my turn to hug her now.

"Thank you. I really needed this."

She wrapped her arms around me. "Stick together, work together, fight together," she said, quietly. I smiled.

Almost by instinct, I started uttering our creed. "I am a Velusan soldier. A fighter, a member of a team."

She pulled away a little, just enough to look at me. "I serve the Council and the House of Cayser. I will always place the mission first."

"I will not be defeated. My spirit is Diatanium; I will never quit," I continued.

Merai grinned. "I have stamina and determination. I am an expert in my field and I am not afraid to do what it takes."

My expression mirrored hers as the fire came back to my eyes. "I am prepared physically and mentally to engage and destroy our enemies and threats to the peace of Cayser."

"I am a protector of the system and defender of my planet."

Together, we both finished the creed. "I am a Velusan soldier."

Chapter Forty-Four: Tessia

Two Repairs, Two Hearts

Andrex's screaming echoed throughout the train.

Every hair stood on end as I could feel my heart shattering in my chest. My mind immediately went to the worst-case scenario.

I turned my head and exchanged a look with Destin. His horrified expression reflected my own. Tears started welling up in his eyes and streaming down his face as we both raced for the passenger car. I let my brother go through the doorway first before barreling after him.

The passenger car's door slid open as Destin crashed through, breathing heavily. As soon as I entered, I recoiled, gasping. Andrex was performing chest compressions on Zephyr. Her eyes were closed, and she wasn't breathing. Siren's tail flicked anxiously around Destin's shoulders as she puffed mournfully.

Andrex was muttering to himself the number of compressions he was on.

I looked around the passenger car, my eyes wildly searching for something to use to help get her heart started again. Anything. Suddenly, I got an idea and raced back into the Silver Dragon's main car, grabbing my katana and running back.

"Destin!" I said, panicked and slightly breathless. "You need to electrocute this!"

Both of them realized what I was suggesting. Andrex perked up a bit.

"Wires... we need wires. Or something Destin can draw power from!" Andrex exclaimed.

My brother snatched the katana from my hands and passed it to Andrex. The doctor grabbed it and held it flat against Zephyr's chest, taking one of Destin's hands and placing it top-side on the flat of the blade. Destin planted his other hand firmly against the floor. He took in a deep breath.

"I can do it here," he determined. I looked over at Andrex, nodding.

"Do it," I said.

Andrex inhaled shakily, but held the blade steadily. "Three... two... one... CLEAR!"

The lights in the passenger car flickered as Destin drew power from the Silver Dragon. His right hand glowed as energy passed from the circuitry under the floor through his body and to my katana held over Zephyr's heart.

Electricity crackled into the sword and shocked Zephyr. Her eyes flew open and she gasped, taking in as much air as she could before wincing and gritting her teeth in pain.

All three of us collapsed in relief. Destin most of all, since he just sucked and transferred energy from a high-powered vehicle to Zephyr.

Andrex wrapped his arms around Zephyr and pulled her to him. She was breathing heavily, be it from pain, shock, or both, I couldn't tell.

I looked over at my brother and noticed a small MA patch of blue had appeared around his pupil, and a thin streak of his hair had turned gray.

"Destin…?" I asked, softly.

There was a long moment before he responded, exhaling. "Y-yeah…?"

Everyone was now looking at Destin and the streak of gray hair that ran down his forehead and covered his right eye.

"Dude…" Andrex started.

"Yeah, I know…" my brother said. "It's… a Mechanical Advantage thing. The more I use it, the more stress it puts on my body. And let me guess. My eyes are turning blue, too?"

"Yep," I said.

Destin didn't speak again. He just nodded, stood up, and shrugged off his heavy aviator jacket. I watched as he went over to Zephyr and knelt beside her, putting it around her shoulders. He took Siren from around his neck and placed the little creature in her lap. Siren puffed happily. Zephyr looked at him with dark gray eyes before he smiled sadly and raised himself up again. He left, making his way back to the locomotive cab, looking exhausted.

Suddenly, a realization hit me.

"Guys," I said. "I think I know what Destin is doing."

"What?" Andrex asked. Zephyr remained silent in Andrex's arms, her chest heaving. She was still in shock.

I started to think back to when my Mom did this on a race with her ship. "He's giving the Silver Dragon his life force in exchange for more speed and power. I've seen my mother do it before. It... can be deadly."

Zephyr looked back at the door that Destin had left through. "W-Why is he doing it then?" she asked after a long moment, clearly trying to hide the strain in her voice.

"My only guess would be because of you," I said, quietly. I watched as Zephyr's facial expression shifted from realization to trepidation. I knew exactly what was going on in her mind. She was the soldier. She thought she had to be the sacrifice to keep all of us alive. Her every action was to keep my brother, Andrex, and me safe with the mindset that we would get off of Earth no matter what. Even if it meant the cost of her life.

Everyone was silent. The only noise that filled the dead air of the passenger car was Zephyr's pained breathing. It made my gut twist to see her like this.

"You... you have to tell him to stop," Zephyr whispered. "He can't die for me. I couldn't live with myself."

Andrex gave Zephyr's arm a light squeeze as he sat down next to her, Siren curling up in her lap. He pulled her into a hug and she just let him. I felt like there was something I missed, but I decided now was not the time to be asking about that.

"We couldn't live with ourselves if we let you die, Zeph," Andrex said. I nodded in agreement.

I took a deep breath. "I'm so glad you're okay," I said. There were suppressed bangs from the locomotive's car. "I'm gonna go check on Des."

Zephyr barely nodded. "Yeah," Andrex said. "I think that's a good idea."

I smiled at both of them before returning to the train's cab.

Destin was leaning with his back against one of the walls, arms folded over his chest. In his right hand lay his smoking pistol.

Now that I truly knew why he was looking so tired, I really saw it. His eyes were sunken back into their sockets. His face looked pale in the night's shadow, dark circles decorating the skin under his eyes. With his jacket on, I couldn't see it before. The veins in his arms were showing through his skin, light blue lines that streaked from his biceps all the way down to his hands and wrists. The gray streak in his hair hung down in front of his face with the rest of his bangs. He brushed it away and turned to look at me as I entered.

"Oh, Destin…" I said, quietly, going up to him.

"Hey," he muttered. "How's Zeph?"

He switched his pistol to his left hand and put his arm around me as I sighed, resting my head on his shoulder.

"She's gonna be okay, thanks to you."

Destin nodded. "Good."

He gestured toward the other end of the cab with his gun toward what used to be Andrex's bow. It looked just like the Silver Dragon's missing driving pin. "I used Zeph's sword to shave it down and shot it a few times. It's not perfect, but it'll do the job."

I laughed softly. "Want help putting it in place?"

My brother nodded. "Sooner rather than later. Let's go."

He removed his arm from around me and walked over to the bow, picking it up. Destin opened the cab door and jumped onto the cold desert sand.

TESSIA

"Here," he said, handing me the new pin. "Lemme get the tools."

He walked over to the tender and opened a toolbox on its side. I watched as he pulled out a huge sledge hammer, a clip thing that looked like a C, and a tube of grease. He hefted the huge hammer over his shoulder and walked over to me.

"Let's put this back together," he muttered, walking toward the rear drive set. My brother motioned for me to hand him the pin. I did, and he took it, squeezing some grease from the tube, rubbing it around the pin with his finger.

"Will this really work?" I asked.

"Oh, it better. 'Cause we're out of options. Here, hold this over the connecting main drive rod hole so I can hammer this in," Destin directed.

"Uh, alright." I said. "Just don't hit me, okay?"

Destin shot me a look. "You're funny."

"I know."

I did as he instructed, watching as he brought the hammer up to swing it sideways to hit the pin in place.

"Watch your fingers!" He shouted as he brought the hammer down hard and fast. I snapped my hand backward and out of the way as the solid metal head hit the pin and drove it in place. Exhaling slowly, we both stood there for a few moments in silence, just staring at the pin. I swear I even saw a small spark of MA blue jump off the hammer as it smacked into the pin.

After a long few seconds, I finally spoke. "Did it work?"

Destin nodded, smiling. "Yeah. It worked."

I put my arm around my brother. "Let's go get some rest now. We're gonna need it."

Taking his hand, I climbed back into the Silver Dragon. I started to pull him toward the passenger car so we could be with the others, but he pulled his hand away.

"I-I think I'm gonna take first watch," he said. "You know, just in case any more guards or Area 51 personnel show up."

I nodded slowly. "Alright. Wake me up in a few hours. I'll go next."

Destin looked away from me. "Okay."

Frowning, I gave my brother a quick hug before heading into the passenger car and pulling down another mattress that Alice had packed. How and when she had gotten everything in here, I had no idea. I was just thankful she did.

Just as I was about to fall asleep, I felt something odd: the hissing of the train's air brakes releasing, and chugging of the locomotive piston boxes as the train slowly began to move again. I closed my eyes as the Silver Dragon gained speed, hoping my brother wouldn't push himself all night. But knowing him, I knew that was a futile belief.

Chapter Forty-Five: Andrex

Drastic Measures

"**G**ods above," I muttered, pacing around the Silver Dragon's passenger car. It was morning now. The early light of day pouring in through the windows of the car filled it with a golden glow, yet I couldn't enjoy its beauty or warmth; not since I woke up to Zephyr shivering as if she were on Zaccoth wearing nothing but a tank top and shorts.

I went over the procedure in my head time and again, but I knew I did it right. I had taken the bullet out of Zephyr properly; there was no way I could've damaged any of her internal organs. Yet her condition said otherwise.

"For the billionth time, Andrex. Answer my question!" Zephyr demanded.

By my orders, which she had refused more than once, she was finally resting, laying on her back, Destin's aviator jacket wrapped tightly around her. Siren was curled up by her side, her small forked tongue flicking in and out.

"What if I don't want to?" I responded, sharply. "I-I need a lab... I need *tools* and equipment. I can't base this on just an educated guess!"

"I'm dying, aren't I?"

"No, no, I'm not going to let that happen, Zeph." I ceased my pace. "I'll be right back."

I left the passenger car and headed up to the train's cab, where Destin and Tessia already were. Once I entered and closed the door, I noticed that Destin was standing up, head poking out of the window, his left hand on the Silver Dragon's throttle. Tessia tapped him on the shoulder. He pulled his head in and faced me.

"How is she?" he asked. He looked dreadful. There were dark circles under his eyes and the streak of gray in his hair wasn't helping his appearance. Then again, we all looked terrible.

I shook my head. "It's not good. Her body temperature is much lower than it should be. I just can't figure out *why*."

"How… long does she have?" Tessia said, softly.

"I give her a week at most, but if she keeps moving and doesn't rest, that time could be limited to about four days." I sighed. "What am I missing?!"

Tessia's face lit up. She stood up, shaking her index finger. I could almost see the gears in her head turning. "What if… what if it's the bullet? What if there were something on it, or what it's made of, that's affecting her?"

I slapped my palm to my forehead. "Of course! Did any of you get shot?"

"I was grazed," Tessia shrugged. For the first time, I noticed that her sleeve had blood on it by her shoulder.

"Let me see that!" I insisted, concerned as to why she didn't come to me earlier. I took her arm, shoved up her sleeve, and examined the wound. I then turned on Destin. "How come you didn't tell me? She's *your* sister!"

"Zephyr was in worse condition," he argued.

"I meant *after!*"

I pressed two fingers to Tessia's neck. Her pulse was normal. The wound didn't look terrible; the blood just made it seem worse. The cut was small and not very deep, so she didn't suffer too much blood loss.

"Am I gonna live, doctor?" Tessia asked.

I gave her a look. "You'll be fine. I can clean that up and give you a bandage from that kit Alice packed." I sighed. "Don't wait to tell me about things like this. That could've been a lot worse."

She nodded.

"We all got a little beaten up," Destin said to me, tapping the side of his head and then pointing to me.

I scowled, remembering the hit to the head I endured while we were fighting. A big purple and black bruise formed across my cheek and next to my eye.

"Tess," I said. "Are you cold at all?"

"No. It just kind of aches like a sore muscle."

"How's your head?"

"Feels normal."

"Okay, then you're good. Zephyr was drawing most of their fire, so whatever was on the bullet, or what it's made of, is really taking a toll on her health. Des, how fast can the Silver Dragon get us to the ocean?" I asked.

"Uh… two to three days tops, but that's if I *really* push the locomotive."

By that, I knew he meant that he'd push himself. I exhaled, slowly steeling myself for their next reaction.

"Hmm," I said. "We're gonna need a hospital."

"*WHAT?!*" Destin and Tessia exploded.

"No way, Andrex! Are you *insane?*" Tessia snapped.

"I'm sorry, but there's no other way! It's either I get her to a hospital where they have the tools to help her, or she dies before we get home!" I shot back. "I need equipment! I'm not gonna let her die! It already happened once, I can't–"

The cab went silent, everyone trying to think of what to do. We were battered, bruised, homesick, and running for our lives.

"Okay... then let's grind the wheel," Destin said, forcing the throttle all the way forward. The roar of compressors got louder and a heavy pounding noise came from outside the locomotive, which I assumed was the piston boxes being put under load. "But you don't let *anyone else* touch her, okay?"

I nodded in reply.

"Is there really no other way?" Tessia asked.

"We have to take the risk."

"Let's do it." Tessia clapped her hands together. "So who's gonna tell her?"

I sighed and headed toward the door. "I'll do it. I need to recheck her vitals and the wound, anyway."

Zephyr was still in the same position, but Siren was trying to use her forehead as a pillow. She moved the neidren off her head when I came in. The lithe creature puffed in protest but just curled up in Zephyr's lap instead.

Gods... I thought. *I guess I'll just have to be blunt. There's no way of sugarcoating this.*

"Zephyr, we've decided that we're going to be making a little detour when we reach the nearest city."

She tried to sit up, but winced, one hand to her head. "And what detour would that be?" she said with a little difficulty. It looked like she was struggling to stay awake. I made a quick mental note of that.

"You need a hospital."

Her eyes widened. "No. No, I can't go there. I can't do it. Not again."

"Zeph, I don't have the equipment here to help you! Whether you like it or not, it's what needs to be done."

"I'm not afraid to die."

"Well, we're all afraid of losing you!" I exclaimed, throwing my hands into the air with exasperation. "This is for your own good!"

"I'm sorry, Andrex. I can't go through all of it again. I can't do the testing and the tables and the white rooms…"

I knelt down next to her and put my hand over hers. It felt colder than ice. "I'm not going to let anyone else near you. I'll make sure I'm the only one working with you, okay?"

"Okay. How… how long do I have?"

"About five days. Maybe more. Maybe less. I can't tell." I exhaled. "That means you need to stop moving. Too much activity could speed up whatever is moving through your system."

"What do you think it is? Lead poisoning?" she asked.

I shook my head. "No. The bullet wasn't in you long enough. Tessia has a theory that it may be something *on* the bullet, like a…" I trailed off.

"What?"

"A poison. Oh, no. Oh, gods, no." I lifted my hand off of hers and said, "I need you to roll over."

Without question, Zephyr nodded and moved Siren off of her lap and onto the mattress. Siren deadpanned in her direction but made no motion to go back to her comfy position.

Carefully, I pushed her on her side before she moved to lay flat on her stomach. I could see something thin but bold underneath her shirt. I pushed the shirt up and removed the bandaging. What I saw chilled my blood and sent a shiver down my spine. I had to stifle my gasp.

Thin black skeins lined in dark purple were twining and weaving their way from the center of the wound. They were climbing up her back and side, reaching around for her heart.

"Andrex?" Zephyr said, quietly. "Andrex, what's wrong?"

"I... I don't know how to help you..."

Chapter Forty-Six: Zephyr

Ticking Time-Bomb

Around three billion scenarios were racing through my head. What did Andrex see? What was he so concerned about? It was just a gunshot wound, and he already took out the bullet. Why did I feel like my gut wanted to twist itself into one of Destin's sailing knots?

"Andrex…" I said, turning my head. "What is it?"

He didn't respond. He was just staring at the wound on my back. Knowing I was about to regret this, I twisted around to see what he was looking at. As soon as I laid eyes on the black veins spiraling away from the shot, my mind went to one thing. Poison.

Andrex looked at me, his eyes wide. He shook his head, standing up. "This is bad," he said, running a hand through his already messy hair. "Very, *very* bad."

I could see the calculations spinning out of control in his mind. He started pacing again.

"Andrex, please stop. You're making me nauseous," I said. Or maybe it was the venom coursing through my body.

Nonetheless, he stopped, kneeling beside me again. He shook his head for the second time. "I don't know what to do," he said, quietly.

I spoke, calmly. "How much longer?" Andrex didn't reply. I put my hand over his and repeated my question. "How much longer, Andrex?"

"F-Forty-eight hours," he stuttered. "Y-You'll be dead in forty-eight hours."

Siren looked back and forth between Andrex and me, and noting the pain in his voice, she slithered over to him and flicked her tail against his leg sympathetically. Andrex hardly smiled.

"I made peace with the fact I had a high chance of dying back in Area 51. I gave myself a side mission to get you guys out at any cost, even if it meant my life," I admitted.

Andrex stared at me. "I will not let you die, Zephyr. I will beg Salutem and Asrea herself to keep you alive. I'm not losing you. And neither are Destin and Tessia."

I nodded, knowing that I was okay with dying. What scared me was everyone else not accepting that fact. They're worrying about me so much, they're hardly taking care of themselves. Especially Destin.

"So when are we gonna tell the Kincaids?" I asked.

"When are you gonna tell the Kincaids what?" Tessia responded. I hadn't even noticed that she'd entered the passenger car with Destin. This poison was clearly taking a toll on my senses as well.

Andrex bit his lower lip, not wanting to say anything to them. I, however, just spat it out. Death was death, after all.

"I'll die in about two Earth days," I said. Destin looked like he was about to throw up, and Tessia's jaw dropped. I watched as Destin left the passenger car with a haunted expression on his face. It's not like I expected him to say anything. Tessia knelt next to Andrex in front of me.

"We need that hospital," Andrex said, looking at her. Tessia just nodded solemnly.

"I know," she breathed. "I… I know. Destin said he could get to the ocean in two or three days… oh, gods. He's gonna kill himself."

My heart squeezed in my chest. I hated that Destin was giving up his life for a glimmer of hope that mine could still be saved, but I knew it wouldn't be worth it. They'd just have two dead bodies to bury if they ever got back to Velus.

"Tessia, you can't let him. You have to stop him."

"I can't stop him! He's the only one that knows this train inside and out. What if we break down again? Plus, I can't just knock him out or tie him up. He's my brother," she said.

Andrex snorted. "I'd love to tie up or KO my brother." We both just stared at him. "What?" he asked. "Just because I miss Zaccoth does not mean I miss my family."

Tessia shrugged. "Okay, that's fair." She looked back at me and sighed, her eyes tired and filled with heartbreak.

I wanted so badly to move. I wanted to get up and pull her into a hug, saying that everything was going to be okay. But I knew better than anyone that it wasn't. I was a ticking time-bomb with hardly anything left on her clock. I accepted it. I just wanted the others to accept it, too.

I closed my eyes, trying to avert my gaze from both of them. Siren slithered over to me and curled herself up into a little ball by my side.

My mind then switched to someone else, and it shattered my heart. Damari. My big brother losing both of his sisters to tragedy. The death of my twin took a hard enough toll on both of us, especially since I was there to witness it. Even though I couldn't see it, I remember so clearly the sound of the Silverclaw slicing my sister in half.

Damari never got the chance to say goodbye to her. And now he wouldn't have the opportunity to say goodbye to me.

I shuddered at the memory, trying to force back tears. It felt like my chest was seizing up, and I couldn't breathe. Panicking a bit, my breath sped up, and I began to hyperventilate.

Andrex sat down next to me, pulling me into a hug and running one hand through my hair.

"Do you want to talk about it?" he asked, quietly.

"My brother," I responded, shakily. I couldn't finish my statement. Saying it out loud made it far too real, and that was one thing I was not ready to accept yet.

Tessia stood up. "Time to… KO Destin, I guess."

Andrex said something to her, but my mind was tuning it out. There was so much fog in my brain. I couldn't think clearly, and my vision started to blur.

There was a twinge of pain from the shot wound, causing me to wince and tense up, which only hurt me more.

Damari… I thought. *Mom… Dad… I'm so sorry…*

Chapter Forty-Seven: Destin Confession

"Tessia?" I said.

"Yeah?" she responded. We were both in the cab of the Silver Dragon. I had slowed the train down to about eighty miles per hour because we were tired, and I didn't want to accidentally fall asleep and crash. The moon was low in the sky, and stars were still starting to come out.

"Could you watch the tracks ahead for me? If something comes up, just pull this lever," I said, pointing to the brake.

Tessia gave me a skeptical look. "Why? Where are you going?"

"I, uhhh… I need to go tell Zeph something…" I said, awkwardly, rubbing the back of my neck. My sister's eyebrows shot up.

"Oh? Are you finally going to tell her?"

I laughed a little. "Yeah, I am. We almost lost her yesterday, Tess. She… deserves to know."

Tessia smiled. "Ooooh, tell me how it goes!" she said, shoving me out of the cab and into the steam compressor room.

"Ack, okay, I will!" I said before she shut the door, leaving me in the darkness of the tender.

Well, I thought. *I'm committed now…*

"Silver Dragon, lights on in the tender," I said, quietly. The bulbs flickered on, their light haloed and bright. Two long tubes that were about the height of my waist were on either side of me. They housed the two compressors that squeezed steam produced by the evaporator cores, which fed the piston boxes to make the locomotive move.

I strode briskly to the other end of the room and opened the door that led to the walkway in the water tender. I continued forward until I entered the passenger car.

Despite the darkness of the car, it was clear that Zephyr was shivering. Whatever had been on that bullet was working through her system very quickly. At the other end of the room, Andrex was sleeping soundlessly with Siren curled around his arm. I realized that Zephyr was sleeping, too.

Swallowing my nerves, I quietly made my way over to her and knelt down. She was on her side, her hands next to her head. She was still wearing my jacket.

Her left palm was facing the ceiling. I carefully placed my hand on hers; it felt colder than ice. I took a deep breath as guilt washed over me. I knew that it wasn't my fault she'd been shot, and I knew it was her choice to follow me when we left Velus, but still it hurt.

"Hey," I said, softly. I didn't want to wake her up, but I thought she had the right to know how I felt. And as much as I didn't want to think about the potential death factor, I knew that this might be my last chance to tell her.

"I-I've been wanting to tell you this for a long time, but I never really got the chance to. You've always been there for me when I've needed you most. You're strong and kind and you never let anyone get you down. You tell it like it is and you're not afraid to fight for what you believe in. I'm not one of those people who wants to be your friend because of your father. I like you for yourself. Your unshakable, stubborn self. You're one of the bravest people I've ever met." I inhaled slowly, looking down. "I guess what I'm trying to say here is that... I... I love you, Zephyr Haldensdottir. I have for a long time." I hung my head, laughing quietly. "Please don't hate me," I whispered, giving her hand a squeeze.

I was surprised when I felt her squeeze back. My head snapped up. In the darkness, I could see her bright green eyes sparkling. She had heard all of it. Now I was a little happy that the car was dark, because I felt my face burn. "Oh, Des," she said, quietly. "I could never hate you."

"Hmmm, yeah, I like ice…" Andrex murmured, sleepily. Zephyr and I exchanged a wide-eyed look before smiling.

"I'm gonna sit up, help me or not," she whispered.

"Seriously? Zeph, you're in no condition t–" Despite my protest, she put her hands behind her and scooched herself upwards to lean against the wall. "Gods, you're stubborn."

"I thought you liked my stubbornness."

I scoffed. "Yeah, yeah."

Zephyr just flashed me a smile before shifting my jacket which she wore, then zipping it up and hugging her arms tightly. I moved over to the wall and slid down it to sit next to her. She closed her eyes and sighed, tilting her head to lean it on my shoulder.

"You know," I said, resting my head on hers, "you look good in an aviator jacket. Maybe you should consider an occupation that would get you out of the front lines."

She let out a breath of laughter as she shook her head slightly. "I'll stick to being a soldier, but thanks."

"I'm serious, Zeph. I don't know what I'd do if I lost you. I... I almost did." I lifted my head and wrapped my arms around her, holding her against me, trying to swallow back the lump in my throat. "I would give up every machine and invention I have ever made if it meant saving your life. My machines I can rebuild and restore, but you... you're irreplaceable."

I felt her gasp slightly, and for a moment, I thought I'd hurt her. But instead of pulling away, she hugged me back, burying her face in my shoulder. "I made a promise to you, Destin Kincaid. And I intend to keep it. You won't be losing me any time soon."

"But you can't promise that..." I said, my voice wavering. "You're dying. You have less than forty hours to live. I don't know if I can–"

"Hey, none of that," Zephyr said, pulling away. "My will is stronger than my stubbornness."

I scoffed. "Well, that's saying something."

She swatted my shoulder, smiling. "We've been together our whole lives, Des. It's gonna take a lot more than a tiny piece of metal to get rid of me."

"Yeah, well, that 'tiny piece of metal' is hurting you. You really need to take it easy."

Zephyr nodded. Was it the darkness or the fact that she was dying? I couldn't tell, but her eyes looked duller. Dimmer. Her fire was still there. It just wasn't as bright as before.

I wrapped my arms around her and hugged her again, wanting to be as close as possible to her if this would be the last time I'd see her. She rested her head on my shoulder and closed her eyes, exhaling shakily. I could only imagine the severe pain she was in. We sat there in silence for a while. I listened to her shallow breathing. It broke my heart.

"I'm not afraid to die, Destin," she whispered. I flinched in surprise. I thought she'd fallen asleep.

I just gave her a gentle squeeze. "But I'm afraid of losing you." A tear slid down my face. I didn't have the willpower or the strength to wipe it away. "Please don't leave me," I said, my voice hardly audible.

"Don't worry," she said. "When I die, I'll make sure to haunt you."

That got a laugh out of me. Here she was with just a little more than a day to live, joking. It did make me feel a bit better, though.

"Alright. I'll remember to watch out for your jump-scares."

Her shivering calmed down a little as she started to relax and drift off to sleep, although I knew it would most likely be restless. I lifted my head off of hers and turned it to see Siren staring at me from within her coils.

"What are you looking at?"

The neidren just blinked in response, slowly retracting her head back into her coils before bringing it up again and resting it on top of them like a scaly pillow. I smiled, and then realized how hard it would be on the little creature as well. Zephyr had been with Siren constantly. You don't get one without the other. They were a package deal. Knowing she would most likely go to Damari, it still hurt.

Suddenly, I heard Tessia hissing my name from the locomotive's cab. I looked back down at Zephyr and carefully removed my arms from around her so that I didn't wake her up. I made sure she was comfortable sitting where she was against the car's wall before standing up and walking to the door. Just as I slid it open, I heard her voice.

"Where are you going...?" she asked, her voice riddled with tiredness and pain.

"I just need to check on something with my sister," I responded, leaving the car. As soon as I slid the door shut again, I turned tail and raced toward the cab.

Tessia whirled around when I barreled in. "Destin!!!"

"What?! What's wrong?! What broke?" I exclaimed.

My sister was grinning. "Lights, Destin!! There's a city!"

Eyes widening, I shoved past my sister and stuck my head out the window to get a better view. Sure enough, she was right. And where there was a city, there was bound to be a hospital. There was bound to be help.

I turned to Tessia and picked her up in a bear hug, spinning her around once. She laughed, hugging me back. I pulled away from her just enough to see her grinning face.

"Tess, this is amazing!"

"I know! Andrex can get Zephyr to a hospital, and we can fix up the Silver Dragon!"

I hugged her again, sighing in relief. Everything was going to be okay. We were all going home.

Chapter Forty-Eight: Andrex

Glevein

Destin shook me awake. At first, it was gentle, and I just shrugged him off. Then he grabbed my shoulder and shook it violently, jerking me awake. After that, I felt a slap as Siren slammed her tail into my stomach. I grunted and sat bolt upright, bleary eyed and confused.

"Andrex!" he shouted. "Andrex, wake up! We're here!"

"Huh...? What– where?"

"We made it to a city. COME ON, GET UP!"

I rubbed the remaining sleep out of my eyes and stood up, brushing myself off. The Silver Dragon was still moving, and it was still night time. I looked out the window, seeing a wide breadth of lights up ahead. Grinning from ear to ear, I turned to Destin.

"How soon?" I asked, my eyes darting in Zephyr's direction. She was still unconscious and so pale. I forced myself to look away from her and at Destin again.

"Ten minutes max," Destin said. I exhaled in relief, giving him a brief hug. Destin quickly scooped up Siren and wrapped her around his neck. The neidren stared at him before accepting her new position of sleep, resting her head on her coils and closing her eyes.

Those ten minutes felt like ten hours. As soon as the train slowed, I slung Zephyr's arm over my shoulder and picked her up. She winced quietly, her head lying limp against my shoulder.

"Shh... it's okay. We found a city," I whispered to her. "You're gonna be okay."

Zephyr didn't respond. The Silver Dragon stopped. Off in the distance, I could see a tall white building with a massive red plus on its front.

That's gotta be it, I thought, climbing down from the Silver Dragon with Zephyr still in my arms.

What looked like some form of hover vehicle had pulled up to the Silver Dragon as the train had neared the city. A human stepped out of the craft, a silver slab pressed against his ear. It looked like a type of comm. The man took a step back as I approached him, eyeing Zephyr.

"Please help," I said. "She was shot. I need to get to a hospital."

The man's eyes widened as he beckoned for me to go into his vehicle. "Come on," he said.

Part of me knew not to trust him. He was human, and he could turn us in at any moment if he knew who we were. The other part of me also didn't care now that Zephyr only had a few hours to live. I'd lost track of time.

As soon as the doors slid shut, the man turned and sped off. I held Zephyr tightly in my arms, careful to avoid her wound.

"Where are we?" I asked the human.

He gave me a side glance. "Reno, Nevada. What happened to her?"

"We were uh… both kidnapped," I said, bending the truth. Then again, it wasn't entirely a lie. I was kidnapped from a field, and she was taken from her crash site. "As we were escaping, she was shot."

"Good grief," the human said. "We'll be at the hospital in a few minutes."

I nodded, looking down at Zephyr's face. It looked like she was trying to force herself to wake up. I just hugged her closer, rubbing my hand up and down her arm.

As soon as the man pulled up to the hospital, I opened the door to his vehicle, thanking him before running inside.

"PLEASE HELP!" I shouted. "SHE WAS SHOT! I NEED HELP!"

Almost immediately, nurses and hospital personnel were swarming me. I could hear chatter over comms, and a few moments later, a gurney was rocketing down the hall toward us. I laid her down on it and took Destin's jacket off of her, seeing that the black skeins were now much higher, stretching around her front and climbing for her heart. I felt nauseous, but ignored the feeling, shoving past the nurses and pushing the rolling bed down the hall from where it came.

I wheeled the gurney until two other doctors beside me directed me to turn into an empty room. They were talking quickly, trading ideas. I pushed it to the center as my eyes took in the room and its equipment. It wasn't Zaccoth or any of the advanced materials the Cayser System used, but it would have to do.

"She needs emergency surgery," I said. One of the doctors gave me a look as nurses bustled around the room.

"Kid, how did you even get in here? How old are you? Like, sixteen?" he said. I remember hearing the doctor's name from his partner. This was Dr. Anside.

Quickly, I calculated Cayser System years to Earth years. Back home, I was fourteen. Here, I would be around sixteen years old.

"Yeah," I said. "You got that right."

"So what are you doing here?" the other physician said. That was Dr. Halford. "If this girl needs surgery, you can't be here."

"I *am* a doctor and I *will* be here," I snapped. Anside and Halford recoiled at my change in tone. The nurses said nothing, leaving the room to get more equipment.

"Andrex?" Zephyr said, quietly. Her voice sounded panicked, and I walked over to her side. "Andrex, where am I?"

"You're in a hospital. I'm going to help you," I said, calmly, trying to get her to relax. It didn't work. She tensed, trying to sit up. When she saw Anside and Halford behind me, her storm gray eyes spiraled into red.

"Andrex, there are two White Coats behind you," she warned.

"I'm aware," I told her. I opened my mouth to continue and tell her they were friendly, but Zephyr swung her legs over the side of the bed and lunged at the doctors before I could stop her. Her moves were weak and encumbered, but a trained military commander against two terrified doctors? She was bound to win.

Dr. Anside shrieked and ducked, narrowly missing a blow to the side of his head. She was using the last of her energy to save my life. I was trying to figure out how to get her to cooperate and not endanger those around her. Just then, I had an idea, but I knew she would really hate it.

Zephyr crouched and kicked, swiping Dr. Halford off his feet. He hit the tile on his back, gasping for air. Anside thought it would be a good idea to try to restrain her, but she mustered all of her remaining energy and backhanded him before landing a swift kick to the gut. He fell back and slammed into a shelf, vials of medicine crashing to the floor and shattering around him. It was now or never.

Forgive me, I thought. Carefully, I slid behind her and touched her lower left-back, right where the wound was. She cried out in agony and collapsed against me, falling into my arms. The pain rendered her hardly conscious.

"You… hurt a patient?" Dr. Anside looked at me in shock.

I scooped Zephyr up and laid her back on the gurney, attaching an IV to her arm and putting an anesthesia mask over her face, flicking a switch to start the gas. "Well, it was either that, or she'd kill you both," I said. The two doctors looked at me in shock. "She has a really strong hate toward… people in white coats."

"Well, that's comforting," Halford grumbled, standing up and brushing off his coat. "What happened to her?"

Using my story from before, I took a deep breath. "We were both kidnapped and as we were escaping, she was shot. I performed surgery on her in the desert or wherever we were and got the bullet out, but I think there was a poison on it that's killing her, hence her veins turning black and whatever those vine-looking things are."

Both Anside and Halford stared at me. After a long moment, I clapped my hands in front of their faces.

"HEY. I just said she was poisoned. She probably has just a few more hours so can we SAVE HER LIFE, PLEASE?!"

The doctors snapped out of their baffled trance, starting to send orders through comms and reorganizing their equipment. Carefully, I rolled Zephyr onto her stomach and looked around for a sharp object. Behind me, there was a table with scissors on it. I grabbed them and snipped the bandages around Zephyr's torso. Slowly, I pulled them away, inhaling sharply when I saw the wound. Halford walked over to me and examined it. He had gloves on and a surgical mask.

"Oh, my God," he said, quietly, doing a double take, his eyes looking at the three claw scars down her back. He then frowned, leaning a little closer. "Wait... I recognize these symptoms. Has she been shivering uncontrollably as well?"

I nodded.

"Glevein," Anside jumped in. "It has to be. But that's an illegal drug. Why would someone–"

"I just told you we were kidnapped, right?" I snapped.

The doctor nodded, a bit embarrassed. "What are your names?" he asked, changing the subject.

"Co–" I was about to say Zephyr's full title by formal introduction instinct, but I cut myself off. "Co... Karia. And I'm Aspen."

A small part of me disliked using my brother's name since I really did not have the best relationship with him, but it was either that, or they'd put down our real names and Area 51 would show up with an entire army.

"Karia and Aspen," Halford repeated. He backed off as the nurses came in with the surgical equipment. Halford grabbed a pair of fine scissors and cut the stitches.

"First, we'll clean it. Then we'll get the antidote and administer it, keeping her on high vital check for the next five hours after that," Anside ordered. "Aspen, I'm going to have to ask you to leave the room."

I shook my head. "Absolutely not. Okay, yes, I'm sixteen here but I am also a trained professional that has been studying this since I was…" I did the calculation from Cayser to Earth years in my head. On Zaccoth, I was five. "Seven. I've been studying this since I was seven."

Snapping gloves over my hands and quickly throwing on a mask, I grabbed a surgical cleansing tube and held it over the gunshot wound.

"It's my way or no way."

Chapter Forty-Nine: Tessia

Here We Go Again…

Wherever we were was torrid, bright, and absolutely dead. The sun had just come up over the horizon and it was already blazing hot, even in shorts and a tank top, spare clothing Alice had packed. Destin was still wearing his heavy work pants and a white T-shirt. His pistol was holstered at his hip, which he hadn't taken off since Area 51. Honestly, I couldn't blame him.

Destin had locked himself in the locomotive's cab. He was there for almost a solid hour, and whenever I'd check on him, I'd hear sobbing. The poor guy was so shaken after everything that had happened. The original *Caroline* was destroyed, he saw his best friend die twice (the first time was a wicked simulated experiment, but the second was horribly real), and then the White Coats threatened him with scrapping the *Caroline II*. He just needed some time to himself; I hoped if I left him alone he'd slow down, easing up on giving the Silver Dragon his life force.

After a long while, Destin came out of the cab. He searched the rail yard for a maintenance shed. The Silver

Dragon had taken a beating, averaging one hundred and ten Earth miles per hour to get here, putting crazy amounts of strain on Destin and the train.

Destin had totally taken apart the locomotive - all of its shiny streamlining had been removed, revealing the huge evaporator core casing behind it. The tender and passenger car had also been completely unhooked from the locomotive, the right middle drive set where the main pin had been replaced. It was completely taken apart from the huge rod. Parts were strewn on the workshop floor. The right side of the train had been jacked up to lift the huge wheels off the ground to replace the parts.

"This is terrible," Destin grumbled, with a fair amount of anger behind his words. He had given me Siren so he could focus on his work. She was sitting around my shoulders, watching him.

"Really? I think this has been *fantastic*," I muttered back.

Destin just sighed and continued to work. "I need to get into the evaporator core," he announced after a long moment of silence.

"What's the problem there?" I asked.

Destin bit his lower lip. "N-nothing."

He clearly wasn't telling me something.

"Do you want my help?" I asked, narrowing my eyes slightly with suspicion.

"Uh... sure? I'm just unplugging the battery." Now it made sense. He wanted me to watch, making sure something didn't happen when he unplugged power.

"Alright then."

We climbed inside the locomotive's cab. Destin walked over to a control panel and grabbed a large switch meant to shut off all the power. He pulled it down. There was a small whining noise as the train powered down. I looked over at Destin and felt my heart drop. His face was as white as a sheet.

Oh, no, I thought. *Oh, gods.*

"Tessia…" he breathed. He sounded exhausted. "I feel cold…"

I ran over to him and he collapsed against me. I felt his forehead. It was as cold as ice.

"Destin? DESTIN?!" I shouted, shaking him gently. He just rested his head against my shoulder. Siren hissed quietly, bumping her nose against his forehead.

"I think I'm gonna sleep…" he mumbled, slurring his words.

"No, stay awake. Stay awake, Destin!" I grabbed his arm and slung it over my shoulder.

I made my way through the cab and climbed out of the train, pulling my brother with me. As soon as he left the train, his eyes closed, and he fell completely limp. We collapsed to the ground and I shook him again. Siren's tail whacked him in the arm.

"DESTIN! DESTIN, WAKE UP!"

I started screaming for help, knowing that we couldn't be the only ones here. I held my brother against me and tried not to cry. He was looking worse by the second, and his breathing became shallow. He had given so much of his life to the Silver Dragon that there was barely any left for him.

Two security guards appeared around the front of the Silver Dragon to find us on the ground, Destin in my arms. I shied away from them and drew Destin's pistol, aiming at them. They held up their hands and stopped advancing. My eyes scanned them. They didn't look like the Area 51 personnel.

One of the guards took a hesitant step forward. "Are you alright, ma'am?" he asked. My hand was visibly shaking as I slowly lowered the gun. Tears started to stream down my face as the other guard advanced as well. Siren hissed at the both of them.

"Please help me," I said, quietly, my voice wavering. "He... he's dying."

The first guard closed the distance between us and picked Destin up while the other helped me stand, eyeing the white neidren.

"Come with us," the second one said. "We'll get you to the nearest hospital."

My heart rate sped up as every instinct told me to go nowhere near a place with White Coats, but I didn't exactly have a choice.

The two guards led me through the rail yard to their vehicle. The one holding Destin opened the door and put him in the back. I climbed in after my brother and hugged him. The guards jumped into the front of the vehicle and started the engine, revving it up before tearing down the road.

"What are your names?" the one driving asked.

"Uh..." I hesitated, trying to come up with aliases. The first two names that came into my head were my parents'. "C-Caroline and Fynn."

"We're Officers Bush and Walters. What happened to you kids?" the driver, Bush, asked. Walters eyed the blood on my arm.

"We were uh... k-kidnapped and..." I said, slowly. "We managed to escape but..."

Officer Bush sped up the vehicle, weaving through traffic toward a tall building with a red cross on it. Destin groaned quietly in my arms and I hugged him a little tighter. His face had completely lost its color, and his lips were cracked and dry. The officer yanked the steering mechanism hard to the left, swerving around a corner, causing the other vehicles to blare their horns by reflex. My shoulder slammed into the door, but I didn't care.

As soon as the officers pulled up to the hospital, I didn't wait for the vehicle to fully stop. I pulled the handle to the door and jumped out, grabbing my brother and dragging him with me. Officer Walters got out of the vehicle as well and ran into the building ahead of me. Doctors and medical personnel started to swarm around us. They helped me lay him on a gurney before wheeling him down a hallway. I started to follow, but Officer Bush held me back.

"Let the doctors work," he said. I shook my head, struggling to get away from him.

"I need to be with my brother," I said, my voice shaking. "You don't understand what we've been through. I *need* to be with D- with Fynn."

Regardless, he held me back against his body. Siren hissed at him, but he didn't flinch. "They need to operate."

"Please!" I shouted, crying at this point. "Let me go! Let me be with him! You don't understand!"

A nurse approached me and looked at the blood on my arm. Officer Bush took my hand and gripped it tightly as the nurse beckoned for us to follow her so she could look at my wound. I tried to get away the entire time without hurting the officer, knowing he was just trying to help me, but I only had my mind set on one thing. Getting back to my brother.

The officer pulled me into a room and closed the door before he let me go. I immediately lunged toward the pad by the side of the door, trying to open it, but it was locked. I slammed my fist against the door and slid to my knees, crying for my brother while the nurse attempted to calm me down so she could patch me up.

Chapter Fifty: Zephyr

Hearing Colors

Everything hurt. My vision was swimming as all the icy and bright colors of the room blended together and spun around my head, making me feel even more nauseous. I put my hands against my face and moaned quietly, the bullet wound burning as I forced myself to sit up.

Slowly, I rose, the room around me pulsing with bright spots. I felt lightheaded, but stood up anyway, my only goal to find Andrex and get out of this place as soon as possible. As I took one step forward, the muscles in my leg failed me. They spazzed, causing me to cry out and collapse on the frigid tiles. I tried to get up, but I had no energy.

Off to my right, someone inhaled sharply, like they'd been shocked awake. I thought I heard Andrex's voice calling my name, but it sounded distorted and far away, as if it were echoing through a cave. I watched as the person I assumed was Andrex stand up and rush over to pick me up. My head rested against his shoulder as my eyes struggled to stay open.

"What have I been telling you this entire time?" he said, sharply, scolding me.

"I wasn't list'ning," I replied, slowly, my words slurring together. He sighed in exasperation and put me back on the gurney.

"You scared the life out of all of us," Andrex huffed, running a hand through his hair in an attempt to tame it. "You'll be okay, though. But only. If. You REST."

"Mmm…" I complained, putting a hand against my forehead. It burned, but I didn't take my palm away. Andrex leaned over me, his eyes studying my face.

"Destin and Tessia arrived at the hospital last night. Des is recovering after he zapped all of his strength, and I've already met with Tess. We're getting you both out of here and back to the Silver Dragon," he said, his voice lowered.

It took me a moment for my brain to register what he was saying, and once I comprehended it, I frowned.

"Wait… what…? Destin is in the hospital…?" I asked, my speech still garbled. How much medication was I on?

Andrex nodded. "He'll be fine." He hesitated for a moment. "I'll be right back."

I barely moved my head in acknowledgement as Andrex left the room, returning a few moments later with what looked like a chair on wheels.

"What's that…?" I mumbled.

"That's our ticket to getting you out of here," Andrex said, hurrying over to my bedside and picking me up. I didn't resist as he set me down in the chair, spinning it around and pushing it out the open door to the room.

I hugged my arms as my eyes darted around the hallway, looking at every White Coat and nurse. My irises flickered between red and gray as Andrex sped up. Just as he turned a corner, he crashed straight into another wheelchair. I grabbed the armrests to prevent myself from falling out, but the motion of it made my wound ache.

"Watch where you're going, you hollow-headed Ori–" Andrex started, snapping at the other person who was pushing the other wheelchair. He stopped himself once he realized that it was Destin and Tessia. I looked over at Destin; Andrex was right. He did look a lot better from the last time I saw him.

"Tessia!" Andrex exclaimed. "You gave me a heart attack!"

She slapped his arm. "Lower your voice, will you?" Tessia hissed. "We're trying to sneak *out*. Not get caught!"

Noticing that Siren was sitting around Tessia's shoulders, I reached out to her instinctively. She slid onto my arm and coiled herself around it as I kissed her small head. "It's good t' see you guys," I said, my words not colliding as much as they were before, but still somewhat slurring. Destin smiled at me.

"It's good to see you, too, Zeph," he said. There was a flash of light blue in my vision as he spoke, and I blinked, thinking I was hallucinating.

"Andrex…" I started, trailing off.

"Yes?" he responded. There was a spot of green this time.

"I think I'm hearing colors," I said, seeing red in the corners of my vision this time. I shook my head and blinked again.

"Yeah, okay. Let's get out of here," Destin said. The others nodded in agreement as they pushed us past medical personnel and out the door.

Destin jumped up immediately and staggered straight into his sister, who yelped in surprise before catching him. He regained his balance, straightening out his jacket which he must've gotten back when I was unconscious.

As Tessia began fussing over Destin while he repeatedly assured her he was okay, Andrex took my arm and slung it over his shoulder before he scooped me up.

"Okay," he said, looking around to see if any White Coats were following us. "Let's move."

We walked in silence for a long time, Tessia and Destin constantly looking over their shoulders and scouring the streets for any sign of Area 51 guards. At one point, Destin shoved both Andrex and Tessia into an alleyway as a couple of officers drove past us. As soon as all was clear, we were moving again.

"Andrex, you c'n put me down. I'm fine," I said. He laughed.

"You most certainly are not, Commander," he replied. I could hear Destin snickering. At least he was feeling much better than I was after his mass energy drain.

Siren wiggled her way up from around my arm to loop herself around Andrex's neck. Her head rose up as she scoped out the streets, hissing at any humans that looked our way. She craned her small head upward and puffed as a massive shadow overtook the streets and blocked out the sun's light. Andrex stopped walking and stared up along with Siren, Destin, and Tessia. All around us, humans were screaming and running in the opposite direction. Human transports sped by as they tried to get away from the shadow. Gray flashed along the edges of my vision as those engines revved.

"What is that?!" Andrex shouted as the wind started to pick up. I turned my head to see what they were all staring at.

"That, my friend," Destin beamed, "is the Velusan command ship. The *Prince of Dragons*."

Damari... I thought, a smile starting to grow on my face.

"We're going home!" Tessia shouted, not caring who heard at this point.

The PoD had arrived along with the Cayser System's best soldiers and my brother. A warm, joyful feeling spread through me as I realized I was going to see my family again and be reunited with the people I love.

Chapter Fifty-One: Andrex

Death of a Hero

We rushed back to the rail yard as quickly as we could despite the distance, keeping our eye on the PoD and what looked like the *Concord*, still hovering above Earth's atmosphere. As soon as we got back, we beelined for the Silver Dragon and our ships. I watched as the Kincaid siblings exchanged a look, like they knew they'd have to say goodbye to someone. Or something.

Tessia climbed into the train and came back with Zephyr's sword. She held it out to her brother and he took it. He then turned back to the Silver Dragon, putting his hand on one of the driving rods.

"I'm sorry…" he said. "I-I will be back for you… I promise, but until then…" He drove Zephyr's sword into the steam and water lines that connected the tender to the locomotive, water gushing out of them. "You will have to stay dead…."

A tear rolled down Destin's cheek. I didn't know what to say to comfort him. This was the machine that had saved our lives, and Destin was now being forced to abandon her here on this planet.

"I will be back… I promise," he said, quieter this time. The phrase sounded more like he was telling it to himself than anything. Tessia went up to him and pulled him into a hug.

"She'll be okay. You *will* be back for her, but now we need to get off this planet."

Destin nodded and walked over to the flatcars holding the *Caroline II* and the *Nautilax*. Using Zephyr's sword, he cut the straps holding them down.

"Alright," he said. "Let's get off this mud ball." He waved his hand at the *Caroline II* and her engines fired up, the sound resonating throughout the rail yard. The cargo door to the ship then opened. "I'm gonna send a radio message to the PoD to let them know where we are. You guys stay here."

"I'm coming with you," Tessia said, following Destin as he climbed up into his ship.

I looked down toward Zephyr and smiled. "I told you I wasn't going to let you die," I said quietly to her. She let out a breath of laughter, hardly opening her eyes.

"I never doubted you," she replied, her voice hardly above a whisper. At least she wasn't slurring her words too much anymore.

"But you did have some doubt regarding that poison affecting you."

She gave a slight nod. "Maybe just a little."

I looked back up at the sky as five sleek, dark missiles rocketed toward the Velusan command ship. I frowned and looked back at the *Caroline II*.

C'mon, Destin, I thought. *Hurry up.*

Chapter Fifty-Two: Damari

Planet Earth

The *Prince of Dragon's* crew and every soldier on board were running around, shouting orders, or slamming buttons on the control panels in the bridge. The comms were firing off commands from the *Concord* every few seconds as both bridges were making contact back with Velus and my father.

My hand gave my sister's pendant a squeeze before I put it back in the pocket over my heart and stuck a comm on my ear. Sorres and Dennett came up behind me, a smirk growing on Sorres' face.

"You ready, Haldenson?" he asked, cracking all of his knuckles.

"I was born ready," I replied, my eyes blazing. "I will shred this planet apart if it means getting the commander back."

Dennett laughed, clapping me on the shoulder. "And we'll be right next to you the whoooole time."

I grinned at him before looking out the bridge window. Earth was a decent-sized planet with mass oceans like Velus, although we had more. Flashes appeared in the atmosphere as lightning in passing storms circled the globe, white clouds swirling over continents and nations filled with the people that had shot down my sister's ship and had taken her away from me.

Across the *Concord* comm connection, I could hear General Kincaid shouting at his crew to prepare a smaller ship to be deployed to the Earth's surface. I walked over to the comm panel and slammed my hand down on it.

"You aren't going anywhere without me, General," I snapped. "That dropship better come and pick me up, or you and I are gonna–"

"Relax, Damari," the general said. "I'm sending it over to you right now– WHAT DO YOU THINK YOU'RE DOING? I said extraction ship! Not a full-blown deployment!"

I held back a laugh as the general continued to screech at his crew. I turned my head over my shoulder and looked at Merai. She was busy fastening her armor and checking her holsters. When she felt my gaze upon her, she looked over at me, giving a thumbs-up and smiling. I smiled back, feeling more confident.

Just then, a comm broke into our signal, a deep and threatening voice booming through the bridges of both the *Concord* and the PoD. "State your name and business, aliens. Or we will shoot you from the sky."

I leaned over the comm panel, nodding at the soldier stationed there to press the button that would let me reply.

"I'm only here for–" I started.

"You are unwelcome. Leave or be shot down."

Behind me, Dennet snorted. "They're hospitable," he grumbled, crossing his arms.

"Haldenson! Incoming!" Braxton yelled. I looked out of the bridge window to see five black missiles streaking toward the *Prince of Dragons*. They were large and fast, but not enough so. The standard pressure and gravity of the planet slowed them down. By the time they reached the Velusan command ship, they bounced harmlessly off the Diatanium hull and fell screaming back to the Earth, burning up in the heat of the atmosphere.

"Who are you?" The distorted voice on the opposing end of the comm didn't sound as collected now. There were certainly hints of panic in the speaker's tone.

I scowled, glaring down at the blue and green marble against the dark bruise of space.

"*I am Command Sergeant Major Haldenson of Velus, and I'm here for my sister.*"

The *Concord's* comm broke into the frequency. "And I am General Kincaid of Velus, captain of the super starliner *Concord.* And I'm here for my children."

"You have no power against us!" I shouted, feeling my temper begin to rise. "Stand down or face the consequences of your mistaken actions. We will not leave until we have retrieved who we came here for. Nothing and no one will stop us. Including *you.*"

There was a static sound as the comms cut off between Earth and us. Their only response to my message was dispatching more explosive projectiles. These, however, were stronger and faster. Two shells exploded against the hull of the PoD, making the command ship shake. Soldiers stumbled into walls and shouted at each other.

"Firing Officer Rondier! Tell the gun crews to target the origin of those missiles!" I ordered. He nodded and relayed the message to the rest of the PoD. "Let's show them what a 110-inch HEPAP shell looks like…."

A split moment later, the PoD's massive main guns rotated in the direction of Earth.

"EYES ON THE BRIDGE!" Rondier shouted. Knowing the warning, I lifted my arm to shield my eyes from the muzzle flash of the guns. Everyone on the bridge did the same motion as the ship rocked, the *Prince of Dragons* firing off a full 110-inch broadside assault.

"Keep going!" I ordered as more of Earth's projectiles slammed into the PoD's hull or rocketed past us. There were more flashes as the guns on the PoD fired off again. Explosions down on Earth's surface lit up like small sparks as our shells collided with the ground.

"Haldenson!" the general shouted over comms. "The extraction ship is ready. Do we have landing clearance on the PoD's top deck?"

I looked over at one of my soldiers, who gave the go-ahead. "Yessir," I replied. "Sorres, Dennett, Merai! With me!"

Turning on my heel and making a circling motion with my hand in the air, I left the bridge and ran down the hall, the others jogging right behind me.

"The sooner we get in, the better," Merai said.

"Agreed," Dennett replied. We all turned the corner and dashed into the lift. I slammed my fist into the button to shut the doors as it brought us up to the top deck. The lift remained shut until the extraction ship landed and the gravity shields safely surrounded the deck. As soon as the doors opened, I ran out, the ship's cargo ramp already being lowered.

The others were close behind me. We sprinted up the ramp as I ordered for its immediate closure once we were on board. The hatch shut as we made our way to the extraction ship's bridge. There was a beeping sound as the PoD command center requested a comm connection to the extraction ship. I answered.

"What happened?" I asked.

"There's an incoming call from Destin Kincaid," one of the crew replied.

"Well, don't just sit there! ANSWER IT!" I exclaimed. I could feel my heart rate starting to speed up, whether it be nerves or excitement, I couldn't tell. Maybe it was both.

"Hello? *Caroline II* to the *Prince of Dragons*. Does anyone copy?" Destin's voice came through. I exhaled in relief.

"Destin, where are you?! We're coming to get you!" I shouted, not caring if I broke everyone's eardrums on the ship. I turned to Sorres and ordered him to contact the PoD to lower the gravity shields.

The comm connection crackled as Destin spoke. "Uh, we're in a place called Reno, Nevada. How soon can you get here?"

Not soon enough, I thought, already punching the coordinates into the ship's locator system.

"About five minutes," Merai said for me. "Are you okay?"

"A lot went wrong," Tessia said, her voice filling the ship as the engines started. Worry started to grow, but I quickly shook it off. I needed a clear head here.

The gravity shields around the PoD's top deck were lowered, and the extraction ship took off, heading straight for Reno, Nevada, the nav system triangulating and pinpointing the signal from the *Caroline II.*

Wait, Caroline II? Where's the original? I thought. Then again, I wasn't quite sure I wanted to know.

General Kincaid walked into the bridge and sat down in one of the chairs as the rest of us strapped ourselves in. The extraction ship entered Earth's atmosphere right as the general buckled himself in. The bridge window lit up like a flare as we shot through the ozone layers, dodging missiles from Earth.

After breaking through the atmospheric resistance, we headed straight for wherever Reno, Nevada was. I watched through narrowed eyes as the land drew nearer, cities starting to appear before my eyes. Our ship's descent began to slow the closer we got to land, the plasma rigid-rotors going into backward thrust and pushing against the gravity so we didn't crash into Earth's surface.

The extraction ship landed in a rail yard. I saw a sleek silver train, a more modified version of what looked like the original *Caroline*, and a Zaccothian subship. The name *Nautilax* was embossed in the underwater-dwelling machine's side.

I looked forward out of the bridge's window and saw Tessia waving, and Destin talking to a blonde boy who was holding–

Zephyr. My mind spiraled into a million different scenarios. It looked like she was unconscious.

Before the ship had fully landed, I had already unbuckled my belt and stumbled out of my chair, crashing into the wall in the corridor on my way to the cargo's landing door.

"Haldenson, wait!" Dennett shouted after me as he quickly jumped up from his seat. The pilot started yelling at us, but I couldn't care less. The ship landed as I made my way to the door and slammed my hand against the button that released it.

As soon as there was a gap large enough for me to fit through, I slid down the ramp as Dennett yelled my name again. I hit the ground and rolled back up to a standing position, sprinting around the ship to where the Kincaids and my sister were. I ran straight over to the person holding Zephyr and took her from him. Siren puffed at me from his shoulders, but I hardly noticed. I could already feel tears welling up and my throat seizing as my eyes scanned her face. Destin pulled the stranger away as I knelt down, cradling Zephyr in my arms.

"Zephyr…" I said, her name barely audible from my lips. Tears started to slide down my face.

She opened her eyes. They were stormy and dark gray, but once she saw my face, they spiraled into green. She smiled at me.

"Hey, Damari," she said, quietly. I let out a half-laugh, half-sob and held her tighter, touching my forehead against her own.

"Oh, gods, Zephyr. Don't you ever scare me like that again."

She smiled. "I'll do my best."

Behind me, I could hear the Kincaid siblings yell "Dad!" as they were reunited with their father. I was happy for them, but my only concern at the moment was my sister. I stood up, carrying her back to the extraction ship; Sorres and

Dennett were already down, talking to the Kincaids and their new friend. Merai approached me before I boarded the ship.

"I told you everything would work out," she said, grinning at me. I smiled back, nodding.

"You were right." I paused, looking back at the sleek silver locomotive, feeling as if it had something to do with the Kincaids. "Check in that train and take anything that belongs to them," I said. She nodded and gave me a pat on the shoulder before walking off.

I carried my sister into the extraction ship and to the bridge, setting her down on one of the seats and strapping her in before kneeling in front of her.

"What happened to you?" I asked as my hand reached toward the pocket over my heart.

"I was shot when we were escaping the facility where we were held prisoner," she said, leaning back.

I pulled the pendant out of my pocket and pressed it into her hand, kissing her forehead.

"You're safe now," I said. "I'm gonna take you home and never let you out of my sight again."

She laughed, looking down at the pendant. "That sounds like a deal."

Merai walked into the bridge with Zephyr's sword and neidren draped around her neck. Siren narrowed her eyes and hissed at me for forgetting her before sliding off Merai's shoulders and onto Zephyr's arm. I smiled at the neidren.

"Sorry about that, Si," I said to the lithe creature. She just puffed at me indignantly before curling up and hiding her head in her white coils.

Sorres, Dennett, and the general arrived on the ship a few minutes later, claiming that the others were taking their own ships into orbit and would meet us up there. I nodded, overflowing with relief that my sister was safe and with me again as everyone buckled in, and the extraction ship took off.

Chapter Fifty-Three: Tessia

Almost Home

Sitting beside my brother in the bridge of the

Caroline II felt like the most natural thing in the world. This ship could honestly be a second home to me, and I would not object.

Destin was grinning from ear to ear. Despite the fact that he still looked tired, he seemed to be feeling a lot better after whatever the White Coats had put him through at the building with the red cross. There was color back in his face, and he wasn't as veiny as before, which I took as *very* good signs.

All seemed so right with the universe. We were free of Area 51 and the cruel experiments, Zephyr was back with her brother, we were reunited with our father, and everyone was going home safe and alive.

The brigantine schooner powered through Earth's atmosphere, the resistance lighting the hull ablaze. Luckily, due to Destin's MA and the Diatanium hull, we were all home free. The PoD's and *Concord*'s comms connected to both the *Nautilax*'s and ours. Our father decided to issue a hyperjump, relaying the information to all of us over the comms. I switched the frequency over to talk to Andrex on the *Nautilax* privately.

"Are you going back to Zaccoth?" I asked.

"Nah," he said. "I've always loved the planet, but honestly, I'd rather be with you guys. I'm–"

"You mean you'd rather be with your GIRLFRIEND," Destin said loudly, cackling. I smothered a laugh while Andrex heavily sighed.

"Good to see you feeling like yourself, Destin. But... yes. Since I'm an adult," he continued, "I can just leave whenever I want. It's not like I missed my family that much anyway. We never really got along."

"Ah," I said. "Then welcome to Velus."

He laughed. "Thanks, Tess."

"Wait, what?" Damari said over the comms. "Do I need to kill someone?"

Destin's face went bright red as I cracked up.

"NOTHING, DAMARI!" he shouted.

"You forgot to disconnect?" I whispered. He shrugged at me. I double-checked our frequency, glaring at my brother when I realized he hadn't. He cleared his throat awkwardly.

"Are we gonna hyperjump back to Velus?" Destin asked.

"The star charts should be updated," someone from the PoD said.

"They are," my Dad responded, having just arrived on the *Concord*.

"Well, what else are we waiting for?!" Andrex exclaimed.

"Absolutely nothing!" Damari shouted over comms as soon as he reached the bridge of the PoD; the extraction ship dropped off his team before the general.

"All ships! Charge your hyperdrives! Set course for the Cayser System!" our father said from aboard the *Concord*. Destin maneuvered the *Caroline II* to hover beside the gigantic *Prince of Dragons*, grinning at everyone in the bridge.

He then flicked the switch to start the hyperdrive, readying it for the jump. The other ships, *Nautilax* and *Concord*, also glided into formation next to the PoD. Damari's voice sounded over the open comms connecting all the ships.

"Prepare to jump in three, two, one!"

Destin pushed the *Caroline II's* throttle forward and one by one all four of the ships made their jump for the Cayser System. The sound of the hyperdrive wound up. I looked out the window as far-off stars became streaks of light in front of us; then suddenly, there was a sharp bang as the ship's hyperdrive engaged and she rocketed ahead at the speed of light back to our system. Back to our home.

As soon as we were within sight of Velus, I could tell there was something very wrong. The entirety of the UDN's ships were surrounding what looked like a fleet of vessels burnt or built from scrap metal. *Grebles*.

Destin stood up, his gaze smoldering. "That bastard is the only reason we were in this mess," he growled, angrily. I watched as his eyes flashed electric blue.

"What are you doing?" I asked as my brother slammed the button on the control panel that activated the top deck's gravity shields.

He turned his head over his shoulder and looked at me. "I'm putting an end to that monster." His eyes blazed dangerously.

With that, he turned and raced out of the bridge, closing the door and ordering the *Caroline II* to lock it behind him. I jumped up from my seat and dashed over, trying to get it to open. I struck the door in frustration, looking through the window in the door at my brother.

"Don't do this!" I shouted. "Destin, open the door!"

He gave me a knowing smile that chilled me to the core. "It's okay, Tess. Now it's my turn to protect you."

I watched as Destin ran down the corridor as I screamed after him, trying to get the door open. After a while, I looked out of the bridge window, all of my anger dissipating once I saw my little brother walking up the *Caroline II*'s top deck and closer to the bowsprit. My heart squeezed with fear as he climbed up onto it and looked out at the Greblin fleet.

"Hey, Mordrar," Destin said, his voice icy. "Remember me?"

Chapter Fifty-Four: Zephyr
To Be the *Dauntless*

Destin stood as still as a statue on the tip of the

Caroline II's bowsprit, his hands at his sides. I stared out of the bridge window of the *Prince of Dragons* at the entire Greblin fleet miles in front of me. My eyes focused on the biggest ship. The *Mennus*. I could hear footsteps behind me, and I swiveled around. Damari was advancing, a grim expression on his face.

I tried to stand up, but my brother put a hand on my shoulder to keep me seated.

"You need to rest," he told me.

I frowned. "But–" Damari cut me off with a stern look.

"Do I actually need to remind you that you were *shot*, Zeph? In all seriousness, I *will* strap you down to your chair for your own safety," he said.

"Okay, fine." I paused. "What is Des doing?"

Damari looked out of the window. His expression went from confusion to shock. "It looks like he's gonna get himself killed!"

I looked back out at Destin, my concern growing. I glanced over at the ship across from the *Caroline II*; the *Mennus*. The Greblin Command Ship. I could just make out Mordrar within his bridge. He was seething.

"You again!" Mordrar yelled. His ship's outside loudspeaker blasted his voice all the way across the gap that separated the UDN from the Greblin fleet.

"HAH," Destin's voice boomed. "I find it funny that you actually remember me."

I turned to my brother. "Does Des have a comm on him?"

"No, why do you ask?"

"Then how is he talking so loudly?" I said. My brother pressed the comm on his ear and muttered a few words to the crew. What they said next clearly shook him. "Are you okay, Ari?"

"We have no access whatsoever to the outside comms in any of our ships. Destin's taken control of them."

My eyes widened.

"Of course, I remember you, *Destin Kincaid*," Mordrar spat. "You're hard to forget. In fact, I would like to settle something with you!"

That made my blood boil. Here I was, incapacitated sitting in the bridge of the *Prince of Dragons*, and I could do nothing to help my friend who was literally the only one standing between us and all-out war.

"And what would you like to settle?" Destin shouted.

"Do you recall when you tore the guns off my battleship?" Mordrar roared back.

"Of course!" Destin laughed. "It was the most liberating thing I'd ever done!"

I smiled, remembering Mordrar's reaction to his ship having just been rendered completely defenseless and disarmed.

"What's so funny?" he demanded.

"Oh, I'm sorry. I'm just laughing at the fact that it was so easy. Aaaand your reaction when I interrupted your little intimidation speech with Commander Haldensdottir."

Now I started laughing, which I quickly regretted, as the bullet wound still ached, and any motion in my torso made that area throb and burn.

I heard Mordrar growl. Destin was laughing so hard that it looked like he was about to fall off the *Caroline II*'s bowsprit.

"How on Oburna do you find any of this funny?!" Mordrar screeched.

"I'm sorry. This is just too hilarious. It's comical to think that after all these years of hiding, you suddenly decide to blast off your godsforsaken planet and say to yourself, 'Oh, I want to conquer the whole galaxy for no reason!' If you just went to war with Velus, I would understand, since you lost the war to us forever ago. But the whole galaxy, in my opinion, is just *absurd!*" Mordrar was speechless. "I mean, come on! How well did you think that was–" Destin was cut off.

"ENOUGH!" Mordrar screamed. "DON'T YOU EVER STOP *TALKING?!*"

"DON'T YOU EVER STOP *TRYHARDING?!*" Destin yelled back.

The entire bridge on the *Prince of Dragons* cracked up, crew members and military alike slapping desks and just flat-out falling over with laughter. My father and brother were laughing the hardest.

"Shut up! You useless, stupid, incompetent Velusan *child!* I *knew* I should have gone after you once I killed your mother!"

The bridge went silent, all traces of former joy were completely gone. There was a long silence. I watched as Destin's hands curled into tight fists.

Admiral Halden grabbed the engine telegraph and ordered the UDN to charge on the Greblin fleet.

None of the ships moved.

"Didn't you hear me?!" my father snapped. "I said, full ahead!"

A voice crackled over the bridge's announcement comms. "I'm sorry, sir! All of the engines have shut down! We can't restart them! It's like they have a mind of their own."

Destin, I thought. *Oh, gods, Destin what have you done?*

"You need to cut power to the ships!" I shouted.

"ALL OF THEM?!" the other commanders over the comm shouted simultaneously.

"I know what Destin is doing! He's drawing energy from the ships; you have to cut power!" Everyone stared at me. I deadpanned. "Are you *deaf? Cut the power!*"

"You heard the commander!" a captain from one of the UDN's ships said.

"Sir!" a crew member called out to my father. "There's something big approaching on the radar!"

"How big?" Admiral Halden stood up and walked over to the man.

"It's the size of Velus, sir!"

For the first time in my life, I knew what it was like to watch fear completely take over my father's features. My gut twisted, and Siren, who was resting on my shoulders, snapped to attention and started tensing. The tip of her tail lashed back and forth.

"Impossible," my father whispered. Suddenly, a huge shadow cast darkness over the UDN fleet, like the sun had disappeared.

The comms started exploding with messages as the fleet commanders and generals began freaking out.

"What is *that?!*"

"What do we do?"

"Admiral, what are your orders?"

"Do we fire?"

"WE'RE ALL GONNA DIE!!!!!"

Damari gave my shoulder a gentle squeeze before walking over to our father. They were feverishly exchanging ideas and trying to figure out what to do about whatever was blocking out Brei, our star. I averted my eyes from the two of them and looked out of the window again.

"Oh, no," I said.

"WHAT?!" everyone in the bridge asked me. I was surprised that they heard me over all the chaos.

I turned around. "How many of you are familiar with the Dauntless Project?"

Recognition and fear flashed across everyone's faces as they realized the impact of my words and what that massive shadow meant.

Over the outdoor comm on the *Mennus*, we heard Mordrar give the order for all ships to fire on the UDN. Explosions from the entire Greblin fleet lit up the dark sky. I watched as all of the shells advanced on the UDN and there was nothing we could do to protect ourselves.

I looked at Destin, and noticed that he looked like he was glowing the same brilliant blue I saw in the Area 51 black light. The circuit board markings covered his body, and they radiated brighter than I'd ever seen. Blue sparks crackled in the palms of his hands. He looked possessed.

His eyes were glowing electric blue. In my heart, I knew it came from all of the hatred and anger that had been building up inside of him ever since he was seven and lost his mom. He was mad at the White Coats, he was furious with Area 51, and he was losing it now with the Grebles. To see so much raw power and fury take over my best friend scared me.

Siren gave me a puff, and we both put our heads down, expecting the explosions and obliteration of the fleet. But it didn't come. I raised my head and saw that Destin had waited for the shells to get close before raising his arm up in a blocking motion. All the shells stopped where they were. They were just… hovering in the middle of space.

Destin's voice was low and threatening, filled with wrath and malice.

"You. Did. *WHAT?!*"

"You heard me!" Mordrar snapped. "I killed your mother. Probably one of the most satisfying kills of my day."

Just by that sentence, I knew Mordrar had just made a very grave mistake. There was a loud grinding noise coming from above us. I craned my neck upwards to see the view of the *Dauntless'* bow opening up, revealing a massive gun barrel. I knew for certain that I didn't want to be on the receiving end.

"Guys!" Andrex's voice crackled over the comms. I was relieved to know that he was okay on his subship.

"What is it, Andrex?" I asked.

"That's a quantum energy weapon!" he shouted. "That thing can take out entire *planets!"*

I exchanged a horrified look with my brother. "How do we stop it?!" my father roared.

"Sir, once the charging process begins, you can't stop it," Andrex said. "The only way to prevent the charging is to kill Destin."

"No way!" I shouted. "We're not killing him. Not after everything we've been through. Can't we just knock him out?"

"Yeah, but who's going to volunteer to go up to him when he has LIGHTNING coming out of his HANDS?!" Andrex shouted.

There was a long silence. Nobody wanted to face the guy who had a hyper dreadnought, a quantum energy weapon, and the entire UDN under his command.

I stood up slowly and started to make my way toward the bridge door. My brother, unfortunately, realized what I was trying to do and lunged at me, catching me around the waist and picking me up. I struggled against him, but his grip was strong, and I was weakened by my wound.

"Let me go, Ari!" I snapped. "I need to help him!"

He didn't put me down. "You need to help yourself."

"He's my best friend," I responded, not realizing I was crying until I could feel the tears falling down my chin. "H-He won't hurt me."

"I am not letting you go up there!" Damari insisted. "I will not let you endanger yourself."

"LET ME GO!" I shouted.

"I DON'T WANT TO LOSE YOU, TOO!"

The bridge went silent, and I finally stopped struggling. My tears were from both physical and emotional pain. My wound throbbed and it was like I could feel my blood rushing through my veins. However, Damari was right. I was being reckless, but it was my nature to put those I care about first before myself. He walked over to my seat and put me down.

"I'll do it," Tessia's voice said over the comms. "After all, he is my brother."

"Tess–" I started.

"Don't say it, Zeph. He's my brother. I'm probably one of the only people he'll listen to. Plus, you're wounded."

I was about to retort, but there was a high-pitched sound that came from the comms. Everyone covered their ears, wincing.

"Just so you know, I can hear everything you're saying," Destin said. There was something *very* off about his voice. It was like there were two Destins speaking at the same time.

"Des, please come down from the bowsprit!" I shouted, still crying. "You're gonna get yourself killed!"

"I'd rather it was me than you. Let us get our revenge."

Damari's eyebrow shot up. "Us?" he asked. The high-pitched sound echoed through the bridge again before silence followed. Ignoring my brother's words and Andrex's orders,

I stood up and stepped toward the window, pressing my hands against the thick glass to keep my balance.

I could see the shocked face of Mordrar in his bridge. Destin's double voice was icy and dangerous. *"We will tear you apart!"* he growled.

"We?" Mordrar squeaked.

"We want revenge," Destin continued. He made a gesture to the *Dauntless*, which Mordrar hadn't noticed until now. It was probably because he lost sight in one eye and has terrible vision in the other.

"Th-that's not possible!" he stammered. Lightning started to crackle and shoot out of the quantum energy weapon, and a loud whirring sound reverberated off of both fleets. My father stormed over to the control panel and started slamming buttons.

"DESTIN KINCAID!" he screamed. "If you can hear me, GIVE ME BACK MY SHIP!"

"You have tested me for the last time! You thought you could get rid of me, Mordrar, but you forgot about three things... the Dauntless Project, my son, and our shared power! This is the rise of a nation, Mordrar! One led by a beast made of Diatanium! Your days of terrorizing the galaxy are OVER! Dauntless is a monster built and designed to stop you! It ends HERE! RELEASE THE WAR MACHINE!!!!"

Destin pulled his right arm back to his shoulder; palm forward and fingers outstretched. After a moment of agonizing silence, he executed a full-force thrust, and every shell, every bullet, and every missile from the UDN, *Nautilax*, and the *Dauntless* hurtled at the enemy. The quantum energy weapon fired, imploding the Greblin fleet.

At first, there was just silence, but then a bang louder than I ever thought possible rocked the skies. A shock wave shot out from the destruction.

"GET DOWN!" my father screamed. It was too late. The wave was fast and powerful. It hit the UDN fleet, knocking everyone over or sending them flying. The *Prince of Dragons* propelled into space as the wave pushed the command ship away from Velus.

My back hit the wall, knocking the air out of my lungs. I fell to my knees and then hit the floor face-down, trying to take in a breath. A loud ringing resounded in my ears as I lifted my pounding head, watching the *Caroline II*.

Destin had collapsed, and Tessia dragged him off the bowsprit and onto the deck, trying to wake him up. Siren nudged my cheek, making sure I was awake.

"Siren," I coughed, still trying to breathe. "I need… a comm…"

She slithered off my shoulders and headed in Damari's direction. The wave had rendered him unconscious. Using her tail, she flicked the comm off his ear and onto the floor. Then Siren grabbed it in her mouth and wiggled her way back over to me.

"Thanks, girl," I said. The adrenaline from before was starting to wear down, and the pain of the bullet wound and my head were starting to take effect. The world was spinning. "Contact Andrex Nivalis over *Nautilax*," I said shakily into the comm.

"Zephyr! Are you okay?"

"No, but I need you to get to Destin first. He needs more medical help than I do right now."

"What happened to you?"

"The shock wave. Everyone in the ship is unconscious…" I trailed off.

"Stay awake! You might have a concussion."

"Get… to Destin," I coughed. Breathing was becoming harder. "Help him."

"I'll head to Velus and get help. Try to stay awake, okay?"

"I don't know if I can." I closed my eyes, trying to block out the spinning motion of the bridge. I could hear Andrex talking to me, but I didn't understand anything he was saying.

I rested my head against the floor. My cranium pounded and my lungs threatened to constrict and suffocate me as the bullet hole in my back burned.

I could hear something over the comms, but it seemed so distant. It sounded like Destin's double voice was glitching.

"Bearing 148.7 degrees of Velus. We're going to win this war."

ZEPHYR

Epilogue

Sixteen Years Later

The sun was low in the skies of Velus as I sat down on the white sand beach behind the Kincaid's household. The golden light of Brei, our star, streaked the ocean and made it sparkle.

I had asked to be alone, leaving my family and friends back inside the house. I just needed a breather, and there was something else I had to accomplish. Straightening out my jacket and brushing sand off of my legs, I pulled a handheld comm out of my pocket. Wind whipped at my dark hair, and I tucked away any strands behind my ear.

After Destin had destroyed the Greblin race, the Cayser System lived in peace since that battle. Destin was proud to serve the System, but ten years ago, he left without a trace, and we haven't heard from him since.

Taking in a deep breath of salty air, I switched on the comm. An AI asked who I would like to send a message to, and I responded with the name Destin Kincaid. Inhaling another slow breath, I opened my mouth to speak into the comm.

"Hey, Destin. I know it's been a decade, and I know that everyone else has given up hope because we haven't had a *single* communication, but I really believe you're still out there. I *know* you're still alive, somewhere in the galaxy."

I squeezed my eyes shut. This wasn't easy.

"My daughter became an adult this week. I just wish you could've been here to celebrate with us. Your nephew is probably going to be taller than you and…" I laughed, shaking my head, "and the twins are just as reckless as ever."

My voice broke, and I struggled to keep my tone steady, despite the fact that tears were already starting to form in my eyes.

"Destin… please come home. Just send us some sign that you're out there." I began to cry. "I just want my best friend back," I said, burying my face in my knees. "Come home, Des. Come back to me. To Tessia and Andrex. Come back to your family."

I switched the comm off and stifled a sob. Even though a decade had passed since Destin's disappearance and everyone else had given up sending messages to him four years ago, I refused to stop. My gut told me he was still out there in the universe somewhere, and I knew he was searching for something.

"Zephyr?" My head snapped up, and I turned around to see Andrex walking out of the Kincaid house toward me. He quickened his pace when he noticed I was crying. "What's wrong?"

He sat down next to me, and I leaned my head on my husband's shoulder as he put his arms around me. "I miss him," I said, quietly, trying to swallow the lump in my throat.

"We all do," he soothed. Behind me, I could hear the door opening, and everyone else followed suit. My daughter, Aralyn, ran out with Talos, Tessia's son, and behind them, Luminara and Lazarus, Damari's twins, followed. Then came Tessia, Damari, and Anisa.

They all sat down around me as our children played by the water's edge, spraying each other and laughing. I swiped at my eyes and smiled at them.

"Do you truly believe Destin is out there?" Tessia finally said. I nodded.

"Then he's out there," Tessia agreed.

"I just hope he comes back," I sighed. "I hope he found what he was looking for."

"He'll be back one day, Zeph," Damari said. He opened his mouth to continue, but the comm in my hands pinged with a message. At that same moment, Brei was eclipsed by a ship the size of Velus.

"This is Engineer Destin Kincaid aboard the *Dauntless*. I'm requesting permission to enter the Velusan atmosphere via the *Caroline II*. Do I have landing clearance? Over."

My heart stopped, and I felt like I couldn't breathe. Everyone went completely silent. Even the kids had ceased playing. They were staring up at the massive hyper dreadnought that consumed the skies. I held the comm to my lips.

"D-Destin?" I stammered, my voice trembling.

"Hello, Zephyr. Tell Lyn I said, 'Happy birthday.'"

I choked on my next words, overwhelmed by emotion. I was feeling happiness, anger, and confusion all at once. "That's a copy. You have permission to dock."

Above us, bright light burned through the Velusan atmosphere as the *Caroline II* made her way to the Kincaid household. She docked in the waters beside the wooden-plank walkway that stretched at least eighty feet out into the ocean. I stood up, beaming, ready to rush over and see Destin for the first time in years.

Destin walked out across the *Caroline II's* top deck and waved at us. He slid down a ladder from the ship's hull, onto the dock.

I wanted to run toward him, but a voice over comms interrupted. "Fleet Admiral, stay back! That man is a wanted fugitive!"

Confused, I turned my head to see twenty of the UDN's soldiers making their way across the beach toward us.

Two of them grabbed me, pulling me away while using their bodies as shields. A third had his gun drawn, and several others took the kids away from the beach and guided them into the house. Over to my right, I could see the flash of a sniper's scope glinting from a reflection of the setting sun through the trees across the narrow peninsula that housed the Kincaid residence. Were they going to kill him?

"Stop! Let me go!" I shouted. "That's my best friend!" The two guards refused as the third approached Destin, the gun aimed squarely at his chest.

"I'm sorry, Fleet Admiral. His arrest was ordered by the Cayser Pentarchy."

"I override!" I snapped, tears of fury streaking down my face at the Council's decree. How *dare* they make a decision like this without me. "Let me go! That is an *order*, soldier! Stand down!"

They didn't release me. Instead, they kept pulling me away, trying to protect me from my own friend. I watched, heartbroken, as the UDN soldiers forced Destin to his knees and arrested him.

The End…?

BOOK TWO:

THE DAUNTLESS CHRONICLES II:
RISE OF THE DREADNOUGHTS

COMING SOON!

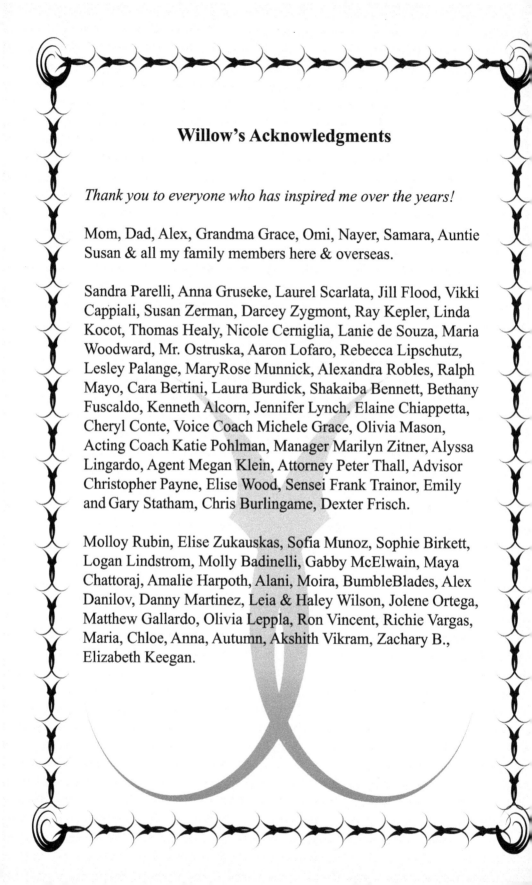

Willow's Acknowledgments

Thank you to everyone who has inspired me over the years!

Mom, Dad, Alex, Grandma Grace, Omi, Nayer, Samara, Auntie Susan & all my family members here & overseas.

Sandra Parelli, Anna Gruseke, Laurel Scarlata, Jill Flood, Vikki Cappiali, Susan Zerman, Darcey Zygmont, Ray Kepler, Linda Kocot, Thomas Healy, Nicole Cerniglia, Lanie de Souza, Maria Woodward, Mr. Ostruska, Aaron Lofaro, Rebecca Lipschutz, Lesley Palange, MaryRose Munnick, Alexandra Robles, Ralph Mayo, Cara Bertini, Laura Burdick, Shakaiba Bennett, Bethany Fuscaldo, Kenneth Alcorn, Jennifer Lynch, Elaine Chiappetta, Cheryl Conte, Voice Coach Michele Grace, Olivia Mason, Acting Coach Katie Pohlman, Manager Marilyn Zitner, Alyssa Lingardo, Agent Megan Klein, Attorney Peter Thall, Advisor Christopher Payne, Elise Wood, Sensei Frank Trainor, Emily and Gary Statham, Chris Burlingame, Dexter Frisch.

Molloy Rubin, Elise Zukauskas, Sofia Munoz, Sophie Birkett, Logan Lindstrom, Molly Badinelli, Gabby McElwain, Maya Chattoraj, Amalie Harpoth, Alani, Moira, BumbleBlades, Alex Danilov, Danny Martinez, Leia & Haley Wilson, Jolene Ortega, Matthew Gallardo, Olivia Leppla, Ron Vincent, Richie Vargas, Maria, Chloe, Anna, Autumn, Akshith Vikram, Zachary B., Elizabeth Keegan.

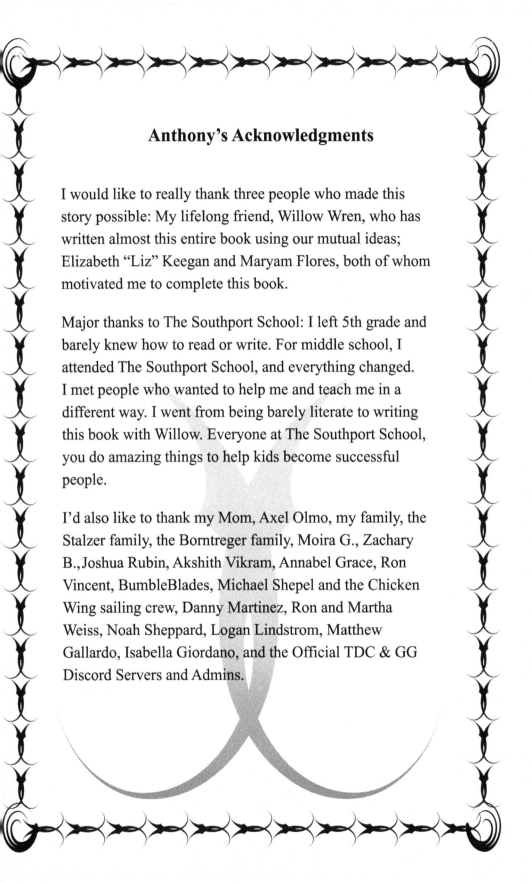

Anthony's Acknowledgments

I would like to really thank three people who made this story possible: My lifelong friend, Willow Wren, who has written almost this entire book using our mutual ideas; Elizabeth "Liz" Keegan and Maryam Flores, both of whom motivated me to complete this book.

Major thanks to The Southport School: I left 5th grade and barely knew how to read or write. For middle school, I attended The Southport School, and everything changed. I met people who wanted to help me and teach me in a different way. I went from being barely literate to writing this book with Willow. Everyone at The Southport School, you do amazing things to help kids become successful people.

I'd also like to thank my Mom, Axel Olmo, my family, the Stalzer family, the Borntreger family, Moira G., Zachary B.,Joshua Rubin, Akshith Vikram, Annabel Grace, Ron Vincent, BumbleBlades, Michael Shepel and the Chicken Wing sailing crew, Danny Martinez, Ron and Martha Weiss, Noah Sheppard, Logan Lindstrom, Matthew Gallardo, Isabella Giordano, and the Official TDC & GG Discord Servers and Admins.

WILLOW
WREN

Author, model, actress, musician and artist, Willow was signed by the FORD agency at age 6 and has modeled for over 60 companies such as *American Girl, Brooks Brothers, Saks Fifth Avenue, Levi's, Aeropostale* & worldwide campaigns for *Adidas, Monnalisa, Vogue Bambini* and *Benetton,* to name a few. She's appeared on TV shows and commercials including *Crayola* and the *WWE,* filmed for *The Goldfinch* and *Infinity Tree* and was proud to have been selected to represent the *American Girl Doll, Samantha Parkington,* gracing 5 book covers. Visit **wow-folio.com** to view her portfolio, reels, and music.

A member of the *National Association for Gifted Children*, she completed middle school with 96 A's including 25 A+s and earned the *President's Award for Educational Achievement* for outstanding grades, intellectual development in accelerated math & science, achievement in music & commitment to her academics while balancing the demands & rigors of a professional NYC career.

In 2018, Willow was teacher-nominated for the *Student of the Month Award of Recognition*, and later that year, she received the *National Novel Writing Month Certificate,* achieving over 20,000 words in 30 days. At age 11, Willow earned her 1st Literary Award in the 38th annual event of the literary competition and at age 12, she earned her 2nd Literary Award.

In 2020, Willow registered the trademark, *Writer's INC*, with the *USPTO*, after purchasing *WH Publishing, LLC.*, when she was 14. She is the daughter of a 3-time award-winning TV journalist mother and a father who's been a multi-award-winning publisher for over 30 years.

Willow received not only the *Governor's Certificate of Recognition*, but also a personal letter from *Connecticut Commissioner of Education*, Stefan Pryor, for reading 2,158 pages & 2,146 pages in consecutive summers for the Governor's Challenge when she was 5 & 6 years old. At 7 & 8, Willow wrote 2 national book reviews for the *We Do Listen Foundation* which publishes stories about confidence, sportsmanship, bullying and self-esteem.

She published her 1st book, *The Healing,* at age 8, based on a true story to inspire other children to always be kind to animals & never give up on a dream. At age 9, she was invited by *Barnes & Noble* to sit on a panel of doctors & healers for a *Health: Mind, Spirit & Body* presentation, speaking professionally about her non-fiction followed by multi-day book signings & bookings for Author's Visits.

In her spare time, Willow enjoys songwriting and plays the piano, violin, Seagull Merlin, harp, dulcimer, harmonica and recorder. In 2018, her school orchestra competed against more than a half dozen schools at *Central Connecticut State University* taking 1st place that year. She enjoys tennis, horseback riding, snorkeling and the school track team, often earning 1st in hurdles & 100 meter. At age 9, Willow flew her 1st plane and by 12, she was certified in CPR. Willow lives in Connecticut with her mom, dad, big brother, 3 cats & 22 fish.

ANTHONY
OLMO